PROLOGUE

CW00664276

Prince Ibraham of Kaiama was not
Cooper was as sure as this as he c
Ibraham had no royal blood ties. Hi:
a goat herder, originally a nomadic tribesman, who had raised
his son on the banks of Lake Natron in the Ngorongoro Crater
in Tanzania.

Not that Charles resented Ibraham's pretence. The
African had immersed himself in the role and there was
something bordering on envy on his own part; not of Ibraham's
duplicity, but the ability to convey such self-belief when all
others were well aware that it was a deception.

But now Ibraham had fucked up, and the dead girl lying
face down on the hotel bed was a testament to that.

Charles Cooper was a little shy of six feet, with a severe
face accustomed to frowning. He had turned seventy last
month, though he had never considered retirement. The
company was all that mattered. The financial rewards were
obvious, but for Charles, it was the sense of procurement that
held precedence over everything, the knowledge that all that
he had acquired had been because of his own talent and
determination.

His brother, Murray, currently pacing the floor like a
caged big cat, was three years his junior, shorter by almost
five inches but much broader. Murray was not comfortable as
a businessman. This was not a disparaging appraisal of his
younger sibling, merely a statement of fact. Murray would
have been quite happy running the original factory they had
inherited through the family decades ago, and to hell with the
other far more lucrative ventures the brothers had built up over
the years. To be honest, Charles believed that Murray would

1

have been content hawking wares from a barrow in Camden Market.

Charles loathed all aspects of manual work and was never more content than when watching others perform menial tasks on his behalf. He would have been quite at home as an overseer in a Dickensian workhouse.

It had been Charles, of course, who had expanded their interests and by the early eighties they were major players in the arms industry; by far the most lucrative enterprise they had ever ventured into. The goods were seldom seen as the Cooper's primarily acted as brokers for buyers and sellers.

The procurement and sales of weapons is a serious and clandestine industry, swathed in red tape with loopholes that are ready to be exploited. The simple fact of the matter is that, although the industry, as a whole, is regarded as immoral and fundamentally distasteful, it is needed, and there isn't a government, corrupt or otherwise, running a country in the world that doesn't recognise that single fact.

Ibraham was a bulk buyer operating out of Nigeria. He had dealt with the Cooper brothers on several occasions, the most profitable being back in the mid-'90s when the state-funded factories producing stockpiles of guns and munitions collapsed following the fall of communism. Renovated and refurbished weapons were readily available and the Coopers brought them in their hundreds of thousands, via Ibraham and his own consortiums. At the time one of the most popular guns in the world was the AK-47 and there were so many of these weapons available that the brothers were able to buy two hundred thousand pieces for just under fifty dollars each. The whole deal cost just under ten million dollars. They sold the entire stock within two months, nearly two-thirds bought by anti-Taliban forces in Afghanistan, the remaining third to various warlords operating out of Central and North Africa. The deal netted the brothers and Ibraham forty million dollars, so it was understandable that whenever Ibraham turned up in London to negotiate more deals, he was afforded the luxuries becoming of a prince - bogus or not.

Ibraham had a weakness for petite, boyish girls, the younger the better. Charles knew the dead girl on the bed was in her late teens, but she looked younger. She had overdosed on a cocktail of heroin supplied by the African and a cheaper synthetic opiate that, according to Ibraham, the girl had upon her person when she met him at his hotel room. Ibraham blamed her death on the lethal combination of the two. When he had called Charles an hour earlier he had sounded put out, as if the girl's death was little more than an inconvenience. Charles had phoned his brother and Murray's son, Clive, and they had met Ibraham in the hotel lobby. It was only a small B&B situated two miles from Hyde Park. Although Ibraham was staying at the Savoy it was not prudent to show up at such a distinguished venue with a girl who looked no older than fourteen years old on his arm.

Ibraham had left the brother's with his key and departed. This was no longer his concern.

Once in the room, Murray had started to pace and Charles made a phone call. Clive Cooper sat on the bed and said nothing. The call was to the girl's pimp. He arrived in five minutes as he was only parked around the corner ready to pick the girl up once Ibraham had dispensed with her services. He had not thought at the time that the phrase would become a fatalistic translation.

Murray ushered him quickly into the room and he stared at the girl for a full minute before saying anything. As usual, it was Charles who took charge of the situation. They had paid the pimp five hundred pounds for the girl. She was to spend three hours with Ibraham.

"A shame," the pimp muttered eventually.

"I'm sorry, Denny," Charles said. He placed a hand on the pimps shoulder. Denny didn't say anything. He had dealt with the brothers on several occasions; his girls and boys were readily available at a moment's notice. Ibraham was a frequent traveller and could turn up out of the blue and expect to be appeased. The brothers had looked after him and his girls in the past, there was no reason for him to think that they wouldn't do so now, in this most dreadful of circumstances.

"You will be reimbursed for this, Denny, you have my assurance. Do you understand that?" Denny turned to face Charles Cooper now. A mean little grin split his face at the mention of compensation. The dead girl was not a significant loss, there were many others willing to step up and take her place, but there was no reason that anybody should know that. Denny knew that he was being paid off, but that fact didn't jar him in the slightest. If he had been a man of integrity he would have become a social worker, not a whore's guardian.

"I need you to go away for a while, abroad, maybe a month, an extended holiday," Charles continued. "It will be an all-expenses-paid trip. You understand that we need to keep a lid on this situation and the fewer people you speak to the better."

"I understand that Mister Cooper, but what about the compensation?"

"I will pay you fifty thousand for the loss of your asset . Does that seem acceptable?"

Murray inhaled deeply beside him but Charles ignored him.

4

"Fifty thousand?" Denny said quietly.

Charles nodded.

"And this does not include the holiday or my..um, expenses?"

"Not at all, that will be an entirely separate transaction."

"That seems," Denny hesitated. "A perfectly reasonable offer, Mister Cooper. I accept."

Charles clapped him on the shoulder once more. "Good man. Do you have a passport?"

Denny nodded.

"Okay, I think you should leave tomorrow before the girl is missed . Does she have a family?"

Denny shrugged. "Junkie mother somewhere, not important."

"What about close friends?"

"Nah, nobody special."

Clive Cooper stood up and glanced at the body. He was as tall as his uncle Charles but also broad and well-muscled like his father, Murray. Clive was an imposing figure, handsome and confident, in his mid-thirties with a dark, swarthy complexion that he inherited from his mother, who had left Murray when Clive was a baby. Clive never spoke of her, but Murray caught glimpses of his ex-wife in his son. The twitch of a lip that would become a sneer, the proud jaw thrust forward, the cold green eyes.

Clive turned from the bed now.

"Where's her phone?" he asked, turning to the pimp.

"I don't know," Denny said. "Her bag?"

Clive knelt on the floor and picked up a small brown suede clutch bag. He opened it, took out the girl's mobile, and glanced down at the screen.

"She made two calls and sent one text message since she came here. First call to you at seven-thirty four p.m."

Denny nodded, "That was to confirm that she was in the room and the mark was here. I always get my girls to let me know."

"A text at eight-forty eight also to you: *Decent smack, high-end grade.*"

Denny held up his hands. "A girl of taste."

Clive looked down at the phone again. "Who is Candy Girl?"

Denny's brow furrowed as he mulled the name over in his head. He looked at the phone as Clive held it out to him at arm's length.

"The girl called her at nine," Clive said, "Ten minutes after she texted you about the drugs."

Denny thought for a minute. "There is a Candy Girl, I recall the name."

"One of your girls?" Murray asked.

Denny issued a small laugh that sounded like a puppy's startled yelp.

"Good god, no, If it's who I think it is then she's a major league player, high-class call girl."

Clive nodded at the dead girl lying on the bed. "Why would she be calling her?"

Denny shrugged.

"Do you know where she lives, this Candy Girl?" Charles asked.

Denny nodded. "No, but I can find out."

Clive smiled. "Then find out," he said.

Two minutes later Denny gave them an address.

"No more killing," Murray hastened. He glanced down at the girl's body on the bed.

Charles laughed. "Oh come on, brother, stop being so melodramatic. We simply need to discern what, if anything, our girl said to this Candy."

Murray bristled at the admonishment. He was a bull of a man, with a barrel chest and thick, muscular forearms. The stomach was a gut now, but he was still a hard, strong, imposing figure.

Despite Murray's larger stature, Charles had never been intimidated, even when they were kids and the spitefulness of youth was prevalent. Murray had never used his size to physically outmanoeuvre or take advantage of his older, scrawnier brother.

Charles Cooper had a presence, the aura of the weak-bodied but intelligent, ruthless man that was enough to make the most zealous bully pull his punches.

Charles turned to Denny. "Leave now, my friend, get packed and call me in a month when you get back into the country. I'll have the money with you in the morning. Don't be stupid and take the entire amount with you abroad, understand?"

Denny nodded quickly. "I understand."

The pimp left the room without a second glance over his shoulder.

Charles looked at his watch, it was nearly eleven p.m. He turned to Clive.

"Go and see this Candy Girl, see if you can get her phone, and get rid of any evidence that she was called from here. Do that and if she does say anything later to the authorities then it will be just the word of a hooker, high class or whatever."

Clive slipped the girls phone into his pocket and followed the pimp out of the room. Murray exhaled deeply and sat on the foot of the bed.

"Just the body," he said absently.

Charles nodded. He was already making his last call.

Murray stood up and headed for the door. "Forgive me if I'm not here when he arrives. I can't be in the same room as that man, you know that."

Charles nodded understandingly.

When he was alone he spoke quickly into the phone. "Mister Skein? I have a job for you."

Denny the pimp didn't receive his compensation or his gratis holiday abroad. His body was never discovered and there was little speculation as to where he went. He was buried deep, alongside the girl who had died in Ibraham's bed. Aside from Denny, not one of the men in the room that night of her death knew or asked her name.

It was Jilly Phelps. She was nineteen from South Shields.

People knew her as *Viola*.

CHAPTER 1

When Gemma Bradshaw was eleven years old her grandmother had died. It was sudden and unexpected, she was seventy-two and it had been the first and only time Gemma had seen a dead body.

Until today.

Her grandmother had appeared tranquil in death. Gemma thought she looked like an angel; her arms folded across her chest, the faint trace of a smile on her lips. Her mother, Angelica, had cried, trails of snot pooling on her top lip as she burbled nonsensical sentiments that were alien to Gemma. She could never recall her mother ever sharing any

8

such recollections when her grandmother had been alive. According to Angelica Bradshaw, gran was an *"overbearing, fucking bitch!"*

The dead guy lying on the floor in front of her now was not tranquil, and most assuredly not an angel. His name was Clive Cooper and Gemma had been staring at his lifeless body for the last three minutes, not wholly convinced that he was truly dead.

He wasn't moving; in fact he hadn't moved for the three minutes she had watched him, but that was no guarantee was it? She'd seen the movies. As soon as she leaned over his body he would draw in a deep, hitching breath and then his hands would be on her throat.

There was no blood, but there was a golf ball-sized lump above his right eyebrow where she had hit him with the bottle. Another smaller lump had appeared on the other side of his forehead where he had connected with the edge of the coffee table on the way down. From where she stood it looked as if he was about to sprout horns.

Quite appropriate, Gemma thought and almost laughed at the notion. Should she feel for a pulse, just to be sure? No, he was dead. Her immediate priority now was to get away.

The apartment was smart but sparse. She spent very little time here; it was more akin to a hotel room, somewhere to sleep and get changed.

Somewhere to fuck.

Gemma took off all of her jewellery; people noticed such trinkets, and if she tried to sell any of it she would leave a trail. She was thinking clearly now, which, despite the circumstances, was as reassuring as it was surprising. She dropped her jewellery onto the coffee table next to the bottle of Jack Daniels *(the murder weapon?)* and walked quickly into the bedroom. She glanced at her reflection in the full-length mirror on the wardrobe door, leaning in close to examine the marks on her face.

There was a discernible handprint across her cheek, and a small cut on her chin where Clive had caught her with his signet ring.

Gemma opened the wardrobe fully and pushed all her designer gear over to the left. She grabbed a handful of items from the rail and flung them onto the bed. These were her nondescript clothes. She took a backpack down from the top shelf and laid it on the bed next to the pile of clothes. She dressed quickly: t-shirt, jeans, fleece, and a pair of trainers, then bundled similar items into her backpack. She zipped the bag up then lifted it with one hand, testing the weight. She turned back to the wardrobe, stood on tiptoe, and reached further back into the dusty confines of the wardrobe's top-shelf. She retrieved a small box, brought it out and set it on the bed next to the backpack. Inside was her personal stuff: Passport, driver's licence, her premium bond details. A different looking Gemma Bradshaw stared back at her from the official documents. Nobody knew her as Gemma Bradshaw, well nobody that mattered. To her clients and a small group of friends, she was Candy Girl. She was popular and expensive, a high-class call girl; the kind that only a select number could afford.

People like Clive Cooper, she thought.

Her client list was recommended, vetted, short-listed, and finally approved. She didn't advertise her services, and she didn't have a website, which was certainly beneficial now as there were no recent pictures of her that could be scrutinised.

Her client list would be known to some; it was impossible to keep all her liaisons a secret, and some would be questioned. Even so, Gemma was certain that many would have no intention of coming forward. The life of a hooker and her client was a clandestine affair, neither courting publicity, the client in particular, for the most obvious reasons.

Gemma bundled her paperwork into the side of her backpack. She had fifty thousand pounds in premium bonds, but that was for her later life; a life away from prostitution. She was twenty-eight now. If things had stayed the way they were, then she may have had another five or six profitable years ahead of her. The death of Clive Cooper had scuppered that prospect. She doubted she could ever go back on the game full time now.

She wondered how she would cope living under the radar. Could she just attempt to fit into daily life? A life consisting of working and sleeping, of making new friends who didn't pay for her company; to socialise without feeling compromised? Gemma wasn't sure, but it was a lifestyle that she would have to try. Fifty grand was a nice nest egg, but that is all it was. For now, and the foreseeable future, she had to look for a way of supporting herself outside the sex trade.

Gemma left the bedroom, her backpack slung over one shoulder. She walked into the kitchen, reached into a high cupboard and took down a dummy can of Heinz soup. She opened it and took out a wad of twenties. This was her emergency stash. Gemma counted the money quickly. There were six hundred and eighty pounds. She stuffed the notes into the back pocket of her jeans then walked back into the living room.

Clive Cooper hadn't moved - he was dead.

His eyes stared blankly ahead and his mouth was slightly open. His teeth appeared alarmingly white. Gemma was surprised she hadn't noticed that before.

So *this is how it feels to have killed somebody,* she thought. She was remarkably calm, but then she had no idea how she was supposed to feel. Guilty, maybe?

No. If she hadn't caught him a lucky blow from the bottle he would have killed her, no doubt of that. It was self-defence, but she was certain that nobody else would see it that way.

She had a bad case of the shakes when she first hit him and had been unable to release the bottle for a few seconds, her fingers refusing to relinquish their hold on the neck. Slowly, the trembling subsided, and she set the bottle down gently on the table. Then she had just stared at him, wondering if he would move.

Would she have hit him again if he had? She didn't know - *probably.*

She bent down and searched his clothes, locating his wallet in the front pocket of his trousers. The search altered his position slightly so that he was now gazing up at her, his stare accusing.

As if killing me was not enough, now you're gonna rob me?

There were only two hundred pounds in his wallet, not as much as she had anticipated. She stuffed his money into her back pocket alongside her own emergency stash. Less than a grand in total. She tossed his wallet on the coffee table.

It was a few days before Christmas, though there were no yuletide trimmings adorning Gemma's flat. In the corner of the living room was a thin, decorative tree with spindly twigs sticking out at bizarre angles. It lit up via rows of tiny halogen bulbs that ran the length of the branches, but it was not a Christmas tree and had no illusions to be. It was here when she moved in and she had never bothered to get rid of it. Clive had made a comment earlier, ridiculing its place of prominence and teasing her over the lack of tinsel and baubles. She hadn't bothered to point out that it was not meant as a festive ornament.

Gemma was not a fan of Christmas. Her own childhood had been a hideous time; her upbringing had been one of deprivation and turmoil, inhabited by nefarious and obscene characters that drifted in and out of her life like warped, spectral wraiths. Her alcoholic mother and her loathsome entourage of depraved clients and disparate groups of acquaintances acknowledged the festive period as an excuse to indulge to even more excess than was customary.

As Candy Girl, Gemma received lots of cards, most of them from clients. She opened them all, as most contained tokens of appreciation. Then she would bin them, never bothering to read the mushy, sentimental crap that was penned within. She was offered presents too, hundreds of them, and not just during the festive season. She had steadfast rules on the receiving of gifts. She accepted cash *(obviously)* dinner engagements *(depending on who was asking and the exclusivity of the restaurant)* and jewellery. Some of the trinkets were hideous, but expensive nonetheless. She sold all of these, normally after a few months or so, making a list of who had bought her what and when. She would wear that item, a necklace or bracelet usually, just to appease the present giver the next few times they met, then it would be re-boxed and sold.

Gemma hated traditional, worthless junk. She saw no reason for adorning the apartment with such trivial items. She loathed artwork on the walls and found no need for ornaments, nick-nacks or souvenirs that, in her opinion, served no practical use whatsoever.

Apart from her monkey, of course.

He was old, and moth-eaten, sporting an alarming smile. Much of the fur around his mouth had perished, accentuating the toothy, maniacal grin, and lending his overall appearance rabid overtones. He was dressed in a purple, velvet waistcoat, and red and white striped pantaloons. He wore a fez on his head; a tassel had hung from his hat at one time, but that had long ago vanished. There was a key protruding from his back, and the clockwork mechanism, though old, was still functional. When the key was fully wound, he would clap frantically, clashing a pair of cymbals together. The monkey had fascinated her as a child. Her grandmother had taken it down from the shelf whenever she had paid the old woman a visit, set it on the table, wound it up and let it play. It was the only keepsake Gemma had, not just from her gran, but anybody. She was not, and never had been a sentimental person.

"Why do you want that thing?" Angelica had asked her on the day of Gran's funeral. wrinkling her nose and shaking her head as if Gemma had brought a decaying rat carcass riddled with disease into the house.

"It was Gran's," Gemma had replied. The poignant moment was lost on her mother who sniffed disapprovingly and reached for the vodka bottle in order to wash away any bad vibes that the foul monkey was evidently leaking into the atmosphere.

After mocking her *"Christmas Twig "* Clive Cooper had plucked the monkey off the shelf. Gemma held her breath, silently praying that he wouldn't damage it. She didn't say anything. The mood he was in she was certain that if he had detected a hint of fondness towards it he would dash it to the floor and crush it underfoot. She had feigned indifference and asked him what he wanted to drink. He had stared at the monkey for seconds longer than she was comfortable with before setting it back on the shelf.

She looked at the monkey now. She couldn't take him with her, much as it pained her to leave him. He was a link to her past. Too many people would be aware of her association with the monkey that it simply wasn't worth the risk. She turned from the shelf and cast a final glance around the apartment.

It was time. She snatched up a pair of sunglasses and a baseball cap from a small table in the hallway, then pulled the straps of her backpack over both shoulders and headed for the front door. She locked the door behind her and posted the keys through the letterbox.

CHAPTER 2

Gemma put on the sunglasses and baseball cap. She pulled the hood of the fleece up over the cap so that only the bill was showing. She tied a scarf around the lower half of her face and hurried to the end of the street. She hailed a cab and told the driver to head towards King's Cross. When he dropped her off, she crossed the road into St Pancras. It was nearly one a.m. At the station she selected a random route, running her finger down the names of stations and picking one about sixty miles from the capital: Wellingborough.

Her first priority was to get out of London. She couldn't travel too far yet, just find somewhere to lay low for a few days. It didn't really matter where, she just needed enough time to evaluate her position and come up with some kind of plan.

She was aware that her movements could be tracked. CCTV could monitor her progress, taxi journeys could be scrutinised, and designated routes could be cross-examined. But her temporary disguise was good, her face wasn't visible for the entire trip. She paid for her ticket with cash, left the station forty minutes later and arrived in Wellingborough at two-fifty a.m.

She walked from the station to the first hotel she could find where the lights were on and checked into a room for two nights, under the name of Katy Coles.

It was a totally random name. A little precarious as she could forget it and get caught out, but she wanted to set the anonymity bar high, and chose not to use the name of anybody that she knew. She paid cash and wasn't asked to show any i.d.

Once in her room, she dumped her backpack on the bed, undressed and took a long shower. She thought sleep would evade her, but dropped off as soon as she lay on the bed, waking six hours later, with the towel across her stomach and a damp patch on the pillow where she had lain with her long hair still wet.

Gemma showered and dressed again. She turned on the news but there was nothing about Clive's death this early. She wondered how long it would be before they discovered his body.

She turned the television off and pulled on her trainers. Her first priority was to change her appearance. As Candy Girl, she stood five feet five, weighed eight and a half stones and had a shock of long blonde curls. Her makeup was subtle and never overstated. Gemma knew that she was attractive. Hookers need a selling point, and highlighting their charms is no different from skilled craftsmen advertising their wares by producing samples and booklets advertising their respective products.

Candy Girl had been a character and, for the most part, she was a cliched Barbie Doll. Punters liked the empty-headed, stereotypical blonde bimbo: Golden locks, big boobs and a simpering persona that she had perfected through repetition. There had been a few clients who had wanted something different, those that wanted an intelligent conversation or, what Gemma called, *a sophisticated fuck.* She could play that part too. The curls could be tamed and slicked back. The basque and stockings could be replaced by a sensible skirt and blouse. The talk was not of TOWIE and latest fashions and trends, but local politics and career-driven professions. It made no difference to Gemma, she was still fucked and she still got paid for it. Clive Cooper hadn't wanted to talk about the economy and he wasn't interested in hack reality TV shows either.

"I'm going to cut you, you little fucking whore!"

Gemma clenched her fists tightly at the memory. Of him advancing towards her, the knife in his hand. He had dropped it when she had swung the bottle at him. She had forgotten that; it must have fallen under the coffee table.

Gemma could do little about her height and weight, but she could certainly change her hair. She watched early morning television until ten o'clock, put her cash back into her pocket and left the hotel. It took her ten minutes to reach the town centre, where she found a hairdresser that advertised: *walk-ins welcome.*

Two hours later the long blonde hair was gone. Gemma now sported a short, black stylish bob, that made her look five years younger and gave her an elfin appearance that was as startling as it was refreshing. She bought a pair of fake spectacles from an optician for forty pounds, insisting that she wanted to get a feel for the look of the frames before committing to paying for the lenses. The optician declared that it was understandable. Why didn't Gemma try them for twenty-four hours and then pop back in later? The forty pounds was simply a precaution, a refundable down payment. Gemma nodded, knowing that the frames and clear lenses were only worth about a tenner, but she was not concerned, as the glasses altered her appearance so much that she viewed them as a necessity. She made an appointment for an eye test that she had no intention of keeping, then left the opticians, slipping the spectacles on as she headed back to her hotel.

She watched TV all afternoon, scanning the news channels. Nothing came on about Clive's death. Gemma turned it off and decided to go back out. She had to feel confident about being in public.

The guy on the front desk was the same person who had checked her in. He was in his mid-twenties, gangly and slightly awkward looking, with an old-fashioned, mullet haircut, and a few acne scars on both cheeks. A name tag on the lapel of his jacket read: Gregory.

They had spoken briefly when Gemma had checked in. Gregory had not appeared curious about the lateness of the hour. His inquiries were perfunctory questions, just a tired receptionist going through the motions of checking in a weary guest.

As Gemma approached the desk, Gregory glanced up. He was resting his head on one hand, a paperback open on the counter in front of him. When he saw Gemma he sat back in his chair, his eyes opened wide. The paperback closed up on the counter.

"Wow!" Gregory breathed. "I didn't recognise you, Miss Coles."

Gemma smiled, pleased that her new look was the transformation that she had hoped for. She glanced down at the cover of the book. It was called *The Kind Worth Killing* by an author she had never heard of before- Peter Swanson

"Please call me Katy," Gemma said. "Miss Coles makes me sound like a schoolmistress."

Gregory nodded. "I must say I like the new look, although I can't think of many girls who would cut off their golden locks. You running from somebody?"

"God no, what makes you say that?"

Gregory shrugged. He tapped the cover of the book with his finger.

"Jesus, I dunno, I guess that was a pretty dumb thing to say. My mind tends to wander sitting at this desk all day. I read a lot." He turned the book over showing her the cover. "Have you read any of his stuff?"

Gemma shook her head.

"Oh he's great. This is only his second book, the female leads are either neurotic, paranoid, or a bit of both, with a twist of psychosis thrown in for good measure, yet you feel empathy for them."

Is that how he sees me? Gemma thought, a character in a book? She relaxed a little, realising that Gregory's musings were little more than fictional comparisons as opposed to astute observations. Still, the conversation had unnerved her slightly and she made her excuses and left.

"Hey, you staying for Christmas?" Gregory called after her.

Gemma turned and looked back at him. "Um, I don't know, maybe."

Gregory nodded. "That's okay, it's no problem. We've got a party of nine arriving on Boxing Day, booked the whole top floor, but they're only here for one night, so until then it's just you and me"

Gemma thought she may stay until after Christmas. It seemed pointless to look for new lodgings at the height of the holiday period. It was the day before Christmas Eve today, maybe she could stay until New Year. The more she thought about it, the more the plan appeared appealing.

"Yeah I think I might, I'll let you know, okay?"

"Sure Katy, see you later."

Gemma turned and waved over her shoulder as she walked through the hotel entrance.

The town centre was busy. Gemma passed people laden down with bags, escorting excited children. A small brass band was playing carols near a sparse selection of market stalls, attracting the attention of a drunken man in his sixties who was performing a stumbling dance in front of the band, a matchstick thin, unlit roll-up dangling precariously from his lips. The band's conductor cast regular glances at the drunk; a look tinged with a combination of annoyance, pity and wariness.

Gemma was nervous within the crowd, but not as much as she thought she would be. She ordered a coffee in a busy Costa and grabbed a window seat just as a young couple was leaving. She stared out the window and people watched. After paying for two nights at the hotel, her train ticket, haircut, glasses and a few sundries, Gemma had a little over five hundred and fifty pounds left of her emergency fund. She hadn't eaten a proper meal for over twenty-four hours, and she suddenly felt ravenous. She caught the attention of a passing waitress and ordered a bowl of soup, a bacon and brie wrap and a slice of carrot cake. If she intended to stay at the hotel until the New Year then that alone would rapidly diminish her funds. She seriously believed that she could live in a world away from prostitution, a life that she had known since she was fifteen, but for now, she needed some instant cash and she could think of no better way than relying on her own experience and expertise for recognising a potential customer.

A man in his early forties took a seat next to her, and they nodded hellos to each other. She wondered whether to strike up a conversation, but then he opened a folded newspaper and started to read as his coffee cooled and Gemma turned her attention back to the steady throng of pedestrians outside.

She thought about Gregory. Gemma prided herself on her ability to read a person's character. Gregory was an innocent, a man swept away by characters of fiction. Stuck in a dead-end job, he was a fantasist, and why not? She wondered if she offered Gregory sex, whether or not she could trade it for a few nights accommodation. Gemma had no qualms about toying with such a notion. To her, Gregory would just be another paying customer, someone to barter with when negotiating a deal. It didn't matter that she was selling herself short, she would simply do what she had to do. Her mission now was one of survival and as a hooker, she could still rely on her talents and abilities to reel in a catch.

She quickly dismissed the idea though. Gregory, sweet and naive as he may be, was still the only person who had seen the *Old Gemma,* before her transformation. She would be foolish therefore to get too close to him, for fear that he may be asked later to describe her. She was under no illusions that her ex-clients would be sought out and they could give a detailed picture of what she looked like, but she had changed dramatically since she fled the capital, and there were no photos, Gemma made sure of that. A lot of the girls advertised their services online; it was a natural progression from cards in telephone boxes, but Gemma had never needed to. Her client base was very select. She had not taken on a new punter in over two years, and she hadn't changed her look for about five. She had been in high demand and, although reluctant to admit it, there were parts of the life that she would miss.

It hadn't always been that way, of course. The road to becoming high class was a literal kerbside crawl, with the bodies of many of the victims who had attempted the progression littering the gutters.

In the early years, when her young age had been a factor, Gemma had witnessed the depravity first hand. The man who had set her on the path was dead now, and good riddance to him. She hadn't thought about him for years. For Gemma, in her sordid world, Frank Davenport stood head and shoulders above the nefarious pack as the *King of Sleaze.*

CHAPTER 3

Two days before her fifteenth birthday, on the day of her Uncle Stan's funeral, Gemma's stepfather, Frank, tried to put his hand down the front of her dress.

It was a fumbled attempt. He was drunk, his watch caught in the straps of her dress and his fingertips only managed to brush the top of her breast.

Angelica had been in no position to defend her daughter even if she had wanted to. Gemma was not certain that her mother was even aware that her brother had died. Such was her dependence on the bottle that she was seldom coherent and spent most of her time asleep on the sofa.

There had been a time when she had genuinely loved her mother, before Frank had moved in, but even then it had been far from an idyllic relationship. Angelica's drinking was becoming tiresome even then, though thankfully she was not a violent drunk.

Her mother was maudling and apologetic once under the influence. So sorry for the life she had foisted upon her children, always maintaining that one day she would make it up to them, forever insisting that she would reunite her family. She had never gone so far as to promise that she would kick the booze, get a job and they would all move to a chocolate box cottage in the countryside, but she came damn close to painting such a delusional picture once the cap of the vodka bottle was unscrewed.

Frank Davenport was the catalyst that drove the final wedge between Gemma and her mother. Gemma couldn't remember how the two of them had met. Angelica was not working, claiming disability for a couple of genuine and a few maligned illnesses that ranged from stress to acute abdominal back pain. It was as if Frank was just there, suddenly appearing like a spectre from the fog; a pencil-thin, wasted figure of a man, who had almost telepathically sensed Angelica's yearning for companionship.

Gemma knew that her mother turned a few tricks in order to supplement her meagre income. She had been a beautiful woman once; not movie star glam, but striking, with a cascade of rich, golden locks, that Gemma had inherited, a small, high bosom, and a killer ass. Angelica rarely discussed the serendipitous meeting with Frank, although she appeared happy that he had taken it upon himself to move in. Gemma knew that Frank and her mother had sex, but she was never certain if Frank was a former client of Angelica's or just a chancing loner who had latched onto her like a limpet on the hull of a boat, drifting through life, forever dependent on its host. To Gemma, he was the most basic, parasitic life form. He had never worked as far as she was aware, certainly not in the traditional way of procuring an honest wage, and yet his wallet always bulged with a wad of cash.

Frank was shark-like, both in looks and temperament, voraciously feeding on the emotions of those around him. His hair was greasy and clung to his forehead in wet strips, his sunken cheeks lending his face a cadaverous appearance. He sported a permanent five o'clock shadow, the stubble coarse and dark, mottled with powdered grey flecks, and he was seldom seen without a black, cracked leather jacket, that he wore *"Fonzie"* style, with the collar turned up. He wore scuffed, pointed boots, and skinny jeans that clung to his long thin legs like damp towels.

Frank moved slowly and methodically as if each stride was purposeful. On one rare occasion when the three of them, Gemma, Angelica and Frank, had been watching a wildlife documentary on chameleons, one segment of the programme showed the lizard clinging to a tree branch, slowly inching its way up the bough towards its prey.

"It moves like Frank," Gemma had observed. Far from being offended, Frank had accepted this as a compliment. He nodded knowingly as if such a comparison had been made on more than one occasion.

Six months after he had moved in Angelica casually announced one morning that she and Frank were married. Gemma was at the breakfast table, a bowl of untouched cereal in front of her. For years she had eaten bran cereals, rich in fibre and whole grain. Occasionally, her mother took it upon herself to set the breakfast table. She filled Gemma's bowl with a sickly sweet concoction of peculiar shapes and strange coloured marshmallow lumps. Gemma moved it around a little with her spoon, creating small whirlpools in the milk. She watched as the cereal pieces swam and danced in one direction and then the next.

"When?" she asked.

"Yesterday, at the registry. It was a quiet affair, it was what Frank wanted."

Gemma nodded. She waited for the small spinning eddies in her bowl to subside. "Is it what you wanted?"

Angelica had laughed at that, but she didn't answer her question.

"It's for the best," she replied.

Gemma seriously doubted that but said no more about it. There seemed to be little point.

Angelica's decline was rapid following the marriage. Her alcohol addiction grew ever more acute until Gemma seldom saw her without an unopened bottle by her side. She lost weight and became gaunt, her eyes dark-rimmed and huge, staring blankly out of hollowed sockets. Her luscious, untamed locks grew listless and greasy, the striking blonde replaced by a mousy, dull ochre brown. At times she was unable to satisfy her dwindling number of clients, lying beneath them like a yielding slab of malleable flesh. On one occasion she fell asleep as one punter mounted her. He continued until he was satisfied, and then simply rolled off and left her snoring. Frank had caught up with him a few hours later. Gemma had no idea what he did, but he had returned with a fistful of notes and a Cheshire Cat grin. Gemma realised that her mother's descent into prostitution was complete by this stage and for all intents and purposes her new husband was her pimp.

Gemma should have felt sorry for her, but she couldn't bring herself to show any sympathy. The twisted, fucked-up mess of a world that she herself inhabited was populated with such nefarious low-lifes that Gemma believed that they were all suited to each other, her mother included.

Gemma still attended school, and for the most part, she was an accomplished scholar. Of course, it was an escape into an alarmingly normal environment and one that she relished. She was certain that she could quite simply have dropped out and Angelica would be none the wiser.

Her brother, Alan, rarely visited. His relationship with Angelica was even more volatile than Gemma's. When he was younger he had spent many years in care, as he was prone to violent outbursts that Angelica was unable to cope with. He told Gemma he had lived for a while in a big house with other youngsters prone to violence. The neighbours had petitioned the council when the decision to house the "Special Needs" kids had first arisen, assuming the premises would reduce the neighbourhood to something akin to a no-holds-barred ghetto. They had failed to prevent the place from opening, and subsequent petitions were also unsuccessful in having the unit closed down. For the most part, Alan told her, they were simply left alone. When the neighbours realised that they were not housing potential murderers or rapists on their doorsteps, the protests abated, but never went away. Prejudice, however unjustified, was a stubborn mule that neither succumbed to carrot or cane.

A few days after Uncle Stan's funeral, Angelica, in one of her rare moments of sobriety, approached her daughter in her room as she was reading. She sat down on the bed and Gemma self-consciously moved away. Angelica frowned at this but didn't say anything. It was as if she was unaware of the environment her daughter was being exposed to, and possibly felt that Gemma, for reasons she was unable to comprehend, was judging her too harshly.

"Gemma, men have needs," Angelica said cryptically. "You're not a girl anymore, you're a woman now." She paused awkwardly and nodded at Gemma's large breasts. "See?"

Gemma almost laughed at the absurdity of the statement, as if she herself was unaware of the changes her developing body was going through and had to rely on the observations of her alcoholic mother to point it out to her. But she didn't say anything, she was intrigued to see where Angelica was going with this. She set her book down and turned to face her. Angelica seemed momentarily dumbstruck by this apparent interest. She coughed nervously.

"Gemma, men have needs," she said.

"You've already said that," Gemma replied, her eyes never leaving her mother's face. "I take it we're talking about sexual needs?"

"Yes, exactly." Angelica seemed pleased that apparently her point had been made, despite the fact that her daughter had decoded her clumsy opening statement for herself.

"I myself am getting old," Angelica continued. Gemma did laugh now and Angelica blinked in surprise.

"Mother, you're forty-two, you're not old. You're mistaking senility with incapability." Angelica stared hard at her for a moment and then smiled herself.

"Gemma, I have no idea what you're talking about. How many teenage girls speak like that?"

"What do you want, mum?"

"I've told you twice," Angelica said, exasperation creeping into her voice.

"You've told me nothing. You just keep saying men have needs, and in a cack-handed way, you're saying that you can't fulfil them. If you propose to prostitute me out, mother, just fucking say so."

Angelica reeled from that, as if she had been slapped, genuine shock on her face. "I had....no , I had no...Gemma how could you think such a thing?" she stammered.

"Mother. What do you want?" Gemma asked deliberately. There was a long pause as the two of them stared hard at each other. Eventually, her mother dropped her eyes and took up her daughter's hand. It was a rare physical moment, and Gemma was too surprised at this sudden act of intimacy to snatch her hand away. The significance was shattered almost immediately though when she realised that her mother, far from showing affection, was merely staring at Gemma's hand intently.

"So small," she whispered. "That's what they like. So very small." Now Gemma did pull her hand away as if her fingers had inadvertently touched something disgusting.

"It's not sex," Angelica said, her eyes still gazing down at Gemma's hands. "It's not fucking, I would never allow that, but they like a small hand encircled around their shaft, you know that? Look at mine." She lifted up her own hand, but instead of presenting it for her daughter to examine she held it up to her own face and stared at it for a full minute, turning it like a prized jewel on a pedestal.

"My hands are big with long fingers." She was mumbling, and although Gemma could not smell the drink on her, it was evident that the years of alcohol abuse had taken their toll. Even when relatively sober Angelica was befuddled, confused. At times there were moments of lucidity; a forgotten memory or distant emotion managed to claw its way out from her comatose state of mind. But the fog bank was down now, and Angelica's self-indulgent appraisal of her own hand was a testament to that. Oblivious to everything else, it was as if Gemma wasn't even there anymore.

"Large hands, a man's hands somebody once said. That's no compliment, is it? I mean, who would say such a thing to a lady?" She blinked and then dropped her hand. "Think about what I've said, Gemma," she said abruptly and stood up as if to go. Gemma stood also and touched her mother on the shoulder. Their eyes met once again.

"Mum, you haven't said anything," Gemma said gently. "Is it Frank? Did Frank tell you to come in here?"

"Frank? No of course not. Your father's a good man."

"Please don't call him that."

"What, father, or a good man?"

"Both mum, he's neither."

They both smiled at that, but Gemma was certain that her mother was not sharing any empathic notions with her. She simply copied others now, repeating their sentences, mirroring their own reactions parrot-fashion."

"There's no fucking, remember that. That life isn't for my girl, I told him that."

"Told who, mum?" Frank?" Did Frank suggest it?"

"I would never allow that, I told him straight, not for my girl" Angelica's voice trailed off like an actor who has suddenly forgotten their lines. She glanced around Gemma's room as if unsure that she should be there.

"Do you remember that mirror?" she suddenly said, pointing at a spot on the wall. "It was your gran's, it used to hang just there. Remember how heavy it was, Gem, how we hung it up with a nail, and your brother said we had to put it up

29

with a screw, or it would just fall down and rip a hole in the plaster. Do you remember?"

Gemma nodded. "Yeah, I remember Gran's mirror."

Angelica stared at the wall for a few seconds longer then abruptly turned and headed for the door, still mumbling to herself.

Gemma followed her mother out, but she had hurried across the landing, her bedroom door already closing behind her.

Gemma headed downstairs, through the living room and into the kitchen. This room was tiny. The paint was peeling from the walls, revealing soiled, cracked plaster beneath. In places the damp was so prevalent, that the plaster had eroded completely, leaving nothing but bare brick.

There were plates, mugs, and dishes strewn across every work surface, some broken, many just piled in the sink, that wasn't even filled with water, so the food stains remained baked hard. Gemma used to clean up. She would clear the dishes, tidy the rooms and perform everyday chores, but the daily mess accumulated so quickly that she eventually gave up this one-sided battle.

Gemma opened the back door and headed out into the yard. She could hear noises from the shed to the rear. The yard was small, enclosed by a wall on the left in desperate need of repointing. Thick ivy roots penetrated the brickwork, destabilising the whole structure further and Gemma feared that a strong wind would bring the whole thing down. An ancient BSA motorbike engine sat forlornly against the side of the house, rusting beneath a torn and degrading piece of tarpaulin, that flapped in the breeze like the tail of a kite.

Gemma headed for the shed. The door was open. It was always open, as only the top hinge supported its weight.

Frank was just inside the door, an open toolbox on the bench in front of him. A part from the BSA's engine was in his hand and he held it like a nugget of gold. His hands were filthy, caked with oil. He turned when he heard Gemma and set the engine part down. He smiled at her.

"Gemma, what a pleasant surprise."

"What did you say to mum?" Gemma demanded.

Frank shrugged. He picked up the spare part again and then started rummaging through his toolbox.

"I've said many things to your mother. What are you referring to?"

He picked up a tiny screwdriver, thinner than the lead inside a pencil, and started to work on a screw hidden deep inside the engine part.

"I'm not going to jerk men off, you filthy bastard. Mum would never suggest that, despite everything, she would never allow that."

Frank smiled. "Despite everything," he repeated. He laughed and Gemma almost cried out in frustration.

"Skinny as you are, you're a real looker, Gemma, you know that? You need to start thinking about your future, a means to support yourself while you're under my roof. Do you understand me?"

"Your roof?" Gemma cried. "My mother....."

"Your mother is fucked," Frank snapped. "She isn't any use to me anymore, Christ, she isn't any use to anybody!" He dropped the engine part and screwdriver onto the workbench. "I'm not suggesting you go out to work, not on your back anyway, but come on girl, even you must have realised that this day was coming. You've got to learn the trade sometime, and what better way to start than with the basics. Things won't change that much, you have your education to think about

31

after all." He sneered as he said that. "A man has needs, and requires a means of release, me included" He lowered his head and grinned at her malevolently. "I'm sure you catch my drift?"

"I'm fifteen," Gemma protested.

Frank shrugged. "So?"

"I will leave. Just because mum's guard is down, I won't let you or anybody else touch me, I'll leave before I do that. I swear I'll bring Social Services down here. "

Frank's hand lashed out like a striking serpent and he struck her hard across the face. Gemma tumbled backwards and fell hard against the precariously balanced shed door.

"Don't you ever fucking threaten me again you little bitch. I will take your throat out with my bare hands, you understand me?"

Gemma nodded dumbly.

"You want to leave, then fucking leave, but both you and I know you're not going anywhere. Beneath that tough exterior, you're just a frightened little girl."

He suddenly spread his hands in a placating gesture and Gemma involuntarily took a step backwards. The anger had disappeared as quickly as it had flared up. Now he was gracious and genial. Gemma was unsure which of these diverse personalities frightened her the most.

"Look, I'm not asking for a lot. We can maintain a cordial relationship, we don't have to like each other, hell, kids aren't supposed to like their parents."

"You're not my parent," Gemma hissed. She tentatively touched a finger to her lips. There was no blood, but she could feel swelling.

"Even better," Frank replied. "There's less guilt to concern us. You ever jerked a guy's cock before?" He laughed now, a deep throaty, hacking laugh that bent him over.

"Of course you have. I bet the boys queue round the block to get a hand inside your knicks and for you to put your own down the front of their fucking trousers. Bet you've taken a few fingers knuckle deep too, am I right? Come on, where's the harm?" How am I any different to the lucky boys on the estate?"

Gemma stared hard at him for a moment, enraged because some of his observations were accurate. It was difficult to conceal what her mother was, and even harder to justify, not that she tried too often. Despite her small stature, Gemma had fought with many of her classmates who piously condemned her mother, though she could never understand afterwards why she felt it necessary to defend the reputation of a woman that she felt very little love for. The assumptions that she herself was easy is what hit home though, and she never added fuel to those flammable accusations by giving any suggestion that she was a sure thing. She had only let one boy put his hands between her legs, and that was mainly to satisfy her own curiosity. It had been uncomfortable and far from satisfying. So different from her own exciting fingertip explorations.

"I don't want to," Gemma said.

"Oh come on," Frank said. "We've passed the stage of worrying about what you want and don't want."

He suddenly reached down and opened the fly on his jeans. He reached inside and pulled out his penis. It was huge and lay against his thigh like a fat, wet slug. It jerked beneath his grip and Frank laughed at the look of disgust on Gemma's face.

"See there, girl, it twitches whenever it smells young cunt! Bet the backstreet boys have never sported an uncoiled python as big as this fucker. Ha, they'd be spurting the sap from their pencil dicks just at the sight of it." With one deft movement, he tucked his penis back inside his jeans and zipped up.

"That's the deal, girl, a select few, including yours truly, and I mean select. Not the lowlife who hump your fucking mum. I ain't trading old for new here, but you will do as I bid, I swear that, otherwise you can fuck off out of my house. I ain't no charity worker, you're not bringing in any real readies and with your mum earning next to fucking nothing, then you're gonna have to contribute in some way."

Gemma said nothing and turned to go. Frank retrieved the motorbike part from the workbench.

"Oh, and one other thing," he said without looking up. Gemma stopped but didn't turn around

"The arrangement with me starts from now, you understand? Nothing like being thrown in at the deep end. Your mum literally cannot handle the big boy any longer. She's either got the shakes and can't hold on, or her grip is as feeble as a politician's handshake. The python demands a strong grip. We understand each other?"

Gemma said nothing. Frank had been right about one thing. She was afraid to leave.

So Gemma had stayed and done what Frank asked her to do .

CHAPTER 4

"It looks like rain," the man in the coffee shop said. Gemma looked up, startled from her thoughts by the sudden interruption. She pushed her empty soup bowl aside and popped the last piece of baguette in her mouth. The man had refolded his paper and was staring at her intently. Gemma was so lost in her memories she was uncertain how long he had been looking at her. She smiled at him, then glanced out of the window as the first few, heavy droplets splattered against the glass.

"Good prediction," she said and they both laughed.

"Would you like another coffee?" the man asked. "Seems pointless to go out in this just yet, and we have the best seats in the house.

Gemma nodded. "Thanks, I'll have a cappuccino."

"Keep my seat," the man said, though he laid his newspaper upon it for added security as he stood up and left to get their coffees.

Gemma identified him as a chat-up artist. She had been on the game long enough to recognize the signs. He was in his late forties, good looking, a businessman or maybe a rep. They would make small talk over their coffees and then he would probably suggest drinks back at his hotel.

Back in the day, Gemma was in demand as Candy Girl. The largest fee she had ever charged was three thousand pounds for an all-nighter with an actor who was in London shooting a new movie. He had been big in the eighties, waning slightly in the nineties and almost off the radar by the time he was making some straight to DVD Anglo/American action nonsense that brought him to Gemma's attention. Still, it had been a great payday. He had been an adequate lover, and she had bolstered his ego by exaggerating his performance. All in all, Gemma believed herself to be a better actor than her punter that night.

The guy arrived back with the coffee. They shot the breeze for a while, and then he made his move. He was a rep from Birmingham, just closed a big deal. He was staying at a

Travelodge on the outskirts of town, would she like to come back for a drink. It was a well-stocked mini bar, yadda, yadda, yadda. Gemma interrupted him then.

"Three hundred," she announced, sipping her coffee.

The man blinked in surprise. "What?"

"You are propositioning me, aren't you?" she asked him innocently.

"Umm, well no, I thought…"

"You thought what? A girl you've never met, twenty years younger would come back to your hotel room. For what reason, an afternoon nap?

"I didn't realise you were a…."

"A hooker? Well, aren't you the lucky one? Shall we go?"

"I don't have three hundred," he said. If his ego had been bruised by the simple fact that his charm alone had not enticed her, he didn't show it.

Gemma shrugged. "Okay, thanks for the coffee."

"Wait," the guy said. Gemma turned. "I didn't say I couldn't get it, it's just that three hundred is a lot of cash. What…. What exactly would I get for that?"

Gemma leaned closer to him and whispered in his ear. "You'll get everything that a few months ago, some lucky bastard was prepared to pay ten times that amount for. Now, are we going?"

Two hours later, back at her own hotel room, Gemma was immediately beginning to rue her hasty decision to sleep with the guy from the coffee shop. She was on the run for killing a man. She was supposed to be keeping a low profile.

She had envisaged a plan for a new life, one that didn't include prostituting herself out, and at the very first opportunity to swell her coffers, she went straight back to the only way she knew of procuring cash.

The rep's name was Mike *(that was the name he gave her).* He worked for a company specialising in chemical solvents and he was often down in Northamptonshire and the surrounding counties. As she was leaving his room, he had begged Gemma for her number. She had refused but threw him a bone by stating that she *may* bump into him again. The suggestion of serendipity did little to placate him and he implored her to arrange another meeting, but again Gemma said that it was impossible. She left him in a state of utter despair, sitting dejected on the side of the bed, his limp, exhausted penis lying forlornly between his legs.

The rendezvous had been extremely foolhardy, Gemma knew that without a shadow of a doubt, and she had been wracked by wave after wave of anxiety and panic attacks as she weighed up the possible consequences of her spontaneous decision to fuck the guy.

For a start, he was a sales representative, a man who made his living by travelling the length and breadth of the country. True, he had assured her that his business was localised and restricted only to the former counties associated with the footwear industry, but he was still a well-travelled man. Secondly, he was not coy around prostitutes. He was well versed in the slang and the appropriate payment methods for the services offered. A man with such knowledge would come into contact with other hookers and escorts and would undoubtedly visit massage parlours, and although the chance of him discussing any previous liaisons with any of them was minuscule, it was still an unnecessary risk that she had taken.

There was a gentle tap on her door and she hurriedly bundled up her cash and placed it under the pillow. She opened the door to Gregory who was standing sheepishly holding a tray of sandwiches.

"Hi," he said, chewing on his bottom lip. "I'm just about to have lunch and was wondering if you had eaten yet?"

Gemma opened the door wider and let him in. "Thank you," she said. "That's very thoughtful."

Gregory shrugged. "There's only you and me here, I hope you don't think I'm being intrusive."

Gemma didn't but still conceded that it was a little odd. She had also just broken a second of her newly established rules; the fact that she was not going to associate too closely with Gregory as he was the only person to see her before her transformation. She chided herself that she was being paranoid, but again it showed that if she was ever going to maintain a subterfuge, then she would need to employ a little more willpower than she was exhibiting at the moment.

There were no chairs in the room, so Gregory sat on a vanity stool tucked under a tiny dressing table, he held out the platter of sandwiches and Gemma took one. He lay the rest on the bed then folded his hands in his lap.

"Aren't you having one?" Gemma asked.

Gregory shook his head.

"Oh god, you're not going to ask me to come and look at your collection of stuffed birds in the parlour are you?"

Gregory blinked in surprise. "What's a parlour?"

Gemma smiled and took a bite of the sandwich. It was tuna and mayonnaise. Too little tuna and far too much mayo.

"Haven't you ever seen *Psycho*?" she asked.

Realisation dawned on Gregory's face and he laughed. "Of course. That's very witty."

Gemma took another bite of her sandwich.

"Are you down here seeing friends?"

Gemma nodded. She chewed for a few seconds, thinking of her reply. She had prepared a tale that was feasible in her head. She just hoped that it sounded as plausible when she said it aloud.

"My sister lives in the town. I've been abroad for a few years and only got back last week. I'm going to visit her in the new year.

Again Gregory looked puzzled. "Doesn't she have room to put you up?"

Gemma leaned forward as if to divulge a great secret. Instinctively Gregory copied her so that their faces were only inches apart.

"Her husband," she whispered conspiratorially. "We don't see eye to eye. He works on the rigs and goes back on the second of January, that's when the coast will be clear and I'll have time to spend with my sister." She tapped the side of her nose.

Gregory stared at her for a few moments and Gemma grew a little uncomfortable under his gaze, then he nodded slowly.

"Do you want a drink?" Gregory suddenly said. "We could share a bottle of wine."

Gemma sat back. "Sure, that would be great. I need to take a shower and then I'll be down. It'll be more comfortable in the bar, don't you think?"

Gregory looked around the room, a slight frown on his face indicating that he evidently found the small room far cosier.

"Okay," he conceded. He stood and picked up the remaining sandwiches on the tray. He didn't ask Gemma if she wanted another.

When Gregory left the room, Gemma hurriedly packed her bag and retrieved her money. She slipped quietly out of her room and headed downstairs to the lobby of the hotel. She glanced inside the small bar area. The doors, although frosted glass, stood ajar. She could hear Gregory behind the bar, the clinking of glasses and incoherent mutterings. She hurried past the doors and out through the hotel main entrance. Gregory was quite possibly a sweet guy, lonely yet a little creepy. She was paranoid enough without having to fuel her anxiety further by subjecting herself to unnecessary cross-examination.

It had started to rain again as Gemma hurried towards the train station.

CHAPTER 5 (4 MONTHS LATER)

"Would you like one?" the woman asked. There was more than a hint of an accent in her voice - Polish possibly, or maybe Czech, Ray Jessop wasn't sure. He glanced down at the fish in her hand. She had filthy nails; long, cracked and caked with dirt. The fish was about six inches long, the hook still in its mouth. Ray recognised it as a mackerel. The Polish, or possibly Czech woman had been pulling them out of the sea with a standard rod and line with alarming frequency. Ray had counted five catches in the last ten minutes. He wondered if she was selling them or maybe just stockpiling for a feast.

She stared up at him, not smiling, but still presenting the fish. She was in her early forties, plump and remarkably plain. Ray had no idea why she was offering him the fish. Maybe she had caught enough, in which case common sense dictated that she could simply stop. Perhaps it was a come-on, but he somehow doubted that. He was guilty himself of cliched opening lines and clumsy proposals, but he had never offered a potential first date a live fish.

"No thank-you," he replied. The woman shrugged, removed the hook from the mackerel's mouth and dropped it into a bucket at her side. Conversation and potential chat-up lines concluded, the woman baited her hook and cast the line out over the sea wall once more. Ray was tempted to wait, merely out of curiosity, to see if she would land another fish, but he had a schedule to keep, so he turned from the proficient angler and started to walk.

Ray Jessop was six feet two, with a dark, olive complexion and a shock of wavy, black hair. He worked out regularly and the gym was doing its job. At thirty-eight he was trim and toned. Not quite as fit as when he had been serving in the military, but that had been a decade ago, and age was never a faithful ally when trying to maintain a strict regime.

He was in a reflective mood as he walked alongside the sea wall. The newly-laid viewing platform at Newton's Cove offered a panoramic view of the wide channel, with the huge scattered boulders hugging the coastline. Nothe Fort, set high on the hillside, stood sentinel over the popular gardens that had adopted its name and he stopped for a moment to gaze out at the shimmering sea.

There were a few more anglers scattered about the stony beach that lined the cove's shoreline. Many seemed to be having great success in landing the ever-popular mackerel, and a few children were crabbing amongst the rock pools at the water's edge.

Ray turned from the viewing platform and started to make his way through the gardens, preferring the solitude and serenity of the tree-lined tracks as opposed to the concrete path that ran alongside the recently finished sea wall. Small patches of burned grass and the odd scattered beer can or discarded Pringles tube showed evidence of clandestine barbecues enjoyed by teenagers who, ever rebellious, were prone to flaunt any rules or regulations.

It had been twenty-five years since Ray had last visited Weymouth. If much had changed, and he assumed that it had, he did not notice it. He had paid little attention to the town, or the layout as a kid.

Ray reached the edge of the gardens and stopped. He was standing atop a high grassy bank. There were a few commemorative benches scattered about and a sloping green led down to the famed Jurassic coastline. The view over Newton's Cove was stunning from this point, the wind flicking at the choppy water, fringing the waves with white spray as they lapped continuously at the steadfast sea wall.

In front of him stood the fort. The impressive building dated back to 1872 and played a vital role in the defence of Portland Harbour navy base during World War Two. Purchased by the council in 1961, the fort was now a museum.

Ray had never visited it; not as a kid, and he had no intention of doing so as an adult. He loathed museums.

It was late April, and a chilly, persistent wind clung to the hillside. Ray buried his hands in the pockets of his jacket as he walked in the direction of the fort.

He spotted his former army colleague sitting on a bench at the top of the hill.

Brian Harrier was gazing out to sea as if in a hypnotic stupor. He was an unremarkable-looking man, pasty-faced with thinning, long hair that cascaded unfashionably over his shoulders; a few rebellious strands dancing fitfully across his balding pate.

Despite the cold, Brian was wearing a thin blue waterproof anorak, burgundy, knee-length shorts and navy plimsolls without socks. His thin legs were tanned a deep mahogany brown, and his face was as dark and lined as aged parchment. He suddenly turned as Ray approached and stood up, an uneasy smile on his face. He retrieved a cane that was standing against the bench and leaned on it. He managed a thin smile. Ray held out his hand and they shook.

"Hello, Brian," Ray said. He noted the cane and gestured for the other man to sit. Brian shook his head and instead reached for Ray's arm, resting an unsteady hand upon it. He nodded and the smile warmed a little.

"How was the trip?" Brian asked. He started to walk, unsteady, small steps. Ray guided him as they made their way across the green, away from the sea wall in the direction of the Nothe Fort car park.

"Took just under four and a half hours from Poole," Ray replied. "Journey back was a little longer."

"The ferry doesn't travel to Jersey from Weymouth?" Brian asked.

"Not anymore."

Brian nodded slowly. "Did you find her?"

"Yes." Ray took out an envelope from the inside of his jacket and held it out.

Brian stared at it for a few moments before taking it from Ray's outstretched hand. The envelope was unopened and Brian flicked at the sealed flap with the tip of his thumb.

"She didn't even open it?"

Ray shook his head. "No."

They crossed the car park and headed for the stone steps that led to the harbourside. A glorious view of the seafront and esplanade was enjoyed from the top of the harbour steps and the two men stood for a few seconds and gazed out across the water.

At the bottom of the stone steps was a small jetty used by hardy boatmen who ferried passengers across the small stretch of water between the harbourside and the seafront.

"Can you manage the steps?" Ray asked.

Brian stared down as if contemplating the descent of Everest.

"Providing you haven't made any immediate plans."

Ray smiled and Brian looped an arm through Ray's, tapping each step with his cane as they slowly descended. When the two men reached the bottom of the steps one of the boats was just docking, the boatman expertly lifting the oars and letting the craft bump gently against the small landing platform. He secured the vessel and started to escort the passengers off, offering a complimentary, almost deferential doff of his cap as they paid their fares.

Ray reached down and offered his hand to a striking woman in her early twenties. She smiled up at him and thanked him for his assistance. She made light work of the steps, bounding upwards with a graceful gait, taking them two at a time. She looked back when she reached the top and waved at Ray and Brian who both waved back. The two men turned and started to walk alongside the harbourside in the direction of the town's bridge.

Ray turned to see Brian glance casually over his shoulder to see if the girl was still watching from the top of the steps. She wasn't and Brian lowered his head as he walked.

They stopped at a cafe on the fringe of Hope Square; the central hub of the old harbour, dominated by the huge *"Brewer's Quay"* complex; an amalgamation of shops specialising in antiquities, arts and crafts and memorabilia. The area drew in the punters with its abundance of pubs, cafes and restaurants that lined the harbourside, tightly packed like a Victorian terrace meandering its way from the square to the town bridge that spanned the harbour.

A waitress showed them to a window seat and handed them each a menu. Brian didn't even glance at his .

"Can I have a large scotch please?" he asked, setting his menu down on the table.

The waitress stared at him as if he had asked if she was wearing a peephole bra.

"I'm sorry sir, we do not serve alcohol." She glanced over her shoulder at a clock on the wall. It was ten-thirty a.m. She sniffed disapprovingly at Brian for having the temerity to not only ask for alcohol but to do so at such an ungodly hour.

"Two regular black coffees please," Ray said, smiling up at the waitress. He picked up both menus and handed them back to her. She took them and smiled back at him.

"And could I get some scrambled eggs on a couple of rounds of wholemeal toast, no butter."

"Certainly, sir," the waitress beamed. She turned to Brian, but he waved her away. She turned abruptly on her heel and left to fetch the order. Brian gazed out of the window as Ray unwrapped his knife and fork from his napkin. They remained silent for a few minutes.

"She liked you," Brian said absently, still staring out of the window.

"The waitress?"

Brian shrugged. "Maybe. Maybe the waitress. Yeah, why not. But I was talking about the girl on the steps, the one you helped out of the boat."

"Yeah, whatever."

Brian laughed. "Christ, that is so easy for you to dismiss isn't it, Ray? It means nothing to you to disregard that tryst as if it was insignificant."

"Tryst?" Ray laughed. "What the hell are you talking about?"

"Only a handsome, confident man can be that blase."

Ray sat back in his chair and smiled.

"Brian, you didn't ask me all the way down here so we could discuss charm offensives." The waitress brought their coffees. Brian glanced out of the window again.

"My wife, Carol, won't speak to me, you want to know why? You want to hear how I fucked up my thirty-year marriage?"

Ray didn't say anything.

"Eighteen months ago, I met a girl, Ray, a beautiful thing in her twenties. I saw her in a bookstore in town. It was only a cheap, second-hand place. They always seem to do so well in coastal towns; them and the charity shops," he added wistfully. "My curiosity was piqued when I heard her ask for a copy of *Christian Meir's* biography of Caesar. You know I have a passion for Ancient Rome, but, of course, the shop only stocked pulp crime novels and trite romances, so I told her about *Ferman's,* the antiquarian book emporium just off The Esplanade. They specialise in literary fiction and biographies, and that's when she smiled at me, Ray. Oh my God, it was a thing of beauty, believe me."

The waitress brought Ray's scrambled eggs, but this time he did not smile at her. He continued to look at Brian across the small table. The waitress appeared hurt by this sudden cold demeanour and left hurriedly.

Ray picked up his knife and fork and started eating.

"Go on," he urged between mouthfuls.

"So I said, if she liked, I could show her how to get there. Not just directions, but walk with her, like a chaperone. I don't know what I was thinking, Ray, I swear that I thought she would say no, adamant like, but she just smiled again and said that would be great. So that's what we did. I walked with her to *Ferman's,* and we chatted all the way. No deep, heavy shit, just shooting the breeze." Brian paused and took a sip of his coffee. "You know what the strangest part was at that time. I mean we had literally just met, and you have any idea what was freaking me out?

Ray shook his head. "Enlighten me."

"It all seemed so perfectly reasonable. Normal. I've been married thirty-one years, Ray, and I've never strayed once, never. Okay, I admit I'm not Brad Pitt, but Carol loved me. She's a good wife, Ray," he added unnecessarily. "Romance never sought me out, but once I'd made a bit of cash, there were opportunities, frequent opportunities, but I was never tempted to take that final step. Thirty-one years, we had to be doing something right, wouldn't you say?"

Ray nodded. "I guess."

"Girls don't notice men like me, Ray. I don't stand out. I have never slept with anyone since the day I met Carol, but her."

Ray set his knife and fork down. He pushed the half-eaten plate of scrambled eggs to one side. "Some people would see that as an achievement of sorts," he said.

"Something to be proud of you mean?"

"Yeah, why not."

"You don't find it a little sad?"

Ray did not know where Brian was heading with this conversation. He decided to steer him back on course.

47

"So this amazing looking girl who showed an interest in you. You fucked her right?"

Brian looked hard at him and Ray was surprised to see defiance tinged with regret in his eyes.

"I did what any red-blooded man would do," he spat. "You show me somebody who would turn down such an offer and I'll show you a fucking liar!"

"Or somebody who is determined to stay faithful to his wife, no matter what."

Brian's eyes blazed with anger now, but Ray felt he had no right to be indignant. He certainly wasn't going to assuage Brian's guilt by justifying his actions.

"Calm down, Brian, I'm not judging you. Just don't play the " *it wasn't my fault"* card either. What happened?"

"She blackmailed me for twenty-five grand. Took me back to her shabby B and B, let me fuck her - twice, filmed the whole thing on a pinhole camera and threatened to put the clip online unless I gave her the money."

"Jesus, Brian. Did you pay her?"

Brian shook his head. "No man, I called her bluff." He took another sip of coffee. "It didn't work. She posted the clip in an email attachment to my wife. Carol left me."

Ray didn't know what to say, so said nothing

"You see that look the waitress gave me when I asked her for a scotch. Haughty bitch. I've never been a big drinker, Ray, but I've reached the stage where it doesn't really matter what I do now."

"How long have you got?" Ray asked.

"They told me not to start any long novels."

"Shit, Brian, I'm sorry."

Brian shrugged. "Pancreatic cancer. I was only diagnosed a year ago, but by then it was too late. Bastard

48

needs to be spotted *asap* otherwise there's no fucking hope. They told me I could go another year, but I'm not buying that. The fact that I can still move around is not the great indicator it should be. At times my back feels as if it's being pierced by hot spikes and I'm coughing up some weird shit. That's why I need to get my affairs in order, Ray. I need you to go back to Jersey for me, force the envelope down my daughter's throat if need be."

Ray nodded slowly but had no idea how he was to attempt that particular task. The meeting with Brian's daughter had been fraught, to say the least.

Brian finished his coffee and winced. Whether it was from the taste or some unseen, unrelenting pain, Ray didn't know.

"There's something else too. One last thing I want you to do for me."

CHAPTER 6

"So what do you think?" Brian asked.

Ray looked around the small lounge and connected kitchen . The cottage was small but tastefully decorated; neutral colours and no excess of nautical paraphernalia that some people found was an ideal complement for a seaside abode.

"It's nice, Brian." He meant it too.

"Carol likes it here," Brian said, opening the fridge and getting them both a can of beer. He handed one to Ray, opened his own and drained nearly half the contents in one long pull. Ray set his own beer down on the table.

"I looked at it as an investment originally," Brian continued. "Holiday lets are quite lucrative, but Carol didn't like the idea of sharing her home with anybody. We've got a big house in Dorchester, but we tend to spend more time here in Weymouth now. I mean we did," he added ruefully. "I'll leave it to Carol once I've gone, the big house too. It won't make amends, but what are you going to do?"

"You did well since we left the unit," Ray said.

Brian nodded enthusiastically. He took another gulp of his beer and set it on the table next to Ray's unopened can. "Property investment really. I was fortunate, buying at the right time, selective tenants, selling once the market was buoyant, it's just anticipating the peaks and troughs, to be honest."

Ray nodded, but he knew there was a little more to it than that. He had always been poor with money, never saving or investing wisely. After leaving the army, he had signed on with an employment agency, wanting a more simplistic life. Most of the work offered was in warehouses or factories, usually on a production line for minimum wage. Ray wasn't bothered, the menial work was banal but surprisingly satisfying. He enjoyed the option of moving on when the tedium became too much. At one point he was offered the job of supervisor in a factory but hated the idea of the authority that would come with the position. After serving in the army, civilian life, by comparison, was far more sedate. At times the repetition of the work threatened to overwhelm him, but Ray was seeking uncomplicated stability in his life at the time.

When Brian had contacted him a couple of weeks ago asking him to deliver the letter to his estranged daughter in Jersey he had been able to accept without having to worry about disrupting any work patterns.

They had spoken on the phone, Brian simply stating that he was ill and unable to deliver the message personally. Ray had let that obvious lie slide. If there was a personal issue that Brian did not wish to disclose that was his prerogative. Ray had picked up the letter from a solicitor's office in Weymouth yesterday, arriving back today. He believed that the job was simply Brian's way of getting him to come down and discuss this secondary matter. It didn't concern Ray. Brian was dying, he was allowed to indulge himself a little.

"Carol will be fine once I've gone," Brian said. "I've put everything in her name, Lucy will be okay too. There's a cheque for two hundred grand in there," he nodded at the envelope that Ray had attempted to deliver to Brian's estranged daughter.

She had stared Ray down when he had presented it to her, then she had asked him what it was. He had simply told her to open it. He had no idea of the contents at the time. Lucy had grown suspicious and folded her arms. Ray thought that she believed she was being served.

"It's from your father," he had said, realising his mistake the moment he had made the declaration.

"In that case, you can take it back and tell him to stick it up his fucking arse," she had spat. Ray had returned with the envelope unopened. He had decided not to repeat her message verbatim.

"I want you to find somebody for me," Brian said. He sat down at the table and stared intently at Ray for a few seconds, then his eyes fell to the unopened can. "You going to drink that?" Ray shook his head and slid it across to Brian. The older man cracked it open and took another long swallow.

"The girl," Brian said.

"The one who blackmailed you?"

Brian nodded. He walked away from the table and opened a small bureau set in an alcove in the adjacent lounge. He took out an A4 cardboard file and sat back down.

"I never saw the video," he said quietly, Carol had a copy, obviously, the one the bitch e-mailed her, and after screaming at me for endless hours, she described what happened in it in great detail. So originally, I had no pictures of the girl. When I met her in the book shop she told me her name was Helena. Helena Landless, but that was undoubtedly a lie."

Ray nodded. "It's a character from the novel, *The Mystery Of Edwin Drood.*"

Brian blinked in surprise. "How did you know that?"

Ray shrugged. "I don't know, a random fact I can recall, I guess. Didn't you go online and look it up?"

Brian nodded absently. " Eventually. I remember thinking that it was risky on her part, using a pseudonym that I may have recognised. I guess it could have been legit. Maybe her parents were fond of the book."

Ray didn't believe that for a minute. *Edwin Drood* was not one of Dickens' most memorable novels. He had died whilst writing it, so it remained incomplete, hardly a foundation for a solid fan base. It occurred to him that the mysterious Helena had proved not only seductive but cocky too.

"You said you didn't have a picture originally." He nodded down at the file. "I guess you have one now."

Brian nodded and opened the folder. "This is her."

He handed Ray a large colour, glossy photograph. The image had been enlarged, but the quality was still very good. The picture showed a striking girl in her early twenties on a dance floor, the camera had caught her as her long hair cut a wide arc in the air as she danced. She was smiling, obviously happy. She was with a handsome man of similar age, also smiling. To their left was a second couple, a man in his forties, slightly overweight and looking a little uncomfortable on the dance floor, alongside a stunning girl about the same age as Helena.

"This was taken in a bar, the night after I had met Helena in the bookstore. I'm what is known as a pillar of the community, or at least I was, so I know people" Brian laughed, the sound came out like a sharp bark. "When Carol left me I was on my own and I started to investigate. I called in a few favours; the owner of the bar is a particular friend, we're both members of the Rotary Club. I thought there was a good chance that Helena would have stayed in the town for a while. The B and B she took me back to is on the front, but I couldn't go asking questions there for obvious reasons."

Ray studied the image. "You recognise the other couple?"

Brian shook his head. "Nah, could be anybody, but this is a good likeness of her, don't know the guy she's dancing with either. You think that will give you something to go on?"

Ray looked up from the photograph and stared at the older man. "I haven't said I would take it on yet, Brian."

Brian smiled. He reached into the file and took out an envelope. He tossed it onto the table. Ray could see that it was stuffed with cash.

"There's five grand in there," Brian announced grandly, "Expenses and a down payment."

"A generous down payment."

Brian sat down heavily. He pushed the half-full beer can away and rested his chin on his open palm. "I want justice, Raymond, the last wish of a dying man. The money means nothing to me now, you know that."

"By justice, you mean having her arrested?"

Brian nodded slowly. There were flecks of white saliva pooled at the sides of his mouth. He brushed his hand across his dry lips and smiled. "I'm not asking you to kill her, Ray. Find her and then hand her over to the police, that's all I want."

"We were never the best of friends in the army," Ray said truthfully. "Why me?"

"Because I know you will find her, Ray, that's what you are good at. It's a business transaction, nothing more" He hesitated, then held out a hand, and for a moment Ray thought he was reaching for the beer. Only when Brian raised it further did he realise that he wanted to cement the deal with a handshake. Ray took the older man's hand in his own and shook it.

"Okay, Brian. I'll find her."

CHAPTER 7

Situated between the coastal resorts of Great Yarmouth and Lowestoft, is the small seaside village of Hopton; a popular location due to its close proximity to it's larger commercial neighbours.

On a large holiday park of over three hundred static holiday caravans is The Elm Tree Carvery Restaurant and Cabaret Bar. Built in the late sixties, it's a sprawling, slightly shabby building in need of an update. The carvery bar is approached via a pair of large double doors, with polished brass handles running the length. A small fish pond sits to the right of the entrance, raised on a concrete pedestal with a brick surround. The constant flow of running water from a decorative fountain set in the centre of the pond can be either relaxing or annoying, depending on the customer's mood.

The carvery bar is panelled in oak; stained and patchy, the area is mainly a holding area for those waiting to use the carvery restaurant, though it attracts many of the park's patrons who just want a drink.

Gemma had been working in the restaurant since Boxing Day. She had no predetermined destination once she left Gregory in the bar at the hotel in Wellingborough. She had spent Christmas Eve and Christmas Day helping out in a soup kitchen in Great Yarmouth. The charity running the kitchen neither questioned her motives or her circumstances, they were simply grateful for the extra pair of hands. They had let her sleep in one of their supported hostels in a rundown area of the town centre. Again she wasn't interrogated.

"The righteous are there to aid the needy, not judge the circumstances that befall them," one helper had proclaimed, rather preachily, Gemma had concluded, but she was grateful for the charity all the same. Her funds were rapidly depleting.

On Boxing Day she had overheard a girl in the soup kitchen mention vacancies at The Elm Tree in Hopton and she had paid over the odds for a cab to make the five mile trip as no buses were running to the village.

There was a cardboard sign in the window, simply asking for relief staff. She knew that they would be busy over the New Year period, so Gemma simply walked in and asked to speak to the manager. He asked her about her experience and she told him that she had worked in several bars in London. Pubs were closing so frequently nowadays that it would be difficult for them to check the authenticity of her story, not that Gemma was concerned. She knew that work would be sporadic for now. Once the holiday period was over she could look for something a little more stable than bar work and waitressing.

The manager's name was Paul Overton. He told her he was mainly looking for people to wait tables in the restaurant.

"It's not difficult," he explained. " It's a carvery , so they help themselves. You just need to take their drink orders and bring them the dessert trolley."

There was a trial period of two weeks. Gemma bonded well with the Elm Tree staff. All those who waited in the restaurant were girls. At twenty-eight, Gemma was the oldest.

Overton was in charge of running everything. The owner of The Elm Tree was a huge Scotsman called Patterson, who spent eight months of the year at his villa in Portugal. His infrequent trips to the Elm Tree consisted of little more than sitting at the end of the bar, downing copious amounts of Port, demanding that the bar staff make a note of the amount he was consuming, and then present him with the bill at the end of the night, that he had never once paid in the twelve years he had run the business since inheriting it from his father.

There were six workers on split part-time shifts who tended the bar, and a bar manager called Nigel Moon, who all the girls warned Gemma about because of his wandering eye and hands.

Gemma had adapted well to her new way of life, even enjoyed it to a certain extent. What she allocated for her entire food budget for a week now she could have easily spent on a single bottle of wine at one of her former, favourite restaurants.

Her digs were cheap (a tiny bedsit above a kebab shop in Lowestoft) and she was able to get a lift into work with other employees who lived in the town.

She knew that her life before was a folly, a succession of debauched and self-conscious days spent in the company of people whom she mainly loathed, and were themselves loathsome because of their desire to associate wealth, and it's abuse, with power and success. If she was being honest, she would have to admit that she missed parts of it. It was nice to be pampered once in a while, even though her treats were little more than rewards for services rendered.

Her new life was far from perfect, but there was a certain stability ensconced within the mundane existence. There was tension, of course, that was inevitable, though she had learned to curb her anxieties slightly, so that not every stranger was viewed as somebody who recognised her from her past.

In the first few weeks after leaving London, it had been frightening how the paranoia enveloped her, so much so that she was convinced that every passing glance was a look of recognition, every perusal or double-take, a calculated observation. The longer she remained *"at large"* (an expression that she perversely relished) the less stressful she felt. She had changed her hair again. Now it was shoulder-length, and auburn. She had kept the glasses, even though they were intrusive and she didn't like the look.

Near the end of January, Gemma had been waitressing in the carvery restaurant. It was Sunday dinner time, one of the busiest periods of the week as the restaurant was open to patrons and others not staying at the park. The chef presented a decent three roasts and seasonal veg. Earlier than morning she saw a piece in *The Sun on Sunday* newspaper. Not front-page news but a story tucked away on page six. The headline read: *Businessman's Son Missing.* Gemma scanned the story thoroughly, the article reporting the disappearance of Clive Cooper on a trip to Bolivia on January fourth. She cut the piece out and filed it away. Clive Cooper was dead, she knew that, but somebody was covering it up. For now, she didn't know why.

Gemma was waiting tables, taking the drink and dessert orders. The clientele was mainly local, though there were a few early season revellers taking advantage of off-peak prices. The restaurant was full.

A man reached out and grabbed her arm as she passed. This annoyed the hell out of Gemma, but it was a common occurrence and she had learned to live with it, even if it was rude to the extreme.

She glanced down at his hand on her arm, and he appeared to realise his *faux pas* and released her. He was sitting with a woman, who Gemma assumed was his wife and two kids both under ten. They were bored, the elder of the two, a boy of about eight was kicking his sibling under the table, who in turn was protesting to his mother. The woman seemed worn down by their bickering and sat stoic-like beside them, oblivious to the older boy's euphoria at having a free reign to continue the bullying, and his brother's protests to his mother for her lack of intervention. Gemma had seen this behaviour on so many occasions. The family was nearing the end of their holiday, and they were getting on each other's nerves. The mothers, in particular, were ground down over the week. Suddenly the man turned and snapped at the older boy.

"George, pack it in, now!" he hissed. Berated, George stopped swinging his legs. His brother poked his tongue out and George quietly fumed. The man glanced at his wife for a second, but she had the glazed expression of someone who had no intention of intervening. The man turned his attention back to Gemma.

"Sorry about that, miss."

Gemma shrugged. It was no big deal.

"What can I do for you, sir?"

"Do you think we could get a jug of water?"

"Yes, of course. If you could just bear with me for a few minutes, I'll get one for you."

She hurried away to where, at another table, three young men in their twenties were seated. They were loud, and growing a little raucous. George's father shot them a disapproving glance. As Gemma approached, one of the three called out to her.

"Yo, Sugar Tits, can we get some beers?"

Gemma ambled over to him, leaned in close and said,

"You'll get a fucking slap if you call me Sugar Tits again." She spoke quietly, but loud enough for his mates to hear, both of whom dissolved into fits of laughter.

"Yo Bazza," one of them cried. "Busted man!" Bazza smiled up at her. He was handsome and confident. He sat back in his chair and appraised Gemma, who simply stared him down. She was fully aware of her own attractiveness and confidence. Then he laughed.

"Hey, I'm sorry babe, but you are the cream on the strudel."

Gemma took out her notebook and pencil. "What can I get for you?"

But Bazza kept on looking up at her. His eyes narrowed and his smile re-appeared though Gemma didn't like this one so much. There was a sly tinge to it.

"Hey, do I know you?" he asked.

Suddenly the room was silent as if she had just immersed her head in a bath of warm water. Gemma stared at the man who had spoken to her.

Bazza?

Did she recognise him? Was he familiar? She didn't think so, but did he really recognise her? In her mind, she heard the sentence over and over.

"Hey, do I know you?"

Then she was back. The hubbub and sounds of the restaurant surrounded her. Bazza was still gazing up at her, but he looked confused now.

"You're not from around here are you?"

When Gemma didn't reply, Bazza stood up and placed a hand over his heart.

"In here, this is where I know you from." His mates laughed at the corny line, but Gemma let out a sigh of relief. She managed a thin smile, but the incident had shaken her badly. As she walked away from the table, Bazza started to sing. *"I want a woman like Marilyn Monroe, the kind of woman that will never say no."*

It was a Prince song that Gemma recognised. Bazza didn't seem to care that he was in the middle of a crowded restaurant. He was spurned on by his mates, even though the audience seemed distinctly underwhelmed. Gemma turned and smiled at him. Encouraged, Bazza's voice rose,

"The kind of woman that'll make you scream, that's the girl of my dreams!"

Gemma had slept with Bazza that night in his caravan. It was the first time she had made love to a man who wasn't paying for the privilege for as long as she could remember.

It was wonderful.

At the beginning of April, Paul Overton called Gemma into his office. He was a fastidious man in his early fifties, bald with small, feminine hands and perfectly manicured nails. He had a peculiar, antiquated turn of phrase, often using words like *marvellous* and *splendid* as if he was an officer in the military during the Second World War.

He smelled of rubbing ointment; an odour that Gemma recognised but couldn't place, Deep Heat or Ralgex, maybe for a niggling shoulder injury, or a stiff neck, as he was always massaging this area. Perhaps it was just the stress of the job. She wondered how he would react if she offered to alleviate some of the tension. She couldn't be a hooker for as many years as she had without inheriting a sense of mischief.

But she had settled into this job and was enjoying it far more than she thought she would, and she didn't want to jeopardise it by making advances that could quite easily be frowned upon. Overton had shown very little interest in her, and although she was not so conceited to believe that every man should swoon or be overawed in her presence, Paul Overton had appeared so indifferent to, not only Gemma but every other girl on his team, that she was convinced he was gay.

"Nigel Moon has left us," Overton said as Gemma settled into a seat across the desk to her superior. He regarded her seriously over the top of his frameless spectacles.

"When you first applied for a job here, you said that you had previous experience in bar work, is it something that appeals to you?"

Gemma rested her hands in her lap. "Are you offering me the position of bar manager?"

"Not necessarily." Overton frowned a little at her presumptuous manner, but Gemma was certain that she was not wrong. She knew that Moon was the only full-time member of the bar staff team, the others were all part-time. Never really looking for full-time work, they were mainly supplementing college courses, working around the kids, or boosting low salaries with other part-time jobs.

"I'm pleased with your work," Overton said. "You're punctual, have fitted in very well with the others and you're not afraid of hard work. If you can show me that you have the capability of managing the bar, then I will consider you for the position."

Gemma nodded. "Okay."

Overton shuffled some papers on his desk. "It would mean taking on some responsibilities in the top bar also, that means some late nights, particularly on Friday and Saturday's."

Gemma nodded again. All the staff referred to the cabaret bar as the top bar. Most of the time it hosted disco's and dinner dances alongside local comedians and singers, although sometimes, in the summer months, a few recognised celebrities would take to the stage, those just closing a summer season at Yarmouth or Lowestoft. On those occasions, the top bar would sell out, and the demands for staff increased.

"What happened with Nigel?" Gemma asked."

Overton coughed delicately into his hand. "I'm not at liberty to discuss that at the moment, safe to say there will be an inquiry by the management regarding inappropriate behaviour. The bar manager's salary isn't high, but it does come with a very attractive fringe benefit."

Gemma raised her eyebrows at that and detected the faintest of smiles dance on Overton's lips.

"Your own accommodation," Overton announced grandly. "All regular full-time staff have their own paid for static on-site." He sat back in his chair and smiled, revealing small white teeth. "I can see that interests you."

"When can I start?" Gemma replied enthusiastically.

"Right away, for a trial period of course," he added quickly. "There's a girl in the outer office here for a job, you think you can interview her, and go through some of the basics?"

"Of course," Gemma replied quickly. *How difficult could it be?* she mused.

Overton nodded again. "Splendid, I'll make the introductions."

He stood up and left the office. Gemma could hear him talking outside and then he reappeared accompanied by a girl in her late teens or early twenties. She was smaller than Gemma, with alabaster white skin, red hair and a small, acorn sized birthmark on the side of her neck. She was pretty, in a girl next door kind of way, and she dressed plainly in clothes that would be more suited to a woman twice her age.

Gemma stood up and the girl smiled shyly. Gemma offered her hand and the girl shook it.

"Gemma this is Carly Decker," Paul said. "Gemma is our bar manager," he announced grandly as if the deal had already been finalised.

"Nice to meet you," Gemma said, not realising at the time that the meeting with Carly Decker was about to change her life dramatically.

CHAPTER 8

The house in Dorchester was set back from the street. A wide, paved driveway, flanked either side by strategically placed cedar trees, hid most of the property from view, lending it an air of mystery.

Ray sat in his car and waited. Carol Harrier had arrived home about an hour ago. He had watched her as she drove up to the house and took two cases from the rear of her parked Range Rover. Then she had disappeared from view as the cedar trees blocked his sightline.

Well, an hour was surely long enough for her to settle, Ray mused. He opened the door of his Audi and walked across the narrow street. There was an intercom housed on the wall by the gate. Ray pressed the call button and a woman's voice answered almost immediately.

"Yes?"

"Mrs Harrier?"

"Yes," the voice was neither impatient or curious.

"My name is Ray Jessop, I served with your husband in the same army unit."

There was a moment's hesitation then: "My husband is dead."

"I know that Mrs Harrier, I would like to talk to you about Brian if you don't mind."

"I do mind, Mister Jessop. I don't open my door to just anybody, and certainly not to a stranger who has been sitting in his car outside my house for the past hour. I take it you are the man in the Audi?"

Ray sighed. "Yes, I wanted to make sure you were settled after returning from your holiday."

"How did you know that I have been on holiday, or was returning on this day as a matter of fact? You're sounding more sinister by the minute, Mister Jessop. Goodbye."

She clicked off.

"Shit," Ray muttered. He pressed the intercom again and as before Carol Harrier answered straight away.

Ray spoke before she had a chance to say anything. "I'm a private investigator, Mrs Harrier, your husband hired me just before his death."

Another pause. "Why would he do that, Mister Jessop?"

Ray pushed forward. "He wanted me to find the girl who blackmailed him."

Carol Harrier didn't say anything and he thought that she had hung up on him again, but then he heard the click of the intercom disconnecting and the gate swung open silently.

Brian Harrier was fifty-four when he died. His wife looked a lot younger, about forty, Ray thought, though he knew she must be older, as Brian had stated they had been married for thirty-two years.

Carol stood about five-nine, slightly taller than her husband. Her shoulder-length, auburn hair was tied in a ponytail, and her face was brown from the holiday sun. There was a splash of freckles across the bridge of her nose, which highlighted her youthful appearance. She was wearing light blue shorts and a loose-fitting chambray shirt, the top two buttons undone, revealing a small bust and a freckled cleavage. She was barefoot and her legs were shapely and tanned. She smelled slightly of coconut oil. Ray thought that it may be the residue of sunblock. Two large cases with small wheels were in the hallway where Carol stood looking Ray up and down, her hand poised on the door jamb ready to slam it in his face if the need arose. She didn't ask him in.

"So did you find her?" Carol asked, shifting her weight from one foot to the other.

"No, I didn't."

"When did my husband approach you?"

"Just over a month ago."

"I buried Brian two weeks ago."

"I know, I was at the funeral."

"I don't remember seeing you."

"You wouldn't have done . I kept a low profile. I didn't think it appropriate to approach you at the graveside or the wake afterwards. It was my intention to meet earlier, Mrs Harrier, but of course, you were on holiday."

Her eyes blazed angrily momentarily. "That sounds very much like condemnation to me, Mister Jessop."

Ray shrugged. "Does it? It wasn't meant to."

"Is that why you came here, to pass judgment?"

"No, I came to give you this." Ray opened a small leather document case that was under his arm and handed her the envelope Brian had given to him in Weymouth.

Carol took the envelope and turned it over in her hands. "What is it?"

"Five thousand pounds. It was what your husband was prepared to pay me for finding the girl who blackmailed him."

"Five thousand? Your fees seem rather steep, MIster Jessop."

"I didn't say that was my fee, I said it was what your husband was prepared to pay me. He took out a second envelope. "This is for your daughter. Brian asked me to deliver it to her before his death but she refused to accept it."

"What is it?"

"I don't know," Ray lied. He had decided to leave the letter with Brian's wife as opposed to approaching Lucy again.

"Couldn't he have just posted it?"

"I don't know, Mrs Harrier. Maybe, yes I suppose he could. I guess he wanted to make sure that she received it, that is why he asked me to deliver it by hand. If she had received the letter through the post and decided to ignore him, then he would have had no way of knowing if she had received it or not." Ray held up his hands. "Well that's it, Mrs Harrier," He nodded a farewell and turned to go, but Carol placed a gentle yet restraining hand on his arm.

"Do you want to come in for a while?" she asked.

"What for?"

Coffee?"

Ray nodded. "Coffee. Yeah, why not."

"I'm not an insensitive person, Mister Jessop," Carol said, "But he hurt me so much. For Brian, money was important, it brought respect and status. I'm not going to lie and tell you that I didn't enjoy the wealth. This house..." she spread her arms wide, indicating the lavish surroundings. The lounge was tastefully decorated, neutral whites, unimposing, expensive ornaments, and as large as the entire floor space of Ray's apartment. "The holiday cottage in Weymouth, the cars, the lifestyle itself. I enjoyed it, I still do," she added ruefully. "But I was also happy before the money started coming in, we both were. I still don't know why he did it. Our sex life was quite active. I enjoyed it, I believed that Brian felt the same way. Evidently I was wrong about that."

"Men have affairs for many reasons," Ray said, realising how trite that sounded almost immediately.

Carol Harrier offered him a wan smile. "I would hardly call it an affair, Mister Jessop, more a brief fling. I can understand a man having his head turned, especially as he gets older, but Brian was smart. Once the hurt and anger had dissipated, I was left feeling disappointed that Brian could have been so easily duped and manipulated like that."

"I take it Lucy felt the same way?"

Carol nodded slowly. "My daughter took it very badly, refused to speak to him, even though I implored her not to take such a defiant stand."

Ray raised his eyebrows in surprise.

"I didn't want Lucy to hate her father, Mister Jessop, I felt that my anger was enough for both of us, but I couldn't force her to forgive him either."

"You didn't speak to him after the…. liaison?"

"Let's agree to call it a fling," Carol said and smiled sadly. "Only to sort out financial issues. We separated almost immediately, I couldn't bear to be near him, the hurt was that acute. I remained here and Brian stayed at the cottage in Weymouth. He tried so hard initially to make amends, but it was still so raw for me, and then I guess once he had been diagnosed, he kind of gave up. What's the point of reconciliation if you've no time to enjoy it?"

"You didn't know about the cancer initially?"

Carol shook her head. "It was so like Brian not to mention it. He would have thought of it as playing the sympathy card, especially after what he had done. He would have hated for me to pity him, I know that. Brian's brother, Michael, called me the day Brian passed away, that was the first time I had heard. It was all so quick, from the time he had been diagnosed until the time he died. I had spoken to Brian on several occasions, but he never once mentioned his illness. It was difficult for me to see beyond the betrayal. I don't know how things would have worked out had he not died, I guess that's all academic now."

"Would you have taken him back had you known he was dying?"

Carol stared hard at him for a few seconds and Ray wondered if his question had crossed a boundary, but then Carol smiled.

"Probably not. The cut was very deep, but I still wish that he had told me. Michael and the rest of his family view me as the bad guy now. I don't really care as I doubt that we will ever see each other again. I would have liked to have spoken to Brian though, at the end I mean. He must have been so lonely and frightened." A sob caught in her throat and she took several deep breaths in order to compose herself. "You can't suddenly stop loving somebody after three decades together, no matter what they did. Are you married, Mister Jessop?"

The question caught Ray off guard. He hesitated then shook his head. "My wife and daughter were both killed in a road accident four years ago."

"Oh how dreadful for you!"

It was an unusual response. Most people would say how sorry they were; the initial reaction to being told such devastating news was always one of concern and condolences. Rarely was the onus of sympathy laid so abjectly at Ray's own doorstep. He wasn't sure how to reply so he said nothing.

"Were you and Brian friends in the army?" Carol asked.

Ray was relieved that she had changed the subject. The fact that he had not offered any further information was probably the reason for Carol Harrier's changing tack. She was an astute woman, the conversation was easy and relaxed, despite the sensitive issues they were prepared to discuss. Her initial hostility, although understandable, was possibly a smokescreen, Ray believed. Considering the animosity between herself and Brian's family, it was probably quite a relief to be able to discuss the positive side of her relationship with her late husband. He hadn't acknowledged his friendship with Brian himself, he saw no reason to lie to Carol about it now.

"No, not really, " he said. "Brian was a warrant officer, I was in military intelligence. We served in the same unit, but our relationship was little more than nodding acquaintances. He called me up because of my background, not because we had any close bonds."

"Military intelligence. It sounds very exciting, can you talk about it?"

"Not really."

"Classified?"

"No, because for the most part, it was incredibly boring."

Carol nodded and they were quiet for a moment. She asked Ray if he wanted a top-up and he declined. "Something stronger?" she asked. Ray thought of Brian; the heavy drinking that seemed almost defiant in light of his terminal illness. He wondered if Carol was aware that the problem even existed. If Brian was to be believed when he indicated that it was a recent thing - the binges precipitated by the notion that he was going to die, maybe Carol had no idea that he had even gone down such a path. He shook his head.

"No thanks."

She sat down on the couch opposite him and folded her hands in her lap.

"So you're a private investigator now then?"

Ray shrugged. "Not really. I find people. That's what I did in the army. Seeking out those lost in conflict, hostages, friendlies trapped behind enemy lines, deserters. Brian was aware of my background and called me to help him."

"But you didn't find the girl who blackmailed my husband?"

Ray shook his head. "I hadn't really started to be honest with you."

"What do you know about her?" Carol asked.

"Very little, but then I didn't know anything about anybody who I searched for and found in the past. I worked from photographs, and for the most part, they were pointless."

"Why?"

"The majority of the people I looked for were kids, runaways as a rule and the parents would always give me a picture in which the kid was smiling and happy. Nobody keeps a photo of a sullen, unhappy child, but they would have been far more beneficial, as it would be a more accurate description once the kid had spent some time on the streets."

"Did you find many?"

"Quite a few. Not as many as I'd have liked, and certainly not as many as the parents hoped I'd find."

"So what exactly have you learned so far?"

"Excuse me?"

"The girl, you must know something about her?"

"I can't discuss that with you, Mrs. Harrier."

"Why not?"

"Because I was hired by your husband, not you."

"Is that a legal thing, like a lawyer/client confidentiality agreement?"

"Not necessarily, but from an ethical viewpoint I think it would be inappropriate to discuss the matter with anyone apart from the person who hired me."

"My husband is dead, Mister Jessop. I saw a video of some slut sucking his cock. I hardly think that anything you divulge now is going to shock me." She sat back on the sofa and crossed her arms defiantly over her chest.

Ray inclined his head, conceding her point.

"Okay, how about if I retain your services so that you can continue the investigation."

"Is that what you want?" Ray asked, surprised.

"Why wouldn't I? That bitch ruined more than one life. It would be insensitive of me to continue seeing my husband as the only guilty party."

Ray nodded. "Very well."

Carol picked up the envelope stuffed with cash and counted out two thousand pounds. She held it out to Ray who took it from her and riffled the notes with the edge of his thumb like a seasoned card player.

"That's another few days, to begin with, but after that, it won't be cash. I'll need a list of expenses and then we can settle on the presentation of an invoice. How does that sit with you, Mister Jessop?"

"That's fine." Ray opened his leather document case again and took out the photograph of the girl who had blackmailed Brian Harrier. He handed it across to Carol who stared at it intently.

"This is the girl from the video. Where was this taken?" she asked quietly.

"A club in Weymouth. Brian acquired it, pulled in a few favours. Do you still have the video?"

Carol shook her head vigorously. "No, I do not."

Ray didn't say anything and Carol reddened slightly.

"I watched it when I first opened the attachment. I couldn't believe it, it still sickens me now just thinking about it, I watched it again before confronting Brian. Once he had admitted to the fling, well how could he not, I deleted the file."

"Did you show it to anybody else?"

Carol snorted in derision. "Of course not."

"Do Brian's family know about the fling?"

"No, I don't think so."

"But you told Lucy?"

Carol shifted uncomfortably in her seat. "She's my daughter, I couldn't just split with her father without telling her why."

"So there are no copies of the video?"

"I just told you, no."

"That's a shame," Ray said.

"You have the photograph,"

"It's all I have to go on."

"So what have you learned so far?"

" She calls herself Helena, I think she's a sex worker."

"What makes you think that?"

"There aren't many girls who are prepared to offer sex for money, even if it is through blackmail. The fact that she is prepared to do so on film also, and would therefore be unperturbed by who sees it, also makes me wonder. Yeah, I think she may be a prostitute.

"That hardly narrows it down,"

Ray nodded. "That's true, but it gives me an opportunity to talk to people who may be able to help us"

Carol Harrier raised her eyebrows. "You know many prostitutes?"

Ray smiled. "I know plenty. Working the seedier sides of the street, you come into contact with many characters, and you have to form some kind of a rapport or they'll never talk to you. Hookers, pimps, fences, petty thieves. Most will talk if you ask the right questions"

"You mean you pay them off?"

"Of course that's what I mean, they're hardly going to do it for a smile and my eternal gratitude.

"Whatever happened to the tart with the heart?" Carol said, a hint of a smile on her lips.

"I've yet to meet her," Ray said. "But rest assured, all fees for services rendered will appear on my next invoice. Have you thought about a reward?"

"For information leading to an arrest?"

Ray nodded.

"How much do you think would be reasonable?"

"It's more a matter of what is viable, Mrs Harrier. The people who associate with girls like Helena are likely to want to be paid well for such information, they're not going to give somebody up for nothing."

Loyalty amongst thieves," Carol scoffed.

"Something like that."

"Shall we say three thousand to set the ball rolling?"

Ray nodded. "I think that will suffice."

Carol nodded. "Okay." She held out a perfectly manicured hand , and Ray shook it. Her hands were small and delicate, slightly oily to the touch as if she had recently applied cream. Again Ray caught the smell of coconut oil.

"One other thing," Carol said. "I don't want to involve the police."

"Why?"

"Because Brian's family knows nothing about this, and I don't think there's any need for them to find out either."

Ray nodded slowly. "You realise that if I find the girl, then the police will have to be informed and it will be impossible to keep it from Brian's family."

"I know that Mister Jessop, but then I will have closure myself. We all have our demons to contend with, the truth about Brian's infidelity will be theirs." She sighed heavily. "There's no point in saying anything now, in case you don't find her, they'd just think I was lying anyway don't you think?"

"Maybe," he conceded. Though he knew that she was probably right.

CHAPTER 9

It had only taken a few days for Gemma to realise that Carly Decker had a crush on her.

This was not immodesty on Gemma's part as there were clear signs that the younger girl had genuine feelings for her. She fiddled with her hair and smiled coquettishly whenever Gemma spoke to her. When they were close enough to touch, Carly would do so - frequently. A brush of hands when stacking glasses, fingers stroking a bare arm when replenishing shelves, and the boldness of a hug when the situation clearly did not warrant it. Gemma didn't mind. Carly was a sweet girl without a hint of animosity in her. Gemma liked her. She was also flattered.

She had attracted admirers in the past; some that were appreciated - the present givers for example - some less so, such as the fixated punters who believed that any form of a relationship between a hooker and a client could exist outside the contractual boundary. Some were merely a nuisance, insisting that there had to be more than just sex. As Candy Girl, Gemma assured them that this was not the case. If their delusions were to be accepted, would they be prepared to let her move in with them? Could they envisage her as a mother to their children? Would they want her to meet with parents and other members of the family? When asked how they met, how would they answer? Infatuation was a clouded emotion, countering rational thought and reason with desire and unrealistic expectations. Usually, a reality check would shatter these illusions and the status quo would be resumed.

Usually, not always. There would always be people like Howard Price.

Howard was a chiropodist, a successful family man who Gemma had been seeing for a little over eight months. He was a regular client, twice, sometimes three times a month, the rendezvous always in a hotel room. There was nothing unusual in this, of course. He always had a bottle of Gemma's favourite wine, and they would chat for up to an hour after sex, sometimes smoke a little weed.

Howard was a poor lover, constantly in need of reassurance. Again this was not uncommon. Most punters are insecure, it is the main reason they seek out prostitutes in the first place, but Howard Price was a constant theme.

A couple of years ago he asked her to go with him to a conference on the coast.

"We could spend the weekend together, the two of us," he had said excitedly. Gemma had smiled and told him quite clearly that that was not the way things worked.

"But I'll pay you, obviously, think of it as a busman's holiday, I'm not asking you to come to the conference, we can eat out, go dancing, it'll be fun."

He had forgotten to include the fact that he would be fucking her, of course, but that in itself was not a new proposition, it was simply a change of location. So Gemma had agreed.

It had been a big mistake.

The holiday itself was okay, it had been the first time Gemma had ever been to the seaside, but Howard was overbearing from the off. It was obvious that his intention was to show her off, although she could never meet any of his colleagues. He was a respected, married man, after all, but that didn't stop him from presenting his trophy girlfriend at every club that his respectable associates wouldn't dream of frequenting.

Pubs and bars were especially embarrassing. Gemma was hit on, as she knew that she would be. In one club Howard had exploded when she had dared to dance with another guy. It had backfired on him, of course. Gemma's admirer had laughed at Howard's fury but had quickly grown angry and indignant at the older man's threats and belligerent attitude.

He had laid into Howard, a flurry of quick punches, that luckily didn't do too much damage because of the other club-goers hindering his swings on the busy dance floor. Gemma had managed to pull the younger guy off, receiving a mouthful of abuse herself for her troubles. That didn't bother her, name-calling was par for the course.

Howard was bloodied but unrepentant.

"We're leaving, come on," he had demanded, grabbing Gemma by the arm and hauling her off the dance floor.

She had slapped him then. Hard.

"What the fuck are you doing?" Gemma screamed. "Do you know who you are anymore Howard? *DO YOU?*"

He had stared at her, his face a mask of confusion. Gemma left him standing there, returned to the hotel, packed her bags and left. She caught an overnight train and didn't see Howard for four days. When he did call on her, he had the decency to do so face to face.

"I'm so sorry," he said as he stood at her front door, his eyes downcast.

"I'm not your possession, Howard," Gemma said, still angry. "I don't belong to anybody. I can be bought, but not owned, do you get that?"

"Yes."

"Do you understand that?"

"I do, yes, I'm sorry."

But Howard hadn't understood. Their meetings after the holiday were fraught with emotion. He had been unable to perform and blamed her for making him stressed. He was angry and emotional, crying on one occasion. He exploded one evening after failing to get an erection and raised a hand to her.

"Don't," Gemma had said simply. "You will regret that Howard."

"I'm regretting a lot of things," he snapped, but he lowered his hand.

After that incident, Gemma had told him not to call her again.

He had called her, of course, he didn't stop calling, pleading, cajoling, threatening, whatever it took. It was all too late now, Gemma knew that and she believed that Howard did also, but that didn't stop him from attempting a reconciliation.

The phone calls became more frequent, flowers and gifts were sent on a daily basis. On one occasion he turned up at a restaurant that Gemma was eating at with an influential client. He was shabbily dressed and wild-eyed, falling on his knees and begging Gemma to return his calls until an embarrassed maitre d had him unceremoniously hauled away.

Gemma had apologised to her client, but he had simply smiled. "I can make this problem disappear for you, Candy," he had said, delicately dabbing at the corner of his mouth with a napkin.

She shook her head. "I don't want to hurt him."

The client tilted his head: *Hey, it's up to you* .

When the frequency of the phone calls increased, and the begging grew ever more insistent - *"My wife knows about us, Candy, I told her everything. I'm a free man now!"* - Gemma called the client.

"Okay, make him stop, but please don't hurt him."

There was silence on the other end of the line.

"Well not too much," Gemma said.

She never heard from Howard Price again.

Carly was not Howard Price. There was a charming naivety about the girl, that Gemma found both endearing and erotic.

She had always liked girls, pretty and slight were a particular favourite and Carly fell into both categories. Gemma was not gay, but she enjoyed the intimacy of making love with another girl far more than the rough and tumble of penetrative sex.

Men could be sensitive lovers, of course, but Gemma had not met many. As a hooker, her requirements were rarely taken into consideration. She had never had a stable relationship, but she knew what she liked, and the intimacy of sharing her body and exploring another girl was high on her priority list. She had decided that she would seduce Carly Decker and see where it took her.

On the sixth of June Paul Overton announced that the restaurant would be closed for the forthcoming weekend following the discovery of an infestation of Powderpost Beetles nesting in the bar.

"The entire room will have to be fumigated," he stressed. The staff were not so downbeat.

"A weekend off, all of us!" Kat Webber exclaimed. "We should go out."

Katharine Webber was a barmaid at The Elm and had been promoted to supervisor as soon as Gemma had been appointed bar manager. There was no ill-feeling between the two girls, even though Kat had been working there for nearly two years. The fact was that Kat didn't want the responsibility of being in charge. She had only accepted the supervisor's position because Gemma had convinced her that it was more money for very little extra work.

Kat was a total contrast to Carly: Early twenties, sassy, and confident She was hard to dislike and harder still to ignore.

Gemma, still wary and paranoid around strangers, had little to fear from Kat's intrusive and forthright insights, as they consisted of little more than observations about soaps, trashy hack shows like *Made in Chelsea* and *Jersey Shore,* drinking, and the size of men's cocks. The latter was a particular favourite topic that Kat deliberately raised in order to shock Carly, who reddened whenever Kat launched into one of her sordid narratives. It was fun banter, of course, and although Kat was obviously exaggerating about her encounters with men, the tall tales brightened an otherwise predictable work routine.

Kat certainly had her admirers amongst the customers, and she did little to discourage many that she herself found attractive. It was little more than flirting of course. Kat was stunning; slim with large breasts, and a shock of luscious blond hair that spilt over her shoulders.

"All of us?" Gemma replied.

Kat nodded enthusiastically

"Did you know It's Carly's birthday on Monday, her twenty-first. We could surprise her with a night on the town this Saturday."

"We?"

"Yeah, you and me, as opposed to just me."

Gemma shook her head. "I don't think so. Carly doesn't strike me as a party animal."

"Shit, that's the whole point. It would bring her out of her shell a bit."

Gemma thought for a few seconds and then nodded. "Yeah, why not. It sounds like the kind of thing friends would do."

"We'd go into Yarmouth though, hit a few bars and then go onto a club."

Gemma could see that Kat was warming to the idea. She tried to quell the voice of concern inside her head. She was hardly maintaining a low profile by working in a public bar, but she remained vigilant. She never drank to excess; being drunk could lead to cataclysmic circumstances, but a girly night out sounded like a great idea. A chance to dress up and really let her hair down.

There had been a follow up to the article in the newspaper, concerning the disappearance of Clive Cooper. It was still vague, and utterly confusing, stating simply that the businessman's son had disappeared whilst on an unsupervised hiking holiday in the Bolivian jungle.

Why lie? Gemma thought. Had they forgotten about her; were they no longer looking for her, if they ever had been in the first place? It was tempting to become complacent, but the very inconsistencies of the story alarmed her, and she knew that she would be crazy to drop her guard and stop looking over her shoulder.

But one night out with the girls?

Why the hell not?

CHAPTER 10

Just before he had left the big house in Dorchester, Carol Harrier had asked Ray one last question.

"Why didn't you just keep the five grand? I never would have known about it. Brian had money all over the place. You could have just kept it and not said a word."

"That's not who I am," Ray said.

It was a glib answer, but Carol had shrugged and appeared to accept it, though she was suspicious enough not to compliment him on his honesty.

The truth of the matter was that Ray could have kept the money. He had come very close to depositing it into his account and forgetting all about the late Brian Harrier, his wife and precocious daughter, but he couldn't do that.

Ray had no true loyalty to his ex-army buddy, in fact, it was stretching it to even call Brian a buddy. They had been in the same unit - The Royal Artillery and they had served together in Iraq, so there was a camaraderie there, but they had never been friends.

Brian had been an aloof, rather unapproachable character, finding it difficult to interact with others. His cynicism and disparaging wit were often rebuffed or taken as insulting, as Brian lacked the charm to offer a caustic remark without a glint in his eye and a chuckle in his voice.

As soon as Brian had died, the need for Ray to continue his search for Helena stopped. His first thought then was to bank the money. It was a few days later that he realised that giving the money back to Carol was the right thing to do, but his immediate response was to keep the cash.

He had not been wholly surprised when Carol Harrier had asked him to continue his search for the woman who had shattered both her and her late husband's life. Ray had no idea if they had problems before the fling, (*surely all married couples did)* but he could understand her wanting him to find the girl who had so tragically tore their marriage apart.

The biggest problem for Ray, of course, was where to start. He had a photograph but very little else, aside from the assumption that she was a prostitute. That hardly narrowed it down or aided his search. For one, he didn't know for sure that she was on the game, and secondly, the network distribution for sex workers was enormous. It was a bit like walking into the bathroom section at a random B&Q store, showing the staff member a photograph of somebody who may or may not be a plumber and asking them if they recognised him.

He decided that it would probably be best to start at the club where Brian acquired the photograph.

It was nearing midday when Ray approached The Revolution . It was a large bar situated on the town side of the bridge, overlooking the harbour. The club was upstairs and closed this early, but the downstairs lounge and restaurant were busy.

Ray headed upstairs. The club was dark, with only a few lights situated above mirrors on the wall at the back of the bar providing any illumination. There was a man in his early twenties leaning on the bar, chatting to a girl of about seventeen. They both turned as Ray approached, and the girl giggled as if they had been caught out.

The man shushed her and turned his attention to Ray.

"Club's closed," he said, matter-of-factly.

"You the manager?" Ray asked.

The girl giggled again, and the young man laughed also. "No I am not, I'm a barman. You want me to fetch him?"

Ray didn't. From previous experience, he had learned that those in authority were far less likely to divulge information than the grunts who toiled below them. He took out the photograph. " You know anybody in this picture?"

The man took it from him and studied it. The girl leaned in and took a closer look. Eventually, he looked up again. "You a cop?" he asked.

Ray shook his head. "Nope."

"Why the interest?"

"Does it matter?"

The young man shrugged. "Dunno. You gonna pay me like they do in the movies?"

Ray sat down at the bar and leaned against it. The girl studied him closely.

"Why would I do that," he said. "I'm only asking if you know anybody?"

The young man frowned. He held the photograph up and pointed at it. "I know this guy, he's been here a few times." He had picked out the older man dancing with the girl, not Helena but the other girl in the photograph.

Ray had not been convinced by Brian's dismissal that the two couples in the picture may not know each other. At this early stage of the investigation he was prepared to explore all avenues. He didn't expect to get lucky so early on and find somebody who could identify Helena straight away, but the fact that the young man had recognised one of the people in the picture was enough to pique his interest.

"Got a name maybe?"

The young man shook his head. "Nah, sorry. You a private eye?"

"Kind of. Could you get a name for a hundred?"

"Pounds?" the girl said, her eyes widening.

Ray nodded.

"I can't, unfortunately, but I know somebody who might try for a hundred," the young man said. "Wait a minute." He turned and walked to the end of the bar, disappearing into the gloom.

"He kill somebody?" the girl asked.

"Who?"

"The guy in the picture."

"Why would you think that?"

"Dunno, guess you must be searching for him for a reason."

"Don't you think the police might be looking for him if he had killed somebody?"

The girl shrugged as if this hadn't even occurred to her. "Yeah, I guess."

"Hey, big fella," the barman called from across the room. "Come on over here."

Ray nodded at the girl and she smiled back. He headed down the bar where the barman was waiting for him. A second, older man stood at his side. The barman simply introduced him as Gully and then he walked back to the girl further down the bar.

Gully was in his thirties, thin to the point of being emaciated. He sported a scruffy goatee, and his left eye was bloodshot. He looked Ray up and down briefly before running the tip of his tongue over his dry, cracked lips. Ray took out the photograph and showed it to him. Gully barely glimpsed at it.

"I know him, this older guy, dancing with the hot chick he said. "I know his name and what he does for a living."

"How do you know him?" Ray asked, knowing that the question was irrelevant, but wanting to see how much Gully would divulge.

"I know a lot of people who come into the club, I sense what they need. Companionship, bit of blow, maybe something stronger." He shrugged. "You know?"

"If I was a cop I could bust your ass," Ray said.

"Yeah but you're not. I can smell bacon a mile off."

"So tell me about him, the older guy."

"I want three hundred," Gully said. The tip of his tongue poked out once more and he clenched it gently between his teeth.

"For what?" Ray said.

"For telling you about the older guy."

"Forget it, I'll give you a hundred, and for that, I want more than just the guy's name and occupation."

Gully shook his head. "One hundred ain't worth my time, man."

Ray shrugged. "Fair enough," he turned and started to walk away.

"Hey, I know you're bluffing, man, come back here and give me my money."

Ray carried on walking until he reached the barman and his girl. He slipped the young man a tenner. "Thanks," he said.

He had nearly made it to the exit before Gully caught up with him.

"Okay, two hundred." He held out his hand and Ray simply stared at it, then turned to leave. He managed five more steps before Gully's arm fell on his shoulder.

"Okay, man, fuck. I'll take the hundred. Ray nodded and reached for his wallet.

Gully snatched at the money with long quick fingers and it disappeared into the back pocket of his jeans.

"Okay, dude's name is Howard Price," Gully said. "He's a corn doctor, been down here several times, dirty weekends, conferences, sometimes with a pretty girl on his arm, sometimes without. When he's without, he usually asks me to set him up with somebody to spend the night with him."

"You get him this girl?" Ray asked indicating the girl Price was with on the dance floor.

Gully shook his head. "Nah man, I don't know any chicks that good looking. She was with Price when he came in."

"When was this?"

Gully shrugged. "Eighteen months ago, maybe a couple of years."

Ray raised an eyebrow. "You're good with dates and faces."

Gully smiled. He had bad teeth, which was why he didn't smile often, Ray assumed.

"Hey man, she's got the kind of face that is hard to forget. Don't you agree?"

Ray stared at the girl for a few seconds. He had to concede that he did.

CHAPTER 11

The building which housed Howard Price's chiropody surgery was a suite of rooms in a converted house in Macmillan Drive, Finsbury Park. It was nearly five-thirty in the afternoon. Ray had driven here straight from Weymouth after Gully had given him Price's name and address, the journey taking a little over three and a half hours.

Ray thought it an unusual trait. Chiropody, dentistry, homoeopathic medicine, many operated from similarly converted rooms such as this one. He reasoned that it was because they were trying to convey a message of reassurance. Home from home or some similar bullshit. There were four names on brass plaques on the wall outside, each of them had a lot of letters after each name that was meaningless to Ray. Howard Price's name was at the top of the list. The initials following his own name were considerable, but no less confusing, as far as Ray was concerned.

Ray pulled the door open and entered the waiting room, which at one point was evidently the entrance hall. There were a few meaningless certificates, framed and hanging on the wall, alongside information posters on the importance of maintaining good foot hygiene. On a low coffee table, there were several magazines and a perspex holder crammed with leaflets on chiropody and podiatry. Ray assumed the two were exclusive but had no idea what the difference was between them.

A middle-aged woman, with startlingly white hair, smiled at him as he approached her counter.

"Good afternoon, sir," she said, eyeing Ray up and down quickly.

Ray nodded. "I was wondering if I could see Mister Price for a minute?"

"Are you registered with this practice?"

"Nope."

The receptionist smiled again. "Well, no matter. I will need a few details to begin with. Could you tell me your name and date of birth?"

Ray smiled back at the receptionist. "I think that you misunderstand me. I don't wish to register or even make an appointment, I just need to see Mister Price very briefly."

"A personal matter?" the receptionist said."

"Exactly."

"I'm sorry sir, that's completely out of the question. Mister Price is very busy today, he is with a patient now, and we close in half an hour."

"Perhaps I'll wait," Ray said cheerfully. He turned from the counter and took a seat, folding his arms.

The receptionist became flustered. She waited for a few seconds, watching Ray, then, after making a decision, she turned and left the desk and entered a door to the rear of the waiting room. The only other person sitting with Ray was an old man, who was looking at him over the top of his magazine. Ray stared at him until the old man dropped his gaze.

The door to the rear of the waiting room reopened and the receptionist walked back inside, accompanied by an overweight, balding man in his mid-fifties: Howard Price. He had gained a little weight since the photograph of him dancing with the girl had been taken in Weymouth nearly two years ago.

The receptionist whispered something to Price, having to stand on tiptoe to do so as he was well over six feet, and he glanced over at Ray. There was a mixture of confusion and annoyance etched on his face. At the moment this was a situation he was still in control of. Ray intended to relinquish him of that authority very shortly. He stood up.

Price walked around from behind the desk. "Can I help you?"

"Is there somewhere private we can talk?" Ray said.

The chiropodist thought about this for a minute. Ray could see him mentally weighing up the situation. Ray was obviously not a patient, and Price had a chequered past; his association with hookers was a testament to that. Both the receptionist and the old man, who had given up all pretence of eavesdropping, were staring avidly at the chiropodist and Ray. Price nodded after a few moments and gestured Ray through another side door. They stood in a small office, with a desk and chairs on opposing sides. A large filing cabinet stood in the corner. A consulting room, Ray assumed. Price closed the door and turned to face Ray. He didn't offer him a seat.

"Well, what is this all about?" he asked. Ray took out the picture from the club and laid it on the table.

Price glanced at it casually, then did a comedic double-take when he realised that he was in the photograph. He slumped heavily into one of the chairs, snatched up the picture and looked at it more clearly. His face dropped, and the colour drained from his cheeks.

"I haven't seen her," he said quietly. "I haven't contacted her and I've severed all ties. You made that very clear before. You must understand, I have had to rebuild my career. My wife…" Price hesitated. "My wife has been very understanding," he added

Ray stopped him there. "Howard, I'm not who you think I am. What can you tell me about the other couple in the picture?" he asked.

Price's brow creased in frustration.

"You're not blackmailing me?"

Ray laughed. "Howard, that is offensive. Do I look like the kind of guy who would need to extort money from you?"

Price looked at him closely. "No, I guess not. Then what is it that you want?"

"Some information."

"Why? Are you a private investigator? Did somebody hire you to look for Candy Girl?"

"Kind of."

"What does that mean?"

"It means that I'm a private investigator, but I'm not looking for Candy Girl. Is that her dancing with you?"

Price nodded. "Don't think the earth is moving for her, what do you think?"

Ray ignored the question. "I'm looking for the other girl in the photograph. Her name is Helena."

"I don't know her," Price said.

"I think the girl is a hooker," Ray said. "Did you speak to this girl that evening in the club?"

"No, she was just a girl enjoying a dance."

"What about Candy, the girl you were with."

"What about her?" Price said defensively.

"Did she speak to Helena?"

Price shrugged. "How the hell should I know, we weren't joined at the hip."

"So she may have done ?"

Another shrug. "I guess so."

"You know where I can find her?"

"Who Candy, Christ no, I told you I haven't seen her for over a year."

"Yeah, but you must have had an original point of contact."

Price waved a hand. "I don't need this, really, please you're going to have to leave."

"If you can't help me, Mister Price then I'm going to have to keep asking around, give me something and I'll be on my way, we'll probably never set eyes on each other again."

"Is that a threat?"

Ray said nothing.

"Okay, okay," Price relented. "There was another girl Candy was friends with, her name is Chelsea, but I don't know her address."

"Then how does that help me?"

"Cos I know who her pimp was, a guy called Cole."

"You've used his services in the past?"

Price nodded wearily. "Yes. Now if I tell you where you can find him will you leave me alone?"

"Of course."

Price gave him the address.

CHAPTER 12

Ray realised as he approached the address Price had given him that each name was leading him further away from Helena. The straws he was clutching at were slipping through his fingers with increased rapidity; the chances of individuals knowing anything about Helena growing more tenebrous. Chelsea, another hooker, was an acquaintance of the girl Price had dated in Weymouth - Candy Girl. Firstly, there was no evidence that Helena had even spoken with Candy, and if

91

she had, it was unlikely that they had discussed any personal issues such as where each other lived and how convenient it was to blackmail stupid, gullible men who should know better. Still, it was a lead nonetheless, and the almost derelict three-storey house in Kings Cross before him was a testament that the people he was looking to aid him were growing ever more seedier.

He hurried up the few crumbling stone steps that led to the front door. It was a huge entrance, no bell or knocker, the green paint chipped and flaky. Scuffed boot marks adorned the bottom panel, where the wood was splintered and rotten. Ray knocked loudly on the door and heard movement inside; shuffled footsteps and then silence. He guessed the person was peering at him through a peephole. Then a girl's voice, high pitched and nervous.

"What do you want?"

Ray leaned closer to the door and shouted. "I'm looking for Chelsea, does she live here?"

There was no answer for a few moments, then the girl's voice again. "No."

Ray shuffled impatiently on the doorstep. "Is there anybody else there I can speak to?"

Again there was a long pause as if the girl was mulling over each word, reconstructing the sentence inside a befuddled brain before attempting an answer.

"What for?" she said. Ray decided to try a different approach.

"Look I need to leave a photograph with you. Hopefully, somebody will recognise one of the people in the picture, somebody I'm looking for."

Silence from within

"I can pay you," Ray said.

The door slowly opened. The girl was tiny, standing only about four feet ten. She was also unattractive. Her hair was dirty and matted; there was a rash of prominent acne spots running down the side of her left cheek, like an angry swarm of midges had taken residence there, and her teeth were bad. Not just cracked and broken, but brown and dirty.

Skinny white legs protruded from a pair of frayed cut-off jeans, with faded white daisies on the front pockets. She wore a threadbare t-shirt with a large bird of paradise emblazoned on the front, it's plumage mottled with rhinestones, half of which were missing so that the bird looked like an incomplete dot to dot picture. Her breasts were small, almost pre-pubescent; two small mounds barely discernible beneath her shirt. On her feet, she was wearing a pair of satin ballet pumps, scuffed and stained.

"How much?" she asked.

"I'm not sure," Ray said, stepping through the open doorway, forcing the young girl to move to one side, "What is the going rate for looking at a photo?"

The girl looked puzzled as if Ray had asked her to calculate the area of a circle by multiplying pi by the square of the radius.

"I dunno," she shrugged. "I guess I won't charge anything to just look. You got any skag?"

"No, just the photo."

They walked further inside the house. The hallway was narrow and smelled faintly of damp and mildew. There was a long dark staircase leading to the upper floors. The girl turned and walked into a large kitchen. Ray followed her. She turned to face him again, leaning against a battered, Formica top table, a design that was popular in the seventies and was making a bit of a revival now. There were several empty coffee cups on the tabletop, all empty with ring stained bottoms. Again there was a prevailing faint odour of dampness. The walls were paperless, the plaster cracked in places. There were a few tiles serving as a splashback behind a cooker similar to one that Ray could remember his gran owning a lifetime ago.

He handed over the A4 blow-up and the girl looked at it fleetingly.

"I don't know anybody in this picture." She handed it back and Ray placed it down on the table next to the empty coffee cups.

"Is there anybody else in the house?"

The girl shook her head. "Just me, the others are out?"

"The others?"

For the first time, a look of suspicion crossed the girl's face.

"You ask too many questions."

Ray nodded. He reached into his pocket for his wallet. He took out a twenty-pound note and handed it over. The girl snatched at it quickly and it disappeared into the back pocket of her jeans.

"You know a girl called Chelsea?" Ray asked.

Recognition flashed in the girl's eyes and Ray smiled.

The girl shrugged again. "I dunno, maybe." When Ray handed her another twenty, the girl smiled. "Chelsea's nice, she's my friend, even though she's older. She ain't with us anymore though"

"How old are you?" Ray asked.

The girl smiled. "How old do you want me to be?"

When Ray didn't answer she sighed. "I'm nineteen now, but Cole reckons I can pass for thirteen. That's a good thing, right?"

Ray thought it was possibly the most appalling thing he'd heard in ages, but he didn't tell the girl that. He was familiar with the terms of soliciting, but considering the girls' unattractiveness, her youthful appearance was possibly the only thing she had going for her in this sordid business.

"You know where Chelsea is now?"

The girl shook her head quickly, as if Chelsea's absconsion amounted to desertion, and if, as she said, Chelsea was a friend, she certainly wasn't going to divulge her whereabouts to a total stranger, no matter how much money he had.

"Is Cole here?" Ray asked. It was the name of the pimp Price had given him.

A brief look of fear danced across the girl's features, her eyes widened and her lip trembled slightly, then it was gone.

"You can't be here," she said suddenly. "I don't know the people in the picture. You going to stay here, you have to pay me."

"I just gave you forty pounds."

The girl shook her head impatiently. "I'm thirteen, you gotta pay more than that, it's obvious."

"We both know that you're nineteen, and I don't require your services. I just want to speak to Cole and Chelsea. I need to know if somebody can recognise the girl in this picture."

"I just told you I don't know anybody."

"But the others may," Ray persisted.

The girl's eyes widened again, and Ray realised that she was looking behind him. He heard a grunt and then a dull thud as something struck him hard against the back of his head. He pitched forward, managing to get his hands out to push the table aside before he hit the floor. Once down he stayed still, a dull ringing in his ears, and a throbbing pain at the back of his skull.

"It's almost impossible to knock somebody out with a single blow to the head, regardless of what Hollywood would have you believe." This was according to Ray's martial arts instructor. He had gone on to say that the assailant who is able to do so would have to be extremely skilled or very lucky, and even the skilled man would still need an element of luck.

Whoever had hit Ray was neither skilled or lucky, but it was still a blow to the head, and that is always serious. Just as likely to kill you than render you unconscious. Ray felt the force, even though he had managed to turn his head slightly, alerted by the girl's quick change of expression, and therefore it was only a glancing blow, the brunt of it absorbed by his shoulder. Even so, it still hurt like hell.

"You've killed him!" A man's voice, high-pitched and worried. "Christ, Cole, why did you hit him so hard?"

"He ain't dead, quit worrying," Cole's voice was complacent, unconcerned.   "He just came in, Cole, I don't know him, honest!" The young hooker cried, her voice bordering on hysteria.

"He isn't fucking moving, Cole! Shit, I think you did kill him,"

"It doesn't matter, he was trespassing, I'm within my rights…"

"I don't want to get mixed up in no murder."

Cole laughed now. "Oh spare me, Conrad, I wouldn't want to implicate you in anything. Forget the fact that you're here to fuck a twelve-year-old girl."

"Hey fuck you," Conrad countered, indignant now. "We both know she ain't twelve."

Cole laughed again. "Maybe not this one, maybe not this time."

Ray slowly got to his feet and turned. The pimp, Cole, drew out a switchblade and popped the blade, then let it hang loosely at his side.

"He showed me that picture," the young hooker said. "Asked me if I knew the girl."

"Distressed dad, get them all the time," Cole said dismissively. "That your fucking daughter, big boy?" Girl's on the fucking lam now, man, taking regular cock, I don't doubt." he sniggered, and expertly twirled the knife between his fingers

"You know her?" Conrad asked, picking up the photograph

"Nah," Cole replied. "Wish I did though, she's a fucking looker." He turned to Ray again. "Your daughter, big boy?" He glanced at the picture again. "Nah, too old. Sister maybe? Runaway?"

Ray said nothing.

"What the fuck!" Cole said stepping forward. "You fucking mute? He eyed Ray up quickly. "What's your fucking problem, man?"

"I don't have one," Ray said calmly. "I just wanted to know if any of you know the girl in this photograph." He nodded towards the picture that Conrad was holding.

"We ain't got time to look at your fucking prints, man, now take a step back, you get me?"

"You don't have time? I'm only asking you to look at a picture, not sit down and watch a documentary."

Cole laughed. "Are you fucking with me?"

Ray looked at each person in turn. The skinny little hooker, eyes darting from person to person, subservient and waiting to see what would happen. Cole, the pimp, thin, but sinewy. Dirty blonde hair, confident and arrogant, cliched tracksuit bottoms, and zippered fleece, drawn up tight to the neck. The fat guy; he of the whining voice - Conrad; a potential client. Cheap brown suit, too long in the arms so that only his fingers poked out from the sleeves. Sweaty and nervous, uncomfortable in his surroundings even though he was probably a frequent visitor; first name terms with Cole indicated a familiarity between the two men.

"So, big guy." Cole stepped forward with an exaggerated swagger, all bad boy attitude and confident with it. "You know you fucking trespassing on my property." He snatched up the photo and flicked at it with his fingers. "I'll ask you once more, is this your girl? Sister, huh; Young lover maybe? Well, we don't know shit, and you don't come round poking your fucking nose in and asking my girl questions, you fucking understand?" As if to emphasise his point, Cole twirled the knife once more with a practised twist of the wrist.

"Shit, Cole, put that thing away," Conrad said, taking a step towards him. Cole rounded on him, the knife instinctively raised, suddenly inches away from the fat man's face. Conrad cried out and stepped backwards. Once he was at a considered safe distance, he quickly regained his composure.

"Are you out of your mind?" he shrieked. Cole ignored him and turned back to Ray. "So you can go now, big guy, okay, I mean get the fuck out, and I don't want to see you round here again, you understand me?"

Ray still said nothing.

"One more thing," Cole said. "You can leave your wallet here. You've caused me some hassle, and you're gonna have to pay for that." He took a couple of steps backwards so that he stood between Ray and the kitchen door, the knife was held loosely at his side once again. Ray glanced around the room. His eyes fell upon a foot-long length of hollow piping set against the wall by the door.

"You hit me with that?" he asked, turning to Cole.

The pimp smiled, revealing twin rows of small, uneven teeth. "Fucking A. I always keep a tool close by and within hands reach. What does it matter?"

"Just curious," Ray replied. "I'm in two minds whether to shove that up your fucking arse, or take that blade you're waving about and cut your balls off with it."

CHAPTER 13

Two hours earlier, as Ray was entering the surgery of Howard Price, petty thief, Spider, was thinking that he just may be onto one hell of a scoop.

Spider had been following the woman for nearly an hour, and for all that time she had been speaking into her mobile.

He kept picking up snippets of conversation, but he paid it no heed. He had first noticed her in the supermarket and stood behind her at the tills. She made no attempt to conceal her PIN. In fact, she actually stepped back to get a better look at the display, then punched in the four digits slowly and methodically. Even if he hadn't been paying attention, Spider would have found it hard not to see. Short of her calling out the number as she entered it, it would have been difficult for her to make a bolder announcement. - *"Hey come and rob me why don't you?"*

From the supermarket, she went to the dry cleaners. Spider waited on the street corner. He didn't have to appear innocuous, the woman appeared oblivious to all around her. Now and again she would laugh or cry out in surprise. She held the mobile in the crook of her neck as she paid her cleaning bill then left the shop holding the cellophane-wrapped item high in order to keep it wrinkle-free, her small bag of groceries were in the other hand She stood at the kerbside and waited.

His real name was Ian Coates, but everybody who knew him called him Spider.

Spider was a prime example of why the word petty was often associated with the lowest of the criminal fraternity. He was a petty thief, for sure, shoplifting and pickpocketing his methods of choice. Although both high risk, with relatively low returns. (far more shoplifters are apprehended these days than most people imagine, with modern cameras and alarms increasing the conviction rate) the risk of capture for many of the felons was countered by the *"slap on the wrist"* repercussions. The most brazen simply didn't care. They would chance the incriminating CCTV footage or the clasp of a security guard's hand on their shoulder if the odds of walking out of a store with an armful of designer goods was about fifty-fifty. The recriminations were often meaningless; fines were often ignored and anti-social behaviour orders were no more than words on paper.

Spider was more cautious. He was a thief, but he wasn't doing it to fund a dependency, it was simply for financial gain. Not that he had progressed very far in that particular field. The odd twenty in a wallet or purse was about the going rate. Most people just paid by card now, but Spider never used them. Cameras were everywhere and the chance of his recognisable mug being spotted outweighed the risk.

He had been apprehended, of course, on many occasions, and each arrest and subsequent conviction resulted in a change of tactics. If he was busted for shoplifting, he would turn his attention to the shoppers at Oxford Circus, or the commuter crowds on the tube and dip a few pockets. When, ultimately, he was caught again, he would change tack, and the cycle would begin afresh.

A huge old Daimler pulled up and a capless chauffeur stepped out and took the woman's dry cleaning and shopping without a word. The woman neither thanked or even acknowledged him. She kept on talking into her phone as the driver put the groceries in the boot and neatly placed her cellophane-packed garment over the backseat before driving off. The woman set off again and Spider followed.

She ordered a latte and a pastry from a small deli, then sat on a bench in a pocket park, that housed a bizarre array of mangled and bent pipes masquerading as kids climbing frames.

What the hell is wrong with swings and slides? That's what Spider wanted to know. He pulled his coat tight around his thin frame and waited outside the park. Stepping inside and loitering was just asking for trouble.

He was wearing gloves, his deformed left hand still noticeable beneath the bespoke garment. It ached like a bastard in the cold weather and he stuffed his hands into the deep pockets of his parka.

Spider was forty-five. He had a pasty, sallow complexion, and thinning, salt and pepper hair, that would have looked neater if it was cut shorter. He was clean-shaven, save for a few rogue whiskers that clung like limpets to his neck. He had a prominent Adam's apple that slid effortlessly up and down his throat as he spoke, like an oiled mechanism. His teeth were white, but a little crooked and overall his whole demeanour, along with his attire, appeared dishevelled and slightly unkempt. Spider didn't hate who he was. He knew that he was little more than pond life, feeding on the unwary or vulnerable, but he was resolute and accepting of his lot. If there had been another way for him to live, he would gladly embrace it. Petty thievery was a way of life, an occupation so ingrained that it would be impossible to turn away from it.

It hadn't always been this way. Spider's father had been a fine sleight of hand magician, who had entertained passengers on cruise liners, restaurants and hotel lounge bars. He was successful enough to make a career out of it, but never resourceful enough to invest his money wisely. For a man whose talent lay in manipulating cards, he was an appalling card player and often left the gaming tables red-faced and with empty pockets. He died bitter and penniless when he was only sixty-seven from peritonitis caused by a ruptured appendix.

Spider's mother was a distant memory. She had run off with the milkman when he was five years old; a realisation so cliched, that Spider had never told anybody the truth of the tale for fear of ridicule. If asked, though few did these days, he would simply say she died in childbirth. In his early years of adolescence, he had recited the tale so often that he himself had difficulty accepting the more embarrassing reality as anything more than a fable.

When Spider was in his teens, his father had shown his son the basics of card sleights, and Spider was a voracious learner. He practised double lifts, false shuffles, and cuts, in-jogs and Biddle grips, riffles and forces, for hours on end. He had no realisation as to just how good he was until his father had seen him unknowingly from the kitchen, whilst Spider absentmindedly spun and cut a full deck one-handed as he watched television, and praised his son on his ability.

But Spider had not been bothered about entertaining folk for a few quid . He had seen just how desolate his father had become and had no intention of following in his footsteps. Years later, after his father had died, he found himself drawn by the sham, brazen displays of the con men who flocked to the London streets, to prey on the unwary tourist.

Street gangs congregated in shop doorways in and around Oxford Circus, Westminster Bridge and in many of the underpasses leading down into the subterranean tunnels of the underground system. Exceptionally gifted at misdirection and sleight of hand, their games of choice were, *"three-card monte,"* *"find the lady,"* and *"the shell game,"* the latter being a deft con trick involving three halved walnut shells and a dried pea. The premise of all three games was incredibly simplistic, consisting of the dealer asking the mark to pick either the card of choice or, with *"the shell game,"* under which nut he believes the pea is secreted. The con itself lay in the belief that the mark thinks he can't lose, and for the first few hands, the dealer lets certain "lucky" punters win by correctly selecting the designated card. What the majority of the onlooking public doesn't realise is that the winner is part of the gang, as are others who will act amazed at the winner's luck. Further gang members act as lookouts in case the police show up and bust the miscreants. The beauty of such simple cons, of course, is that there is very little set up involved. A collapsible table, that can be folded and whisked away in a matter of seconds, and a few cards or walnut shells that are pocketed and hidden.

Spider was aware of the gangs. As a street wanderer, it was only a matter of time before he came into contact with them. At first, he had been amazed that people could be so gullible and fall for such an obvious con. But for all the people who were duped, there were so many more who believed they could buck the system and win. Spider quickly realised that people didn't like to be tricked, and many were convinced that they would not fall for such a blatant deception. If the lady *(so often the queen of hearts)* was obviously in the middle, then pick the card to it's left or right. When they still got it wrong, they became even more frustrated and angry, much to the delight of the dealers, who were quite happy to take them for more money.

Spider practised the sleights on his own at home, changing the routine ever so slightly, making the trick appear even easier to win. He favoured *"find the lady"* as his opener, and perfected the manoeuvres until he was so adept at the routine that he could perform it at incredible speed without having to look down at the cards as he flipped them down onto the pavement.

Spider's biggest mistake was to simply set up on his own.

One Sunday afternoon he laid a small plain tea towel on the path on the South Bank of Westminster Bridge and harried the passing tourists for business. He had no lookouts and no bogus punters who would win a few of the first hands. Spider's plan was to let the genuine marks win themselves. Their responses would be far more convincing than the pantomime theatrics performed by the successful gang stooges.

The best customers were Asian tourists. Chinese and Japanese teenagers who flooded to London for the sights. Wary at first, they would only wager a quid or two, and these preliminary hands were the ones Spider would let them win. When the other tourists saw how easy it was, they were ready to wade in with fivers, tenners and even twenties. Spider fleeced them mercilessly. When the punters caught on and realised they were being scammed they quickly moved on, but not before Spider had taken nearly two hundred pounds in a little under an hour.

Spider had hurried away, hastily pocketing the money. He waited until the area was clear of all those who had been watching before setting back up again in exactly the same spot. As the next wave of marks jostled for position, he was unaware of the black transit that pulled up to the kerb. Two huge guys got out, opened a side door and strode over to Spider who was oblivious to their presence, as he was in the process of taking a brash, retired American telephone engineer for a quick fifty. The crowd parted when they sensed trouble and the two heavies pushed aside the Yank, who complained bitterly, but was ignored.

The largest of the two guys lifted Spider from his crouched position, turned and flung him into the transit. The second guy snatched up the stake money from the pavement. The American guy was about to protest, but a withering stare from the heavy brought him to his senses, and he hurried his family away, rueing his losses and contemplating his own stupidity.

Spider was terrified as they drove. The largest guy had a knee across his neck, burying his face into the dirty floor of the transit's rear.

The journey was short, maybe twenty minutes. The van screeched to a halt, tyres on gravel. Spider remained pinned to the floor as the doors were flung open. He was manhandled out and pulled to his feet. He was standing in a small courtyard of industrial units. Each was no bigger than a thousand square feet, some even smaller. All appeared deserted, except for one. The guy shoved Spider hard in the direction of the occupied unit. The roller shutter was open, and there was a large car lift inside. The unit was obviously being used as a mechanic's workshop. Spider stumbled and only just managed to keep his balance. The huge guy stood a few feet behind him, a stupid grin on his face. The other heavy stood by the transit, leaning against the passenger door, his arms folded across his massive chest. Spider just stared at them. Were they hoping he would run, then enjoy chasing him down? The guy by the transit nodded his head in the direction of the open door, and Spider walked towards it.

He stepped inside the cool interior. There was a car on top of the hoist. A brand new Audi, that looked as out of place in a ramshackle backstreet garage like this as a Fiat Punto would in a Bentley showroom. Closer inspection showed that the car was in the process of receiving a brand new spray job. Spider peered around the corner of the door. A man of about sixty sat at a desk. Despite the dim interior, the man was wearing sunglasses. He glanced up but Spider had no idea if he was looking at him. It was only when the man spoke that he realised that he was.

"Sit," the man ordered in a heavily accented Slovakian accent. Spider sat in the chair opposite the older man.

"You must stop the cards, right now," he said. "It is our patch, our income. Do you understand?"

Spider nodded vigorously. He opened his mouth to speak, but the man held up a hand to silence him. Before he knew what was happening, the two heavies appeared behind him. The first grabbed Spider around the throat, choking off his air supply. As the world around him started to swim, the second guy pulled Spider's left arm forward until his hand rested on the desk in front of him, fingers splayed. As he surrendered to the darkness he just caught a glimpse of the older guy's raised arm, the lump hammer gripped tightly in his huge fist.

"A reminder, just so that you don't forget," the man said, and the hammer came down, once, twice, three times, smashing every bone in Spider's hand and fingers.

The woman he had been following was in her late fifties, Spider surmised. Not unattractive and exceedingly well dressed. Her coat had a fur-lined collar and reached to her knees. She was wearing black boots with a zip down each side. He couldn't see from where he was standing, but Spider guessed she was clad head to toe in designer labels. She had a large cream coloured leather bag over her left shoulder. The strap was long and when she walked it slapped against her hip. Spider knew that her purse was near the top. The bag was open and only a bright, rainbow-coloured scarf concealed the purse. Spider could never understand the carefree attitude people adopted towards their possessions. Most were either forgetful, careless or even just downright foolhardy, believing that there was no chance of themselves being robbed. The woman, so absorbed in her conversation, appeared to be an amalgamation of all three. For the first time, Spider wondered what it was she was talking about and with whom. She had barely come up for breath.

He would have to make his move soon, perhaps when she got up from the bench. There was no telling when she would be heading home, and if the chauffeur in the Daimler was to pick her up, then he would have no chance.

Spider normally liked to work in more crowded areas than this, but the woman was so absorbed in her conversation that he believed that would prove distraction enough. He could easily maintain a non-hurried pace behind her, pick up speed at the right time and snatch the purse and bury it within the confines of his coat before she had time to register his passing by. When the woman eventually stood up to go, he was already in position behind her, his pace matching hers, speeding up only at the very last moment. She wasn't even aware that he had even passed her before he was away, her purse tucked away in a deep pocket of his coat.

Spider ducked down several alleyways, listening for a cry from the woman, or an order to stop from a vigilant copper forever on the lookout for suspicious characters. When he heard neither, he squatted down beside a Biffa skip, filled with empty fifty-litre drums of cooking oil. He took out the purse and opened it.

There were sheaves of notes. He riffled then with the edge of his thumb and then took them out. He counted the money quickly. Two hundred and sixty pounds, all in twenties. Who carried that amount of money around these days? He ignored the cards, credit and debit. Despite the convenience of contactless payments now, which in his opinion, was a huge step backwards by the banks regarding security, and the fact that he knew her PIN, he never dipped his sticky fingers into that area of thievery. Too many fucking cameras about these days watching your every move. Cash was a godsend, and this was a veritable windfall. He stuffed the money inside his pocket, and tossed the purse up and into the skip. First things first, he was going to get a girl, and he knew exactly the person would be to help him out.

CHAPTER 14

There it was, a twitch at the side of Cole's mouth; a hurried glance at the other man in the room. Would he provide backup, if need be, now that the big guy in front of him was suddenly imposing and threatening, a million miles away from the desperate, grief-stricken brother or lover that Cole believed him to be?

Ray thought he'd help him along with that particular dilemma.

"Hey," he said, turning to the fat man, who looked up and shook his head, although Ray hadn't asked him anything specific yet. "What's your name?"

"Conrad. Look I don't want any hassle man, I ain't involved in anything."

"You sure about that, Chunky?" Ray replied. "What about her?" He nodded at the young hooker. Conrad glanced in that direction and Cole instinctively turned also. Ray moved with lightning speed, kicking out and catching the pimp hard on the wrist. Cole cried out and the knife spun across the kitchen floor coming to rest underneath the table. Ray stepped to his left so that he was now between Cole and the weapon. Cole grabbed his wrist and looked up at Ray with fearful eyes.

Ray knew that look.

Most fights are won or lost before a punch is thrown. Confidence in your own ability and the belief that your adversary is either incapable of handling themselves, unsure, or even frightened by the dire circumstances they find themselves in is a good indication that the bout is over before it has begun. Intimidation is a deflator of bravado, but in order for it to work the person being threatened has to feel overwhelmingly intimidated. Ray knew that earlier Cole had not sensed any steel in Ray's manner. He had, mistakenly, mistook him for a man on a desperate quest; unsettled and out of his comfort zone amongst the lowlife of the city, certain that he would have Ray's wallet in his possession, and be kicking his arse in the bargain.

The game had changed now, and Ray could see that the pimp was scared. He hadn't turned and ran, and he quietly commended him for that. He evidently had a reputation and he had to save face somehow. Perhaps his only chance of gleaning anything now was for Ray not to humiliate him any further.

Ray turned to Conrad. "I guess you'd rather be anywhere else than here right now, ain't that right, Chunky?"

"Who are you?" Conrad answered.

"Your worst fucking nightmare," Ray hissed, laughing inwardly at the cliche. He was enjoying himself, relishing the men's discomfort. He hit Conrad quickly in the stomach, pulling the punch so that he didn't rupture the fat bastard's kidney, but with enough force to knock the wind out of him. Conrad doubled over dramatically and Ray assured himself that the fat man had no fight left in him, if he ever had any to begin with.

Conrad held up a hand. Still doubled up he lifted his head. Tears were running down his heavily jowled cheeks. His hair was greasy and swept back over his balding pate.

"Wait a minute, please," he wheezed. "I didn't hit you, look I objected to the violence, you must have heard that."

"Oh that makes you a veritable saint," Ray said.

"Who are you to judge me?" Conrad snapped, indicating that there was still a modicum of defiance left.

Ray hated both of these men equally. The provider and the perpetrator. They both lived for and craved the abuse and suffering of those less fortunate than themselves. For the most part, they had a charmed life, these men who lived off the proceeds of those that they tormented and persecuted. Their nefarious activities were often condoned yet rarely challenged. Ray found that from time to time that air of arrogance and confidence needed to be pricked.

He laughed out loud at the attempt at piety. "Judge you? You want to be careful I don't take on the role of jury and

110

executioner, you perverted bastard, now sit your fat arse down and shut the fuck up."

Conrad did as he said and slowly lowered himself into one of the chairs around the kitchen table, still clutching his stomach as if Ray had impaled him with a samurai blade.

Cole stood stock still. Ray wondered if the pimp would attempt to go for the knife, hopefully restoring the balance of power, but he didn't move. He probably realised that even with the switchblade he would still be no match for Ray, whose swiftness at disarming him had been rapid.

Ray turned to the young hooker, who stood by the wall, her arms held rigid at her side and her fists clenched tightly into balls.

"What's your name, sweetheart?" Ray said gently.

"Trixie," the voice barely raised above a whisper.

"Well, Trixie, why don't you pop out and get yourself some lunch or something."

She glanced fearfully at Cole. "You're not going to hurt him are you?" Ray knew that her question was more than likely borne out of fear of reprisals. If Cole detected a hint of disloyalty from the girl, he would make her life even more miserable than it already was. She probably wanted Ray to carry out his threat more than anything and cut off the scumbags balls, but instinct took over, especially when there was the chance of later repercussions and Trixie's plea to spare her boss any further pain or humiliation was unflinching.

He turned and detected a hint of a smile dance on Cole's lips before the pimp dropped his gaze like an admonished schoolboy.

"Go on," Ray urged, and Trixie hurried out. Ray reached down and picked up the switchblade. *Too late to make a defiant last stand now, Cole old boy,* he thought. He folded the blade and pocketed the knife.

"Sit down," he said to Cole. Cole dragged his feet and slumped down into the seat next to Conrad. The two men looked up at Ray expectantly.

Now he had them where he wanted them - A standing man always has a more powerful position than one that is seated.

Cole glanced down at the photo and his eyes widened in surprise.

"Hey, I know this guy," he said, pointing at the picture.

Ray stepped over to the table and looked. Cole was pointing to Howard Price. He could say that it was Price that had put him onto Cole in the first place, but he didn't hate the chiropodist so much to endanger his life. And he was certain that Cole would seek retribution if he found out that it had been Price who had told Ray where he lived.

"I don't care about the man, you know the girl?"

Cole leaned forward and slitted his eyes. "Her face is familiar, but I don't know."

"What about her?" Ray asked, pointing to Helena. *No harm in asking,* he thought. But Cole shook his head immediately. "No, I don't know her, never seen her."

"You know a girl called Chelsea?" Ray asked.

Cole nodded eagerly. "Yeah, I know Chelsea, but that ain't her, man. Why are you asking about her?"

"I heard she may know this girl. She's called Candy Girl, that name ring a bell?"

Cole shrugged. "Don't mean shit."

"What about you, Chunky? You know anybody?"

Conrad glanced at the picture. "No," he said sulkily.

"Chelsea used to be one of my girls, but she ain't no more, she moved away, but her mate is still around here, in King's Cross, man. Her name is Pippa, she knows this guy in the pic, think she fucked him a few times. I know where she lives. I can give you her address," Cole said.

"Aren't you forgetting something?"

Cole and Conrad glanced at each other. "What?" Cole asked.

"You fucking hit me. With that." He nodded at the piping still lying against the door.

What remained of Cole's resolve crumbled a little further. He attempted a small laugh, but it came out more like a plaintive cry. "Look man, I'm sorry, but you were just in the house, man, you could have been anybody. What was I supposed to do? You're a big guy, I had to give myself the upper hand from the off. I didn't know who you were."

"You don't think I'm entitled to some form of compensation? You could have killed me with that thing."

"I'll give you two hundred," Cole said quickly.

Ray laughed. "I don't want money, you little shit, I want a comeuppance."

"The fuck, man?" Cole said.

"How about I bust your nose," Ray said matter-of-factly. "Break it. I can do that with a single blow, do you believe me? Busted nose is gotta be worth a whack on the head with a pipe, what do you say?"

Cole stared at him with widened eyes. He wiped a shaking hand across his dry lips.

"I know people," Cole said quietly.

Ray lashed out with a boot , catching the edge of the table and sending both men sprawling backwards over their chairs. Conrad cried out and hit the floor hard, his bulk not allowing him to prepare for the fall, and there was a loud crack when the back of his head hit the hard surface. Cole was skinny and much more nimble. He rolled over when he hit the floor and found his feet quickly. Ray knew that he had cornered the pimp, by telling him that he was going to hurt him, whatever compromise Cole offered.

And a cornered rat had no option but to fight.

Even so, despite Cole's agility, Ray had anticipated his intentions, and as he rose, Ray slammed a huge thigh against Cole's body, sending the smaller man sprawling.

"You fucker!" Cole cried. Ray kicked him in the ribs and heard a crack as Cole crumpled. Ray lunged for him, grabbed him by the lapels of his fleece and hoisted him to his feet. Cole groaned and then cried out again as Ray slammed him against the wall.

"You know people do you, you scraggy fuck! You wanna call a friend right now? You don't know who you're fucking dealing with, you fucking lowlife. You're a bottom-feeding, scumbag, that's all. He pressed his forearm against Cole's windpipe, shutting off his air supply. Cole clawed at Ray's arm, but it was like spun steel, and Ray only pressed harder until Cole's eyes started to bulge. Then Ray stepped back and let him fall. Cole wheezed and drew in huge lungfuls of air, grasping his busted ribs in the process.

"Please," he whimpered, all the bravado was gone now. "Please don't hit me again. I'll give you Pippa's address. She knows the dude in the picture, fucked him, several times."

"How do you know that?" Ray demanded.

"I just know it man, please."

Ray glanced over at Conrad. The fat man was either unconscious or pretending to be. Either way, it didn't matter to Ray.

"Okay," Ray said. "Get me the address." He stepped closer to Cole, who had managed to struggle to his feet once more, and the smaller man flinched.

"But you listen to me, pond life. You ever disrespect me like that again and I'll do more than bust your ribs and bruise your windpipe, I'll wring your scrawny neck, you understand?"

Cole nodded dumbly. "Yeah I got it," he said.

CHAPTER 15

The Saracen's Head in Whitechapel is a villain's pub.

Not in the traditional sense. There are no desperados cleaning their fingernails with pocket knives sat at the bar, or gangs of thieves with bags of booty secreted under the pool table. It is a place where the underworld meet up, exchange views, talk deals and, on occasion, fall out.

The pub was relatively quiet. A couple of teenagers playing pool on a table with a drink stained cloth. Two older men deep in conversation like Fagin and Bill Sikes huddled together in a booth, a garishly dressed woman in her late sixties feeding a fruit machine on a loop.

Spider recognised a few of the faces, but there were no close acquaintances here. It was 11 a.m the following morning. He nodded a hello to the barman and ordered a beer, taking his drink to an empty booth. He glanced nervously at his watch. At precisely 11.10 Cole Waters walked through the front door of the Saracen's Head and strode over to the bar, just as Spider knew he would. The skinny pimp was holding his left side, and even from this distance, Spider could see that he was grimacing with pain.

Spider knew people's routines; it was all part of being a petty villain. Cole and he were not friends, they were barely nodding acquaintances, but they were aware of each other, in the same way that an ice cream salesman is aware of the guy who sells burgers and hot dogs at the same venue. Similar trades, not rivals, aware of each other's business.

Cole spoke to the barman for a few minutes. A bear of a man, with a huge gut, and a beard that would make a Norse god envious. They nodded a few times. Cole pointed to his ribs and the barman shook his head solemnly. As Cole turned, Spider stood up and waved. Cole narrowed his eyes and stared in his direction. He then said a few more words to the barman and headed over towards Spider. He slid into the chair opposite the petty crook. He didn't have a drink and he glanced at the screen of his phone. His time was important, and evidently too precious to be wasted on the likes of a nobody like Spider.

"What do you want, Spider?" Cole muttered, foregoing any pleasantries such as *hello* or *how are you?*

"What happened to you?" Spider asked, taking a sip of beer.

Cole waved a hand irritably, dismissing his concern. "Never mind that. What do you want?" he repeated.

"I want a girl," Spider declared proudly.

Cole laughed and then winced again, clutching his ribs, "Sure you do, Spider, try searching underneath the arches in Haringey, you could probably get two for the price of one there." He slid out of the booth and made to stand up when Spider threw two hundred pounds onto the table.

Cole stared down at the money. "Where'd you get that kind of cash?" he asked.

"Who are you my fucking banker? I told you I want a girl, for a few hours."

Cole sat back down. "How much you got there?" he asked.

Spider sighed, knowing it had been a mistake to throw the money onto the table. It was a grandiose gesture. Cole would insist that he would need to part with all of it, and once he knew the amount that Spider had, it would prove difficult to haggle. Spider hadn't been with a girl for over a year. He wasn't exactly a catch, and even those who were aware of his reputation, and were in a similar boat themselves weren't exactly falling over themselves to get in his bed.

But now he had a spare two hundred pounds. Not a great deal of money by anybody's standards, but enough to pique Cole's interests. Spider knew that Cole provided girls for the amount of money that he was showing here; the lower end of the market for a few hours of their time. He could have gone for a five minute blow job or a knee-trembler up against a back alley wall for a quick fifty, but he wanted to indulge himself a little. He knew that he would never accrue enough money to aim higher. He had made more money than this before, but this was a single lift and he regarded it as disposable income. Something he could spend and get pleasure from. So Spider had decided he wanted a girl.

Cole had his phone out and brought up the gallery app. He handed it to Spider.

"Scroll along, until you see one that takes your fancy," he said.

Spider nodded and stared down at the screen. He took his time, his mouth moving as he viewed each picture as if he was reciting a mantra. After a minute or so Spider turned the phone around. The picture on the screen was of a gangly girl in pigtails. She was wearing a cheerleader outfit, but her demeanour showed a distinct lack of enthusiasm. She was sitting on the floor, cross-legged, her short, pleated skirt had ridden up to her waist and her long thin legs were splayed out in front of her. She had scuffed knees and was wearing grubby white plimsolls. Her hands were in her lap. Two forlorn-looking pom poms sat discarded and redundant by her side.

"Desi," Cole said. "Nice girl, Spider, very physical."

Spider shook his head. Physical was out of the question. He wanted an active girl, but not somebody who was going to exhaust him. He turned his attention back to the screen and started scrolling once more.

"Do you still do tricks?" Cole asked.

Spider bristled at the question. "No," he replied bitterly. He held up his misshapen left hand. The knuckles were lumpy and the fingers pointed in different directions like a splayed vine. On the day, and for several afterwards the pain had been excruciating, almost unbearable. The surgeon at the hospital Spider managed to stagger to after he was dumped back on the South Bank of Westminster Bridge, had attempted to reset the bones in his hand and fingers, but was simply unable to do so as most of the bones had been reduced to miniscule fragments. Even now after nearly fifteen years, Spider still had acute, agonising bursts of pain in the hand, running from the tips of his fingers to his wrist. It was the onset of severe arthritis, doctors had warned him, more prevalent because of the damaged tissue. He glared at Cole "I can barely pull my own pants up, let alone deal a deck of cards."

Cole nodded sympathetically. "It's just that I saw a magician on TV once, he only had one arm and he performed some amazing card magic."

Spider knew the man Cole was referring to. He was from Argentina and his name was Rene Lavand. He was also right about him being a brilliant magician.

"You've got to want to carry on doing something to show that amount of dedication," Spider said. "For me, the tricks were just a means of making money, I never wanted to entertain people. My dad attempted that for years, and he died a penniless drunk."

"Whereas you?" Cole asked.

"You know what, you're a cheeky cunt!" Spider said, getting up from the table.

"Oh come on, I'm only fucking with you," Cole said. Spider stared at him for a few seconds and then sat back down. They sat in silence for a few minutes, Cole glancing around the bar, Spider staring rigidly at the phone screen.

"So, seen anybody you fancy?" Cole asked. Spider shook his head.

"I haven't looked at all the girls yet, but Jade seems nice."

Cole picked up the phone and quickly scrolled through the gallery once more. He found the person Spider was referring to, a doe-eyed, Asian girl, with prominent teeth. She was wearing glasses and her black hair was braided into a long ponytail. In the picture she was sitting on the end of a desk in an ill-fitting trouser suit, chewing on a pencil. Spider reckoned Cole was going for the secretarial look here, knowing that the boss and secretary relationship was always a stalwart of the male fantasy.

"Jade's a delightful girl, Spider, a real beauty," Cole enthused. "She was born within sight of Mount Fuji." Spider didn't believe that crock of horseshit for a second but guessed that it sounded better than the truth; that Cole and Jade's relationship probably started after he found her rummaging through litter bins on Islington High Street.

"Okay," Spider said. "How much?"

Cole nodded at the sheaf of notes on the table. "How much have you got there?"

"That's not what I asked you," Spider snapped, annoyed. He picked the money up and stuffed it back in his pocket.

"Three hours with Jade, we're looking at two-fifty," Cole said.

"Two hundred," Spider replied, and Cole smiled and offered his hand. Spider knew that the pimp had deliberately gone higher knowing that Spider would come down to the amount that he actually had. He felt duped, but not so much that he would pull out. He offered his own hand and the two men shook, cementing the deal.

CHAPTER 16

"Do I know you?" Pippa said as Ray approached her outside her flat in King's Cross. He had found the address that Cole had given him, but after trying several times yesterday and finding nobody at home, he had given up. Today he was up early and recognised Pippa from the description Cole had given him. He called out her name and she turned. She was exiting the flat, and he assumed that she had either returned very late last night after he had given up, or she had just ignored the doorbell yesterday.

"No, I don't think so," Ray said. She was an extremely attractive girl, tall and lithe, with an athletic build, short, brown hair, and huge green eyes that stared unblinking at Ray. She was wearing a khaki parka over tight stonewashed jeans, which accentuated her figure. She pulled the door shut and trotted down the steps to stand next to Ray.

"How can I help you, mister?..." she asked.

"Please call me, Ray," he said. Pippa stopped and he offered her hand.

Pippa shook it and Ray was surprised by the firm handshake. "I'm looking for someone," Ray said. "Somebody told me that you may be able to help.

"You a cop?"

"Nope, a private investigator."

"Who are you looking for?" Pippa asked. They started walking again.

"You want to grab a coffee?" Ray said.

"Sure, there's a place on the corner here."

They entered a small cafe that advertised *"Full English breakfast for a fiver!* on a battered peeling sign in the window. The glass was streaked with condensation, rivulets running down the interior like a fine rain, so that it was impossible to see clearly inside the cafe, except to glimpse human-shaped silhouettes milling about like lost wandering souls in the fog. Nevertheless, they chose a window seat and Ray ordered two coffees.

When the waitress had left, Ray took out another copy of the photograph. He had left one copy at Cole's house, the pimp assuring him that he would show it to some of his girls and clients. Ray didn't believe that for a second, but he had plenty of copies of the picture , so it hardly mattered. He handed it to Pippa who studied it intently.

"Somebody said you may know the girl in this picture," Ray said, sipping his coffee. It was scalding hot, and he sucked in his cheeks before swallowing his first mouthful.

" You going to tell me who this somebody is who seems to think that I know so much?" Pippa asked, still looking at the photo.

"His name is Cole," Ray said.

"I know Cole," Pippa replied, still not looking up. She didn't say anymore, and Ray accepted that. Any individual would be reluctant to expand on advertising the fact that they had anything more than the most basic of dealings with such a lowlife as Cole Waters.

"This guy's name is Howard Price," Pippa said, turning the photograph around and pointing to Price. He was a chiropodist with a practice in Finsbury Park."

"Was?"

"Maybe still is," Pippa replied. "I wouldn't know, I haven't seen him for over a year."

"A former client?"

"No, we shared a box at the opera."

Ray smiled. "Guess I asked for that. You know anybody else in the pic?"

"The girl with him is Candy. Candy Girl, like in the song."

"What about the other two?" Ray asked.

Pippa shook her head, and Ray sighed, unable to mask his disappointment.

"I suppose that Howard might know them. They could be a foursome out for the evening, but then again they could just be two random couples on a packed dance floor. I guess you're looking for the girl with the long hair?"

Ray nodded. "With not much luck, I'm afraid. I've already spoken to Price, he says he doesn't know them. What can you tell me about Candy?" He paused. "That's if you don't mind talking to me, of course."

"Tell you what," Pippa said. "You treat me to a full English for a fiver and I'll tell you everything I know. I'm a working girl, but times are hard, and I'm barely making minimum wage. Deal?"

"It's a deal," Ray replied, and called the waitress over.

Pippa ate quickly, the voracious appetite of the very hungry. She mopped everything up with a slice of bread and washed it all down with her second cup of coffee.

"I don't know Candy that well, we both had Howard as a client, so there was some communication. Howard was nice, but a bit familiar," Pippa said. She laughed when Ray looked puzzled. "Yeah I know how that sounds, I'm getting paid for him to fuck me, but there are rules and boundaries, and Howard sometimes crossed them."

"You mean like kissing and stuff?" Ray asked.

Pippa snorted a laugh again. It lit up her face and he was warming to her laid back personality and easy air.

"Nah, nothing like that. Kissing is a bit of a grey area with some of the girls, but it's not strictly off-limits. I mean you let a guy fuck you and you'll suck his dick, but suddenly you're indignant if he suggests a peck on the cheek?"

"I thought kissing was a personal line being crossed?"

Pippa shrugged. "Well maybe to some girls. Howard used to think that because he was paying for something, then it was his to do with what he liked. Oh don't get me wrong, there was no physical shit, Howard was meek, a bit of a pussy, but he simply expected too much sometimes. He never tried it on with me, but he pissed Candy off really bad, she had to call somebody in to get him to back off."

"That sounds ominous."

"Well we girls run in some tight circles, we know some bad boys. Candy was seeing a mobster from Leeds, not some small-time hood but a serious boy; daddy ran a haulage firm, and they used to transport all kinds of shit on the side. Anyway, he had a word with Howard, and that was it. Candy never had any problems with him again."

" She still around?"

Pippa shrugged. "I guess so, I haven't seen her since about November come to think of it, but girls move on."

"You got an address for her?"

"Nope and even if I did, I wouldn't give it to you. Cute and generous as you are, I don't really know you from Adam, and I wouldn't betray a girl just like that." She clicked her fingers. "Cole should have known better giving you my details unless you paid the prick."

"I didn't pay him."

Pippa shrugged. "He give you my mobile too?"

"Nope, just the address."

Pippa took out a card from her purse and handed it over. It was plain, except for the one word: *Pippa* and a mobile number underneath.

"What's this for?" Ray asked, turning the card over in his hand and noting the blank rear side.

"Like I said, you're cute, though I guess you know that. I do sometimes date guys you know, it's not all strictly business. Sometimes it's nice to go out for a meal, or to the pictures."

There was no urgency to the statement, no desperation, just a simple request for company. Ray felt flattered, and almost desperately sad for Pippa at the same time.

"Tell you what," Pippa said. "I'll speak to Candy and see if she wants to speak to you. Fair?"

Ray nodded. "Fair."

They left the cafe and Pippa thanked him for breakfast. Ray tried to come up with an excuse to walk with her, but couldn't think of any, and after an uncomfortable pause, they said goodbye and set off in different directions.

CHAPTER 17

The girl turned up at Spider's apartment at five minutes after seven p.m. She was quite tall, something that Spider had not been able to discern from the pictures on the phone as she was sitting down. She wasn't stunning; she was not even attractive, but what the fuck, Spider wasn't leading man material.

She was probably only half Chinese or Japanese, Spider didn't know. The girl was pencil-thin, wearing a linen, floral dress with pastel flower designs. Her skinny arms and bony shoulders were dotted with small clusters of flat, lightly pigmented moles, and her black hair was long and tied in a ponytail. There were flakes of dandruff on her scalp where her hair parted. She wore frameless, round spectacles. Her front teeth were large and when she smiled she revealed a large, prominent gumline. She introduced herself simply as Jade and Spider stepped aside as the girl walked into the apartment.

He had tidied it the best he could. There was little furniture, no ornaments to speak of and no carpets in the small living area. Spider had lived here for over ten years; the seventh floor in a high-rise in Harlesden. He had bought it after selling his father's house in Tottenham, which suddenly seemed huge with just him living there.

Jade glanced around, actually turning her body to get a clearer view.

"Small," she said matter-of-factly. Her brief appraisal complete, she stopped turning and stood in front of Spider, her hands placed on her bony hips.

"Cole says I have to be back by ten, so that gives you three hours." She shrugged. "So you want to go into the bedroom?"

"Do you..um.. you want a drink first?" Spider said, his nervousness making him stutter.

Another shrug. "Sure, you got any Southern Comfort?"

Spider almost laughed. She may as well ask him for a quart of plutonium.

"I've got a couple of bottles of beer in the fridge."

Jade looked around once more, seemingly uncertain if there was room for a fridge in the tiny apartment. "Okay, why not."

Spider uncapped two cold ones and handed one to Jade. She stared at the label for a few seconds as if unsure of the contents then took a sip. Spider drained half the bottle in one long gulp. They stood quietly for a minute, both staring at the beer bottles. Jade seemed unperturbed by Spider's hesitancy. He supposed she wasn't in any rush - why should she be?

Spider finished his beer. He wished he had some more and he glanced longingly at the almost full bottle in Jade's hand.

He held up the beer cap and pressed it into the palm of his scarred and distorted hand. He performed a simple French Drop, spiriting the cap deftly from one hand to the other, then opened his hand to show the cap had vanished. He clicked the fingers of his good hand and the cap rose up to the tips. Jade stared at it.

"Do it again," she said, so Spider did. The second time she wasn't so impressed. Then she went into her sales pitch.

"I'll do blow and straight fucking. Anal depends on the size of your cock, girth more so than length, too thick and you can forget it, I tear. I'm not even kidding with you about that. Condoms obviously except for a blow job, things haven't gotten that bad yet. Watersports are okay, but not scat, and you can't hit me cos I bruise and I'm simply not into pain. Now I know you've cleared some deal with Cole, so I won't

126

go into prices, but I ain't going to turn down any tips, if you catch my drift." She took a deep breath, reached behind her and undid her dress. She stepped out of it and stood naked before Spider.

" You have any preferences?" she asked, folding up her dress and draping it over the arm of the sofa.

Spider nodded slowly, gazing longingly at Jade's skinny body.

"Yes, yes I do."

He dropped her off at the house in King's Cross, exactly three hours later. The session had been wonderful, and Spider told the cab driver to wait for him. He escorted Jade up the steps to the door like a considerate partner seeing home his prom date.

They walked into the kitchen, but nobody was there, not even Cole.

"Well I'll see you around," Spider said nervously. Jade turned and looked at him quizzically as if wondering why he was still here. He said goodbye to Jade, but she was already on her mobile tapping keys and ignored him. Spider turned and left. On his way out he caught sight of the photograph and snatched it off the table. He stared at it for nearly a full minute.

"Jesus fucking Christ!" he whispered.

He tucked the photograph into the confines of his coat and hurried out the front door.

CHAPTER 18

On the morning of the 8th June, the girls from the Elm Tree Carvery restaurant were getting ready for their big night out.

Carly had called Gemma four times already. The first time was to check that she was still going. When Gemma had assured her she had no intention of dropping out, Carly's sense of excitement escalated. She told Gemma that she and

Kat had booked appointments at nail bars and that Kat was going to make her up later that afternoon. She asked if Gemma wanted to come, and had been a little surprised when Gemma had replied that she was fine and would do her own makeup. Subsequent calls had simply been excited updates of how the transformation was going, and Gemma quietly applauded Kat for taking the time and effort in looking after her colleague so well. It was a big deal for Carly and Gemma was acutely aware of that. To her credit, it appeared Kat did also.

By five-thirty in the afternoon, aside from a few last-minute touch-ups to her make-up, Gemma was ready. Although there were another two hours to go before she was to meet up with her friends, she liked to make her preparations early. She carefully removed her recently purchased party clothes, folded them neatly over a wooden towel rail, that doubled up for her wardrobe and sat on the edge of her bed in her bra and panties. She picked up a new copy of the latest Conn Iggulden bestseller and started to read. She could think of no better way to spend the next couple of hours before her big night out.

Carly and Kat were seated at a booth in the pub when Gemma arrived by cab. She walked into the bar and many heads turned, including those of her two workmates. Gemma spotted them, walked over and took a seat next to Carly. There was a bottle of Shiraz on the table and three glasses. Kat's was half empty, or half full depending on your outlook. Carly's hadn't been touched. Gemma filled the third glass and took a long sip. She was aware of the girls staring at her. Kat looked her up and down and then shook her head.

"Jesus Christ," she whispered. "Aren't you a dark horse?" Carly simply gawped at her, her mouth open.

"You look gorgeous," she whispered. Gemma smiled. and sipped her wine. Kat was wearing fishnet stockings and a dusky pink t-shirt with an intricate and unnervingly realistic caricature of a multi-tattooed Audrey Hepburn emblazoned on the front. She wore a light green jacket, with the sleeves rolled up. A thin, Gucci watch hung limply on her wrist, and she sported a pair of heeled boots that reached just below the knee, plus a tight mini-skirt that barely covered her ass. Her long hair was loose, and hung over her shoulders, a thin, multi-coloured Alice band supporting the fringe.

Carly had been transformed, and Gemma was aware that most of this effort was due to Kat herself. Carly was not unattractive, but her shy demeanour and introverted nature did not allow her to experiment. Kat had, probably for the first time, brought her out of her shell, and possibly her comfort zone, though Carly still appeared nervous, chewing distractedly on the fleshy base of her thumb. She constantly pulled her cardigan around herself, covering her breasts, that were not exactly exposed, but were exhibiting more cleavage than was normal. Carly had opted for a short, pleated tartan skirt and black, lacy tights. She wore flat shoes, insisting that she could barely stand, let alone walk in heels. A shiny, round badge clung loosely above the top button of the cardigan. The slogan "21 TODAY" for all to see.

But it was Gemma's appearance that was the real talking point. Kat was always glamorous. Carly was pretty, though her outfit was still too reserved to render her anything more than attractive.

But Gemma was stunning. The frumpy, tied to the neck shirts and dull skirts of work had been replaced by skin-tight leather trousers and a plunging cream blouse. The glasses had gone, the make-up was flawless. It was all Kat could do to maintain her incredulity.

"So what's the crack?" she said. "You turn up out of the blue, looking how you do and start working at a rundown bar. Jesus, who are you running from?"

Carly smiled and ran the tip of her index finger over the rim of her wine glass.

"She has secrets, it's obvious."

Despite the unnerving aspects of the conversation, Gemma attempted to fob off the girls questioning with a nonchalant wave of her hand. They had all talked of the past before, of course, but the recollections, especially from Gemma, were always fleeting and brief. Now, however, in a more relaxed environment than that of the workplace, the restrictions and boundaries on probing were temporarily lifted. By agreeing to meet socially, the three girls were almost obliged to discuss matters of a more personal nature, and Kat, in particular, was quick to seize the initiative.

"You've got a past, lady, tell us about it," Kat grinned mischievously and took a long sip or wine.

"You've both got active imaginations," Gemma said. "Everybody has secrets, it doesn't make them a double agent, or a fugitive from the law. Shit, Kitty Kat, look at you, dolled up to the nines, you look about ready to step out onto the catwalk. We could question what you're doing at The Elm."

Kat shrugged her shoulders, seemingly unaware how subtlety Gemma had shifted the conversation away from herself.

"I'm saving myself." She smiled and fluffed her hair, throwing back her head and adjusting her Alice Band.

"Saving yourself for what?" Carly said.

"I don't intend to spend all my life behind a bar, I've got plans."

"Like what?" Carly insisted.

Kat sipped her wine. "I want to find a sugar daddy. Some rich old bastard who will sweep me off my feet and pamper me."

"In exchange for what?"

"Well, what do you think?"

"You want to become a prostitute?"

Kat laughed. "Of course not. Christ, Carly!" She pinched the folds of her Audrey t-shirt and thrust it towards her. "Have you ever seen *"Breakfast at Tiffany's?"*

Carly nodded.

"I wanna be like Holly Golightly, a good time girl."

"I think you'll find that was a polite way of saying she was a prostitute," Carly replied. She took a miniscule sip of her wine, made a face and set the glass back down on the table.

"Oh my god, Carly, she was not. Holly liked the men, but she wasn't a fucking hooker!"

"I think you'll find opinion is divided on that," Gemma said.

"Whose side are you on?" Kat said, but there was a grin on her face. "Anyway, what is wrong with having good sex? I love it and to get paid for it would just be an added bonus as far as I'm concerned."

"You're condoning prostitution," Carly said.

"Condoning?"

"It means you're agreeing with something that is abjectly wrong."

"Whoa, hang on, hang on. Are you saying that all the glamorous women on the arms of rich, older men are prostitutes? Movie stars date younger, beautiful girls, singers, sportsmen as well, and some of them are such ugly twats that the young pussy wouldn't give them a second glance under any other circumstances, except for the fact that they're either rich, famous or both."

"No of course I'm not saying that, but what about love?"

Kat shook her head dismissively. "Overrated. Should be reserved for mothers and small dogs only"

They all three laughed at that. Gemma was enjoying the banter. Playful though it may have appeared, she was aware of an underlying, serious tone to Carly's objections, and she was certain that if the younger girl had a few larger sips of wine then she may be able to back up her arguments a little more forcefully, instead of having to defend them against Kats barbed witticisms.

"I could never sleep with anybody unless I loved them," Carly said almost wistfully

"Never underestimate the power of a one night stand," Kat replied. "Are you going to drink that wine or dribble into it?"

Carly shook her head. "I don't really like it"

"Then why did you order it? I was going to line up three vodka and cokes , it was your idea to buy a bottle."

Carly looked bewildered. "I don't know. I just thought it would be a good idea to order a bottle, I haven't done this kind of thing before." She laughed, perhaps realising how staid and square that sounded.

Gemma reached across the table and picked up the bottle. She topped up her own and Kat's glass and set the bottle back down. "Why don't you let me and Kitty Kat finish this off, and the next round, I promise I'll get you a drink that you're going to enjoy."

"Will it be alcoholic?"

Kat laughed. but Gemma shot her a look that said lay off the teasing for a while. Kat read it right and held up her hands in mock surrender.

"Carly I'll get you a cup of cocoa if you like, but trust me, you're going to feel better with a few stronger drinks inside you."

Carly nodded. "Well, okay then, but do you think you could get me some crisps too. I haven't eaten, and this wine has already gone to my head."

Carly relaxed considerably after Gemma had bought a round of cocktails. She didn't tell her that it was laced with rum. They all sipped them slowly. They were delicious with hints of cinnamon and ginger. Gemma had also insisted that they get something to eat and between them, they shared a chorizo and cheese panini cut into three equal portions.

Now they were in a karaoke bar and Carly was on her fourth drink of the night. It was busy and the only table available was next to the toilets. Gemma had lost count of how many drinks Kat had consumed, but she knew that Carly was watching her closely. She was probably aware that she, Gemma, herself was drinking very little.

"The Power of Love" came on. Not the *Frankie Goes to Hollywood* version, but the rousing ballad by *Jennifer Rush.*

"Oh I love this song," Carly said. At that moment Kat's cell phone beeped and she took it out, smiling as she saw the caller's name.

"Hey, I've got to get this." She took out a twenty and dropped it on the table. "My round, get them in and I'll be back in a min ."

Gemma snatched up the money and headed for the bar. It was busy and she had to ease her way in between impatient customers who seemed to believe that if they waved their money furiously in the air they would alert the bar staff to their urgency far earlier, who, in turn, would drop whatever they were doing and hasten to complete their order. Gemma knew better. She managed to squeeze in between two guys and patiently waited until she could get the attention of one of the male bartenders. She was aware of somebody belting out the song in the background, a pretty good, yet rather aggressive rendition in her opinion. The song finished and there was a smattering of applause and one or two over-enthusiastic whoops. She caught the eye of one of the barmen, and blew him a kiss. He made a beeline straight towards her.

"Hey!" the guy next to her complained. "I was here first." The barman ignored him and Gemma didn't even give him a sideways glance as she placed her order.

As she turned around, she spied a group of four girls. One of them was pointing in Carly's direction and whispering to a second girl, who put her hand to her mouth and started laughing. Gemma recognised the group as troublemakers. As they headed towards Carly and Kat, she left the drinks at the bar and stepped away.

She took a meandering route, skirting the fringes of the room, watching the giggling group of girls as they approached her friend's table. She managed to get behind Carly and Kat without them seeing her. She sat down at a table directly behind them. A young couple already seated at the table looked up. The girl frowned at the intrusion, but Gemma ignored her.

Gemma listened to Carly and Kat for a few seconds, but her eyes remained on the group of girls. They had all stopped about six feet away from where Kat and Carly were sitting. Two of them whispering and sniggering. The other two girls held back, seemingly reluctant to take part in whatever scheme they were hatching. Although Gemma didn't dismiss this pair they would be the least of her concerns. The other two, however, were trouble . The first, the whisperer, was a dark-skinned girl about the same age as Carly. She had shiny black hair and a lithe, slim figure. She was quite tall, about five-nine. The second girl was shorter but stockier. She looked hard. Her eyes were slits, and her smile was more of a sneer. There was an aura of malevolence about her; a stoked up boiler about to explode, and the darker-skinned girl was fanning these tempestuous flames. Gemma clenched and unclenched her fists mechanically. She listened to the snippets of conversation from Carly and Kat.

"Steady with these cocktails, hon," Kat said. "They may taste like pop, but they'll put you on your back if you're not careful. How are you feeling?".

Carly smiled. "I feel great, Kat. Look, thanks for everything, I know you think I'm a bit of a bore, and you'd probably rather be anywhere else but here right now, but it's great that you're doing this for me, I really appreciate it, honestly."

Kat smiled genuinely at her. "That's bullshit, babe. Don't put yourself down, I'm really enjoying myself, and I know that Gemma is too."

"What do you think of her?" Carly asked, glancing over at the bar.

"What do you mean?"

"What we were talking about earlier, about her having a history and that. You notice how she quickly changes the subject whenever we bring up any questions about her past?"

Kat shook her head. "Not really, babe, why, what are you getting at?"

Carly shrugged. "I don't know, I really like her, but there's something about her, I don't know...."

"Hey, hey, hey...... Carly Beech!" the stocky girl cried as she tottered in front of their table, the dark-skinned girl was scanning the room. She didn't spot Gemma. The other two girls stood a distance away.

The colour drained from Carly's face. "Oh... hello Jazz." She swallowed and glanced at the dark-skinned girl. "Hello, Pinto."

The stocky girl, Jazz, laughed and tottered slightly on her heels. "Carly, my girl, I haven't seen you since we were at school together. Fuck, what are you doing out, it's not a full moon, is it? And look at your outfit girl. What happened, did your fucking granny die and leave you her wardrobe?"

"Leave her alone," Kat snapped. But she was not a brave girl and her voice quavered. She didn't like confrontation and rarely found herself in situations such as this. Normally when she went out, she either had a strapping guy on her arm or was in a large group of girls, and there was always safety in numbers. She didn't recognise either of the two girls in front of her now, but she certainly recognised their type. Swaggering, confident bullies who had honed in on, and selected, possibly the most vulnerable prey in the room; a pretty girl and her shy friend. This wasn't going to end happily and Kat felt her stomach clench and knot in fear.

"Piss off, bitch," Jazz said, staring Kat down. "We're just asking the birthday girl here how things are." She turned to Carly. "We got shit in common today. Now, what do you say we have a celebratory drink? You're twenty-one and probably never been fucked, I'm getting hitched and gagging for cock. "So what will it be, Carly Beeeeeech?" She staggered again and set a steadying hand on the table before her.

Carly managed a weak smile. "I'm okay thank-you, I have a drink."

Jazz and Pinto exchanged glances and smiled, Jazz winked at her friend knowingly.

"No, no, no, Missy. I mean you're going to buy us a drink."

"Oh, right." Carly managed a weak smile. "I'll get you a drink, what would you like?"

"What I would like is a fat cock on a toned body," Jazz laughed. "What I will settle for is a margarita jug for me and my bitches."

"Okay," Carly said, taking out her purse. "How much is a margarita jug?"

Jazz shrugged. "About thirty quid, but don't bother queuing at the bar, that'll take all fucking night. " She held out her hand. "Just give me the money and I'll get it, I mean what are friends for?"

Gemma stood up and headed back in the direction of the bar, but then she cut straight back and headed for Carly's table, pushing her way between the two girls hanging back, evidently not wanting to get involved. They looked her up briefly but said nothing. As Gemma watched Carly's hand waver with three ten pound notes in her fingertips she stepped up behind Jazz.

"Put your purse away, Carly," Gemma said.

Jazz spun around and was immediately in Gemma's face.

"Fuck off, Princess Daisy, this has got nothing to do with you."

In a single fluid motion, Gemma grabbed Jazz by the hair and shoved her towards the toilet door. The momentum pushed both girls through, and once the door swung back to close, Gemma, still holding Jazz by the hair, head-butted her full in the face. Jazz went down, poleaxed, and Gemma turned back to the toilet door. As expected it opened and the dark-skinned girl hurried in, but Gemma was waiting for her and as Pinto glanced down at her stricken friend groaning on the tiled floor, Gemma swung her arm around and elbowed Pinto in the face before she had time to react. She also dropped. For good measure, Gemma gave Pinto a couple of hard kicks in the ribs. She turned back to Jazz who was crying and holding her nose, blood pouring through her fingers. Gemma crouched down beside her and Jazz flinched. Most girls will back down from a fight, and those that are prepared to go a few rounds would hardly resort to head-butting or a well-judged elbow to the nose. Gemma knew this, and she was acutely aware that Jazz knew it also.

Jazz glanced over at Pinto but her friend remained curled up on the floor in the fetal position, her hands clutched to her stomach, moaning softly. Jazz gingerly touched the tip of her own nose and cried out. She glanced down at her fingertips, covered with blood.

"Get up," Gemma demanded.

Jazz tried to stand. "You've broken my fucking nose!"

"No, I haven't. If it was broken you wouldn't be able to touch it, now get up."

Jazz struggled to her feet. Gemma grabbed her hair again and pulled her head back. "Now you're going to clean yourself up and then you're gonna fuck off, you get me?"

As far as she was able to, Jazz nodded.

"And if you have any thoughts about having a go later with a few extra friends, let me warn you. Next time I'll do more than just put you down. You get me, you nasty, sadistic, fucking bitch?" She yanked harder at Jazz's hair until the girl cried out once more.

Yeah, I get it...Please."

Gemma let her go, turned and left the toilet.

The remainder of the night was a blur for Gemma. With Carly and Kat's constant praise for her standing up to the bullies and the celebratory atmosphere this single act of heroism produced, the girls were keen to party.

As expected Kat met a dashing guy in the final bar and suggested they all proceed to a nightclub. His mate was eager to agree, especially with Gemma on the scene, but Gemma was aware that Carly had had enough. The alcohol and the excitement had proved too much for the birthday girl, and Gemma cried off insisting she would have to get her friend home .

As they waited for a cab, Gemma reflected on the last couple of hours.

The attack on the bully in the karaoke bar had been beyond foolish. If she had been arrested, what would have happened then? Despite her threats, she knew that a girl like that would seek revenge. She didn't really regret any of her actions, as she had let her hair down and gone wild for a single night and it had been great fun, especially seeing a pair like Jazz and Pinto get their comeuppance. But there were too many possible repercussions to take into account now. Perhaps one more week at work, and then move on to another part of the country. She had gotten close to both Carly and Kat in the short time that she had known them, but her life had always consisted of many relationships that were no more than fleeting.

The cab pulled up and Gemma bundled Carly inside then got in beside her.

After she arrived at the holiday park, the driver set off to drop Carly off. When she was alone Gemma made up her mind what to do. She would let the girl's know on Monday that she was finishing at the end of next week.

She had messed up big time tonight. Too many careless moves; too many disruptions to her set routine. Far too many risks.

It was time to move on.

CHAPTER 19

It was Sunday morning when Pippa knocked on the door of Ray's hotel room and offered him that gorgeous smile.

Since the death of his wife, Ray had had many casual relationships. He had felt guilty in the early days, as if allowing himself any moment of intimacy was still a betrayal; not that he had ever been concerned about his infidelity when his wife had been alive.

For that reason his guilt was short-lived. The stark reality was that Ray had never been a great husband or father when his wife and daughter had been alive. To even allow himself a modicum of self-pity now following their tragic deaths was hypocritical and frankly sickening.

Not that he hadn't loved them both, he had unquestionably. He had been able to convince himself of that one fact, despite the cheating and the months spent away.

He had been a self-indulgent man, still was, he conceded. It was all about him; his happiness, his sense of self fulfilment. Ray's womanising had become the elephant in the room. His late wife, Julia, had been aware of it before they married, believing that she could change him, despite strong reservations from her mother. Ray knew that the nights she stayed awake, whilst he was out philandering were torturous, but she still maintained that it was simply a phase that her husband was going through and he would come to appreciate her in time.

It was a frustrating attitude, even Ray himself concluding that maybe if Julia had lost her temper, slapped him or even asked him what the hell he was playing at , he may have opened his eyes and realised the irreparable damage that he was doing. But she hadn't done so. Julia remained calm and even a little contrite, rarely bringing up the subject and continuing her early married life as if everything was mighty fine.

After nearly two years of marriage, Julia suddenly realised just how stupid and lacking in judgement her assessment was. Nobody could live the way she was supposed to live, not as man and wife, she had told Ray. Unbeknown to him, she had already set the wheels in motion to leave him, discussing her feelings with her parents, who remained steadfastly non-judgemental, despite their dire warnings they had issued their daughter of marrying Ray in the first place.

Then Julia fell pregnant, and everything changed.

Ray was certain that his wife stopped caring about what he did on the day their daughter was born. She was reliant on Ray for money, for security, and he never denied her either of these things, but suddenly the infidelity wasn't so important anymore. She wasn't even bothered about sex with him now, even though, despite everything, it had always been mutually satisfying. That in itself was a component of her frustration. She had said to Ray on the rare occasions they had broached the subject - *"Why fuck around when we satisfy each other?"* But even that had been more of a statement of fact rather than an accusation. She hadn't screamed at him: *"Why are you screwing around when we're so great together, you fucking moron!* Which would have been completely acceptable. It had merely been a shrug of the shoulders, confirming that after so long apathy was becoming an overriding factor concerning the reasons as to why Ray was almost deliberately going out of his way to hurt her.

For Ray, it was as if he was given free rein to do whatever he wanted. He was never certain if Julia herself had been unfaithful to him, and he pretended not to care. She would have a good reason after all.

But he did care. He still loved Julia, and he adored his daughter, Sophia, but he was unable to say no to frequent, no strings sex. He knew that his own excuses had been trite and pathetic, yet Julia's acceptance of his screwing around alleviated the guilt to such an extent that he simply stopped bothering to hide the affairs and his own culpability.

Following their death, Ray left the army. Financially he was okay. The house was paid for, and a hefty insurance policy provided stability; the mundane jobs were simply a way of alleviating boredom. Following the funerals, Julia's parents disowned him, confirmation that the tenuous ties that had existed between them before had been severed permanently.

The weirdest thing of all was that once Julia had gone, was no longer a part of his life, relationships were forever fraught with guilt.

He had never felt quite so pathetic in his life.

He opened the door wider and Pippa stepped over the threshold.

"Sorry, Ray, but Candy Girl's a no-show. She's either changed her number or has moved on. It happens. The simple fact is, I can't get hold of her, I'm sorry."

She was dressed in the same clothes as yesterday, and though she still looked smart, Ray noted that the outfit was slightly shabby. A few innocuous stains on the cuffs of her parka that had been scrubbed at but not wholly removed, her hair a little greasier than before, the trainers scuffed and worn down upon closer inspection

Ray closed the front door and Pippa followed him inside. She gazed around but either she was not impressed or didn't bother to offer an opinion. Ray surmised that she was often escorted to numerous hotel rooms for one reason only. Why would she be impressed with this uninspiring location? She sat on a small, two-seater sofa.

"Not to worry," he said, though he was uncertain how things would proceed from here. " Do you want a drink?"

Pippa shook her head. "No, I'm good."

"You sure?"

She looked up at him. "You have any milk?"

"Yeah, sure. You don't want anything stronger?"

"Not unless you've got Nesquik."

Ray smiled. He pressed play on his MP3 player on the bedside table. Elvis Costello came on singing a slowed down, melodious version of My Funny Valentine through the portable speaker.

"It's semi-skimmed, is that okay?" Ray asked.

"Yeah, that's cool. I like this song."

"Me too. Elvis is one of my favourites."

She turned her head, regarding him quizzically for a second. "You're joking, even I know this isn't Elvis."

"Costello, not Presley. One of this country's most gifted songwriters." He handed her the milk and she took the tiniest of sips.

"I'm sorry it's not cold. I don't have a fridge here, I just got a drop for my coffee.

Pippa shrugged. "Did he write this?"

Ray took the chair opposite her. "No, actually."

She took another sip of her milk. "I like his voice."

They were quiet for a while, listening to the music. *My Funny Valentine* finished and segued into *Accidents Will Happen.*

"What do you want?" Pippa asked eventually, setting her milk down on a small coffee table in front of her.

"What do you mean?"

"Do you wanna fuck me?"

Ray paused, and Pippa smiled at him. She looked beautiful when she smiled.

"I don't know," he said eventually.

She laughed at that. "Well, I don't usually encounter that sort of indecision. If not, then what do you want? We both know that I could have told you what I knew about Candy Girl over the phone. You didn't have to ask me over to your hotel room."

Ray inclined his head, conceding the point. "I like you," he said. "I'm leaving the day after tomorrow, going down to Weymouth for a few days."

"And?"

"I want you to come with me."

"Really?"

Ray nodded. "Why not? You said yourself that you went on dates."

"I said we could go to see a movie or grab a bite to eat, not go on holiday together." She laughed again, but Ray sensed that she wasn't totally opposed to the idea.

"We can go see a film and go out for plenty of meals together. Look, everything here has come to an abrupt halt. I need to go back to Weymouth, see if I can get anybody else to

144

shed some light, but at the same time, we can have some fun. What are your plans for the next few days anyway?

"Nothing that can't be rearranged."

"Is that a yes?"

" That's a maybe ."

Ray smiled.

"Can I take a shower?" Pippa asked. "My boiler is fucked and my landlord is trying to botch it instead of paying for a new one. I've been taking cold baths for the past two weeks."

"Sure, it's through here."

Ray stood up and walked Pippa to the bathroom. He opened the door with an outstretched arm and she ducked beneath it. She started to undress. Ray turned to leave, but she put a hand on his arm.

"Please, don't go."

"Okay," Ray said quietly. He watched her undress, revealing boyish hips, a sparse, downy patch of pubic hair and small, shapely breasts with large erect nipples. Pippa stepped inside the cubicle and turned on the water. She stepped under the spray immediately and cried out as the cold water hit her body.

"Give it a minute to warm," Ray said.

Pippa laughed. "This is a Roman bath compared to what I'm used to, come on in."

Ray undressed slowly and stepped into the cubicle. Pippa reached between his legs and grasped his penis with a soapy hand. There were no preliminaries and he didn't expect them. Ray closed his eyes. He turned from her and leaned forward, his arms outstretched, palms flat on the tiled surface of the shower cubicle, balancing his weight. Pippa moved around so that she was standing behind him. She reached between his legs and cupped his balls before grabbing his penis again. Ray could feel the hot spray on his back as the girl slowly manipulated him, expertly stroking his length. Ray was rock hard by the time he spun around. He grasped Pippa around the waist, lifted her high, and pushed her back against the tiles. He entered her with one long thrust and she gasped. She threw her hands around his neck until his face was buried between her small breasts. Ray took a nipple in his mouth, and thrust again, deeper and with more urgency. Pippa pushed back against him and locked her ankles around his waist. She was tight but then almost at once, mercifully yielding, allowing him to press forward so slowly, an inch at a time until he was buried deep inside her. Ray took measured, assured thrusts, and all the time she contracted and then gripped him as assuredly as a closed fist. The spray of water was warm and luxuriating as the couple enjoyed each other's bodies. When Ray climaxed, he lifted her from him and they soaped each other, down, Pippa giggling as she made him kneel down and shampooed his hair.

They headed into the bedroom after the shower and made love again. Then they talked and laughed like an established couple, surprisingly relaxed in each other's company.

Afterwards, they dressed. Ray in fresh clothes, Pippa back in the crumpled garments she had arrived in. Ray reached for his wallet on the nightstand, then hesitated, his hand hovering over it. Pippa put her own small hand on top of his.

"Please don't," she said. "I know what just happened, I know what I am, but on occasion, it's nice to forget. To believe it was something else, you know."

Ray nodded. "Yeah, I know."

146

Pippa left and Ray closed the door behind her. He was only half expecting her to come with him to Weymouth on Tuesday, but that expectation was enough to get him excited.

CHAPTER 20

Spider liked to consider himself *"The word on the street"* As a petty criminal he moved in circles inhabited by those of his ilk - the pickpocket's and the shoplifter's, the bottom feeders and junkies, those that considered fifty quid a result.

Spider had no true friends. Those that would sell the blankets of their own hypothermic grans were unlikely comrades, despite being cut from the same degraded cloth.

However, Spider listened. Eavesdropping or the grapevine, whispered accusations and scurrilous gossip, it really didn't matter, all information was stored in his vast memory banks.

It wasn't a trick, a technique proven by the likes of Paul Daniel's who insisted that word association was the key to a perfect train of recollection. For Spider there was no technique involved, none that he could recall ever having to master. He just remembered shit. He couldn't always recall where he had heard it, or even who had said it, in much the same way that he couldn't always recall the singer of a song that he knew all the words to, it was just there filed away, accessible when needed.

Spider took out the photograph that he had taken from the house when he had dropped Jade off on Friday evening and studied the faces once again. He smiled to himself and slipped it back inside his jacket pocket.

He stood on a street corner and watched as Murray Cooper entered the restaurant. It was 1.20 p.m. on Sunday afternoon. Murray always ate at this particular restaurant on a Sunday, always alone.

As Murray entered the front door, Spider hurried across the road and stood at the window watching as Murray took his seat.

The restaurant was Thai and provided a buffet service on Sunday's. Murray ordered a drink then glanced across at the buffet table. There were about ten people making their selections from the extensive range. He remained in his seat as Spider entered the restaurant. The waiter took in the dishevelled appearance but was courteous enough to offer no more than a cursory glance. Spider despised oriental food, but that was neither here nor there. He wasn't here to eat.

He strode over to Murray's table and sat opposite the big man.

"Hello Mister Cooper," he said. Murray looked up.

"Who the fuck are you?" he snapped.

"We need to talk," Spider said.

Murray Cooper stared at him for a few seconds longer "You know me?" Murray said. "Know who I am, what I do?"

Spider shook his head. "I know of you. I know your son, Clive. Well, no, that's not altogether accurate. I was aware of him also. He used to speak loudly, Mister Cooper. Now whether that was because he had a naturally loud voice, or he wanted people to hear what he had to say, I can't say, though if pressed I would plump for the latter. He was surrounded by sycophants, those who would hang onto his every word, laugh at his unfunny jokes and indulge his nastiness. People with money attract these kinds of people, as I'm sure you are aware"

Murray listened but said nothing. If he was pissed at Spider for insulting his son he didn't show it.

"Do you know where he is, your son?" Spider asked.

Murray nodded slowly. "Yes. Do you?"

"No, I do not. I have read about him in the paper."

"And?"

"I don't believe that your son is missing in a Bolivian jungle, Mister Cooper."

"What do you believe?"

Spider ignored the question. "I know you always eat here on a Sunday. Clive told his friends about it. He said, " *My father loves Thai food, but orders the same shit every time, never experiments, also the same fucking restaurant.*"

Murray shrugged unimpressed. "So fucking what. He tells you that and you turn up here. If there's a point to this charade why don't you make it."

"Clive didn't tell me anything, I overheard. I played the bandit a lot, in the club he frequented, it was a good central location. I have exceptional hearing, and I remember stuff, a real benefit in my line of work."

"And what is your line of work?"

"I'm a petty thief, Mister Cooper. A pickpocket primarily, though I'm on the lam for almost anything. I frequent bars in which people boast and talk loudly. I hide in the shadows at bus terminals and in the echoing tunnels of the subway. I know the girls who hustle on the streets and the men who prey on them, the bent cops and the fences, the charlatans and the pimps, and they all know me. Everybody knows Spider, Mister Cooper and because I am a petty, innocuous man, nobody pays me any heed. I know that your son disappeared a few days before Christmas because the same sycophants that were with him before still frequent the same bar in which I still play the same fruit machine, and one of them spoke of a meeting between your son and Candy Girl. I know that she went missing at the same time. I think your son is dead, Mister Cooper, and the fact that Candy Girl disappeared when your son did, leads me to believe that she had something to do with it.

Murray Cooper sat back in his chair and smiled. "You're right, Spider, you're a very petty man. I don't have time to deal with petty men. You think that just because you have heard a few unguarded conversations, that you have uncovered a family conspiracy? That is your proof?"

"I never mentioned a family conspiracy," Spider said. "But your son is missing, presumed dead. I also think he's dead, Mister Cooper, and that Candy Girl is mixed up in it."

"Now you're starting to repeat yourself," Murray snapped. "The traits of a desperate man, with so little to go on." He stood up and headed to the buffet table. The waiter waved a palm in the right direction as if Murray had somehow lost his bearings. Murray picked up a plate and started piling on food as if he hadn't eaten in a week.

Spider followed him but didn't pick up his own plate. "I want five grand," he said.

Murray laughed and he turned to Spider. "Listen to me, you little prick. You may think you're a hot topic just because you've overheard some shit that amounts to no more than speculation. We both know that, but if you go on believing that whatever scant evidence you possess is enough to blackmail me, then you're wrong, and if I were you, I would think very carefully about your next move. I don't take kindly to being threatened."

"Blackmail?" Spider smiled. He took out the photograph and held it up in front of Murray Cooper's face. He held it there for a few seconds then slipped it back inside his jacket pocket. He was quick on his toes and Murray was laden down with Thai food, but he wanted to be prepared in case the big man tried to make a grab for the photo.

Murray shrugged. "I have no fucking idea who that is," he said

"Of course you don't," Spider agreed. "I don't want to blackmail you, Mister Cooper, I want to help you."

CHAPTER 21

"What the hell is this?" Paul Overton asked, holding up Gemma's hastily penned resignation letter. It was Monday morning, just before 11.00 am and Gemma had arrived a little earlier in order to catch Overton in his office before the rest of her crew started their shift.

"It's my resignation," Gemma said.

Overton sighed, exasperation creeping into his voice. "I can see that I was being rhetorical. Why are you leaving?"

"It was never a long time thing, Paul, I thought you were aware of that."

"Of course I wasn't," Overton sniffed indignantly. "If I had thought that you were about to desert us so soon, I would never have offered you the position of bar manager in the first place. This is most inconvenient, Gemma. Bad form."

"I was under the impression that I was on trial for the time being. The decision pending on whether I was suitable or if I found that the position itself desirable."

"Evidently you don't," Overton said, holding up her letter.

"I'm sorry," Gemma said

"Hmm," Overton was convinced that she wasn't sorry at all "Very well, I don't suppose I can persuade you to stay," he said dismissively.

You haven't actually tried, Gemma thought. Not that he would have much luck persuading her. Her mind had been made up.

"I can't pretend that only offering me a week's notice is anyway beneficial either. Managerial positions normally require at least a month. It will be extremely difficult to find a replacement at such short notice."

"I'm sorry," Gemma said again. She had reached the stage where she was finding it pointless to counter any of Overton's arguments with an excuse in order to justify her decision, so she continued to apologise hoping that he would tire of believing that she was going out of her way to actively betray his trust, and just accept that she was leaving a dull job working in a bar for pastures new.

Her decision would hardly have a detrimental effect on the company. The way Overton was portraying her resignation suggested that her departure would wipe off millions of pounds in the value of shares in a huge conglomerate. Eventually, Overton ceased the interrogation and waved her out of the office.

"What are you talking about, you can't leave!" Carly cried. It was half an hour later. Gemma had entered the bar and was preparing for the dinnertime customers. Carly had rushed in, Kat at her side. Carly was crying, her cheeks two dark rivulets of black mascara. She held her apron in her hands and threw it down on the bar next to Gemma.

"We've just heard," Kat said. She smiled sympathetically.

"When were you going to tell me, were you ever going to tell me?" Carly said

"Of course I was," Gemma replied.

"Can I come with you?" Carly said.

"What?"

"I'll hand my own notice in. Let me come with you."

Gemma laughed uneasily. "Don't be silly, you can't just pack your job in ."

"My job!" Carly cried. She was close to hysteria now. "It's hardly a career!"

"You don't know anything about me," Gemma said, unsure how to placate the girl. "I like you, both of you, but we're little more than work colleagues."

That didn't work, and a sob caught in Carly's throat. She took a deep breath.

"How can you say that?" Carly said, her voice had dropped to a whisper. "After Saturday night."

"Look whatever you think may have happened…"

"I love you," Carly said.

Gemma stopped speaking and stared at the younger girl. Kat looked awkwardly at her feet.

"I love you," Carly said again.

Paul Overton entered the bar, alerted by the raised voices. He glanced uneasily at the door, but there were no customers at this early hour. He turned to the three girls, his bar staff for that day. They were standing in a triangle staring at each other, like combatants in a Mexican stand-off.

Overton was no expert when it came to gauging other people's reactions, especially women.

"Okay, okay," he proclaimed a little over-enthusiastically, clapping his hands, as this was, in his opinion, the only way to gain attention.

The girls all turned to face him. None of them spoke, and he felt uneasy, as if he was intruding upon a clandestine meeting, the proceedings of which he had no reason to be privy to.

"That's better," he said, unsure if he had actually achieved anything or not. "Now Carly, I can see that you're upset, but can you be upset on your own time. There are mixer shelves to be filled and the bar needs cleaning.

"Fill your own bloody shelves," Carly said quietly. She turned and walked out of the bar.

Gemma followed her.

Overton held his hands up in the air. "You're leaving as well, are you serious?"

"Apparently so," Gemma replied as she hurried out of the bar. She caught up with Carly as the younger girl was opening the door of her small red Saxo. Gemma said nothing as she got into the passenger seat and they drove off.

"Be upset on your own time? Really, Paul?" Kat said.

CHAPTER 22

"You live here?" Gemma said. Carly nodded and smiled. She parked her car on a wide gravel driveway adjacent to a huge double garage. The house was located on the border of the villages of Blundeston and Corton about two and a half miles from Lowestoft. They both got out of the car and Gemma looked up at the property.   The house was huge, at least five, maybe six bedrooms, Gemma mused. It was a looming, imposing property, old too, possibly Victorian. There were two massive bay windows situated on the ground floor, and a solid wood front door, richly stained, that was big enough to drive a car through.

"I'm sorry I said I loved you, that was embarrassing," Carly said.

"It doesn't matter, it was a spur of the moment thing. I know you didn't mean it."

"Who says I didn't mean it?"

Gemma ignored that for now. She started to walk up the long driveway to the house as Carly seemed rooted to the spot and quite happy to stand on the gravel surface indefinitely. After a few seconds, she followed. Gemma let her overtake when they reached the front door. Carly opened it and they both stepped into the hall.

The house interior was magnificent. The hall floor was laid out in large black and white marble flagstones, with a decorative, diamond-patterned border. Several doors led off the hall, each one appeared original; flawed patches and welts in the woodwork enhanced the natural beauty. A long, sweeping staircase led up to the first floor landing, fringed by a magnificent balustrade.

"Jesus," Gemma breathed. "Is Scarlett O'Hara home?"

"It is a bit OTT," Carly said. "Come on through to the lounge, I'll get us some coffee."

"Who else lives here?"

"My dad and brother, although they're both away at the moment."

"So you have this whole house to yourself?"

Carly laughed. "Yeah, weird isn't it?"

Carly opened the first door on the left and Gemma followed her in. After the magnificence of the hall, this first reception room was a bit of a disappointment. The floorboards were sanded but not stained, a bare wall of unpainted plaster loomed behind them like an imposing screen, the incomplete job lending the room a shabby, unfinished look. A huge cast iron fireplace dominated the far wall; above it was mounted a seventy inch plus television that looked so out of place as to feel intrusive. A large, four-seater sofa, draped in multi-coloured throws was situated in a prime position in front of the TV. Gemma sat on it and Carly left the room to make the coffee.

When she returned, Gemma had taken off her jacket and slipped off her shoes. She sat with her legs beneath her on the sofa. She took a coffee from Carly who set a tray on the floor in front of them. She picked up her own coffee and sat next to Gemma. Both ignored the sugar bowl and biscuits that were left on the tray. Gemma blew on her coffee and took a sip.

"You don't love me, Carly," she said gently. "You don't know me."

Carly sipped at her own coffee. She avoided looking directly at Gemma.

"I think it's more a case of loving who you are," she said, picking her words carefully. She sighed. "I'm not good at expressing myself, conversations are hard sometimes"

"You seemed okay when we were in the pub."

"Yeah maybe, but I was relaxed then, and besides I know you and Kat now, almost as well as anybody, but it took me ages to reach that stage. To maintain that level of confidence was really, really difficult, you don't understand."

"Why wouldn't I?"

Carly set her coffee cup down on the floor and turned to face Gemma now. "Because I bet you've never been nervous in your life. You ooze confidence. From the very first day I met you in Overton's office, I could see that. It took me days to muster up the courage just to talk to you, and then it was no more than pleasantries and brief exchanges.

Gemma remembered the soft, delicate touches and the unambiguous flirting, and thought that Carly was not the shy shrinking violet she was pretending to be.

Gemma laughed. "You think I've never been nervous? "Oh wow, girl, that is fresh, believe me, I am not a confident person and my nerves are only a car backfire away from being shredded."

Carly shook her head. "I don't believe it."

Gemma stood up, took a deep breath and looked around the room. "Carly, who owns this house, your dad?"

"Yes. He and mum split up years ago, dad bought her out. She met a guy online and she lives in Utah now."

"He's rich then your dad? What does he do?"

Carly shrugged. "I dunno. Something to do with telecommunications, he co-owns the company with a friend. Michael, my brother, works for the firm too."

"But not you?"

Carly shook her head. "No."

"So there's just you, your dad and your brother?"

"Yes, but they're in Asia at the moment, Vietnam I think. They're often away. I see mum from time to time, but she's a resident in the United States now. She has no cause to come over here, does she?"

Gemma shrugged. "How would I know, baby girl? Are you close?"

"Very."

"Do you miss her?"

"Of course, what kind of question is that?"

"Then why not move out there, start a new life in America.?"

Carly thought about this for a moment. "I love my dad too, Gemma, I don't want to be seen taking sides."

"Maybe your mum thinks you have already."

"She had the affair, not my dad."

"So your dad has always been faithful?"

"As far as I know."

Gemma sat back down and sipped her coffee.

"What about you?" Carly asked.

"What about me?"

"Are you running from somebody?"

Gemma looked down into her mug. "What makes you say that?"

"You turn up out of the blue, nobody knows anything about you, then at the pub. Wow, I couldn't believe how you looked! I said to Kat that you were an enigma, you have a past. And now you're up and leaving, just like that."

"Carly, it's a carvery restaurant in a holiday park, people come and go all the time. Why are you even there if your dad owns a huge company?"

"There you go again, changing the subject."

"People who have a past, usually don't want to talk about it."

"So you admit it then?"

"I'm not admitting anything, I'm not on trial," Gemma snapped.

Carly blinked in surprise at the sudden harsh tone and Gemma placed a hand on her shoulder. "I'm sorry, didn't mean to bite."

"It's okay, I was getting a bit nosy." She glanced down at her empty mug. "You want a top-up?"

"Yeah, why not."

Carly stood up and headed for the kitchen, Gemma followed her. The kitchen was as large as Gemma's entire floor space in her old London apartment. A monolithic American style fridge stood in the corner and a solid stone effect free-standing island worktop unit sat in the middle of the floor, though there was still plenty of room to negotiate around it. There was so much cupboard space on the walls and below the units, that Gemma wouldn't know where to begin looking for anything. The worktops were polished black, mirror-chip granite that gleamed as the late morning sun struck the surface through the slatted blinds at the window. Gemma peeped through the gaps, out into the back garden that was set on two levels. The foreground was a huge paved patio area, with a wall running around the top. Reaching waist level. Steps were cut into the wall, rising to an expanse of lawn that appeared as big as a football pitch. There were tubs and troughs adorning the patio all emblazoned with colour.

Carly filled the kettle and set the empty cups on the drainer . "Where did you learn to fight?" she asked.

Gemma turned from the window. "My brother taught me."

"Wow, is he Bruce Lee?"

Gemma smiled. "No, just some guy who used to look out for me."

"Used to? He's not around anymore?"

Gemma shook her head. "No he's not around anymore." She took the mugs from the drainer and swilled them under the tap.

"Where will you go?" Carly asked quietly.

Gemma turned off the tap and turned to face her. There were tears in her eyes and Carly opened her mouth in shock. She took a step forward as Gemma fell into her arms sobbing uncontrollably. Carly wrapped her arms around Gemma's head and soothed her as best she could as the older girl continued to cry into her shoulder.

After a couple of minutes, Carly drew back and looked at Gemma ."Are you okay?" she asked.

"So much for oozing confidence," Gemma said and she laughed uneasily. I don't know what came over me for a moment then."

"Was it talking about your brother?"

Gemma nodded and took a deep breath, she didn't want to start crying again. "Amongst other things."

"You want to talk about them now?"

"Oh god, more than anything."

"Go ahead then."

"I can't, Carly."

"But you just said…."

"I said I wanted to talk about it, that doesn't mean I can."

"It can help, I know that if I had somebody…"

Gemma leaned back against the sink. "I've got to go, I'm sorry I can't do this...this agony aunt bullshit."

"I'm only trying to help," Carly protested, hurt.

"But you can't help me, not you, or Kat or anybody."

"Why won't you let me try, please Gemma, you're my friend, I want to help you."

"You're not my fucking friend," Gemma cried. "You don't know anything about me. You...you spend a few hours a day with me in a fucking bar and one evening out, and all of a sudden we've bonded? What...we're obliged to share one another's secrets? You don't want to know about me, it would give you fucking nightmares for months. Jesus Christ, Carly, you've got a beautiful home, a family who still love you and prospects far greater than working in a shithole restaurant, and yet you mooch about and whine as if you've got the whole fucking worlds problems on your shoulders. Well you don't know anything about grief, about hardships, about being totally shit-scared every fucking waking hour of the day."

Carly stepped away from her, her hands to her mouth. She stared up at Gemma with terrified eyes.

"My god, what did you do?" she whispered.

"Do? I did something terrible, Carly." Gemma took several breaths. "I'm sorry I frightened you, I didn't mean those things I said. I'm sorry, you are my friend, perhaps my only friend."

160

"Really?"

"Gemma managed a wan smile. "Of course, you love me don't you?"

Carly smiled back. "I didn't really mean to say that."

"I know, I know, but the important thing is that you did say it."

Carly shook her head. "Why is that so important?"

Gemma turned to face her. "Because nobody has ever said it before."

CHAPTER 23

Spider had never had anybody take him into their confidence before.

Murray Cooper poured a large scotch and handed it to Spider, who took it gratefully. They were in an office with a large open window that looked down onto a factory floor. Twin rows of sewing machines were all hooked up to industrial sockets on either side of the factory, like intravenous drips feeding a multitude of automatons. Murray's brother, Charles, an imposing figure, sat at his desk and stared at Spider over his bifocals. The stare unnerved Spider and he gulped his Scotch, draining the glass in one loud swallow.

Behind Charles hung a portrait of the brother's great grandfather, Sir Conrad Cooper, who had started the family business in the 1870's. He was a stern, pompous looking man, as was befitting his status and disposition of the day. Those who stood before Charles at his desk often glanced at the painting, perhaps with a sense of foreboding, maybe a little awe. The cocksure amongst them may wonder if there is a safe behind it.

There isn't.

"What do you know about ballet, Spider?" Murray asked. He cradled his own drink in a huge fist, gently swirling the whisky around the glass.

"For poofs and girls with bad feet, so I've heard," Spider said, and laughed nervously. Murray sat on the edge of the large, scarred, mahogany desk. The brother's both stared at him. An old fashioned steel filing cabinet stood next to the side of the large viewing window that looked down onto the factory floor. In an age of computers, Spider was surprised that anybody used filing cabinets to store information these days. The whole office had an old-fashioned air about it.

"You may be right," Murray said, "But I was referring to the manufacture of the slippers as opposed to the performance side."

Spider stared down into the darkened factory floor. " That what you do here, make ballet slippers?"

Murray walked over to the window and stood by his side. "Amongst other things, yes. My great grandfather was in the shoe trade when he set up the business. He wasn't making ballet slippers, of course, but work shoes and boots.You have any idea how much money we made last year, Spider?"

Spider shrugged.

"About seventy million," Murray said "And about fifty-five per cent of that was legit.

"What did you make the forty-five per cent on?" Spider said quickly.

Murray and Charles exchanged glances then both men laughed. Murray produced a large guffaw, whereas his older brother snickered quietly into an open palm, like a coquettish debutante.

"Easy there, cowboy, you're still at the apprentice stage," Murray said. "I can't tell you too much. Safe to say there aren't many businessmen who make a lot of money who don't have their fingers in a few, how should I put it? Dubious pies." He laughed again and turned from the window, Spider turned too. He was beginning to warm to Murray Cooper. After he had shown the photograph of Candy Girl to him at the restaurant and told him who it was Murray's features had relaxed and his whole persona had changed from barely concealed hostility to admiration and maybe a little respect. Spider was quick to discover that despite the vast difference in their financial circumstances, Murray Cooper was not unlike him. A man with a wealthy , as opposed to his own, humble background, raised by a single parent. That said, of course, Murray's ambitions superseded Spider's own limited prospects immensely. And yet there was a common touch about the big man, a trait that Spider was able to empathise with.

Murray had told him that he would gladly pay him five thousand for the photograph, but how would he like to make a lot more than that?"

"Come and work for me," he had said. *"I need men with their noses to the ground, somebody with initiative."*

Spider had been sceptical at first. He didn't work, not in the traditional sense, and he certainly didn't want to be employed by anybody, however enigmatic they appeared.

But Murray had shrugged off his qualms and had insisted that it was merely contractual work, outsourcing, whatever you wanted to call it. Spider was intrigued enough to agree to meet Murray at the factory the following day, and now, here they were.

Murray opened the desk drawer and took out an envelope. He tossed it onto the desktop. It was open and a few notes spilled out. Twenty pound notes. There were a lot more inside. Spider glanced down at the money. He resisted the urge to lick his lips, like a salivating wolf who has just stumbled across an elk carcass, and made do with a quick wipe across his mouth with the back of his hand. Murray's face turned serious.

"There's five thousand pounds there," Murray said. "That pays for the photograph as we agreed. We'll pay you another twenty for a couple of weeks of your time."

A couple of weeks! Spider thought incredulously. He had never seen so much money in his life.

"Do we have a deal?" Murray said.

It was difficult for Spider to tear his eyes away from the money - *his money*. Eventually he met Murray Cooper's gaze and smiled.

"Yes we have a deal, Mister Cooper.

Charles Cooper had not risen from his seat when Spider had walked into the office with Murray. The man had barely smiled, aside from the schoolboy giggle earlier, that Spider felt was more a case of being laughed at as opposed to sharing the mirth, and there was no offer of a handshake. As Murray outlined his proposal and enthused over a profitable relationship, Spider could sense Charles staring at him constantly as they walked around the office. Now that they were finalising deals, Charles coughed loudly into his hand. The two men turned towards him.

"That's a lot of money," Charles said, nodding at the envelope on the desk.

Spider said nothing, but just nodded his head slightly.

"How do you know her, this Candy Girl? It would appear to me that what we have heard about her, she is way out of your league." A brief smile danced on his lips as he stared intently at Spider. He made no attempt to mask his distaste, and the petty crook felt a swell of anger rise.

"I didn't know her on a professional level," he said, meeting Charles's penetrating gaze, "I move in nefarious circles, Mister Cooper, I hear things, and I store that information, sometimes it can prove fruitful, like now."

"Extremely fruitful," Charles said, glancing at the money once more.

"For both of us," Spider countered.

"Well that is yet to be decided."

Charles stood up and walked over to the window. It was nearly six p.m and the workplace was dark and quiet. "So how did you know her?"

"I just heard about her on the streets, I kept my ear to the ground."

Charles turned from the window. "And the pimp, where you obtained the picture, she worked for him?"

Spider laughed. "Cole Waters? Christ no, Candy Girl was way out of his league. They call her ``The Queen of Downtown."

"An oxymoron." Charles said.

"What?"

"A term that appears to contradict itself," Charles explained. "A queen is a person or regal quality, but downtown is a derogatory term in this context, almost as if her kingdom is nothing more than a slum."

Spider nodded. "It's a degrading profession, no matter how high you climb and how much money you make."

"So what was the photograph doing in Cole Water's possession?"

"I have no idea."

"We need to check out this pimp," Murray said, "Find out what he knows, why he had the pic."

Charles nodded. "I agree. I'll speak with Mister Skein."

Murray opened the drawer of the desk and took out a cheap prepaid mobile phone. He handed it to Spider.

"This has my number in the address book. It's the only number, so don't use it to call anybody else. I will be in touch with you very soon. When we find Candy Girl, I want you to be amongst the team who pick her up. She will have changed her appearance, and you are the only person who knows her."

Spider swallowed. "I didn't think my involvement would be that..." he struggled for the right word..."demanding."

"The fuck you think we're paying you twenty- five thousand for; to shout advice from the sildelines?" Charles sneered.

"Well no," Spider glanced at the money on the table again. "I'm not going to kill anybody,"

Murray put a reassuring arm around his shoulder. "Nobody is going to kill anybody, Spider, we're businessmen, not gangsters. Come on take your money." Murray scooped up the notes and pushed them back inside the envelope. He folded it in half and handed it to Spider. The petty thief took it and secreted it quickly within the folds of his parka.

"Now come on," Murray continued, his arm still around Spider's shoulder as he led him out of the office. "I want you to tell me all you know about this Cole character, and then I'm going to tell you what the Queen of fucking Downtown did to my son. I don't want you feeling any pity for her when we pick her up."

Once they had left, Charles pressed a button on an innocent looking intercom on his desk. Skein's voice crackled and then cleared on the other end.

"What do you think?" Charles asked.

"My guys are working on the photo, " Skein said. " The facial recognition shouldn't prove a problem. If there's a pic out there we'll be able to compare it, if not then we'll have to trawl CCTV. Don't worry we have the contacts."

"I want you to speak to this pimp, Cole Waters, Mister Skein. It worries me that this photograph has suddenly surfaced without my knowledge.

"I'm on it," Skein replied indifferently. "What about Spider?"

"Oh he's a fucking liability. "My brother has taken him under his wing, but once we've found the girl, he will definitely have to go."

There was a low chuckle from the intercom. "That's good, Mister Cooper, at least we're on the same page there."

Charles nodded and killed the connection. He self-consciously wiped his hands on his jacket. It was strange but he always felt slightly grubby after talking to Mister Skein.

CHAPTER 24

Carly and Gemma were back in the lounge, two more coffees once again on the tray on the floor. Neither girl had touched the second cup. They were sitting facing each other. Carly had pulled one of the throws, a bright orange fleece, around her shoulders and hugged it to her chest.

"I was the only one who could really see how upset mum was," she said. "I'm not condoning what she did, my dad has always been a fair man. This house, the holiday home, the cars, everything was provided by his work, his hard work and determination." She shrugged and pulled the fleece tighter around her shoulders. "But at the end of the day it wasn't enough. Mum needed more than financial security. She wanted a man at home and dad couldn't be that man. He has always enjoyed the business life, the travelling, the deals , the respect. I don't know if he has always been faithful, who can say with him being away so often, but he was still shocked when mum announced that she had found somebody else. I guess some people get so wrapped up in what they're doing they can't see what is happening to other people around them. My dad loved my mum, still does , I guess, but love can be so fickle can't it? He just assumed that she was happy with her lot but he was wrong. My brother never forgave my mum, they haven't spoken since she left, and that's been over five years now."

"Do you get on with your brother?" Gemma asked.

"Not really. He's very selfish, we've never been really close, even before mum and dad split up. He works with dad all the time now, and that suits me."

"So when are they coming back?"

"Next month, maybe. My dad rings me every other day, but I kind of like it here on my own. We've got a place in Nice and I go there as well just to chill out."

"On your own?"

Carly laughed. "Not as a rule, but on occasion I prefer to go alone."

"Some people crave solitude."

Carly shook her head. "It's better when you're with a friend, or somebody a little more than a friend. She laughed and blushed, "But there isn't anybody really special. I guess I haven't found the right person yet. They'd be in for a treat you know, I'm loaded." She laughed again. "But they're not falling at my feet Gemma. That's why I took the job at the restaurant, so I could meet people."

"What about Kat?"

Carly shook her head in confusion. "What about her?"

"Haven't you ever asked her out?"

"What?" Carly said, horrified. She stood up suddenly, the fleece crumpled to the floor and she kicked it away. "Kat isn't into girls!"

"How do you know?"

"Are you serious? She's always going on about the men she fucks, their cocks and everything."

"Carly," Gemma said patiently. ""She does that for shock value, to get a reaction out of you."

"I know that, I'm not completely naive."

"Yeah, but there's no real malice there, she does like you."

Carly shook her head furiously. "Not in that way, I'm sure of it. Besides you're making a hell of an assumption that I'm gay also, aren't you. I mean I should be insulted. You don't know anything about me."

"I'm a pretty good judge of character."

Carly laughed. "It's still a little presumptuous, don't you think?"

"Only if I'm wrong. Am I?"

"Stop it, Gemma."

"You said that you loved me."

"Yeah, well."

Gemma reached down and picked up her coffee. She took a sip and grimaced. "Getting cold. Shall we have a proper drink?"

"My dad has a cellar full of wine."

Gemma shook her head. "Best not touch that. What else?"

Carly spread her arms wide. "Whatever you want. I'll show you." She led Gemma out of the lounge and back into the hall. They crossed it and entered another room. It was a study; cluttered and a little gloomy. Carly flicked on the lights.

There was a large, walnut desk with a high backed leather chair tucked underneath. On the wall was a row of shelves filled with business folders, all dated and in meticulous order. A tall Welsh dresser stood against the wall. Carly headed for it and opened the twin doors. It was filled with an assortment of bottles. Carly knelt down and looked inside. Gemma knelt down beside her. She reached over and brushed a wisp of Carly's hair behind her ear, then gave her a light peck on the cheek. Carly flushed but didn't object, and moved in for a kiss of her own, but Gemma put a restraining finger on her lips. "Don't rush it," she whispered.

"Are you going to seduce me?" Carly asked quietly.

Gemma nodded. "Yes."

"Oh my god!"

"Shh."

"Don't you want to go to the bedroom?"

Gemma laughed. "It won't be much of a seduction if we start making plans, baby girl. Let's have a drink. Here." She took out a bottle of spiced rum and a second bottle of ginger beer. "I'll make us a *Jamaican Mule* ."

Back in the lounge on the sofa, Carly sipped tentatively at her drink, though she didn't wince at the taste as she did with her previous encounters with alcohol.

"This is nice," she said.

Gemma took a long swallow of her own drink and then leaned forward and kissed Carly fully on the mouth. Her tongue darted forward and after a few seconds Carly reciprocated. They held the kiss as Gemma reached around and gently stroked the back of Carly's head, her fingers running through her hair, pulling her gently forward until the kiss became more urgent. Then, slowly, Gemma leaned back. Carly licked her lips with the tip of her tongue, then opened her eyes and smiled. Gemma lifted her own sweater over her head. She took Carly's hands and placed them on her large breasts. Gemma leaned forward and they kissed again. This time, Carly was eager and ready. She let her fingers slip under the fabric of Gemma's bra and stroked her firm breasts and hard, erect nipples. Gemma sighed and put her hands on the back of Carly's head once more. She broke the kiss then unclasped her bra and tossed it onto the floor. She pulled Carly's head down to her breasts. Carly took a nipple between her teeth and nibbled gently. Gemma giggled.

The giggle soon became a moan of pleasure as Carly turned her attention to the second breast and sucked hard on the nipple. Gemma entwined her fingers in Carly's hair and ruffled it, then raised her head and kissed Carly again. She stood up and slipped off her work skirt and panties. She stood in front of Carly who was flushed and panting. Gemma picked up her drink and took another sip.

"Shall I get undressed?" Carly asked.

Gemma shook her head. "Uh huh."

"You're beautiful," Carly whispered.

Gemma reached forward and took Carly by the hands and lifted her into an embrace. Carly's hands slid down Gemma's back and cupped her small buttocks. Gemma rocked slowly in the girl's arms, loving the feel of her own nakedness against the clothed form of the younger girl. Slowly they turned in each other's arms and Gemma slipped her hands up and under Carly's sweater. She expertly unclasped the bra strap and brought her hands around and cupped Carly's small breasts. They kissed again, with a little more passion now. Carly slipped a hand between Gemma's thighs and probed gently with her fingers. Gemma spread her legs a little and let her new lover explore her deeper. Despite her shy

171

exterior, Carly was far from inexperienced, and Gemma moaned in delight as Carly slid two fingers inside her and gently manipulated her. She reached forward and slipped Carly's sweater over her head and took her nipples into her own mouth. Soon they were both naked and fingers and tongues gently stroked and probed. Gemma knelt before Carly as she sat on the sofa. She raised the younger girl's legs and gently explored her with the tip of her tongue. Carly cried out and gripped the cushions on either side of her.

"Oh God, please don't stop," Carly purred. Gemma didn't and as Carly arched her back as she approached climax, Gemma wondered who exactly was seducing who.

CHAPTER 25

"So what did you do, kill somebody?" Carly asked.

They were in the bath, the water luxuriously hot and filled with bubbles. The bathroom was huge, the bath sunken into the floor and circular like a kids paddling pool. Gemma lay with her back against the tiled wall, Carly was lying in front of her between her legs. Gemma was shampooing the younger girls hair.

"You're not going to let that drop are you?"

Carly turned around to face her, splashing water over the rim of the bath. "Hey we're lovers now, we confide. It may be a brief encounter, but you're still my lover." She turned back and laid her head on Gemma's breasts. Gemma started slowly shampooing her hair again.

"You've been with other girls?" Gemma asked her.

Carly smiled. "Of course, but it was never like this. Stop changing the subject, Gemma. You owe me a little info, surely, tell me about your brother."

"He was my rock, I wouldn't have survived without him. He's dead now."

" I'm sorry. Was he a bad boy?"

"Yeah, but that didn't matter to me. I'm no angel myself. Al died nine years ago. He was shot outside a club in Manchester. Drive by, gangland killing."

"What about your mum and dad?"

"Mum died just before my sixteenth birthday from a brain hemorrhage. I never met my dad. On the day of my mum's funeral, my stepfather was stabbed in the pub, we were using to hold the wake. He died from his injuries."

"Gemma that's awful."

"No it's not, he was an absolute bastard. He had a lot of enemies."

They were quiet for a while, then Carly said: "We could go to Nice."

Gemma stopped the head massage. "What?"

Carly turned around again. Her small breasts bobbed just above the surface of the water

"You need to get away for awhile. We could go to the holiday home, make love, chill on the beach, maybe get a job in a bar or a club. We could be like Thelma and Louise."

"That's crazy."

Carly scoffed at that. "Why because it's a good idea that is mine?"

"No."

"Then why is it crazy? Where were you planning on going at the end of the week?"

"It doesn't concern you."

"What are you talking about? I must mean something to you or you wouldn't have made love to me."

"Carly, you were always aware that I was leaving. I made love to you because I desired you, and I wanted you to experience it too, but don't invite me to come away with you.

173

Within a week I'd probably fleece you for every penny you had and leave you stranded in the South of France without a passport or a penny to your name."

Gemma stood up and stepped out of the bathtub. She grabbed a towel and started drying herself off. Carly leaned on the edge of the tub and stared up at her with wide, unbelieving eyes.

"I can't believe that you would do that."

"Neither do I, Carly, truly. But I don't want to be in such a position that temptation may sway me. And being alone with just you on a sun drenched beach may just prove too irresistible."

"But…"

"No, there are no buts, baby girl. I've been running for so long that I can't say what I would do if such an opportunity came my way. I mean it's a good thing I don't know if you have money in the house, because believe me."

"Twenty-five thousand pounds," Carly said. "My dad has twenty-five thousand in a safe. I know the combination, it's taped to the bottom of the desk drawer in his study. Come with me and we can take it with us."

"Gemma tossed the towel at her and Carly fumbled it before getting a grasp and flinging it aside.

"You're a silly, silly girl," Gemma spat. "Get dressed."

Carly stood and picked up the towel. "I'm beginning to realise that for myself," she said.

Gemma shook her head and left Carly alone in the bathroom

Gemma fixed herself another drink and sat down on the sofa. She turned on the huge TV and began to flick aimlessly through the hundreds of channels stored on the system.

Carly didn't appear until an hour later, dressed in a long, pink robe.

"I thought maybe you had left," she said.

Gemma didn't say anything. She shook her head slightly, but offered Carly a small smile. Carly smiled back. Gemma turned off the TV as Carly slumped down beside her.

"Tell me about the girl in the pub," Gemma said.

"Her name is Jazz," Carly said. "She's awful, a really nasty person. She made my life a misery at school, but It wasn't just me. There was another girl. Victoria her name was. She had really bad acne, all over her cheeks, angry, huge red spots and whiteheads. Victoria only had one friend, you know who that was?"

Gemma nodded. "You?"

Carly shook her head slowly. "No, not me. It was Pinto. You know the girl who was with Jazz Saturday night. Pinto's father is Mexican and Pinto's real name is..." Carly looked up at the ceiling, her teeth chewing on her bottom lip as she searched the depths of her memory. "You know I can't even remember what Pinto's real name is, isn't that weird?"

Gemma sipped her drink.

"Go on," she said quietly.

Pinto and Victoria came through primary and junior school together, they lived on the same estate. They were very close as I remember. Victoria was never an attractive girl, but she didn't have the spots when we first met her. When she hit thirteen or fourteen they really broke out. God they were bad. But Pinto was always there to look out for her. That was until Jazz started at our school. She was called Victoria too, well Vicky, but everybody called her Jazz. Cool nickname isn't it?"

Gemma shrugged.

"Anyway, Jazz liked Pinto. They were both tough girls, though Pinto hadn't adopted a vindictive streak at that time, not like Jazz. The problem was Victoria. Pinto still liked her initially, but Jazz hated her from the off. Jazz hated anybody who she believed was weaker. She was a really cruel girl, Gemma, so nasty. Children are the most wicked aren't they?"

Gemma nodded, but she didn't actually agree. Her own experiences with the adult scum she had encountered in her life put adolescent bullying, despicable though it was, clearly into perspective. Yet victims of bullying all relive their own traumatic experiences as they get older, the hateful memories thankfully fading with time. Gemma sympathised with the girl, Victoria, who had evidently endured her own personal hell on earth in the confines of the classroom, and perhaps in the office or factory later. The weak will always be singled out. Dedicated tormentors grow older, but, in her opinion, are no less vindictive. Same demons just wearing different colour jackets.

"There was never going to be a triangle of friends there," Carly continued. "And Pinto liked Jazz, everybody could see that. Pinto went very quickly to not hanging about with Victoria, to not speaking to her, to mocking her then beating her up. She's not as bad as Jazz, never was. I guess she was just influenced by her."

"You didn't do anything about it?"

Carly looked hard at her. "What do you mean?"

"Not you personally, your classmates? You said they all saw what was happening, but none of you raised an objection, or even a hand to stop the bullying?"

Carly laughed, but it was without humour "No, of course not. We were barely in our teens. We didn't rally round or form vigilante groups, nobody does. You simply look on and thank god that it isn't you bearing the brunt of it."

"But you got some stick later on didn't you?"

Carly nodded her head sadly. "Well, yeah, but it was never as bad as it was with Victoria. And I had friends. Mousy friends admittedly, but people I could confide in and turn to even if they weren't prepared to stand up for me against the likes of Jazz and Pinto. Victoria had nobody and that made it ten times worse. She left the school about six months before we all would have finished our final year. Her dad got a job in Kuala Lumpur. Jazz put yogurt in her hair, and we all laughed except for Victoria, who tried to wipe it off with a damp tissue."

Carly stopped talking and gazed off into space for a few seconds. "I looked her up on Facebook a few years ago. Not my account, I don't have one, it was my brother's. Just typed her name into the search bar. She was there. The acne was gone, but she still wasn't smiling. She lives in Berkshire now, married with two young boys. She has two-hundred and twenty-seven friends. I wondered how many of them are from school."

"Do you want a drink?" Gemma asked.

Carly shook her head. "I left school at sixteen and applied to go to university. I wanted to train as a veterinarian, but around November of that same year, my mum left and I just kind of gave up on stuff. Dad had business in The Netherlands in the middle of December, and although mum hadn't left for the States by then, the wheels were in motion. Michael was being a real pain in the arse. He's two years older than me, and he was seeing this lovely girl called Eleanor. She was nearly twenty at the time and I think they came close to splitting up over mum's affair.

"How come?"

"Well Ellie sympathised with my mum. She didn't say as much, knowing how volatile Michael was, but she would always play devil's advocate, attempting to see both sides of the argument, and I think Michael, who was *"Team Dad"* all the way, felt as if she was betraying him somehow. She was a tough girl, Ellie was, and she wouldn't take Michael's shit. He backtracked when he realised that maybe he was pushing her too far. Michael's a good looking guy, and has always been successful with the girls and he adored Ellie. I always thought he was punching above his weight with her. Ellie was gorgeous."

Gemma set her empty glass down and turned on the sofa to look at the younger girl.

"Anyway, dad came back for the New Year and we had a party. Mum was living with her new guy by then, but they were still in England. Dad had sealed a new contract in The Hague, and he was determined to celebrate, despite the devastation of the split. Most of the people at the party were work acquaintances, and some of Michael's friends. He was happy because he was surrounded by his kind of people. Michael was always going to follow dad into the business, so the work colleagues would soon become his friends also. I remember he spent most of the night laughing and drinking with them, though my dad stayed sober. Dad never drinks to excess, even though the party was his idea. I hung out with Ellie all night, cos she was getting ignored by Michael. She introduced me to Pernod. God I've never touched it since." She laughed. "You know what a lightweight I am when it comes to alcohol. We talked for ages and she was trying to set me up with some of Michael's mates. It was not overly persuasive, just banter and fun really, like we were two twelve year olds. It was just before midnight that I think the realisation hit her. She just stopped talking and looked at me, a little bit like the way you are now. She was so kind to me, so understanding. I had never raised the subject of my sexuality to my mum. I don't think she ever suspected I was that way inclined. She told me to be careful, as all mums do, but there was never any inkling that she believed I was gay. Christ, I wasn't even certain myself then. But Ellie saw it. We went outside and stood on the patio. I remember it was drizzling so we stood under the large umbrella, me wondering why it was still up in the winter. Dad usually sorts that sort of thing out, but he hadn't taken it down for some reason. I kissed her under the umbrella and she let me. I told myself later that it was the drink. Ellie wasn't gay, not even bisexual, but it was the most wonderful moment of my life. Okay, perhaps she was as curious as I was, but as I moved in for a second kiss, she took a step back. She still let me kiss her, but I knew then that nothing was ever going to come of it. That's when my dad came out and saw us."

Carly stood up, undid the cord on her robe and then re-tied it tighter around her waist. She shook her head at the memory.

"When he was about fourteen, mum caught Michael masturbating. He wasn't sitting at the computer, but in bed with a magazine. Mum had brought him a bedtime drink, and he immediately threw the book onto the floor and feigned sleep. Mum put his cocoa on the side, picked up the magazine and then she lifted the sheets. Michael couldn't do anything about that. If he had protested then she would have known he was pretending to be asleep, and would have had to explain the wank mag. So he just lay there with his eyes closed and let mum gaze at his erection."

Gemma smiled. "He told you this?"

179

"In a roundabout kind of way. It wasn't anything pervy on my mum's side. I guess she was just reassuring herself that her son was normal. Michael said it was the most embarrassing thing ever, although he's probably forgotten all about it now."

"I wouldn't bet on it."

"That's how I felt when dad discovered me and Ellie on the patio on New Year's Eve, though neither of us could pretend that we were sleeping.

"What did he do?"

"Nothing. But I can remember the look of shock on his face. Just for a moment it was there, but it was like, *"not you too?"* How much betrayal do you think one man can take?"

"You didn't betray anybody, Carly."

"My dad thought that I was betraying his son, my brother. I was kissing his girlfriend."

"Did he ever tell you that?"

"No."

"Then he probably didn't think it . He didn't tell Michael did he?"

"No, I don't think so, but he may have said something to Ellie, she and Michael split up in February the following year."

"Maybe that was just a coincidence. That probably had nothing to do with what happened on New Year's Eve."

Carly shrugged. "It would be nice to think that. Would you really steal my dad's money?"

"Maybe not."

"Will you make love to me again?"

"I'd like to."

"In bed?"

"If you like."

"Even though you think I'm a silly girl?"

"Yeah."

"Gemma?"

"What?"

"Did you kill somebody?"

Gemma leaned towards the younger girl and undid her robe. She ran her hands up the front of her body. "Yes," she said.

Carly bit on the skin at the base of her thumb. It was hard enough to draw blood. "I think I'll have that drink now," she said.

CHAPTER 26

Cole hadn't heard from Conrad since the incident with Ray Jessop. He had hoped to make a cool five hundred from the fat man. Despite Trixie's tragic appearance, she was still a good fuck, and the pervs loved her youthful appearance, skanky as it was.

Problem was, she earned next to nothing when she was on the street.

He was standing in the kitchen. It was approaching nine p.m and Trixie was still sleeping. She'd been on the streets last night and didn't get in until five this morning. He knew that she'd shot herself up as soon as she arrived home, which was annoying as in another hour he wanted her up for a private job.

Trixie would just sleep though; days on end if Cole didn't drag her out of bed and at least make her presentable. There was a pile of crumpled notes on the breakfast bar, a used syringe with droplets of blood crusted on the needle tip and her front door keys with a small wooden keyring in the shape of a hedgehog attached.

Cole counted the cash, his fingers skimming the notes like an experienced bank teller. It was just under two hundred pounds. This was an average street haul for Trixie. Sometimes she earned a little less than that, but on a good night she could double it. Weekends were obviously more profitable, and despite her rough exterior, Trixie was relatively popular. Cole preferred not to put the girl on the streets. She was so frail that her very presence on a street corner not only highlighted her vulnerability so much as advertised it. Easy prey for the trawling sharks.

He never dressed her as a child when she was working at King's Cross. That was far too risky. Her youthful appearance was her greatest (her only) asset and it was this that attracted the more discerning punter; the man who would come calling, not some fly-by-night, chancing kerb-crawler who wasn't going to risk picking up an underage girl on a street corner.

He stared down at the money now. Two hundred pounds seemed a pathetic amount. His ribs hurt like fuck, and stabbing pains racked his body if he dared to take a deep breath. Suddenly he was furious about everything. He stormed into Trixie's bedroom, snatched the duvet from off the bed and threw it onto the floor. Trixie was lying in the fetal position, her knees drawn tightly up to her chest. She was wearing retro *Magic Roundabout* pyjamas. She blinked awake and sat up to see Cole standing over her.

"What?" she asked, still sleepy and unable to mask her irritation. Cole grabbed her by the arm. Trixie cried out in alarm, fully awake now as Cole lifted her off the bed and dragged her from the room. He released her from his grip once they were inside the kitchen, and Trixie rubbed at her arm, knowing she would be bruised. She remained on the floor on her knees

"What, Cole? What have I done?"

"Is this it?" Cole shouted at her. He waved an open palm over the money on the breakfast bar. "This is all you have to fucking show after a full fucking shift?" He was screaming, spittle running down his chin. Trixie looked down at the money and then back at Cole. She didn't know what to say to him. This was an average haul for a weekday.

"What?" she said again, scared now.

"Is that all you can fucking say, What? What? What? Fucking What!"

He lashed out at her with the back of his hand, slapping her hard across the face. She fell backwards and lay on the floor, her hand on her cheek. Cole grabbed for her again, but Trixie was quicker. She leapt to her feet and headed for the bedroom door, slamming it behind her. Cole raced after her, yanking the door open and letting it crash hard against the wall, the handle gouging out a deep furrow in the plaster. Trixie sidestepped him as he lunged at her, ran to the bathroom and tried to shut Cole out. But the pimp was fuelled by rage now and he slammed a shoulder against the door, ignoring the pain that flared like white heat in his side.

Trixie was thrown off her feet and fell heavily against the side of the bath. She held out her arm to ward him off as he approached, but Cole simply grabbed the outstretched arm and yanked her to her feet. He drew back his fist and punched her in the face. Trixie grunted and her head lolled onto its side. Cole released her arm and she crumpled to the floor unconscious.

Still raging, Cole kicked her hard in the ribs.

Let's see how she likes it, he thought wildly.

He reached over her lifeless body and turned the taps on in the bath. As it started to fill he bent down and propped Trixie up against the toilet. Once the bath was a quarter full, he hoisted Trixie off the floor and dumped her into it. Trixie gasped and then thrashed about in the water like a hooked fish. Cole reached over and grabbed the girl by the hair. He pushed her head under the water, held her there for nearly a minute then pulled her up. Trixie coughed and spluttered. She was crying now, heaving sobs between breaths as she gulped in huge lungfuls of air.

"Cole, please," she wailed. "What have I done?"

"What have you done? It's what you haven't done." Cole spat. Still holding Trixie by the hair he manhandled her out of the bathroom, and dragged her back into the kitchen. Trixie screamed and grabbed her hair at the base, just below Cole's clenched fist in an effort to relieve the pressure.

Cole released the girl and she scooted on her rear until her back was against the wall of the kitchen. Her arms clutched her side and she reached up and gingerly touched the tip of her nose. Water from her sodden pyjamas puddled around her and she shivered miserably.

"You've busted my ribs," she cried. There was snot running down from her nose now and she rubbed defiantly at it with her sleeve. She was still crying and gasping in pain as she drew in ragged breaths.

"What did I do?" she asked again.

Cole's temper had abated a little now. He knew that he was taking out his rage on Trixie, who had become a convenient punch-bag allowing him to vent his anger, but he was not in the mood to be questioned. He grabbed a handful of bills from the breakfast bar and flung them at the girl. She instinctively flinched, her defences so attuned now, as the notes fluttered harmlessly down by her side.

"Two hundred fucking quid!" It's hardly worth it. "Costs me a fucking fortune to keep a roof over your head and you pull in a measly two hundred." He pointed an accusing finger at her. "You better not be skimming off the top girl, because if you are, so help me."

"I'm not," Trixie wailed. "Jesus Cole, I'm really hurting. You need to take me to a doctor."

"Fuck doctor's. You've got money for this shit haven't you?" He snatched up the syringe and flung it at her. Trixie threw an arm across her eyes, but the syringe clattered against the wall and fell down by her side.

At that moment the kitchen door opened and a thin man, immaculately attired, entered the room. He took in his surroundings and seemed completely unconcerned by the melee before him.

"Did I call at an inconvenient time?" he asked, his tone slightly effeminate.

Cole was not in the mood. It was time to get a fucking lock put on that front door he mused, as he turned to face the stranger.

But then the big man entered the room. A gigantic brute of a man, and Cole realised that just as he thought things couldn't get any worse they probably just had.

The giant's name was Big Jackie, and he had worked for Mister Skein for nearly nine months. Skein turned to him now and smiled. It was a lascivious grin, wolfish and unnerving. The grin of a man unaccustomed to grinning. Big Jackie shifted his gaze. He was nearly seven stones heavier than Mister Skein, and he towered over him. To all extents and purposes, Big Jackie was the most dominant of the pair. But physical stature alone was not an indication of power. Big Jackie knew his place and it was well below the thin man's own standing. Big Jackie did most of the hitting. Mister Skein talked a lot, and on occasion, smiled his alarming smile.

Big Jackie was a six foot plus slab of sheer muscle. Ranking amongst the lowest of the pecking order, the grunts were recognised for what they were: The finger-breakers, the eye gougers, the gorillas who stood in the shadows with their arms folded, ready to carry out whatever was expected of them - no questions asked. Big Jackie, like so many others that found themselves embroiled within the criminal fraternity, had been foster-home raised, spent most of their formative years in juvenile and then later, adult penal institutions. Few of the grunts had an orthodox upbringing. Their size and background attracted them to the criminal gangs, and once initiated, they felt respected for the first time in their lives. It was no wonder that they were to repay that trust with unyielding obedience. Big Jackie and his ilk rarely asked why they were to break a guy's kneecaps, or dislocate his fingers, they just did it. They may have stood firmly on the bottom rung of the ladder, supporting the hierarchy that lorded above them, but they were rewarded accordingly.

"What's going on?" Cole asked the two men standing in the kitchen doorway. The thin man looked at him for a long time, and Cole did not feel comfortable under that gaze. He was staring at Cole as if he had uttered the most heinous of insults. Eventually he smiled, but the grin unnerved Cole even more.

He did not know the two men, but he was certainly aware of their standing. *Suits and Boots* they were sometimes referred to within the criminal fraternity. A twisted, and far more serious version of good cop, bad cop. The suit, in this case the skinny one in the immaculate pinstripe, was the reasonable one (and nine times out of ten, the craziest) the guy who usually had a proposition. The bad cop, the hulking gorilla, who had not taken his eyes off Trixie, was the punishment provider. Dispensing whatever passed for justice was usually dependent on the answer given to good cop's proposition.

"My name is Mister Skein," good cop said. He turned his head a fraction of an inch. "My associate here is Big Jackie. You're Cole?"

Cole nodded dumbly. It didn't do any good to piss these guys off by lying or giving them the runaround.

" We interrupting anything here?" Skein said. His eyes drifted lazily across the room and fell on the huddled, still sodden form of Trixie.

Cole laughed. It sounded forced, though Skein acknowledged it with a smile.

"No, nothing at all, Mister Skein. In fact Trixie was about to leave." He hurried across the room and hauled the girl to her feet. "Go and get yourself smartened up," he said, attempting to shoo her out of the room. Trixie shook his arm off angrily.

"You busted my fucking ribs," she snapped. Cole laughed again, but this sounded even more desperate than the last time.

Skein and Big Jackie exchanged the briefest of glances.

"Sit down, Cole," Skein said. Cole sat down quickly at the kitchen table. Skein pondered the chair opposite him, and Cole wondered for a moment if the thin man might produce a silk handkerchief from his jacket pocket and dust the seat of the chair before sitting down himself. He didn't, though, he sat just how Cole imagined he would do so. One leg crossed over the other, just above the knee, his hands folded in his lap.

"Where did you get the photograph?" he asked.

Cole was completely thrown by the question. "Photograph, what photograph?"

"The photograph of Candy Girl."

Cole shook his head. "I don't know…"

"He's talking about the picture the detective brought in the other day," Trixie said. "The girls in the nightclub."

Skein continued to stare at Cole. "Smart girl," he said. "I'm beginning to wonder if she deserved a beating."

Cole said nothing. The thin man raised his eyebrows and Cole shifted uneasily in his seat. Big Jackie took a step closer towards the table and folded his arms across his massive chest.

"Some private detective brought it in," Cole said.

Skein took out the photograph and pointed Candy Girl out in the picture. Cole didn't ask them how the picture came to be in their possession.

"He wasn't looking for her, he said he was looking for the other girl in the picture.", "Are you sure?"

Cole shrugged. He turned slightly to see if Big Jackie had moved a little closer towards him. He hadn't but he was staring at him now, his face unreadable.

"Well, it's what he told me, why would he lie?"

"Why indeed," Skein said. "What can you tell me about Candy Girl?"

Cole snorted "Me? I don't know her, Mister Skein. She, um.. Well, look at her she isn't one of my girls"

"They call her The Queen of Downtown."

The three men all turned to look at Trixie who was standing by the far wall. Her pyjamas clung to her thin frame like a second skin, and she shivered as if caught in a freak snowstorm. "That's what they called her," she said. "The

Queen of Downtown, cos she was high class. My friend knows her."

"Does she indeed, now that is interesting," Skein said, the lupine grin once more fixed on his face. He stood up and walked over to Trixie. Her head was bowed, and he lifted her chin with his finger. She looked into his face and recoiled a little.

"Who is this friend, the one who knows Candy Girl?"

"He busted my ribs," she said quickly. "I didn't do nothing , mister, but he still busted me up. I brought in two hundred, and he just kept hitting me, threw me in the bath and nearly drowned me, the fucker!"

"So I see."

Big Jackie moved over to the table and picked up the remainder of the money. He rifled through it and tossed it back down.

"I know where the detective is, he's in Weymouth," Trixie said suddenly. "I've got the address and I'll tell you if..." she broke off suddenly, aware that if she was about to attempt to negotiate a deal here, there would be no going back. Everybody has a breaking point, even the downtrodden Trixie's of the world. It would appear that she had reached hers.

"If what?" Skein said. He tilted his head slightly, his eyes keen and alert.

Trixie took a deep breath and then pointed at Cole. "Do him over for me."

CHAPTER 27

In Weymouth Ray parked near the Nothe Fort, in the same car park where he had walked with Brian back in April. From there he and Pippa walked down the narrow street to Brian and Carol's holiday cottage. Pippa looped her arm through Rays

189

and smiled up at him. Once inside Ray flicked on the kettle. Pippa collapsed onto the sofa and flicked her shoes off onto the floor.

"Didn't you bring any clothes?" Ray asked.

Pippa shrugged. "Only the ones I'm wearing. I'm not sure how long I'm staying for." Ray took some milk out of the fridge, sniffed it, nodded and then put a little in two cups. He added coffee, then flicked on the kettle. Pippa knelt on the sofa and leaned over the back, her chin resting on her arms.

Ray brought their coffees over and set them on the table. Pippa didn't touch hers. Instead she turned around and sat facing him. Her face had grown serious and he smiled as he settled himself into a chair opposite her.

"What's going on here, Ray?" she asked,

Ray blew gently on his coffee and took a sip. He had been preparing what to say to her from the moment he decided to ask her to come down here. He took a deep breath and set his cup down on the table.

"I like you Pippa," he said. "I like you a lot."

Pippa didn't say anything.

"I find you very attractive. You're witty and intelligent too; that's a bonus. I enjoyed fucking you, and I just want us to spend some time together. I've got some stuff to sort out while we're here, but we can have some fun too. Go out for some nice meals, find a few trendy bars, catch a movie."

"And what happens when you get fed up with me?"

"I won't."

Pippa snorted. "Ray, you call me intelligent and then you treat me like an idiot. I'm a hooker, and my best days are behind me. I'm thirty one now, I'm not going to get away with playing the lusted after school girl for many more years I'm afraid."

"You're thirty-one?"

"See you're having second thoughts already."

"Okay, there may come a time,"

"There will come a time," Pippa corrected him.

Ray reached into his pocket and took out an envelope. He tossed it onto the coffee table. Pippa stared at it.

"What's that?"

"There's five hundred pounds in there."

Pippa stood up, a flash of anger on her face. Ray stood also and placed his hands on her shoulders.

"Listen, it's not what you think. I'm not paying you for that. When we go out, I will pay for drinks, meals, entertainment, but I'm not paying to fuck you. I wouldn't insult you like that." He nodded at the envelope on the table.

"I'm your guest, right? Pippa asked

He nodded slowly, not sure if she was being sarcastic

"That's for you to buy yourself some new clothes, get your hair done, stuff like that."

Pippa still stared at him.

"Look it doesn't all have to be about hookers and punters," Ray persisted. "You're entitled to a bit of fun, surely."

"But I don't know you,"

"I'm not asking for your hand in marriage, Pippa."

"No strings huh?"

"There doesn't have to be."

"Okay, where do I sign?"

Ray sat down and took a sip of coffee. "What?"

" You ever seen *The Big Bang Theory?"*

"I've never heard of it? What is it a TV show?"

Yeah, an American comedy."

"Gangsters and whores?"

Pippa laughed. "Hardly. One of the main characters, a brilliant scientist, who has no social graces at all, sets out an agreement with his potential girlfriend, listing numerous rules and regulations that have to be adhered to if they're going to have any kind of relationship. The girl has to sign this to make it binding."

"Is this how you see our relationship?"

"Don't you?"

Ray nodded slowly. "Yeah, I suppose so." He sighed. "I don't know why this has to be so difficult." He stood up and walked across to the sofa and then sat down beside her. He slipped a hand under her sweater.

"This doesn't have to be complicated."

Pippa reached up and ran a hand through his thick hair.

"What happened to the scientist and his girl, are they still together? Ray said.

Pippa shook her head. "Nah, they split up at the end of the last season. She dumped him, but next season, who knows?" She raised her arms and Ray lifted the sweater over her head and tossed it onto the floor.

"She dumped him, well what do you know " Ray said, unclasping her bra and teasing a nipple between his fingers.

Pippa leaned back as Ray's hand slipped beneath the waistband of her jeans.

"No strings," she murmured.

In the afternoon Pippa bought a new dress. It was not a designer label, that had never been her style, but it was pretty and red (her favourite colour). It was also snug against her body in all the right places.

They had made love twice that morning. The first time was a quick tumble on the sofa, the second time was in the bedroom, taking their time, exploring each other's bodies and indicating to each other what they both liked. Nobody had ever asked Pippa what she desired; where she liked to be touched, and the notion, absurd as it was to her, that this man could prove to be more than just a brief encounter was starting to take shape in her confused mind.

It was not just the lovemaking, (*she had quickly embraced the idea that they were making love as opposed to fucking)* they were relaxed in each other's company. The conversations were devoid of awkward silences and they made each other laugh. After their second bout of lovemaking, as she was dressing, she turned on her i-pod. *"A Good Year For The Roses"* by *Elvis Costello* came on, and Pippa started to sing along.

Ray looked at her in surprise. "You know the words already?"

Pippa nodded. "To some of them. I particularly like this one. It's achingly beautiful, how sad he feels about losing his wife."

Ray snorted. "That's not what it's about."

"Really?"

"If you listen to the words he states most clearly that he's pleased with how the garden is coming along, he don't give a shit about anything else."

Pippa laughed and punched him on the arm. "Are you messing with me? This is a song about guilt and denial. Every recollection for the man in this song, every significant memory, from his wife's lipstick print on her coffee cup, the unmade bed, the sound of the door closing behind her, are all poignant reminders to him that she just left. It's his fault even though we don't know the root problem here, but it's certainly his fault," she reiterated. "Looking out into the garden and thinking about giving the lawn a final trim and how well the roses are looking is just a momentary respite, something to draw his attention from the devastation of his wife leaving him."

Ray frowned. "I've been listening to this song for years, I just thought he was content with the manure he was using."

Pippa swiped playfully at him again, knowing he was making fun of her.

The late afternoon sun was still hot as she ambled happily amongst the shoppers and browsers. As she left the town centre, heading towards the harbourside, she thought once more about the longevity of the relationship. She hadn't been one hundred per cent truthful with Ray concerning their serendipitous meeting, but she had genuine feelings for him, and that unnerved her. But did he feel the same? No, of course not, don't be ridiculous, she chided herself. He had shown a genuine interest initially, but how long was that going to last; the remainder of the break maybe? To believe that it was anything more than a holiday romance, a dirty weekend, was crazy, but she couldn't help thinking to herself...what if?

She knew a few working girls that had hooked up with clients. It never worked out.

Punters enjoyed the anonymity of a no strings fuck, that in itself was the thrill of it. Steady relationships were a no-go area, there were simply too many secrets shared by both parties. What had gone on between them would invariably become sordid and spiteful when inevitable arguments ensued.

For the punter, he would never get over the fact that his new, steady girlfriend fucked other men for a living. In his mind she would be forever making comparisons, and as the paranoia took hold, those comparisons would seldom be favourable.

For the ex pro, she would have to contend herself with the fact that her new man was a guy who used prostitutes. That was it. If he's done it in the past, then he would certainly do it again. The entire relationship was a prelude to stepping out onto a frozen lake as the sun sits high in the sky above. Few, if any, are prepared to take further steps together as the sound of cracking grows ever louder.

Ray Jessop was not an ordinary punter of course. For a start he wasn't even a customer. He had never paid for her services, and Pippa had never asked him to. This break was a treat in itself and they were both treating it as such. She knew that she must accept this for what it was. Maybe, for Ray, it was a prestige thing. Pippa wasn't high-class, never would be, but she had that certain something, and he wasn't paying for it, not directly of course.

It helped that she was amazing in bed. Lonny, her ex-pimp, had screwed her hundreds of times; every night in the first few months of meeting her. He couldn't get enough of her

She was a street girl when she met Lonny twelve years ago. She had been about nineteen then, but looked a lot younger. He had found her in a shop doorway just off Leicester Square. She sported a crew cut, and had the requisite nose studs and tribal jewelry; hoops in her ears, lips and chin. He bought her a pizza and sat and watched her eat it all, slice by slice. No street kid refused pizza.

Her past was plotted and linear. Absent father, indifferent mother, bit of sexual abuse by sundry *uncles* to act as a catalyst, and then she was off and out. Her story was not rare. Most runaways returned home. Those that didn't were forgotten about. Pippa - that was her real name, and Lonny decided to let her keep it, had left home at sixteen, slept rough for about a year but then had been lucky enough to spend two years in a doss house with a couple of other girls. Eventually that relationship became strained and Pippa had left. When Lonny met her she had reached the point where she needed looking after. Ninety per cent of the girls Lonny had working for him were street girls (and a few boys). He offered them their own place, which in itself was a godsend. Pippa would have gladly signed a contract if he had produced one. A year later Lonny was killed in an argument over a drug deal gone bad. He was stabbed to death in a car park near Watford Gap services on the M1.

Pippa stayed in the flat, kept her regular clients, paid the landlord on time, and was amazed at how much money she could make without having to pay her pimp.

She decided she never needed another one.

A few of Lonny's girls drifted away, others were taken on by other pimps. Trixie was one such girl. She was very vulnerable, and although Pippa had told her that she could move in with her, Trixie had taken up with Cole Walters. Cole had asked Pippa to join him too, had cajoled and even threatened her at one point, but Pippa had resisted, and thankfully Cole had let her go. She still spoke to Trixie, and she knew that Cole treated her badly, but there was little she could do there. Trixie was pretty helpless, but as a call girl she wasn't naive. It wasn't Pippa's place to make any demands of Cole. He was a pimp, not a care assistant.

When she reached the holiday home and let herself in, Ray was sitting on the sofa, the photograph of the girl he was looking for lay in front of him. He was staring down at it.

"Everything okay?" Pippa asked.

Ray looked up "Hmm?"

"You okay?"

"Yeah, I'm good. Can you help me with these cuffs?" He held up his arms, an open palm revealed a pair of cufflinks with an ace of hearts motif on each face. Pippa took them and fixed his shirt sleeves. He stood up, his arms straight by his sides. He was wearing a shirt and a pair of boxers. For an older guy he really had a tremendous physique.

"This shirt seem okay for tonight?" he said. The photograph had fallen to the floor, he bent to retrieve it now, glancing at it once again before putting it on the sofa.

"I don't know, you haven't told me where we're going yet."

"You get a dress?"

"Sure, you want to see it?"

"Of course."

Pippa took the red dress out of the bag and held it up for Ray to see.

"I want to see it on, baby, put it on and let's have a proper look."

Pippa nodded. "Okay." She lay the dress carefully over the arm of the sofa and slipped off her outer garments.

"So you know her?" Ray asked. He had picked up the picture again and was staring intently at it. Pippa, in her bra and panties took a step closer and looked at the picture. She had a small butterfly tattoo on her left breast, just the tips of the wings visible above the material of her bra. Ray was staring at her body. She caught him smiling.

"What?" she said

"Nothing. Christ you're sexy."

Pippa pushed her hair behind her ears and then placed her hands on her hips. Her body was lightly tanned, and smelled faintly of vanilla - a cream she used. Ray had commented on it earlier and the fact that he was aware of it after only a few days of knowing her alarmed Pippa slightly.

She took a step towards him and he drew her into an embrace.

Later as they started to get ready for dinner, Ray shouted to her from the bathroom.

"Hey, you didn't answer my question."

"What question was that?" she called back from the bedroom

"About Candy Girl, how well did you know her?"

"Yeah I know her pretty well, well kinda, we weren't really on the same page you know."

"What was she like?"

Pippa walked naked into the bathroom, and adopted a carefree pose by the side of the door, one arm draped over the top of the frame. Ray was fixing his hair. He was dressed, aside from his jacket. He ran his fingers through his thick locks and then nodded at his reflection in the mirror. He rarely used products or any kind. He turned to Pippa. Kissed her on the top of the head and gently pushed her aside. She turned and followed him into the bedroom. Her dress was on a hanger.

"Why?" she asked

Ray shrugged. "Professional curiosity, I guess. I'm not looking for her, but she has cropped up in the investigation. She's intriguing."

Pippa took her dress off the hanger, and started to put it on. "If I tell you what I know about Candy Girl, then you'll know more about her than you do about me."

"Why should that bother you?"

There was a flash of fire in her eyes, and then it was gone. She looked at him for a few seconds, and then pulled the dress up over her hips.

"I didn't say that it bothered me, it's just, well...oh fuck it, I don't know."

"Hey don't be like that," Ray said. He slipped his jacket on and flexed his shoulders. "I told you we'll be together for a while yet, plenty of time for us to get to know each other." He could see that she didn't buy that, but they'd already covered this particular conversation several times and he couldn't be bothered to discuss it again.

Pippa adjusted the straps of her dress and looked over her shoulder, surveying her lines down the back.

"Jesus, you going commando?" Ray said.

Pippa nodded. "Of course. Dress like this, you don't want to be showing any VPL. Besides, no panties means you can finger me under the restaurant table if you like."

Ray made a face and Pippa laughed. "Oh shit, did I offend you, Mister Jessop? But we are fuck buddies aren't we? I mean underneath all the pretence and bullshit, you just really want to fuck me, or finger me under the restaurant table. Let's not kid ourselves, okay?" She was suddenly angry, and he wasn't really sure why.

"Yeah, okay," he conceded.

"Attaboy. So what do you want to know about Candy?"

Ray sat down carefully on the edge of the bed so as not to crease his jacket.

"How did you meet her? She's not..."

"Like me?" Pippa finished for him.

Ray could feel himself growing angry now. He was tiring of this sudden spiteful banter. "I wasn't going to say that."

Pippa smiled, and it softened her features. "No you didn't, but you wouldn't be wrong. A whore is a whore at the end of the day, but there are so many levels. You remember Trixie, Cole's girl at the house?"

Ray nodded.

"Well Trix is one step away from the gutter. Now that's not me being elitist, I'm only just hovering above Trixie myself, but I don't have a pimp, and I'm not dependent on smack or even weed. Even so, working alone isn't all it's cracked up to be." She smoothed the dress down over her body. It fit her frame well, and Ray could see that she was pleased.

"You look stunning," he said.

"Thank-you. Anyway, pimps have pluses and minuses; the biggest downfall is the cut they take. Some girls count themselves lucky to have a roof over their heads, but at the end of the day most pimps look after their girls, especially if they're young and especially if they're pretty. Though the pretty ones tend to move on quickly. Cole is a prick. He's been around for quite a while now, but he's got a terrible temper. Pimps by nature aren't known for their manners and charm, but Cole lashes out frequently."

"How did you know him?" Ray asked.

"Only through some of his girls, Trixie in particular. We were together for a while, I was a tomboy then, that was my look - a punky , spiked hairdo, Dennis the Menace jumper and Doc Martens." She laughed at the memory. "An opportunity arose to move on. I did, Trixie didn't."

"So Candy Girl was never a part of Cole's entourage?"

Pippa laughed. "Christ, no. She was well out of Cole's league. To be honest we never really socialised, few girls do. I know her through the vine."

"What's that? Ray asked, genuinely interested.

Pippa sat down next to him. He placed a hand on her thigh.

"A lot of the girls use a grapevine, doesn't matter if you're pedaling from the gutter or a West-End penthouse, as I said earlier, a whore's a whore, and sometimes even the Saudi princes and Mayfair bankers like a bit of rough. So there's an information site we use, groups can login and see what's been posted. It's a list of people to stay clear of, for a working girl it's invaluable. You have a bad experience and you want other girls to tread warily, put it on the vine. Believe me, it's a messed up world we inhabit, and there are some serious scumbags out there, so you definitely need a heads up."

"So Candy used this, I thought she was high class?"

"Believe me, Ray, the rich fuckers can be just as brutal as the bottom feeders. A while ago, Candy posted a warning about Howard Price after he went a bit nutso."

"But you haven't heard from her for awhile?"

Pippa shrugged. "Nobody has. I checked with a few of the other girls and nobody has heard from or seen Candy Girl since Christmas. It's strange, it's as if she's just disappeared into thin air."

CHAPTER 28

"His name was Clive Cooper," Gemma said. She was sitting in the armchair opposite Carly now. If she was going to tell this story, and it looked as though she would, she had to compose herself, and sitting on the sofa next to her new young lover, dressed in only a toweling robe would prove too much of a distraction.

"Clive was a total bastard, Carly. Evil. Believe me, he was the single most despicable person I have ever met, and the world I lived in was inhabited by many of them. "

"Was he a client?" Carly asked. Her eyes were huge, staring at Gemma over the crystal tumbler that contained her drink that she had no intention of drinking.

Gemma shook her head at that. "Now who's being presumptuous?" she asked.

Carly shrugged. "I think I've gained a little insight into your past life. As I told you before, I'm not quite as naive as you may think."

"Fair enough, but you can't interrupt me, baby girl. If I'm going to get through this it's not going to be in installments, you understand?"

"Of course. But you were a prostitute weren't you?"

"Gemma nodded. "Yes. Yes I was."

"So can you go back a bit?"

"Jesus, Carly this is me baring my soul here, you have no idea how difficult that is for me."

"Yeah, but Clive, whatever his name is, is the denouement isn't he? You're starting the story at the end. Just back up a little bit."

Gemma took a sip of her drink. It was gin and bitter lemon. She had never tried it before, but Carly's father's drinks cabinet was so well stocked that it seemed almost rude not to try something different.

"When I was sixteen, my brother Alan killed our stepfather on the day that my mother was buried. You remember I said he was stabbed in a pub. Well, it was Alan that killed him."

"How did your mother die?"

"Carly!"

"Sorry."

"She had a brain haemorrhage. She was an alcoholic."

"Is that connected?"

Gemma shrugged. "I don't know. I guess it didn't help. Anyway, my stepfather, Frank, and Alan got into a fight at the wake And Al just snapped.

"Wow."

"It never came to anything. Frank had previous form, was on the sex offenders register. The CPS dropped the charges, stating that Alan had acted in self defence. No witnesses denied this, in fact, a few had said that Frank had attacked Alan in the first place. I don't know what happened, I wasn't at the wake . The authorities accepted that Frank had started the argument, Alan had wrestled the knife out of his hand and stabbed him. They offered him counselling and he accepted. We were tight them , closer than when we were really young and mutually dependent on each other's company in order to survive the twisted world my mum lived in.

"I moved in with a woman called Samantha. Alan had a bit of a reputation. He knew her and painted a rosy picture of her as a matronly, kind woman, with moral overtones and a forgiving demeanour."

"I take it she wasn't?" Carly set her untouched drink down on the floor and drew her knees up to her chest.

Gemma shrugged. "No she wasn't, but she was okay. She had about half a dozen girls working for her. She advertised in the back of local newspapers. Escorts, massages that kind of stuff. I didn't actually go onto the game for another two years, and to be fair she never pushed that hard, but once I made the transition she never tried to dissuade me. Still, Frank had introduced me to punters when I was fifteen, so I was no novice."

"You don't look like a prostitute."

"What does a prostitute look like Carly? Julia Roberts in Pretty Woman? Believe me if I'd carried on down the track I was on, I would have been dependent on drugs, alcohol or both, but I shifted gear . I left Sam and went freelance. I never worked the streets and most of my clients were rich. Alan was rising through the ranks of the criminal underworld and got me invitations to exclusive parties. I attended Ascot, Henley, fucked the most influential people; actors, politicians, the big boys in the gangster hierarchy."

"You must have made shit loads of money?"

Gemma nodded. "It was obscene, but it was easy come , easy go. Alan had lots of palms to grease in order to obtain these exclusive invites. And the lifestyle itself was extravagant. Christ, girl you wouldn't believe the money we spent!"

Gemma finished her drink in one gulp and set the glass down on the floor.

"What happened next?" Carly asked.

"Long story short?"

"Not too short. Why are you here, where you are now ?"

"A girl I knew died, an overdose. It happens, and the authorities don't go to town trying to find out what really happened. Some people are still of the opinion that she had it coming because of what she did, but she didn't. Her name was Viola and she called me on the night that she died. People representing her client were keen to keep his name anonymous so they wanted to know what she had said to me when she called, but she didn't tell me shit."

"That was it?" Carly said.

""What do you mean?" Gemma replied.

"Viola died of an overdose, what did that have to do with you being on the run?"

"Clive Cooper happened, and that is definitely a story for another night." Gemma said.

CHAPTER 29

Cole held up his hands.

"Whoa, now hold on guys," he said. "This isn't playing by the rules. You know how this works. Fuck, I give the bitch a little slap now and again, no harm done. My ribs are busted up too, by the way, courtesy of the fucking detective. Christ I should be hiring you guys to beat the shit out of him, and yet here you are considering bartering with this little whore."

Skein stood up slowly and Cole flinched. "I don't believe that I've agreed to any transaction at the present time. I agree that we are in the business of settling disagreements, and the prices vary, depending on circumstances. But you must appreciate that this young lady has some information that we desire and the price she is asking appears most fair, wouldn't you agree?" He turned to Big Jackie who nodded thoughtfully.

"It's what we do," he admitted.

Cole laughed uneasily and ran his hands through his lank greasy hair. He pointed a trembling finger at Trixie. "I can retrieve that information for you within seconds. Leave me with her and I'll get the detective's whereabouts for you, and it ain't gonna cost you shiit."

Skein appeared to consider this. "What do you think?" he said to Jackie.

"I think we go with the girl," the big man replied.

"Me too," Skein agreed.

With alarming speed that belied his stature, Big Jackie lashed out and grabbed Cole by the scruff of the neck. A single quick punch to the stomach was enough to make the pimp crumble in agony. The beating he had received from Ray Jessop was still fresh, and he knew that there was a chance that the big guy could kill him. He held up both his hands but then spotted a figure silhouetted in the frame of the kitchen door. Big Jackie had his back to the door, and Skein and Trixie were both watching the big man bear down on him, so only Cole could see that Jade had entered the kitchen. She screamed and ran across the room and leapt onto Jackie's back.

Big Jackie spun around in surprise and the girl was thrown off. She landed heavily on her backside, but was up on her feet again almost immediately and she raked her nails down Big Jackie's face.

"You fucking bitch!" he cried and punched her hard in the face. She crumbled to the floor in an unconscious heap. Cole seized the opportunity the distraction presented, and he slipped the flick knife out of his pocket. With a single deft movement he punched the blade upwards, the blade burying itself into Big Jackie's chest.

"Ha, you big fucker, how'd you like that?" he screamed, flecks of spittle running down his chin

Big Jackie grunted and stared at the knife sticking out, blood oozing from the wound and staining his shirt like a Rorschach Blot. He started to make a mewling sound, growing in pitch, His fingers hovered inches from the knife, uncertainty vying with fear. Should he pull it out now and attempt to stem the flow? His breath grew laboured and the blood stain grew larger. He looked up at Skein, with saucer shaped eyes.

Skein ignored him. This was a dog eat dog world, the big man was surely done for, and now Skein was in trouble. Without his muscle, his aura of menace diminished considerably. The pimp was staring at him now, his fingers opening and closing. He reminded Skein of a wild animal suddenly freed from captivity. Big Jackie slumped against the table, leaving a bloody handprint on the Formica top. Skein reached into his jacket pocket and withdrew a pistol.

Skein hated using a gun, and only did so as a last resort. Guns attracted the police and investigations were far more thorough once a firearm was involved. This particular weapon was a Russian made Baikal pistol. Originally built to fire CS canisters, it had been modified to use live 9mm ammunition. Because of the modifications, the weapon was unregistered, and untraceable. He pointed the gun at the pimp now.

Cole dived for cover as Skein fired, the slug catching him in the shoulder and spinning him over onto his back as he hit the floor. Within seconds he was back on his feet and running for the door. Skein aimed again, but the pimp was lightning fast and the second shot hit the door frame as he leapt through it. Skein followed, but by the time he reached the open front door, Cole was already running up the street, clutching his shoulder.

Skein put the weapon away and walked back into the kitchen.

Big Jackie was slumped against the kitchen table now, his legs splayed out in front of him. His breathing was shallow and labored. His shirt was now completely red, and blood was still pumping steadily from the wound where the knife had entered his chest. Skein knew that the big man was going to die. He stood by Big Jackie. The huge man's eyelids fluttered and he looked up at Skein, his face ghostly white. He tried to lift an arm, but it shook uncontrollably and fell limply back into his lap. Skein pulled a few sheets of kitchen roll from a dispenser on the wall and reached down and pulled the knife out. Big Jackie groaned, and then he mouthed a wordless curse before his head dropped and came to rest on his chest. Blood pumped from the wound for a few seconds longer and then stopped. Skein slipped the knife into his pocket. He turned towards the small skinny girl.

Trixie was against the wall, her palms by her side, the fingers gripping the plaster. Her mouth was open and she reminded Skein of a shocked cinemagoer watching a particularly nasty horror film. He walked over to her and snapped his fingers in her face. She blinked a few times and then her gaze fell upon him. He thought she might scream, but she checked herself and managed a thin smile. She has bad teeth, Skein thought.

"Where is she, your friend and the detective?" he said.

CHAPTER 30

Cole had never experienced pain like it. Despite the suspicious figure he must have portrayed he was unable to do anything more than stagger from one lamppost or low wall to the next. His feet shuffling on the pavement as if he was picking his way through a particularly tricky dance routine.

The shoulder, where the bullet hit and was still lodged, was a dull throb, though the numbness that ran down the entire left side of his body was cause for concern.

But it was his guts that doubled him up, forcing him to clutch at his stomach every few steps; stabbing spasms forcing him to cry out and fall to his knees. Cabs ignored him and passers-by gave him a wide berth. He knew that he should get to a hospital and to hell with any repercussions. Gunshot wounds were apt to bring out the detective in the most lowly, unambitious uniformed copper. It was for this reason alone that he still hesitated. Maybe he wouldn't have to explain anything if he could make it to where he was going.

He staggered again, and his knees buckled. He hit the pavement hard, and as he knelt there, his bloodied hand supporting his weakened frame, he thought *I'm not going to get up from this.*

Cole dragged his phone out of his pocket. He sat down on the pavement, oblivious to the stares , and his fingers hovered over the keypad. He was limited to who he could ring.

It was at such times as this that Cole realised just how few people he could call actual friends. He picked a name now.

Spider was counting his money. It was something that he enjoyed doing. Stacking the notes into piles and then sitting back and staring at them, before fanning them out like a deck of cards. He actually clicked his tongue in annoyance when his mobile rang, an inconvenience that was interrupting his new avaricious hobby.

He didn't recognize the number, but answered it anyway. The voice that greeted him was laboured and hoarse, a low whisper, barely audible through the tinny speaker of the phone.

"It's Cole," the voice rasped. "Help me, Spider."

Spider's first instinct was to hang up. *Why the fuck was Cole calling him for help?* And from the sound of him Spider believed it was the kind of help he would not be able to administer. The pimp sounded as if he was breathing his last.

"Are you there?" Cole said weakly.

"Yeah, what happened?"

"I've been shot, you've got to help me."

Christ! Spider thought. *Hang up, hang the fuck up right now!*

"Don't you fucking hang up on me, Spider," Cole wheezed, anticipating Spider's motives. "It's your fucking fault that I'm in this mess in the first place."

"What are you talking about?"

There was a long pause, the silence only broken by Coles irregular, strained breathing. Eventually he said: "It was you who took the fucking photo, Spider, don't deny it, I know it was you."

Spider helped Cole inside. The cab he had called was not an ordinary hackney, it was a discreet firm, the owner an associate of Spider's who asked no questions, but expected an inflated fee for allowing such indiscretions to go unchecked. Spider was keeping a tally of the fees. He would present them to Cole when the pimp had recovered, though looking at his pasty white complexion, Spider was not certain that Cole would pull through. He manhandled him into his small living room, and Cole slumped onto the sofa. Spider reached forward to undo Cole's jacket and examine the wound further, but Cole slapped his hand away angrily.

"What do you plan to do, heal me by simply staring? Get somebody over here."

Spider was annoyed at being spoken to in such an abrupt manner. Cole didn't know for a fact that he had taken the photograph from the pimp's house, and even if he had, what did it matter, he didn't really owe Cole anything. Cole couldn't push him around like one of his girls.

Cole coughed and grasped his stomach. He groaned loudly, rocking backwards and forwards on the couch. "I'm sorry, man," he said eventually. "It's not your fault, but I'm hurting so fucking much"

The ingratiating tone went some way to placate Spider. He nodded slowly. He didn't like Cole, but he was intrigued as to why Cole suddenly placed so much emphasis on the photograph. Spider had realised the importance of it as soon as he had seen who was in the picture, but Cole had not been aware of the significance, otherwise he would have seen fit to negotiate with Murray Cooper himself. So what had changed in such a short period of time?

"You got somebody you can call?" Cole said.

Spider stared at him. "Like who?"

Cole groaned and leaned forward in the chair. He took a few deep breaths and shook his head slowly. "I don't fucking know, man, somebody who can help me! I thought you were the word on the street"

"You need to go to a hospital,"

"No," Cole shouted. "No fucking hospitals. Jesus, Spider, you know how it is. I turn up at a hospital with a bullet lodged in my fucking shoulder, then the Old Bill are gonna be asking questions before the morphine has worn off."

"I may know somebody," Spider conceded.

"Then fucking call him man!"

"This is gonna cost, Cole, you're not a charity case."

Cole waved a blood-soaked hand in his direction. "Whatever, man, back pocket."

Spider felt inside Cole's pocket and took out his wallet. It was crammed with cash. He counted out a hundred and pocketed it.

"For the cab," he explained.

Cole waved his hand irritably.

"I may need another two for the guy I know."

"Whatever, just fucking call him will you."

The guy in question was Mal, no surname, and no questions. Not that Cole was in a fit state to interrogate the man.

Mal was another associate of Spider's, a number he had acquired in the past but had never had to use. He was in his mid sixties, with a few wispy strands of grey hair framing a speckled head that resembled a large egg. They were on nodding terms whenever their paths crossed, and that was as far as the relationship went. Spider assumed that Mal had some kind of a medical background; you did not acquire such an anonymous status without having some knowledge within a specialised field. He could have been a vet or a dentist, but he patched Cole up pretty well after removing the slug. Spider

211

handed Mal a fistful of notes, making sure that Cole witnessed this transaction, then Mal nodded to both men and left.

Cole propped himself up on an elbow. His right arm was in a sling, and Mal had swathed his ribs in bandages.

"Haven't you got any fucking scotch?" he said, positioning a pillow behind his back. If he was at all grateful to Spider for helping him out, he was concealing it admirably.

"No I don't."

"Can't you pop to the fucking offy and pick up a bottle, I almost fucking died."

"I'm not your fucking slave, Cole, you ungrateful prick. How long are you going to be staying here?"

Cole narrowed his eyes and glared at the petty thief. "I told you, if it hadn't been for you, I never would have been in this fucking position. Skein wanted the fucking photo that the detective brought round, the one with the girls in the club. You took it didn't you?"

Spider shrugged. "Yeah, so?"

"Why?"

Spider didn't want to tell Cole why, because Cole was crafty and he certainly didn't want to reveal his association with Murray Cooper. Even though Cole obviously hadn't made the connection between Candy Girl and the disappearance of Clive Cooper there was no need to offer him any clues.

Spider's phone vibrated in his pocket and he took it out. It was not his own mobile but the one Murray had given him. "I got to take this," he said.

Cole shrugged. "Secret is it?"

Spider smiled. "Course it fucking is, especially from you."

Spider left the small living room and stepped into the kitchen, pulling the door behind him. He left it slightly ajar so he could observe Cole through the crack, but the pimp simply

212

lay back on his cushions with a weary sigh and aimed the remote at the TV. Satisfied that Cole could not hear him, Spider answered the phone.

"Hello, Mister Cooper."

"Spider, listen to me, we've found her, the girl," Murray sounded excited and impatient at the same time.

"Already, Christ that was quick!"

"Have you ever heard of facial recognition?"

"I've heard of it, not sure how it works though."

"We have the most advanced technology money can buy. Once we scanned your picture of the girl from the club we got an immediate hit on Facebook. How about that?"

"I can't believe that she would be stupid enough to open a Facebook account," Spider said.

Murray laughed. "She wasn't, it was somebody else's page, but forget about that. I'm getting some people together, they'll be picking you up first thing in the morning."

"Hey, whoa, Mister Cooper, what's going on?"

"You will still recognise her?"

"Yes, but.."

"No but's Spider, we know where she is and we're picking her up tomorrow. I need you to be there."

Spider suddenly felt cold, and the phone shook in his hand. "You really need me there?"

"You signed for this deal on the dotted line. You're the only fucker who knows her in the flesh, that's why you're going. You won't be alone, that's what I want to talk to you about. We've been through this before, Spider."

"But."

"I said no but's ." Murray paused. "We get her, Spider and you get to keep your money. All you have to do is point a finger and say there she is, Skein and his boys will do the rest. Tomorrow morning, 6:00 am. Be ready."

"Okay."

"One other thing." Murray hesitated. "Watch Skein, okay?"

"Watch him, what do you mean?"

"I don't mean anything. Just be aware of him."

Murray ended the call and Spider stared dumbly at the phone for a few seconds. Watching somebody and being wary of them sounded like two different things to him. He was suddenly very uncomfortable. He pocketed the phone and hurried back into the living room. Cole briefly glanced at him before returning his attention back to the TV.

"So who was it?" he asked. "Or is that a secret?"

"You need to leave, right now," Spider said.

Cole muted the sound and turned fully to face Spider now, wincing as he did so.

"The fuck you talking about man?"

"What part of that didn't you understand, Cole. Leave now, or so help me I'll throw you out myself."

CHAPTER 31

Ray liked shellfish and the restaurant he had chosen that night, a small, Portugese family run place that specialized in Mediterranean cuisine, was a delight.

They had made love again before they had left for the restaurant, and that had cleared the tension between them. Pippa looked divine in the red dress that she had bought earlier. After their meal they left the restaurant and found a trendy wine bar on the old harbourside. The evening air was chilly but they took a balcony seat upstairs where it was quieter and they gazed out over the still waters as the final few fishing boats chugged gently into the harbour and moored for the night.

They were sharing a bottle of Chilean Merlot and as Pippa sipped her wine she took in her surroundings and relaxed further.

"It's nice here," she said.

Ray nodded. "It's been years since I was last here. I was only a kid then, twelve or thirteen. It was just me and mum."

"Tell me about her." Pippa said.

"Why?"

"I dunno, something to talk about."

"She was scatty, a bit of a hippy. Her first husband was a maintenance electrician for British Leyland. He died from a heart attack when she was twenty-seven. He was forty-eight. She met my father, Marco, at a life modelling class in Hackney."

"Marco was a model?"

Ray shook his head. "Nah, mum was. She posed naked for the adult art classes. They wanted a nude model, mum stepped up to the plate. I told you she was a bit of a hippy. Marco was a student in the class. They had a fling and then got married. He left her as soon as I was born. She still kept some of his pictures, though god knows why, they were shit; thick, acrylic paint on bare white canvases. I was never sure what he was trying to say"

"Did she keep the one he painted of her in the nude?"

Ray shook his head. "Don't think so, though it would have been the sort of thing she would have done. Maybe have it framed and hung over the bed."

"Is she still alive?"

"No, she died from breast cancer the same year as my wife and daughter were killed."

"I'm so sorry. What was your daughter's name again?"

"Sophia and my wife was Julia and before you say anything I don't talk about them or the accident."

Pippa took a sip of wine. "Why?"

"Because it doesn't help. It didn't help to talk about it at the time, and it doesn't help to talk about it now. You can't resolve anything by talking about something that personal, I can't anyhow. I've never been able to and I don't want to attempt to start now. I like the anger and hatred I felt and still feel. I need to embrace that even now after all these years. I don't want to soften that edge by talking about it. I don't want to resolve anything. The resentment and bitterness are familiar bedfellows, I don't want to replace them even if I could."

They sat in silence for a few minutes, watching the waning activity around the harbour. Pippa finished her wine and stood up.

"Be back in a minute," she said. Ray nodded.

Pippa left the balcony and headed for the stairs that led down into the main bar. In a corner of the room a couple had set up a small stage. A girl was singing. She had a haunting, melancholy voice. She was accompanied by a ginger-haired guy on an acoustic guitar; the strings wound so far above the head they resembled the whiskers on a back alley tomcat.

The girl was sweet looking, but the guy was unattractive. Pippa couldn't imagine them as being a couple, but who was she to comment on the idiosyncratic nature of relationships. The girl finished her number, a depressing lullaby with an Irish lilt that earned her a smattering of applause.

Pippa spotted the toilets and headed in that direction. She noted a group of younger people, one guy and two girls seated by the bar. There were a lot of empties on their tables and they were in a party mood. The guy looked up as she passed and nodded appreciatively. She smiled back and made her way to the toilets.

Pippa entered and stood by the sink. She liked the way she looked in the mirror. The dress was rather ostentatious, and she felt a little overdressed for the wine bar, but she didn't really care. Most of the clientele were smart casual. She adjusted her hair a little and applied a touch of lipstick. She wasn't sure why she brought Ray's wife and daughter into the conversation on the balcony. His reluctance or even inability to broach personal topics did not concern her; they scarcely knew anything about each other, therefore why should he feel obliged to share his most innermost thoughts with her so early in the relationship?

A chain flushed behind her and the booth opened. Pippa stared into the mirror, her mouth open as the girl from the photograph, Helena, stepped out from the cubicle. She looked even more beautiful in the flesh. Tall and tanned. she smiled courteously at Pippa before quickly rinsing her hands in the sink. She was wearing a short black dress and heels. She looked at Pippa in the mirror and spoke to her reflection in the way girls do when standing at sinks together.

"Nice dress," she said. "Is it Louboutin?"

"Not really," Pippa replied.

"Whatever. It suits you," the girl said, shaking her hands dry by her side. "Are you here with friends?"

"Just my boyfriend. A few days away."

"That's nice. Okay, see you." The girl turned and left the toilet. Pippa let out a long breath, not realizing she had been holding it. She straightened her hair again and then followed the girl out. As she walked back into the bar she saw the girl in the black dress sitting with the group she had spotted earlier. They nodded to each other and Pippa again saw the guy look up at her. As she passed she saw him lean in towards the girl with the black dress and ask her something, but Pippa was past the table before she could catch a reply.

She hurried back up the stairs to the balcony. Ray was standing now, his jacket over his arm.

"You ready?" he asked as she walked back into the booth.

"She's here," Pippa said quickly. "The girl from the photograph, Helena, she's here in the bar downstairs with two other girls and a guy. They're all sitting at a table having a drink together."

"Jesus Christ," Ray breathed. "You're sure?"

Pippa nodded enthusiastically. "Positive. What do you want to do?"

"Show me," Ray said and they headed for the downstairs bar.

They found an empty table in the corner. The couple had stopped singing and were taking a break.

Ray scanned the group. Helena sat facing Ray and Pippa, the guy on her left, the other two girls in the group sitting across the table to them, their backs to Ray and Pippa. They were all talking at the same time. The guy, a lean, handsome man in his early twenties put his arm around Helene's shoulder, but she shrugged him off. He leaned in and said something to her and her eyes blazed with anger. The guy slumped back in his chair, and Helena stood up. She said something else to the handsome man, but he ignored her. She walked away from the table towards the exit.

"Check the group out for a while and then head back to the cottage," Ray said to Pippa.

"Where are you going?"

Ray shrugged. "I don't know yet, wherever she goes, I'm making this up as I go along."

Pippa nodded. Ray stood up and followed the girl out of the bar.

CHAPTER 32

As Ray and Pippa were ordering dessert at the Portugese restaurant, Skein was sitting in his car scanning the cottage. Trixie sat beside him in his old Jaguar Mark 2, picking absently at a loose bit of skin at the base of her thumbnail. She alternated between bites and delicate pinches and it was beginning to irritate Skein. Eventually he slapped at her hand and she yelped like a sticken puppy.

"Doesn't seem to be anybody here," she said absently

"This is the address that Pippa gave to you?" Skein said.

Trixie nodded. "Yeah."

Skein waited a minute longer. He was double parked and the road was narrow here. The cottage sat on the corner, the road sloping down a steep hill towards the harbour. Cars were parked on both sides and Skein breathed a sigh of relief when he noticed in his rear view mirror, a car vacating a space. It was a much smaller vehicle than his jag and he had difficulty in negotiating the big car into the gap. Once parked he opened the door and stepped out onto the street. Trixie got out of the passenger door and stood on the path. Skein closed the car door and walked quickly over to the cottage. Trixie followed him.

Skein felt for the converted pistol in his jacket pocket, slipped it out and let it hang loosely by his side. He then rapped quickly on the door, looking around as he did so. There was no answer so Skein knocked again, louder this time. When nobody came to the door, he slipped the gun back into his pocket and headed round to the side of the cottage, Trixie following in his wake.

As the cottage was situated on the corner, Skein was able to walk around the property unhindered by adjoining houses. The road sloped down the steep hill, so the height of the wall surrounding the rear of the property increased. At the furthest point of the cottage's boundary line the wall was so high that Skein could not see into the back yard. He walked back towards the front. Opening the boot of the jag he took out a crowbar and approached the front door once more. Then he glanced down by the side of the gate. There was a small box with a rubber cover - a secret key compartment. He pulled up the rubber sleeve and the front flap of the box fell open. It was not locked and there was a spare key inside. Skein turned to Trixie who shrugged. He unlocked the front door and stepped inside the cottage placing the crowbar down on a small hallside table.

Skein took out the gun and called out. "Hello?" There was no answer. He searched the cottage swiftly, upstairs and down, Trixie watching him from the centre of the living room.

"The photo is here," she said as Skein hurried down from the upstairs bedroom. She pointed at the picture on the dining room table. Skein snatched it up and looked at the image from the club.

"I wonder where Pippa is?" Trixie said, glancing around as if expecting her friend to be hiding behind the sofa. The girl was so innocent, Skein thought. Following her betrayal of Cole she had latched onto Skein as if he was a new guide and mentor, and had willingly followed him to his car like an obedient puppy. And now here they were at the address she had given him, where one of her friends was supposedly staying and yet she appeared nonchalant and unaware that Skein was conducting a meticulous search. It was naivety bordering on utter stupidity if the girl thought that Skein was here to pass on his best wishes to the girl and the detective.

He conceded that anybody who has survived as a hooker for as long as she has, must possess a modicum of street cred, yet Trixie seemed oblivious to the fact that she was just an accessory here, a literal sacrificial pawn in Skeins game; a game, he concluded, that was drawing towards its inevitable conclusion.

Trixie said, "Okay, what now?"

Skein was intrigued by the girl. He was a cold, calculating man, with no self-pity. He suffered fools gladly, as he enjoyed mocking and teasing their inability to grasp the most simple premises.

"Do you know what it is that I do?" he asked her, gesturing to the sofa for her to sit down. Trixie did so and Skein took a seat beside her.

"You beat Cole up for me," she laughed. "He had that coming, know that for sure."

It wasn't entirely accurate of course. The pimp had killed Big Jackie, and Skein had lost a grip of the situation for a while, but now he had located the whereabouts of the detective, things were back on track.

"Do you know what leaving a trail is, Trixie?" Skein said.

"Like breadcrumbs?"

Skein laughed again. "No, not like breadcrumbs. Not a literal trail my dear girl, but things that are left behind after the fact. A trail of clues; footprints in the snow, a bloodied smear on a whitewashed wall?"

Trixie stared at him with a look of utter confusion on her face.

"Who aside from that dreadful man, Cole, knows about this photograph and the whereabouts of the detective and your friend Pippa?" Skein asked.

Trixie continued to stare at him.

"Come on, girl, for Chrissakes, this isn't difficult, aside from me, who else?"

"Me!" Trixie suddenly announced triumphantly, and Skein slipped Cole's knife out from his pocket and pushed it up between the ribs of the girl. Trixie managed a faint "Oh!" before crumpling at his side.

"Of course you," Skein said. He slipped off the sofa and knelt down by Trixies still form and wiped the blade against her t-shirt, then he stepped back from the sofa. This was the second body left in the wake of the investigation for the pimp and the detective, and he knew that the chances he was taking were becoming more reckless. His phone rang and he glanced at the display before raising it to his ear.

"Hello, Charles."

"Where are you?" Charles Cooper demanded.

"In Weymouth. I've found the detective and the girl. You want me to bring them in?"

"No, there's no need. We've found her. Candy Girl. I need you to get back here straight away. I want you to get a team together and pick her up."

"Okay I'm on my way."

Skein pocketed the phone and stared at the lifeless form of the dead girl. He consoled himself with the sombre belief that she was probably better off now. Skein had always been able to justify his actions thus and he smiled and prodded her lifeless form with the tip of his shoe, until her head slumped to the side. He stood and stared at her for a full five minutes.

The recent dead fascinated him.

He was christened Thomas Richmond Skein but he preferred the relative anonymity of a single name and had always been known as just Skein. Originally from Lancashire, he had lost all trace of his accent when he had moved to the capital with his uncle when he was seventeen years old.

Now in his late fifties, Skein had negotiated a hazardous course that had led him to relative respectability within the criminal underworld.

His uncle Marius had worked on a sprawling market for a while as a kosher butcher, just outside Charing Cross and Skein had been expected to follow him. Both his parents were dead; his father in a bizarre boating accident in which he fell overboard and drowned in the river Calder when Skein was only three years old. Bizarre, because his father had not been drunk, and the water had not been terribly deep. This coupled with the fact that his father had been a strong swimmer, simply added to the mystery. Many conclusions had been drawn, the most obvious being that Skein's father had become entangled in reeds that were prolific on the river bed. Skein's mother had died just before his sixteenth birthday from a heart attack. She was thirty-six. After a year in a foster home, Skein moved in with his late father's older brother, Uncle Marius.

Marius was neither a good butcher or a successful businessman. Skein himself had no interest in becoming the former, but excelled at the latter. His very first perusal of his uncle's slap-dash accounting books threw up some curious and disturbing statistics.

"What is this two hundred and fifty pounds for?" Skein had asked Marius, his finger tapping at the open page of the ledger.

Uncle Marius waved a dismissive hand. "Oh don't worry about that."

Skein set down his pen. "I have to worry about it. Aside from the meat itself, this is the single largest outgoing payment. You can't expect me to ignore such an invoice, now what is it for? There is no mention of it in the proceeding columns."

So Uncle Marius told him, and Skein had sat and listened in silence, his face unable to mask the conflicting emotions of bewilderment and, if he was being honest, admiration.

The next day Skein spoke to as many of the other market stall holders that were prepared to divulge information. Many were not forthcoming, as it was obviously demeaning, and many were too proud to admit to such a shortcoming. An old porter, by the name of Betts was the one who finally told Skein everything he needed to know.

"They call it protection," Betts wheezed. He sat on a crate of cooling pork dripping and proceeded to roll the thinnest cigarette Skein had ever seen. Betts was in his seventies, but looked ninety. He was one of those characters who looked dirty all the time. He wore what Skein believed must have been a yellow high-vis jacket at sometime, but was so caked in grease and dirt, that it was almost black.

"Yet the only people who they are really protecting you from are others who maybe want in on the racket. That's a paradox." He squinted and looked at Skein closely. "You know what a paradox is, boy?"

Skein nodded and Betts shook his head, certain that, like all teenage boys, Skein was obviously lying.

"So people just pay them, that's it?" Skein asked.

Betts licked the edge of the rollup and stuck it in the side of his mouth. "That's about the size of it."

Skein thought about this for a while. "My uncle pays them two hundred and fifty pounds every four weeks, how many others?" He paused taking stock of the extraordinary amount of money the gang must be making for literally doing nothing.

"But why?" he suddenly asked. Betts blinked and then laughed. It was a dry, mirthless cackle, the roll-up bobbed precariously on his bottom lip but managed to stay put long enough for Betts to light it and take a long draw.

"They pay because they're scared."

That last statement had resonated with Skein. He was not a naive youngster, unaware of such exploitation, he had spent enough time in the capital to witness unscrupulous behaviour first hand. It was simply the sheer audacity that somebody could fleece the stallholders so unconditionally that amazed him. The supposed protection itself was an anomaly, since the only thing the gangs were actually protecting were the assets themselves, namely the stall holders, from interlopers stepping in and taking over, as Betts had stated. The more Skein delved into the practice, the less sympathy he felt for his uncle and his compatriots and the more he wanted a piece of the action for himself.

He started to follow the men who collected the money. Two hulking brutes, who swaggered confidently through the market, spending a little more than a couple of minutes at each stall, sometimes only a matter of seconds, for that was all it took for the stallholders to hand over an envelope. No pleasantries were exchanged, and seemingly there were no requests for protection. Within the space of an hour, the two heavies had collected thirty-eight payments. If they were all paying the same as his uncle, Skein estimated that the men had taken nearly ten thousand pounds.

Simple as that. As much money as his uncle made in a year. Skein decided he wanted to be a part of this.

Over the next few weeks Skein learned the routes of the men, where they stopped to eat, who carried the satchel filled with the envelopes, (it was always the larger of the two, a man named Blu Jarvis) which of the stall holders protested, and, most importantly, the man they worked for.

His name was James Nelson, he was in his late sixties, with a mane of silver hair, that hung in a long ponytail and reached the middle of his back. His office was a small room above a taxi rank in Charing Cross. Jarvis always entered alone, his accomplice sat in the waiting room of the taxi rank, where he joked and laughed with the drivers.

After three months of spying on the operation, Skein had formed the nub of a plan. It was dangerous to the point of being foolish, but Skein was already well on the way to becoming a psychopath. Even the most amateurish psychologist would have enough evidence available to make a half decent prognosis. Parents early deaths; bizarre kinship with his late father's brother, in which the older man depended on his brother's son to aid him in the most perfunctory tasks. And yet the truth was probably nothing to do with any of these particular circumstances. It was apathy that truly fuelled Skeins motives, apathy and a total disregard for the well being of his fellow man.

To Skein, he had witnessed an easy way of making money. The villain's world was one that was fraught with danger, but they continued nevertheless. Nelson's operation was small. For the protection racket, there appeared to be nobody aside from Nelson himself and the two heavies who collected the money. This entire notion appeared absurd to Skein, surely there must be more involved. There were hundreds of workers at the market, how could they allow themselves to be intimidated in such a way? He spoke to Betts about it, and the old porter tapped the side of his nose.

"Why do thousands of wildebeest scatter at the approach of a single lion?"

Why indeed, Skein had thought.

"Fear," Betts concluded. "Simple fear, boy."

The next day Skein, after months of careful planning, made his move.

CHAPTER 33

The girl calling herself Helena exited the bar and lit up a cigarette. She was not aware of Ray behind her as he held his phone to his ear and followed her out of the bar and onto the pathway beside the harbourside.

There were quite a few people here so Ray held back and started to follow the girl as she walked quickly alongside the harbour wall. As they moved away from the bars and restaurants, the crowds thinned out. Ray knew that there was always a risk involved when snatching somebody on the streets, especially on the hop as he intended to do now. But he was ever an optimist and he quickly spied an opportunity.

Helena was approaching a large building that looked, to Ray, like a kids indoor adventure playground; the ones with cargo nets, ball ponds and crash mats. But it was late now and the building was closed and silent. It acted as a huge shield, obscuring onlookers in the short narrow side streets leading to the town centre.

As Helena approached the building, Ray broke into a trot. He swept her up into his arms, one large hand clasped over her mouth, then, heaving her off the ground, he flung her over the side of the harbourside wall and into a moored fishing boat.

Helena cried out as she hit the boat's deck, but the whoosh of air expelled by her lungs masked the sound and before she had time to right herself Ray had landed almost silently beside her.

Ray clamped a hand over her mouth again and pushed her quickly inside the small compartment of the wheelhouse.

The boat was a Trap Setter, and rows of drying lobster pots hung over the side. The vessel was not large, only about twelve metres in length, and there was a small crane to the stern in order to retrieve the pots. The wheelhouse was small, but it offered enough concealment for Ray as he crouched over the stricken Helena who regarded him with wide eyed terror. Ray's hand was still clamped firmly over her mouth, but he wasn't going to remove it, not yet. He had seen the cliched movie scenes in which the abductor states that he will remove his hand now, so *don't scream.* Nine times out of ten, they would. Ray took out a knife from a small, bespoke holster in his boot and held it up to Helena's face. She shook her head desperately, but Ray's grip didn't waver.

"I will stick this straight through your palm if you scream and pin you to the deck. It won't kill you but it will fucking hurt, do you understand?"

Helena shook her head, and Ray cuffed her hard across the face with the back of his hand. Instantly he covered her mouth again.

"Shaking your head is a negative. Are you telling me you don't understand what I have just said to you?" As if to accentuate his point, Ray pressed the tip of the blade into Helena's palm, not hard, but enough to allow a pinprick of blood to escape.

"Now, do you understand not to scream when I remove my hand?" Helena nodded her head furiously and Ray took his hand away.

"Oh my god, are you going to kill me?" Helena gasped. She closed her hand into a fist. A trickle of blood escaping through the fingertips.

"No," Ray said, glancing around the small wheelhouse. "But you tell me why I shouldn't."

"What? Why shouldn't you? Because I haven't done anything to you. Please."

"You call blackmailing my best friend for twenty five grand nothing?"

Referring to Brian as his best friend was stretching things a bit here, but Ray was aiming for maximum reaction. This particular revelation hit home. Sudden realisation dawned on Helena's face and the terror level was upped a notch. Ray turned back to face her

"What did you think? You'd just keep playing your sick games with no consequences?"

"No, oh no, please, it wasn't me, it was Matthew. It was always his idea. Oh god please don't hurt me."

"Who the hell is Matthew? I don't think it was Matthew who asked for directions to the bookshop or seduced my friend, or sucked his fucking cock!" Ray slapped Helena quickly and hard across the face, once, twice, three times. The girl reeled from each blow and immediately blood started to trickle from a split lip. She groaned quietly and Ray lifted a hand under her chin. He drew back his open palm again and she flinched.

"Now listen to me carefully. I'm going to ask you some questions. You lie to me, and I'm going to knock out your front teeth. Do you understand me?"

Helena nodded her head, still groggy from the quick succession of slaps Ray had just admonished.

"What's your real name?"

The girl's eyes seemed unfocused, and Ray regretted hitting her so hard at the beginning of the interrogation, but he needed to terrify the girl quickly. She had to be one hundred percent certain that he was not playing games. If she sensed for one second that he was going to go easy on her then she would lie. People engulfed by an unyielding sense of dread will do anything to be released and will tell you anything you want to hear. Catch them quickly enough and they don't have the capacity to lie. The reality of their situation is numbing and to lie effectively means that you need time to invent and corroborate a story; a fabricated version of the events. To all intents and purposes this is difficult to do under normal circumstances. Facing a genuine threat and even fear of death heightened those circumstances ten fold. Whatever Helena told him now, Ray was certain it would be the truth.

The girl blinked and tried to focus on his face. She attempted a smile but was unable to manage anything other than a sneer. Fear was evident in her eyes and she stared intently at Ray, her eyes swimming into focus, as he moved closer towards her.

"Well?" He asked.

"My name is Zoe, Zoe Corbett."

"Who's Matthew,? The guy sitting with you in the bar?"

Zoe nodded.

"So it was his idea to blackmail Brian ?"

Zoe stared at him for a few seconds. "No, not initially."

Ray raised his hand and Zoe flinched again. "What's that supposed to mean?"

"Matthew came in later, organised the bed and breakfast, filmed the seduction."

"So who was behind it all, who paid you to blackmail Brian?"

"His daughter," Zoe said. "Lucy."

That stunned Ray. He leaned back from Zoe and regarded her.

"Lucy? What are you talking about?"

CHAPTER 34

Pippa sat and watched the remaining group of friends that the girl had been sitting with for a while longer. They were sullen and quiet now, and after twenty minutes, the man stood up and left, leaving the two remaining girls alone. Pippa finished her drink and left the bar also. The sun had gone down now and there was a chill wind around the harbour. She rubbed her upper arms vigorously, wishing she had brought a jacket with her. She could go back to the cottage, but didn't want to do so alone. She walked around the harbour. The bars and pubs were still quite busy, and she was whistled at and propositioned more than a few times. Pippa didn't mind, she even found it complimentary. In her profession it was churlish to harbour any anti-sexist views. She didn't want another drink, she had never been one for alcohol, so she found another bar, ordered a coke and found a window seat and sat for an hour watching the harbourside activity wind down.

After leaving the bar she headed back to the cottage, glad that she had the keys in her bag. There was a spare set in a lock box on the wall in the front garden, but she couldn't remember the code.

She saw the police car parked on the corner of the hill a few doors away from the cottage and she paused for a few seconds. Working girls are always wary of the law, even when they have done nothing wrong. She took a few more steps, and that's when she was seen. A policeman had been sitting in the car. He had obviously spotted her in his mirror and stepped out. He stared down the hill at her. Her hesitancy would appear suspicious, so she continued to walk. The copper watched her as she walked up the steep hill. Pippa was tempted to walk past the cottage, but she hadn't done anything wrong, so she quickened her pace and forced herself to appear confident. The cop continued to watch her until she reached the corner. As she turned it she saw another police car parked out the front of the cottage, it's lights flashing. The front door of the cottage was open and several cops, both uniformed and CID were milling about outside. All activity stopped when Pippa reached the front gate. She had to know what was happening, despite her reluctance to involve herself with the authorities. A man in a heavy trench coat that appeared to possess as many pockets as a magician's cape turned and looked at her. His face was instantly alert, and Pippa had him labelled as the lead detective before he had the chance to introduce himself. He stood before her, his hands buried in his deep pockets.

"Help you, Miss?" he asked.

"I'm staying here," Pippa said confidently. "What the hell is going on?"

Trenchcoat barked a quick order at one of the uniforms standing by the gate and the man ran to his car. Suddenly the activity around the cottage intensified. Trench coat stepped towards Pippa.

"Where is Ray Jessop?" he asked brusquely.

Pippa's heart dipped and she sucked in a quick breath. *Christ, what had she gotten herself into?*

CHAPTER 35

"Are you telling me that Lucy blackmailed her own father?" Ray said. The shock of Zoe's statement had stunned him and the girl could see that. Her demeanour changed slightly from the utterly terrified captive to the quietly confident owner of undisclosed knowledge. Ray could see that she was not so confident to believe that she was out of the woods, but she had a card to play and it was definitely a high roller.

"If you let me go, I'll tell you everything," she said quietly. "Please."

Ray nodded slowly. "So tell me."

"First you have to promise me"

Ray grabbed Zoe by the hair and yanked her hair viciously to the side. The girl cried out in pain and surprise.

"I'm not promising you anything," he barked, giving her hair a quick jerk to emphasise that her idea of bartering did not constitute a level playing field.

"Now tell me why Lucy did such a thing and I may consider *not* snuffing out your sad, nasty life."

So Zoe told him. When she had finished. Ray tied her securely in the cabin, binding both her hands and feet, and gagging her so she couldn't cry out. Fishermen were early risers, so she would be freed at dawn. Although she was hogtied he took her phone and then left the boat.

His car was parked in the car park near the Nothe Fort. He took the back road up to the car park as it was quicker than going via the cottage. He texted Pippa a quick message saying he would be a few hours following up a lead. He would let himself in using the key in the box by the front gate. When she didn't reply after ten minutes he considered calling her, but decided it was not urgent. He turned off his own phone, not wanting to be disturbed. Pippa was more than aware that the trip was a working holiday and the main reason for them coming was to continue the investigation into finding the elusive Helena. He hadn't anticipated, however, the job taking such an unexpected turn.

Thirty minutes later he was parked once again outside Carol Harrier's house, though this time he had taken the precaution of parking a little further up the tree-lined street, so that he could not be seen from the property. He was surprised to see a police car drive up to the gate, pause whilst the driver activated the intercom button, then carry on up to the house. He sat back in his seat and watched. Ten minutes later the police car drove away. Carol Harrier was sitting in the back. She didn't glance in Ray's direction as the police car passed him.

His phone vibrated in his pocket and he instinctively reached for it. When it was in his hand, however, he realised that he didn't recognise the ringtone. He glanced down at the handset and realised he had taken Zoe's phone out. On the dial the caller's name flashed on the screen.

Lucy.

He let it go to voicemail then listened to the message. Lucy was agitated, almost panic stricken, but nothing could prepare Ray for the message she left.

"Zoe, if you're in Weymouth, for god's sake get out. Ray Jessop, the detectve my stupid fucking mum hired to track you down, is here and he killed a girl at mum's holiday cottage. They haven't said as much, but we think she was a prostitute and she was stabbed. Mum's down the station now giving a statement, but get out, go back to the house in Jersey. Ring me as soon as you get this message."

Ray stared at the phone for a minute, his thoughts in turmoil. He listened to the message again. *A girl stabbed? A prostitute? Christ it had to be Pippa, and the police think he had done it!*

Of course, he knew that he was innocent, but his alibi after leaving Pippa in the bar was shaky at best and downright unbelievable at worst.

"Couldn't have been me officer, I was kidnapping and interrogating another girl at the time, if you don't believe me, you can ask her. I left her hogtied in the cabin of a fishing boat on the harbourside!"

Christ, what the fuck was going on? He had to glean more information. Suddenly he had an idea. It was probably foolish but he had to give it a go. He clicked on Zoe's phone, found Lucy's number and pressed ring . It was answered almost immediately.

"Zoe, where are you?" Lucy's voice was still frantic.

"It's Ray Jessop," Ray said quietly. "Don't hang up. I didn't kill anybody, and if the police haul me in, the first thing I'm going to tell them is that you blackmailed your own father."

Ray could hear Lucy breathing. He was about to ask if she was still there when she spoke. Still nervous, but Ray detected a hint of defiance.

"What do you want?"

"To talk," Ray said.

CHAPTER 36

The cop in the trenchcoat was Detective Inspector Paul Jackson. He sat Pippa down at a low desk in a small interview room and brought her a coffee.

"I'm very sorry," he said, taking a seat opposite her. "Were you friends?"

Pippa nodded slowly. He had brought her a cup of coffee. It was strong and sweet even though she had asked for it without sugar. She didn't complain though. Taking slow sips of the hot drink allowed herself to collect her thoughts. She hadn't been arrested and Jackson had reiterated several times that she was free to go at any time. She knew they all said that and she wondered fleetingly what he would say or do if she took him up on that promise. For the moment she was proving to be a staple of the never tired cop rhetoric - She was helping them with their enquiries.

"Try Jessop again will you?" Jackson asked.

Pippa took out her phone and dialled Ray's number. Nothing.

"It's still switched off," she said. They had both read Ray's text message and tried every half and hour since then to contact him to no avail.

Jackson sighed.

"So her name was Trixie, do you know her real name?" he asked. He was short for a cop, maybe five, eight, but still fit looking, with a trim waistline and a good head of greying hair. He had rolled his shirt sleeves up to reveal hairy forearms, covering faded, blue ink tattoos. One was of a galleon under full sail. Pippa wondered if he was an ex-naval man.

"I didn't know her real name. She didn't tell me and I never asked." She shrugged. "We just don't"

" Who's we, you members in a club or something?"

Pippa forced a thin smile. "You want to play games or just shoot the shit?"

Jackson held up his hands in mock surrender. "Okay, just didn't want to jump in there too quickly and make assumptions."

236

"How long you been on the force?"

"Thirty one years."

"Fine, let's not dance with each other okay?"

Jackson nodded. "Fine by me."

Pippa had been shocked by Trixie's death, but hadn't cried. She might later, but for the moment she had too much to consider. Jackson had shown her a picture of Trixies face. When Pippa said she knew who she was, he had allowed her to see the body, only briefly though. She hadn't been sure why he had done that, seeing that she had identified Trixie from the photograph, but now she thought that it was probably to shock her; see how she would react. He evidently had suspicions, and was hoping that she would confirm most or all of them. After a few perfunctory questions (she told him where Trixie lived) he had brought her to the police station in Dorchester and she had sat in this room for just under an hour. She knew they were sweating her out a little, but she wasn't concerned, not yet. She hadn't done anything wrong,

What the hell was Trixie doing at the cottage?

"Okay Pippa," Jackson said suddenly. "I want you to tell me where Ray Jessop is."

They were piecing the puzzle together very quickly. This is where she had to tread carefully. Just tell them the truth and let them fill in the gaps. Did she think Ray had killed Trixie? She wasn't sure. If he had, then she certainly hadn't seen it coming, and it made no sense to her whatsoever. But then what the hell did she know? She had only known him for a few days.

"I don't know. You obviously know that we were staying at the cottage together."

Jackson shook his head. "Actually I had no idea who you were until you turned up at the front door. Mrs Harrier, who owns the cottage ,confirmed that Jessop was staying there whilst investigating a case on her behalf. You w eren't mentioned."

"I know about the investigation."

"Why were you with Jessop?"

"He invited me down."

"What for?"

"What do you think?"

"He a client?"

"No."

Jackson frowned. "Okay, so now I'm confused."

" It was no strings. He had the use of the cottage, while he was conducting the investigation and asked if I wanted to tag along. Have a few drinks, some nights out, you know?"

Jackson shook his head. "Frankly, Pippa, I don't know. You said you didn't want to dance, but I feel you're feeding me a line here, cos from where I'm sitting, this doesn't make any sense at all."

"What, that I could possibly want a few days away?"

"Have you known Jessop long?"

"Nope."

"You want to give me a clue?"

"Three days."

Jackson threw his hands up. "What the hell, you are dancing with me! Shall we start again?"

Pippa closed her eyes and ran her fingers through her hair. "Look, I know how it sounds, but just listen. I met Ray in London a few days ago. He was looking for somebody, a girl. I helped him a bit, we hit it off and he asked me out. We don't plan to elope, I'm sure when this is all over, we'll go our separate ways. It was just a few days away together.

"No strings?"

"Right."

Jackson shook his head and Pippa could see he was still unconvinced. "So where is he?"

"I don't know. You heard the message, he's chasing a few leads. We had a meal together then went to a bar on the harbour. I spotted the girl he was looking for, told Ray and he followed her out. I had another drink, headed back to the cottage and then met you."

Jackson nodded slowly as if absorbing this information. "Did Ray know Trixie?"

"He didn't know her, but he met her."

"Really? When?"

"In London the day before we met. He went to the house rented by Trixie's pimp. She was there. The pimp put Ray onto me, thinking I may be able to help him recognise the girl he was looking for."

"And did you?"

"No, but I recognised another girl in the photo. Because they were together, Ray was wondering if they knew each other."

"You think he did it?"

The question was unexpected and caught Pippa off guard. "What?"

"Do you think Ray Jessop killed Trixie?"

"How the hell should I know?"

"You got an opinion?"

"I thought that was your job."

Jackson shrugged. "Anybody can have an opinion. You think he killed her or not?"

Pippa paused. "I don't know."

Jackson smiled. "You had to think about it."

"I don't know," she repeated.

"Think of anybody else who had a grudge against the girl?"

Pippa shrugged. "She worked the streets, her clients were whacko's and junkies. Life in the big city."

"Know any of these whacko's who might happen to follow her down to Weymouth and then murder her in the same cottage you were staying at with your no strings attached boyfriend?"

"I suppose you haven't ruled me out either?" Pippa said.

"Not entirely, but to be honest I think Jessop is good for it."

Pippa didn't say anything. Part of her felt as if she was betraying Ray. It was a ridiculous notion, for sure. All evidence pointed to Ray and yet she couldn't understand the motive. Unless he was an out and out psychopath, of course.

"What do you know about him?" Jackson asked.

"Very little. I told you."

"You know about his wife and daughter?"

Pippa nodded slowly, not knowing where Jackson was going with this.

"I know they were killed in a car crash."

"Do you also know that the guy driving the other car, Matthew Silk, was drunk, and then fled the scene, escaping with no more than a twisted ankle.

"No."

"Then you also wouldn't know that this same guy broke his neck after falling down the steps in prison?"

Pippa took a quick breath in. "Why are you telling me this?" she said.

Jackson spread his hands. "Just shooting the breeze."

"How could Ray have killed Silk whilst he was in prison?"

"I never said that he did."

240

"Was anybody convicted of killing him?"

"Nope. Official enquiry stated that it was an accident."

Pippa sighed. "But you don't believe that?"

Jackson shrugged. "Doesn't matter what I believe."

"Then why tell me about it then?"

They were both silent for a while. There was a light tap on the door and a uniformed officer entered. Jackson stood up and met him by the door. They talked for a full minute before the officer left and Jackson turned back to face Pippa.

"That address you gave us earlier for the pimp. Was his name Cole Waters?"

Pippa sat up quickly. "Yes, why?"

Jackson stared hard at her for a few seconds." Waters is missing and there's a dead man in his kitchen."

CHAPTER 37

Lucy Harrier was not as attractive as her mother. She had a thin, oval face, with long, stringy brown hair. She wore no make-up, and had dark rings under both eyes. She had looked better when Ray had seen her back in April.

She walked down to the gate and met Ray there, her hands folded over her thin chest. She wasn't going to let him in, understandably concerned for her own safety. Ray surmised that she hadn't considered the notion that he may have a gun. If he had and it was his intention to kill her he could quite easily have done so through the bars of the gate.

She didn't ask Ray how he had found out about her blackmailing her father, and he believed that she didn't really care. Zoe Corbett had told him that Lucy hated her father, not stating why, and she had approached Zoe who offered her services online as an escort, working on the Channel Islands. The two girls had struck up a friendship and Lucy had pitched the idea of blackmailing her father, something that Zoe had not wanted to do, she had insisted to Ray, but had gone along with it for the money. Lucy stared at him defiantly now. Anybody who could be so cruel to conduct such a callous act in the first place would surely be unconcerned about how people judged them once they had been discovered.

"Where's Zoe?" she asked.

Ray ignored her. "What happened with the police?" he said.

Lucy pursed her lips and Ray thought she was simply going to clam up and not answer any of his questions. Then she sighed and let her arms fall limply by her side.

"A neighbour noticed the open door of the cottage, went inside and found the girl's body. He called the police, they came here and spoke to mum."

"Did they say who she was, the girl?"

"No, just that she was a young girl. One of the uniforms said she looked like a hooker. He got a bollocking for that. They asked her who was staying at the cottage and she said you ."

"Did she tell them I was working for her?"

"She told them you were looking for a girl, she didn't go into details."

"Why not?"

"How the fuck should I know? Ask my mum."

"Did they say they considered me a suspect?"

Lucy rolled her eyes. "Duh? Whaddya think?"

She was beginning to piss Ray off, but it was clear that the police had revealed very little to Carol Harrier about the murder, and rightly so. He saw no reason why Carol wouldn't tell them she had been working on a private investigation on her behalf. Even so, it wasn't an alibi.

"Where's Zoe?" Lucy asked again.

"I haven't killed her," Ray said. "Why did you do it?"

"You wouldn't understand?"

"Try me"

Lucy stared at him for a few seconds, a trace of a sneer curled her bottom lip.

"No, she said. "I don't believe that I will." She turned and started to walk back to the house.

Ray took his phone out and switched it on. He had three missed calls from Pippa. Almost immediately it rang.

"Pippa?"

"Hey, Ray, where are you?"

"Pippa, thank Christ, I thought you were dead!"

There was a long pause. "Ray why would you think that?"

Ray sighed. "It's a long story, look where are you?"

"At the police station, they want you to come in, you need to clarify some stuff."

"I didn't kill anybody, Pippa, you've gotta believe me."

"I know that, the police know that, but they still need you to clear some shit up. It was Trixie, Ray. Somebody killed Trixie at the holiday cottage."

"What the hell are you talking about?"

"Hang on Ray."

The phone went quiet for a while, then a man's voice came on the line.

Detective Inspector Jackson introduced himself and reiterated what Pippa had said about just answering a few perfunctory questions. Ray detected unease in Jackson's voice though, as if he expected Ray to hang up, ditch his phone and then disappear, but he consoled himself with the fact that he himself knew that he was innocent. Once Jackson gave him directions, he pocketed his phone and headed back to his car.

He glanced over his shoulder and saw Lucy Harrier silhouetted in the doorway of the big house, as he turned again he heard the door slam shut behind him.

CHAPTER 38

Ray told Jackson everything about his search for Zoe Corbett, though he never used that name, from his original meeting with Brian back in April, to Carol taking on his services, the subsequent meeting with Cole, and then teaming up with Pippa and spotting Zoe in the bar earlier that evening. Of course he skipped the part about abducting Zoe and leaving her tied up on a boat in Weymouth harbour, telling Jackson that he lost her in the crowd after following her out of the bar.

Jackson picked him up on a couple of points, but his questions seemed more inquisitive than probing. He had already told Ray that they were looking for a guy named Skein.

"Have you heard of him?" Jackson asked.

Ray shook his head. "No."

"You're not a real P.I. are you?" Jackson said abruptly.

"I don't think I ever said I was," Ray countered. "All I've ever said is that I investigate. I look for people and on a lot of occasions, I find them, I don't need a registration or a diploma from the SIA for that."

"Well the Security information authority is looking to tighten regulations, so I've heard."

Ray shrugged. "And when they do, you can bet I'll be sure to abide by them."

Jackson grunted. "Can I get you to look at a video?"

Ray nodded. "Sure."

There was a laptop on the desk. Jackson turned it so that they could both see the screen. A flash drive was plugged into the USB port. Jackson opened the video app and pressed play. A remarkably clear image filled the screen. He could see the holiday cottage on the far right. The video picked up an old Jaguar as it pulled to the kerb, the driver expertly maneuvering the big car into a small gap. A skinny man exited the driver's side and then Ray recognised the petite hooker from King's Cross - Trixie get out of the passenger door. The video clip showed them both walking over to the cottage. The thin man was looking around. He slipped a gun out of his pocket and held it loosely at his side. Fascinated, Ray leaned in closer. The skinny man knocked on the door. When nobody answered he walked around the house, Trixie following him. Then he walked back to the Jag, popped the boot and took out a crowbar. Back at the front door he glanced down and smiled. Jackson paused the clip and then zoomed in. The image pixelated slightly, but it was clear enough to discern the man's features.

"Recognise him?" Jackson asked.

Ray shook his head.

Jackson played the clip to the end, showing Skein discovering the key, then exiting the cottage eighteen minutes later. Alone.

Jackson studied him for a moment. "Metro picked up Cole Waters a couple of hours ago, after Pippa told us about him being Trixie's pimp, and the London boys tied him to a killing in the house in King's Cross, Cole started singing. Said that Skein killed the guy and that he was looking for you. We believe him after seeing this video. The victim was John Sansom, known as Big Jackie, and a known associate of Skein. Question is why did Skein bring the girl to Weymouth, and kill her in the cottage you happen to be staying at? You have any idea why this guy was looking for you and why he would be with a girl that you only met briefly on one occasion with him?"

"Not really," Ray answered.

Jackson studied him for a few long seconds as if mulling over an important decision. Then he shook his head and stood up.

"You're free to go, don't want to but can't hold you for the killing of the girl, and that's my investigation. Skein is good for that, but if you turn anything up, you'll contact the police straight away. You okay with that?"

"Sure, why shouldn't I be?"

"You probably won't talk with me again. Metro will be swarming over it now. You reckon they'll let a country bumpkin like me get a foot in the door?"

"A killing took place on your patch, that's got to amount to something."

Jackson sighed, and ran a hand through his hair. "You'd have thought so, wouldn't you? You planning on going back to London?"

Ray nodded.

"You find out anything then you keep me in the loop, not just the London boys, Jessop, you understand?"

"Of course, we're on the same team here, Detective.

Jackson nodded, a little reluctantly, Ray sensed.

"The video, where did you get it?" he asked.

Jackson paused and Ray thought he wasn't going to tell him, but then the cop nodded slowly to himself.

CEFAS over the road from the cottage. State of the art. They were broken into a year ago and upgraded all their equipment.

"Lucky."

For you," Jackson said, with a hint of a smile.

"I guess."

"You planning on going back with Pippa?"

Ray nodded.

"She doesn't know about the video, it came in after we finished questioning her. She may still think you're good for the killing."

"Did she say so?"

Another pause. "No, she didn't. Goodbye, Jessop, and remember, keep me informed should you hear anything." He stood up and Ray did too. He thought that Jackson would reach across the table and shake his hand, but the detective didn't do so. Instead, he tilted his head slightly and chewed absently on his bottom lip.

"You're mixed up in some nasty business here, Jessop," he said pointedly. "Once we bring Skein in you still may have some explaining to do."

"You make it sound as if I'm hiding something."

"Are you?"

"No," Ray admitted. "If I find anything else out, I will contact you."

CHAPTER 39

At ten-fifteen the next morning, Gemma sat in the expansive living room of Carly's house and looked at the money strewn on the table before her.

She was going to steal it. It had never occurred to her not to after Carly told her about it. She really liked Carly, but not enough not to betray her over such a tempting amount of cash. As soon as the younger girl had mentioned the money in the safe, and the whereabouts of the combination, Gemma knew that the final chapter of this brief story would end here, with her alone with the money in her possession and Carly out of the house on a foolhardy mission that would lead to inevitable disappointment.

She had not slept in the night. All she could think about was the money, and how far away it could get her. It was ironic that Carly had mentioned travelling abroad and finding work in a bar. With this little windfall Gemma herself could do exactly that, and not have to touch her own reassuring nest egg.

The lack of sleep allowed her to formulate a plan. When Carly woke in the morning, Gemma announced that her idea of them going to Nice together was a good one. She, Gemma, had thought long and hard about it and she could definitely see the advantages.

Carly bought this sudden change of heart without a second thought, squealed with delight, and leaped around the bedroom. Gemma had felt the first pangs of guilt witnessing the girl's euphoria, but she remained stoic in her belief that her main priority was to look after herself. She told Carly to go shopping. Get some summer gear, bikinI's, sunglasses, shorts and sun cream. Carly had wanted to make the shopping trip a joint adventure, but Gemma had insisted that she needed to tie up a few loose ends first. This was a huge commitment for her, she said. There were people she had to speak to before she could just up and leave the country. She reiterated the point that to begin with they would be holidaying together, and it would be fun, but Carly would return home eventually, she would not. Her convoluted past had lent credence to the lies and Carly had nodded her understanding. Gemma felt another pang of guilt, but she forced it down.

Now, with Carly on her way to a shopping centre in Lowestoft, and Gemma staring at the money on the coffee table, she couldn't understand why she was still here. She had watched Carly leave in the car. Waited twenty minutes before retrieving the combination and opening the safe, but now here she still sat.

Get up, take your money and leave, she chided herself. The fact that she was referring to the cash as *her money* was the clearest indication yet that she was going to do this. So why did she just sit here and wait?

Because a part of you wants to go to Nice with Carly?

She tried to push that thought away rapidly, confine it with the momentary feelings of guilt over her betrayal, but it was difficult to lie to yourself, especially when you were alone.

She tried to convince herself that they were probably not looking for her anymore, if they had even bothered in the first place, but it was a ridiculous proposition. Of course they were. She didn't know too much about Clive's father, but she had killed his son, and from what she did know, through rumours and gossip, he was not the kind of man who would just accept the killing of his son and move on. Oh, he was looking for her alright, and she had to consider herself incredibly lucky that he hadn't found her yet.

She had never met Murray Cooper, but she had researched him online. Alongside his brother they ran many lucrative businesses, some quite shady if the speculative musings of the tabloids were to be believed.

He was a squat, stocky man, with a boxers face and a crooked, insidious smile. So unlike Clive, who was alarmingly handsome. She had met Clive before the night he had turned up at her apartment, though she had never fucked him, he wasn't a client. So when he knocked on her door shortly before midnight she was curious but not initially alarmed by his appearance.

249

CHAPTER 40

"Candy, right?" Clive Cooper said, pointing a finger at her as he leaned on the door jam and flashed a toothy grin.

Gemma nodded. "Clive Cooper?"

He looked surprised momentarily, but also pleased that she knew him.

"I didn't recognise your name when I first heard it, but your face has a ring about it. So we have met then?" he asked pleasantly.

"Not intimately, but you have a reputation."

"Ah. Good or bad?"

"I'm a hooker, I rarely meet men with good reputations."

He laughed at that. "Hey you're a witty girl, can I come in?"

"What for?"

"To talk."

"That's not an answer."

A flash of anger touched his eyes and Gemma stepped back momentarily.

Clive smiled as if she was being willingly complicit and stepped inside the apartment.

"You want a drink?" Gemma asked

"Sure, you got any scotch?"

"I got Jack Daniel's"

Clive sneered. "Fuck's sake, I thought you were supposed to be high class. I was talking about a decent malt. Fucking Jack Daniels. Haven't you got any Chivas?"

Gemma walked over to a sideboard and picked up a bottle of Jack Daniel's. "Actually, Chivas is a blended whisky," she said. "But never mind."

She had no time to avoid the blow. She set the bourbon down on the coffee table and he struck her, hard with the back of his hand across her face. His ring caught her on the chin and she reeled from the slap, sinking to her knees.

"Witty is one thing," he said, his face red with anger, "But disrespect is something else altogether."

"I'm sorry," Gemma said. She was genuinely scared now. She had encountered violence in the past, it was a way of life, and she usually recognised those prone to flare ups. Clive Cooper's reputation preceded him. The son of a wealthy businessman, she knew that he was a callous and vicious individual. She had to tread very carefully now. Men like Clive Cooper trod a very linear line on the cusp of barely maintaining their temper and flipping out completely. She was acutely aware that he could kill her tonight if she pushed him. She struggled to her feet. When she touched her chin her fingers came away dotted with blood. Luckily it was only a glancing blow and the cut was not deep.

"You're not a huge fan of Christmas I see."

Gemma shook her head. "No"

"That is the most fucked up tree I have ever seen," Clive said. "There's no fucking tinsel or baubles, not even any chocolate, what's the point? You're definitely lacking creativity my girl."

Clive snatched her beloved monkey off the shelf and turned it over in his hand.

"What's this piece of shit?"

Gemma shrugged. "It was here when I moved in. "What did you want to talk to me about?"

Clive stared at the monkey for a few more seconds before setting it back down on the shelf.

"You got a call tonight from a girl, one of Denny's whores. What's her name?"   Gemma thought it prudent not to lie. The fact that he knew about the call indicated that he was privy to certain information.

"Viola."

"Why did she call you?"

"She told me she was with a rich African guy and that he had some good skag. I told her to be careful. That was it."

"So Viola was a friend of yours?"

"We never worked together, so you could hardly call us friends."

"So why did she have your number in her phone?"

"We were associates. Is she dead"."

Clive raised his eyebrows. "What makes you say that?"

"You just referred to her in the past tense."

She's dead," Clive said matter-of-factly."

Gemma put a hand to her mouth. "Oh no."

"She didn't say anything else to you about the African, his name, what he did?"

"No."

"You're sure?"

"I'm sure."

Clive cocked his head to one side and smiled. "What if I say I don't believe you?"

Gemma sighed. "Then I don't know what I can do to convince you otherwise."

"Funny," Clive said. "I use a lot of hookers, but I've never fucked you. We both move in the same circles but have never bumped into each other. That's weird, don't you think?"

"They're wide circles," Gemma said.

Clive nodded. "I guess. You know Denny, Viola's pimp?"

"I know of him."

"But you don't work for him?"

"You know I don't."

"So how do you know Viola?"

"She's an associate, nothing more"

"What else did she say to you on the phone?"

"I told you, nothing."

You expect me to believe that crock of shit? This whore is fucking one of the most important men she will ever meet and all she does is tell you that he has a good supply of H? You gonna pour me a couple of fingers of Jack ?"

Gemma nodded dumbly, and reached for a glass. As she handed it to him he slapped her hard across the face. She cried out and the glass crashed to the kitchen floor. He swung his arm backwards and she managed to step back, but he still caught her again, a resounding slap.

"Stop, just stop, will you!" she cried. "Look I don't know what it is that you think I've heard, but…."

"What did Viola fucking tell you?" Clive suddenly screamed at her, spittle spraying from his mouth onto her face. "Did she tell you his name, who his associates were? Tell me!"

"No, she didn't tell me anything!"

Why would she call you?" Clive shouted. "You hardly fucking knew her, so you want me to believe. Why would two whores talk to each other if they weren't friends?"

"It's a hooker's grapevine," Gemma cried. "There aren't that many people out there prepared to look out for us, so we have to look out for ourselves. One of us has a bad experience with a punter we pass it on to other girls. Viola had never met this guy before but she was just saying that he seemed okay. If we come up against somebody nasty we let each other know. On this occasion there were no alarm bells. Surely you can understand that. He was a newbie, that's all. If things had gone South I would have known about him and put it on the grapevine.

He stared blankly at her for a few seconds then smiled and wagged his finger.

"See that wasn't too difficult now, was it? I want us to be friends, Candy, truly I do, but you just lied to me, that's a bad start. Now what about that drink?"

He was crazy, she knew that, and she had no idea how to handle this. She herself had heard from others on the grapevine to stay well clear of Clive Cooper. She stepped away from him and poured another shot of Jack in a fresh glass. Her shoes crunched on the shattered glass that he had slapped from her hand moments ago. She held the drink at arm's length and he smiled again. He reached for it and took the glass from her hand. He took a sip and continued to stare at her.

Gemma got a dustpan and brush from a cupboard and cleared up the glass.

"What do you want?" she said quietly.

Clive turned to her. "What do you mean?"

"I mean, whatever I tell you, you're not going to believe me, so what do you want?"

"I think you should apologise for wasting my fucking time."

"I'm sorry," she said automatically. "I don't know what you want me to say. I'm sorry."

Clive nodded slowly. "You know what, Candy, I don't believe that you are. People say sorry for many reasons, but from your tone I would suggest that you're far from apologetic."

Gemma sighed and looked down at the floor. She had no idea what to say to this man. She was frightened because she knew that he was capable of killing her, and there would be no recriminations against him, for she doubted that the finger of suspicion would ever be pointed at Clive Cooper. Her body would probably be dismembered and buried deep, never to be found. Would she be mourned? Maybe for a few weeks, and only by a few clients and they would soon move on. She knew that she was probably being ridiculous. He was pissed at her for sure, but was he angry enough to kill her?

More precisely, was he crazy enough to?

"I am sorry," she said again.

Clive laughed. "Yeah? Okay I believe you."

"You want to know what happened to Viola?" he said. " How she died at the hotel?"

"No."

Clive picked up his drink and took a sip. "Fucking Jack," he sneered. "Now I don't believe you're following the thread of the conversation, Candy Girl. You telling me you don't want to know?"

Gemma shook her head. " I'm sorry, what?"

"No need to apologise again, girl, we both know you don't mean it. I asked you if you wanted to know how Viola died and you said no, the right answer is, yes"

"Yes, tell me."

"You sure?"

She nodded.

She overdosed on the skag. There was a half empty bottle of gin that probably contributed." He clicked his fingers. "Boom, out like a light. The African would have knocked her about a bit if she hadn't died; he's got a bit of a reputation, but that's one of the perils of the game isn't it? If she'd had lived you could have put a notification on your grapevine. Men are such cunts to women." He laughed. "I think it's the

255

vulnerability. You're not called the weaker sex for nothing, you know. I'm no different. On occasion I just can't stop myself. I was with a whore one night and she fell asleep on the floor. I bust her jaw just for the hell of it. Sometimes I will step back and think, am I going to do this? Should I do this? Occasionally I just go straight ahead and do it, then think - should I have done that? But this was just spontaneous, I didn't even think about it. I just kicked her as hard as I could in the face and bust her fucking jaw. She spat two teeth out. I've only read about that happening in hack adventure novels, but she literally spat out teeth. That's power, Candy. It's such an adrenaline rush, honestly it's like no other feeling in the world. That feeling of complete domination over a weaker person, the sheer brutality of the act."

He turned away from her and started gesticulating with his arms like a stage actor swept away by a powerful narrative.

"For centuries women were used and abused by men, sold with dowries to rich landowners old enough to be their grandfathers. Fucked every which way, beaten for daring to have a fucking opinion. Can you imagine how wonderful that must have been? Do you have any fucking idea? I can barely comprehend."

"Jesus," Gemma breathed. "What kind of a man are you?"

He took a step towards her and she flinched. "A powerful one," he said then burst out laughing. "What's your name?" he said suddenly.

"Candy Girl."

Clive shook his head. "No, no, your real fucking name, and don't lie to me."

"Gemma."

Gemma what?"

"Bradshaw." She felt no need to hide the truth from him. She didn't believe that he would see through her lies had she deemed it necessary to keep this information from him, despite his boasts to the contrary. She could not remember the last time she had ever told anybody her real name, but then she was unable to recall when anybody had even asked her. Why should they even bother?

"Well, Gemma," Clive said leaning against the far wall. "Here's what we are going to do." He pushed himself off the wall and started ticking things off on his fingers as if he was reciting a meticulous plan of action. "Firstly you will need to be punished, secondly we need to determine the severity of the punishment, and thirdly we have to decide who will administer the punishment." He started to walk towards her. "Third part is simple. I will carry out the punishment, I'm not the kind of guy who gets others to do the dirty work." He tilted his head to one side as if pondering the validity of that statement. "Actually I am," he laughed. "Now the severity, that's an important issue. Lying is a real no no as far as I'm concerned, fucking heinous, is that the word? So the real question at the end of the day is what punishment does such a crime warrant?"

"You're fucking crazy," Gemma said quietly.

Clive stopped walking and smiled at her, nodding slowly. "Take off your clothes."

She took a step backwards and shook her head. "No."

Clive reached into the pocket of his jacket and took out a switchblade. He pressed the button and the wicked blade sprang forward.

"You know in Tudor times a whore was branded. They would literally carve a W into her cheek, then rub soot into the wound, therefore all men would be aware of her wickedness.

I'm gonna cut you, you little, fucking whore. Only a little and not on the face, but somewhere where all will know that you have wronged man. Now take off your fucking clothes."

For a few seconds, Gemma was unable to speak. Terror had restricted her windpipe and she was mute. But anger was welling up too. She started to undo the buttons on her blouse.

Clive nodded his head and managed a wan smile. As he turned from her, Gemma stepped forward and snatched up the bottle of Jack Daniel's by the neck. She drew back her arm and as he turned back to face her, she swung the bottle round in a wide arc hitting him high on the side of his head. Clive dropped immediately. His head struck the edge of the coffee table and he was still. The knife slipped from his fingers. He didn't twitch or spasm. Gemma gently set the bottle back down on the table and took two steps back.

She stared at him for a long time, wondering if he was really dead.

CHAPTER 41

The sound of breaking glass startled her from her recollections. She hurried into the hall and towards Carly's father's study, and the sound of the tinkling glass. She opened the door to see a man climbing through the open window. He was large and was having difficulty getting through the tight space. He spied her and grinned. He managed to get a leg over the window sill and set it down on the floor when Gemma snatched up a silver plated pen holder from the desk and swung it at his head.

He managed to get an arm up, deflecting the blow, but it had still hurt him, Gemma decided with some satisfaction.

"Fucking bitch!" he screamed.

He fell into the room and Gemma turned and ran. She made it to the front door, but the heavy wood was unyielding and she tugged it several times before it opened.

A large hand fell on her shoulder and she was yanked back into the hallway. She landed hard on her backside and sat still, realising the futility of a fight at this stage. The large man was in his early twenties, handsome in a grungy way with a mass of unruly black curls and tribal tattoos running up both arms and onto his neck. Gemma heard somebody else moving about in the study. The tattooed man turned and called out: "Is this her?"

Gemma watched in stunned disbelief as Jazz, the bully from the karaoke bar, stepped into the hallway.

"Oh, year," Jazz said. "That's her alright."

CHAPTER 42

Spider sat in unmarked transit watching the house. He was in the passenger seat. Behind the wheel was Oz. That was as much as he knew about the man who happened to be the largest individual he had ever met.

They had discovered that Gemma, aka Candy Girl, was staying here after investigators working for Skein infiltrated the girl's place of work - a carvery restaurant on a sprawling caravan site five miles from Great Yarmouth.

The whole operation had a military ring to it. There had been the initial euphoria when Murray's people, working from the photograph Spider had provided, found a comparison on Facebook. It hadn't been Gemma's account, of course, Spider knew that the girl would not be so stupid as to set up a Facebook page whilst on the run from a pair of shifty gangsters posing as businessmen.

No, the Facebook page belonged to a girl called Kat Webber. The photograph showed Kat alongside another girl, who they now knew was Carly Beech, whose house they were watching, and, on Carly's left, her face turned slightly away from the camera, was Candy Girl. Spider recognised her immediately. Charles's man, Skein, had descended on the restaurant, never approaching management for fear of attracting suspicion. He had used cliched and well used objectives to extract information from staff. Long lost relatives were searching for this girl, look at this picture, do you recognise her? Will Twenty-pounds refresh your memory? Wink, wink, you help me out, scratch my back. It seemed that Candy Girl, now known as Gemma Btadshaw had caused a bit of a scandal, and scandal loosened lips .

"Only been here five minutes and fast-tracked to bar manager…. Fucking the boss, must have been…...Left with another girl, possibly lovers, both a bit strange, if you know what I mean?"

Skein and two other hulk's, named Tonka and Pell, stayed at the restaurant, trying to glean more information, leaving Oz on surveillance point with Spider. Oz told Skein that Carly Beech had left the house alone when they saw the girl get into a battered Saxo and drive away. Skein told them to hold on.

Oz liked to talk. He was in his late fifties, with a shaved head that practically glistened as if it had been polished like an immaculate bowling ball. He had the seat of the transit pushed all the way back, but still had to raise his knees so they sat in line with the middle of the steering wheel.

He wore loose, grey jogging bottoms and a green t-shirt, with *University of Michigan* emblazoned on the front. His muscular biceps not so much bulged as shifted occasionally like drifting icebergs beneath the protesting fabric. His left arm was a sleeve of ink, old school tattoos mingled seamlessly with, crisper, more radical designs. His right arm was completely bare, the forearm bristling with a rough down of course brown hair. On the knuckles of his right hand were the letters WHFC.

"My mum has moved into this over fifties housing project," Oz said, in a broad East London accent, not looking at Spider but keeping his eyes on the house. "She's eighty-two, and since dad died two years ago, she's been finding it tough in her old flat. This new place is warden assisted but he's a fucking queer, so that put me right off from the start. Anyway, this housing project is a new build, and only half the units have been sold or let, about twenty in total, but they've all been sold to people like my mum, her age group you know?"

Spider nodded, but as Oz was staring at the house he didn't notice. Not that it mattered, he continued with the story as if Spider was an appreciative audience.

"Cept for one. One guy moved in who's fifty, just turned fifty, as if he was waiting for the fucking opportunity. Can you fucking believe it?"

Spider turned slowly and looked at the huge man, who was shaking his head in disgust.

"But he's fifty," Spider ventured. "Didn't you say the housing project was aimed at those aged fifty and over?"

Oz snorted in disgust. "Yeah they say that, but who the fuck moves into a warden assisted flat at that age? There's nothing fucking wrong with him, not physically anyway as far as I can see."

"You think he has an ulterior motive?"

Oz shrugged his huge shoulders. "It's gotta make you wonder."

"But what would it be?"

261

"How should I fucking know," Oz snapped. "Guy moves into a warden assisted flat at fifty, what's that all about?"

Spider had no idea what any of it was about. He wasn't sure if Oz had that much of an idea, but he wasn't about to argue the toss with a man who outweighed him by about eight stone and had a good seven inches on him in height.

"How do you know Skein?" he asked.

Oz turned now and looked Spider up and down as if seeing him for the first time.

"You've never worked with him before?"

"I've never worked with anybody before."

It was a stab at levity that fell a little flat. Oz arched his eyebrows, perhaps contemplating if Spider was taking the piss, then he smiled.

"Okay, you'll like this story."

Spider doubted that. If the tale of the interloper who dared to infiltrate an old folks home, for apparently unexplained motives, was an indication of Oz's ambiguous storytelling, he doubted that the story of how he met the psychotic hitman Murray had warned him about would prove more entertaining.

He was to be proved wrong.

"See this," Oz said, spreading his hand and showing Spider the tattoos on his fingers.

"West Ham," Spider said.

"Damn right. Inter City Firm. I was never a top boy, but I met a few in my day. Carlton Leach, Cass Pennant."

"Skein was in the ICF?"

Oz laughed. "Fuck no, you seen the size of him? Skinny little runt; top boys would never let him run with them. Glory days they were, Spider. Millwall away was a fucking blast. I was eighteen when I first met Skein, he was about the same age, maybe sixteen or seventeen. He walked into our pub, on our manor, bold as brass. Nobody did that. Place fell silent. Fuck, if they'd been a piano player he would have stopped mid-tune." He laughed at the memory.

He singled me out, cos I was the biggest. A few of the lads shouted him down, they would have given him a kicking there and then for his damn cheek, but I reined them in."

"Why?"

"I was intrigued. I could tell straight off he wasn't a supporter, rival or otherwise and there was no fear in him. It took a lot of bollocks doing what he did so I took him aside and listened to what he had to say. He had a proposal. Oz changed position so that he faced Spider. The van lurched a little as he shifted his bulk. "Skein's uncle had a stall at a market near Charing Cross. He was a butcher; Skein's parents were both dead and he lived and worked with his uncle. Anyhow there was a protection racket going on, Skein wanted it shut down and asked me if I was interested ."

"In what?"

"Taking them out, of course. The racketeers were a small outfit, or so we thought at the time. Skein had watched them for weeks. The grunt who took the money was just muscle, his name was Blu Jarvis, always accompanied by a dumber sidekick. Their boss was a guy called James Nelson, in his sixties, soft, taking his position for granted because nobody ever challenged him. Skein just wanted the heavies out of the way. He offered me three grand. I could divvy it up any way I wanted with however many guys I think I needed. So I got three lads who were up for a tussle, and we kicked the shit out of the two grunts and took the takings from the market. I kept fifteen hundred for myself and I paid the other boys five hundred each."

"The takings from the market was three grand?" Spider asked.

"Nah, nearer five," Oz admitted.

Spider shook his head. "I don't get it, why didn't..."

"Why didn't we keep the whole five k for ourselves?"

"Yes."

Oz smiled, but he considered his answer for a few seconds. "Because the deal had been for three thousand. I know that Skein was little more than a kid, but there was something about him. You know I told you earlier that I was never a top boy with the ICF?"

Spider nodded.

"That was through choice. I could have been, I was approached on several occasions, but I didn't want the responsibility. I just enjoyed kicking a few heads in on a Saturday afternoon. There was politics involved, Spider, I didn't want a part of that."

"Leaders and followers," Spider said.

"Yeah, exactly. Skein was a natural leader, and I know that if I'd fucked him over he would have hired tougher guys than me to get back at us. Besides, if I took only what I had been promised then there would be more paydays to follow. I wasn't wrong. Nearly forty years later I still get a call now and again. That's trust. It goes a long way."

"What happened to James Nelson?"

The big man shrugged. "Skein killed him, no doubt about that." Oz spoke as if reminiscing about a wayward childhood prank. "He was found in his health spa three days later. He had drowned"

"Could have been an accident. People do drown."

"Yeah," Oz laughed. "In the middle of the ocean or caught in the rapids of a raging river, but not in a fucking jaccuzi. Skein killed him."

Spider considered this for a while. He was a petty thief by trade, but he relied on being privy to information about nefarious activities. He was not a grass, but information gleaned could be information passed on, providing he didn't step on too many influential toes. He was surprised that Skein had never cropped up on his radar before, especially when he considered the man's almost brazen bravado.

"Sounds like gangland retribution," he said. "You told me earlier that Nelson's operation was small, or so you thought at the time, but I gather that was not the case, could have been somebody higher up the tree, taking Nelson out for fucking up after Skein and your boys took the protection money from the market."

Oz shook his head. "Nah it was Skein, no doubt about it. He's always been one to tie up the loose ends."

"You're making a seventeen year old kid sound like Al Capone."

"You ever met Skein before today?" Oz asked.

Spider shook his head and Oz didn't elaborate.

"Of course we all thought we were hot shit for a week or so after the robbery, as if we'd achieved some huge fucking takeover just by giving a couple of brusiers a bit of a slap. We were fucking wrong. As soon as Jarvis got over the humiliation of taking a kicking, he turned up at the market two weeks later with twenty blokes. They trashed every fucking stall, razed a few to the ground. The market foreman was found face down in Camden Lock. Jarvis wasn't calling the shots, but he was certainly carrying out orders." Oz shrugged his huge shoulders. "Coincidence? I dunno, but we all shifted out pretty sharpish. All of us except Skein, of course. Skein stayed and watched, made a few moves. He wasn't a suspect; fuck he was a seventeen year old kid. Balls of steel, Spider, I'm telling you... Hey who's this?

Spider looked out of the window as a car pulled up over the road. He focused his attention on the three people getting out of the car and heading up the long driveway of the house belonging to the Beech family: One guy and two girls. Oz was already on the phone, speaking hurriedly. As the group of three disappeared behind a row of conifers flanking the driveway, Oz hung up. "We're to wait until Skein and the other boys get here, ten minutes."

Spider nodded.

He was not sure that he was cut out for this shit.

CHAPTER 43

Jazz didn't love her fiance. Despite the fact that they were getting married, she had come to the conclusion that she simply didn't like him. In fact she probably hated him. It had never been her intention to jilt him at the altar, she would tell him before that, perhaps tomorrow, maybe later today. She was unsure how he would react. His pride would be wounded, for sure, but Ricky Mayes was too stupid to feel strong emotions. He was attractive in a grungy kind of way. He was stocky and dark, with an unkempt beard, that would look so much better if it was trimmed and tidied. Ricky would go up to a week without shaving, until he resembled a homeless, apathetic punk. He was a good fuck, but lately he hadn't been able to get hard as he was either stoned or pissed. Jazz still had a tough girl image, she liked bad boys and that was something she was trying to maintain, especially after the humiliation of the incident in the karaoke bar, but she had noticed the changes. Friends would stop talking when she entered a room, and they did not appear so awed by her presence. Jazz knew that part of this was down to paranoia, but the biggest change had been her relationship with Pinto. She wasn't one hundred percent sure, but she reckoned her best friend somehow blamed Jazz for the beatings dished out at the karaoke bar.

Although convinced that the bitch had broken her nose, Jazz was relieved to find that it was no more than a little swollen the following day, though it was tender and she could hardly touch it. Pinto however had fared worse. The elbow to her face had spit her lip and although her own nose also hadn't been broken, there was a deep gash across the bridge and she sported two black eyes. Of course Pinto hadn't come out and said that it had all been Jazz's fault, but she was cold, almost aloof in her presence. Jazz had cajoled and humoured her friend to no avail. She had lost Pinto on some level and although she had come close to issuing threats, she somehow thought they would have no real effect. Her aura of invincibility had been punctured, the desertion of her once loyal troops was testament to this fact.

But now she had tracked down the girl who had been the catalyst of her fall from grace. She seethed with hatred, and that one emotion was enough to fuel her anger and restore a little of her shattered pride. Pinto had come, but she appeared to agree to accompany her simply out of curiosity as opposed to wanting to wreak a terrible revenge. Jazz turned and grinned at Pinto now, as they saw their prey cornered. Pinto didn't smile back. The swelling around her eyes had receded and the bruises were yellowing, replacing the angry, ugly black panda eyes from earlier. Jazz may have hated Ricky, but he was a big guy, and she was intrigued to see how this would play out. Try and see the bitch punch her way out of this scenario.

Ricky had pissed himself laughing when she told him about the incident at the bar, and that had angered Jazz more than anything she could remember. They had never considered each other's feelings; it was a relationship composed of a mutual desire to satisfy each other's needs, a singular, selfish, linear partnership that had worked for a while, but could hardly sustain a long term commitment. Jazz realised that now and she thought Ricky must surely see that the relationship was doomed also; but, such was his ignorance, that he semed content to stumble blindly forward, occasionaly fucking her like a rutting stag, and accepting marriage as if it was an inevitable progression, in which nothing was expected to change, and his downward spiral into drug and alcohol dependencey was a decline that, not only was his new wife to expect, but actively encourage.

Fuck that.

It hadn't been difficult finding the profiles on facebook. Carly Beech wasn't on there, but Kat Webber was and from there they had found out where the girls worked and more importantly where they lived. They watched Carly leave earlier that morning and then moved in. Their plan to locate Gemma had been similar to the Cooper brothers own, both fuelled by revenge.

Jazz watched the girl now. She stood by the window, her arms folded over her chest. If she was scared, she didn't show it. Their eyes met across the room and neither seemed to be willing to be the first to drop their gaze. A sudden exclamation from Ricky made Jazz instinctively turn towards him. She cursed him silently and was certain that a faint, knowing smirk danced on the girl's lips for an instant.

"Look at this fucking cash!" Ricky squealed excitedly. His voice always rose in pitch when he grew excited. When he was high and playing *Call of Duty* on an endless loop, Jazz was convinced that only dogs were able to hear him.

"Holy fucking Jesus, you have any idea what I can do with that!"

And there it was, a single sentence that dispelled any doubt that Jazz was making the right decision about finishing their relationship. Ricky's immediate reaction on seeing the cash, was not how it would affect a future with himself and his bride to be, but how it would benefit himself, the selfish cunt! Knowing him as well as she did, Jazz believed he would piss it up the wall and roll it up and smoke it. Within six months the money would be gone.

That could provide a deposit on a flat, Jazz thought, but Ricky had not even contemplated that particular scenario.

"You won't be doing anything with it, pond life," the girl said, without a tremor in her voice and they all turned and stared at her.

"Fuck you say, bitch?" Ricky said. He strode over to the girl and roughly grabbed her face, pulling her cheeks in tight. She slapped his hand away with surprising force and Ricky punched her then, hard in the stomach. The girl doubled over and fell to her knees, and suddenly Jazz knew this was going to work. Ricky was a prick, but today he was her knight in shining armour.

Pinto knew this was wrong. She had agreed to accompany Jazz because she had felt a surge of anger at the girl who had beat the shit out of them both, but something didn't feel right. Her relationship with Jazz had suffered after Saturday night, the problem for Pinto was that Jazz didn't see it. She still swaggered and lorded over the others as if nothing had happened, as if she hadn't had the wind knocked out of her sails. Pinto had put the other girls right, told them what *had* happened, and there was a sniff of rebellion almost immediately. Pinto didn't want to take over. The girl had humiliated her, and she realised that she wasn't quite so tough after all. She had been humbled and for the first time in years she welcomed the humility. That night as she lay awake in bed, her lip throbbing and her nose clogged and tender she thought about Victoria, the spotty girl who had been her friend through primary and junior school. She found herself wondering what Victoria was doing now, how she would react if Pinto contacted her on Twitter or Facebook.

They had laughed and played together as kids, but Pinto found that the only lasting memory was the look of utter despair on Victoria's face when she discovered that her childhood friend had become her tormentor. She had giggled nervously as if Pinto had obviously been joking, and had laid a hand upon her shoulder. Pinto had brushed it away and spat at her. Jazz had laughed . Victoria withdrew then and endured the torments with dreaded acceptance.

She glanced at the money on the table.

There had to be tens of thousands of pounds there. Who had that much cash lying around?

Who was this girl who showed no fear, and what was her connection to the people with that much cash? Suddenly she was scared.

"Ricky, Jazz let's get out of here," she said quietly.

Ricky was still standing over Gemma, his balled fists hanging limply at his sides. He turned slowly to face her.

"What?" he said, his eyes flicking from her to the money on the table.

"We need to get out of here," Pinto repeated.

Jazz had removed her jacket and was hovering near the girl. She didn't turn around.

"What are you talking about, Pinto?" Ricky said, his eyes still on the cash.

"Just fucking look at me, Jazz" Pinto shouted, and Ricky flinched as if he'd been slapped. Jazz paused and slowly turned around to face her friend.

" We can't take this money, we need to get out of here," Pinto said.

Ricky just stared at her, a perplexed smile on his lips. He threw a quick glance at Jazz who continued to glare at Pinto.

"You may not want the money, bitch, but I'm taking it," Ricky said, striding over to the table and grabbing a handful of notes and stuffing them in his pockets.

"You fucking, stupid, moron," Pinto said quietly. "How can you be so dumb?"

Now she did have his attention. The blank, childish mask of confusion slipped from his face, replaced by one of anger and humiliation.

"Who the fuck do you think you're talking to?" he spat angrily, the fists instinctively balled up once more.

Pinto smiled sympathetically. As Jazz's best friend she had known her moronic fiance for just as long and had weathered his anger on so many occasions. Despite his swagger and threatening demeanour, Ricky was not a tough guy. Oh he could hold his own, but he was more at home in a gang, reliant on those who blundered in without reason or apparent fear. Ricky would inevitably be in the second rank, wading in after the psychotic charge of the frontrunners had already done the damage. Kicking somebody when they were down was so much easier than putting the person down in the first place. Pinto didn't blame him. Estate life was tough, and there were constant expectations. Still, Pinto recognised Ricky's bluff and bluster for what it was, and sure enough, after a few seconds of posturing, he smiled and then shrugged.

"I can't leave it," he said. "I just can't."

"We're out of our depth here, Jazz," Pinto said, hoping that her friend would see the sense of what she was saying. Ricky was consumed by greed and could no more give up the money than stop taking food for sustenance.

"Think about it, just for one minute, Jazzy. Who the hell has this much cash lying about on a coffee table? Dealers? Pimps? Christ, not the guys we know. This is more money than they could make in a year. This is serious fucking shit, and I don't want to be hanging around here when they turn up, or have them looking for us if we take it. I'm going."

"You going soft on me, P?" Jazz said menacingly. She took a step towards her and Pinto was suddenly angry. If it came down to it, she'd fight her. She stood her ground defiantly, and Jazz paused momentarily.

"You're not going anywhere," a softly spoken man's voice replied.

They all span round as a thin, immaculately dressed man stepped into the room, accompanied by three huge guys and a scruffy little runt who seemed to be hiding at the back.

The thin man turned to the runt and smiled. "Which one, Spider?" he asked.

The scruffy man stepped from behind the bodyguard barricade and pointed at Gemma.

Then Ricky made a bolt for the door and all hell broke loose.

CHAPTER 44

The journey back to London from Weymouth was fraught and tense. A single question that had hung in the air like an unfounded accusation was the catalyst. It still remained unanswered and Ray glanced at Pippa as she stared out of the car window refusing to look at him..

An hour ago they packed their bags and left the cottage. Ray hoisted his own suitcase into the back of the car as Pippa laid her carrier bag on the footwell at her feet, the new red dress, carefully folded on top. They had driven for only ten minutes when Ray had to ask her.

"So did you think I'd killed Trixie at first?"

"What?"

"When you arrived back at the cottage with the police there and realised what had happened. Did you think it was me?"

Pippa shook her head and glanced out of the window.

Ray was immediately annoyed, and he slammed his hands down on the wheel, startling Pippa until she finally glanced over at him.

"Jesus, Ray!"

"Well?"

"I don't want to talk about Trixie right now."

Ray was not prepared to let that go. "Are you going to answer the fucking question?"

"Not when you're in this kind of mood."

"What kind of mood do you expect me to be in? Fuck, I don't believe this!"

Pippa clammed up after that.

She finally turned away from the window, when they passed Southampton on the M3

"Okay, I don't know what I thought. That's the god honest truth Ray." She waited for his reaction, not sure if he was going to explode once more, but the rage seemed to have left him and he nodded thoughtfully. When she realised that he wasn't going to reply, Pippa continued. "We've barely known each other, Ray. When you left the bar after the girl I didn't know what to think, and when I saw the police at the cottage, the detective told me what had happened."

"You thought it was a possibility that I could have done it?"

More than a possibility, she thought, but didn't voice her opinion. "Yes," she replied.

"Okay," Ray said. "I guess I get it."

Pippa wasn't sure that he did. In the short space of time that she had known him, she believed Ray to be a very insecure man, though not openly. In fact he was introverted to the point of being non-commital. He didn't want to discuss the death of his wife and daughter, which was quite understandable, but he was also reluctant to open up about his past, his mother, his time in the army. Pippa realised that by thinking any of these things were important, she was questioning her own commitment issues regarding the relationship. It had been she who had consistantly reiterated the fact that the relationship itself was little more than Ray fucking her and then justly awarding her performances. Okay, so expensive, dresses and dinner in fancy restaurants sure beat the hell out of a doped-up gangster wannabee, pissing on you in a seedy hotel bathroom, but it was still prostitution.

And what the fuck were you expecting? She asked herself.

More, she concluded.

Ray told her about Zoe. She was shocked when she heard how he had tied her up in the boat and as far as Ray knew she was still there.

"She'll be untied by now," Ray said matter-of- factly.

"She could go to the police," Pippa said.

"She won't."

"She might."

"And say what? *I was abducted by a man who was a friend of another guy who I blackmailed by fucking him and sending the video to his wife?* " Ray laughed. "I don't think so. When you called from the station I was at Carol's house. Helena or Zoe if you prefer told me that Lucy, Brian and Carol's daughter, had set up the blackmail."

"Jesus," Pippa whispered. "Why?"

Ray shrugged, "Don't know, she didn't tell me?"

"You spoke with her?" Pippa said, astonished.

"Yep. Cold bitch; didn't seem to care if her mum knew, or what my plans were. I reckon if Brian had paid the blackmail demand, she would still have sent the video to Carol." He paused. "I think she knew, Carol I mean. I think she knew that it was Lucy blackmailing Brian."

Pippa shook her head. "But why, Ray? Why would she have bothered to take you on and…"

"No, no, I don't mean initially. I think she found out later. Maybe Lucy told her when she realized that her mother had hired me to look into things, I don't know. Fact is, Carol knows what her daughter did, I'm convinced of it."

"Christ, Ray, this is really bad. What are you going to do?"

"I don't know yet, I really don't."

When they reached the M25, Ray reached across and lay a hand on Pippa's thigh. "I'm sorry," he said. "For shouting earlier."

She nodded. "Okay."

He gave her thigh a gentle squeeze. He looked at her briefly, probably wondering if she would say more. When she didn't, Ray removed his hand and concentrated on the road. The traffic was dense and slow moving, a light persistent drizzle welcomed them as they approached the orbital ring road, filled with impatient truckers and tetchy commuters; heavy trucks and fast vans threw up fine sheets of spray, hampering their progress.

When they reached Pippa's flat, it was dark. Pippa opened the door and Ray waited. He wondered for a moment if she would ask him in. Their relationship was on a knife edge. Then she flashed him that winning smile once again and he relaxed a little.

"Come with me, " she said. "I've got a proposal for you." As he sat on the couch, Ray could hear Pippa rummaging about in her bedroom. He glanced about the tiny room. The couch was threadbare, with worn patches on the cushions and arms. There were a couple of chairs, both mismatched. There was no carpet on the floor, but a large, brightly coloured striped rug covered most of the floor area. There was a small TV and a rather smart but old stereo on a sideboard that was missing a drawer, and a home phone with a red light flashing indicating she had two messages on her answerphone.

Everything was crammed into the space allowed. There was no need for a remote control, even if the old TV had one, Ray thought, for he could simply lean forward and reach the controls from the couch. If the TV had been any bigger, he would have gotten neck strain from having to lean back as far as the couch would allow so that he was able to watch in comfort.

Pippa came back into the room. She was holding some money in her hand and looked down at it sheepishly. Then she regained her composure and held the cash out to Ray who stared at her in utter confusion.

"There's nearly twelve hundred pounds there. I'm not sure how far that will go but I want you to find the man who killed Trixie."

"I don't want your money," Ray said softly. "The police know that Skein killed Trixie, they will…"

"The police don't give a shit about us," Pippa interjected, and Ray was surprised to see her crying. "We exist in a nether world, Ray, police are just onlookers. They'll go through the motions, but what's another dead whore, one less burden on society? She tossed the money at him and he jumped, the notes spilling onto the floor.

"You're a private detective, and I'm a paying client, now are you going to take on my case or what?"

Ray stood up, the rest of the money tumbled to the floor. He reached for Pippa but she folded her arms tightly around her chest. She was suddenly angry and Ray had no idea why.

"Why are you acting like this?" Ray said. "Is it because I got mad in the car?"

Pippa shook her head. She was still crying, but he knew that tears of anger now took precedent. She wiped a sleeve angrily across her face, leaving a mask of mascara.

"I just thought that there was a spark there. Three fucking days we were together, and for those three days I didn't feel like a hooker, I felt like a girl who was admired and who had an opinion, but it was just an empty fantasy. I don't know anything about you, not important stuff, you probably don't want to know anything about me and I understand that. That's how it works, Ray. The register rings, we both post on

277

fake smiles, nod respectfully and leave, a cash transaction completed, both parties satisfied.

"That's not how it is, Pippa," Ray said.

"Isn't it?" We have this bond now do we? You're reluctant to even take on my case now as a legitimate, paying customer because you want to sever all ties. Oh I reckon you had a pretty good time, and I do love the dress, all said." Pippa barked a laugh at this "But it all ends here, Ray, it always was going to, let's not kid ourselves."

"I killed the man who killed my family," Ray said suddenly.

Pippa stopped talking. She blinked rapidly a few times, tears pooling on her lashes. She sat down on one of the chairs as Ray seated himself back on the couch, their feet touched because of the confines of the room, but neither of them drew them back. Ray absently leaned forward and started picking up the money, turning each note around so they were all uniform. He straightened the edges off and then handed the pile back to Pippa who took it from him without speaking.

"You know where I was when I got the call that my wife and daughter had been killed?"

Pippa shook her head.

"In bed with my wife's best friend. We had spent the afternoon fucking. I remember she had her hand on my cock. I was getting hard, and ready to go again when my mobile rang. It was my mother-in-law. She didn't ask me where I was, by then I think she was aware of my adultery, and was beyond caring. *There's been an accident,"* she said. " That's how I found out about it, as cold and direct as if she was telling me the result of a football game. There was blame in her voice, anger and undeniable hurt. But I recall the blame as much as anything. It was as if I had been the drunken bastard that had hit them both and then sped away."

Ray sat back and sighed, recalling memories that had been hidden away for so long that he felt no satisfaction in picking at them now like a festering scab.

"His name was Jeremy Silk, good looking guy, medium build, thirty years old. He mounted the kerb hitting my wife and daughter as they walked hand in hand from the local shops. Witness said that he struck them with such force that Sophia was knocked into a neighbouring garden, clearing a four foot high fence without glancing the top. She was killed instantly. Julia wasn't so lucky. Silk put her in a coma, but she was conscious long enough for us to tell her that her daughter had been killed.

"Hey honey, you want the good news or the bad?!"

They picked Silk up three days later, unapologetic, still high. We buried Sophia a week before Julia died, then we had to go through the whole process again. At my daughter's funeral my mother-in-law slapped me, like the woman who hit the police chief in Jaws. Somebody clapped, I don't know who. When we buried Julia two weeks after Sophia's funeral, Jullia's mother contented herself with screaming accusations - " *Murderer! Adulterer!* Nobody applauded her outburst this time. All the people who were at Sophia's funeral were at Julia's. Perhaps they were too numb to appreciate the encore. Anyway, the best friend didn't show up, and I never fucked her again.

"At his initial hearing, Silk pled guilty, and was charged with causing death by careless driving whilst under the influence of drugs or alcohol." Ray paused and collected his thoughts. Pippa didn't say anything.

"I was sitting in the public gallery when the case came to trial. It was the smirk and the victory salute Silk gave as he made his way to the witness box, to a friend sitting only two seats from me that pushed me over the edge. I just lost it and leaped from the gallery across the courtroom. There were two cops escorting Silk. The first one was fat and I just bowled straight into him and knocked him over like a skittle, The second cop was reaching for a can of mace on his belt, but I grabbed his wrist, twisted and turned so that I had his arm in the classic arm break position and then pushed him over too. I got to Silk; could have snapped his scrawny neck there and then, but I didn't. Seeing the look of terror on his face was enough at that moment. So I turned from him and slowly made my way back to the public gallery.

Pippa nodded. "I remember reading something about this. Oh my god, that was you? Didn't the judge get pissed?"

Ray smiled. "You bet. He slapped me with a twenty-eight day prison term for contempt of court and advised me that I should consider myself fortunate that I wasn't also charged with assaulting a police officer."

"Did you do the time?" Pippa asked. She was leaning forward in her chair now regarding Ray with a mixture of pity and awe.

"Yes I did. The press had a field day, running features highlighting the absurdity of a custodial sentence, citing me as a war hero, which I wasn't, who had been pushed to the limit by a sneering scumbag who had savagely killed my wife and daughter and showed no remorse whatsoever. But the judge was unrepentant. And rightly so I guess."

Ray stood up and so did Pippa at the same time. She stepped up to him on tip toe and kissed him hard. Ray encircled her waist and drew her closer to him. When they finished the kiss he grinned at her.

"I guess I'm forgiven," he said.

"For now."

"Don't you want to hear what happened to Silk?"

Pippa shook her head. "Not yet. I want you to make love to me."

She led him to the bedroom.

Later as they lay in bed together, Pippa said, "So tell me, what happened to Silk."

"Sebastian Green is what happened," Ray said.

CHAPTER 45

When Ray had been on leave from the army six years ago he had saved a young man's life.

His name was Barratt Green and he was nineteen.

Ray had been out with friends, in a pub just off Leicester Square. Ray spotted Barratt as he entered the pub with two friends, one male, one female. The girl was drunk, and Barratt and his male companion were supporting her. The pub was busy and loud. Ray was with three of his buddies, none of them army. When he was on leave it was the only chance they had to catch up. All four men turned to watch Barratt and his two companions as they stumbled into seated drinkers and diners on their precarious trek towards the bar. The bouncers quickly interceded, but instead of showing Barratt and his two companions the door, they actively escorted them towards the bar, glaring at any customers who dared to complain.

Interesting, Ray surmised, but once he had lost sight of the trio he returned his attention to his own mates.

Twenty minutes later, a woman screamed and there was a surge of movement at the bar. A nearby table was overturned and people spilled about it as if it's upended state suddenly rendered it a tripping hazard. Customers hurried towards the exit, hampering the bouncers attempts to get to the disturbance at the bar. Ray saw the drunk girl pitch backwards and fall onto the floor. Barratt stumbled away from the bar, his hands on his head as if defending himself from an airborne attack, his male companion staggered after him, his face covered in blood.

The crowd at the bar parted and revealed a leather jacketed man in his early fifties. He was a huge guy with a plaited beard like a Viking warlord. The jacket sleeves were cut off high at the shoulders, the frayed edges fringing skull and dagger tattoos that winked and pointed accordingly as his huge biceps were flexed. He brandished a switchblade, gripped so that the blade pointed downwards as if he was determined to deal a definitive, penetrative stab as opposed to a slice or a cut.

The crowd surrounding the bar was frantic with panic now. The Viking was howling like a wolf, grabbing at those near to him, the knife still poised high at shoulder length. He spotted Barratt and lunged for the young man. Barratt's colleague was in no fit state to defend his friend, and as The Viking's arm encircled Barratt's neck, Ray leaped forward.

He caught The Viking's arm as it was completing its deadly arc towards it's victim. The knife was only inches from Barratt's chest when Ray halted it's advance. The Viking rounded on Ray, his face a mask of rage and surprise. Catching the big man momentarily off guard, Ray butted him full in the face, feeling the man's nose crunch under the force. Under normal circumstances a victim would have crumbled after receiving such a powerful blow from a large man like Ray, and although The Viking staggered he neither dropped

282

the knife or relinquished his hold on Barratt, who was now clawing at The Viking's arm as the huge man cut off his air supply.

Levering his body forward Ray pushed with all his strength against The Viking's arm, managing to slam the back of the hand down on the bar. The Viking grunted, but still held onto the weapon. When Ray attempted to smash the hand back onto the bar a second time, there was fierce resistance, and he moved it barely an inch as the huge man pushed back against Ray with apparent ease. The Viking grinned revealing bloodied teeth. There was a neat, deep gash across the bridge of his nose, and blood stained his grey flecked beard.

Ray still had an advantage though, as The Viking held the knife in one hand whilst the other was occupied in holding onto his hapless victim. Ray took a step back and lashed out with his boot, catching The Viking hard on the knee. It is an effective, quick disabling move. Ray's boot caught The Viking square on the right knee, bending the leg back. The reaction was immediate. The Viking screamed in agony and fell to the floor, landing on his good knee. The knife dropped from his hand, and his deadly choke hold on Barratt was relinquished. The young man pitched forward, clutching at his throat and drawing in huge lungfuls of air.

Ray brought his knee up swiftly, hitting The Viking full in the face and the fight was finished.

The panicked pub goers, quickly realising that the immediate danger was over, watched in awe as the bouncers, better late than never, piled on top of The Viking. It took four of them to drag him away from the bar.

Once he had regained his composure, Barratt had been unable to express his gratitude enough. He had sustained a cut above the right eye and he had been lucky not to lose it, Ray learned later.

"My dad wants to meet you, will you come?" Barratt asked Ray, once the excitement at the bar died down.

"What for?" Ray asked.

"You saved my life, he wants to thank you personally."

Barratt seemed to have forgotten about his companions, as he whisked a bemused Ray out of the bar towards a waiting BMW, the tinted windows obscuring the driver. Ray's friends declined Barratt's half-hearted invitation, but insisted that Ray go with the young man. They were as keen as Ray to see how this story panned out.

Once they settled in the rear of the car, Barratt said to the driver. "The club, Marco." and the car sped off.

"Jesus, I've never seen anybody fight like that, man!" Barratt enthused. "God you got some moves."

Ray was surprised by the young man's euphoria. He accepted that it was adrenaline, but Barratt had nearly died, and yet he seemed to have forgotten about this unnerving chapter of his life as if the assault had been no more than a push and tumble resulting in grazed palms.

"Who was that crazy bastard?" he asked. "He was going to kill you."

Barratt shrugged. "No idea. Nicky said something about his beard and the guy just went fucking schizo. Why would they let somebody like that in a trendy West End bar, seriously, did you see a Harley outside, or what?"

Barratt spoke with an undisguised feminine manner. As he rattled on like a speeding locomotive, Ray found himself warming to the carefree, relaxed manner of the young man. He quickly learned that Barratt's father was a businessman, very wealthy, but Barratt was unsure exactly what it was that he did. "Inherited wealth, initially," Barratt said cryptically, leaving Ray to make of that what he would. Nicky was Barratt's current beau,

"Bit of a sycophant, but aren't they all once they discover Daddy's a billionaire."

He told Ray they picked the girl up outside The Comedy Store a few hours earlier. "Nicky swings both ways, and she was a peach, but such a lightweight."

"They knew you in the pub," Ray said. "I saw the bouncers giving you free reign when you walked in, normally you'd have been out on your ear."

Barratt laughed. "Sure. They're okay, they all know Pop. I'm not a bad boy, Ray, but I'm nineteen and fucking minted, it's almost obligatory to misbehave. The car stopped and Barratt glanced out the window. "We're here," he said.

"Here?"

"Dad's club." Barratt opened the car door and stepped out onto the path. Ray slid across the seat and joined him. He glanced up at the formidable building in front of him. There was no name, but that didn't surprise him; exclusivity and anonymity usually went hand in hand.

"It's called Cody's," Barratt said. "Very exclusive, but this is Park Lane. "Well this is where I must leave you. Thank you again Ray, you literally saved my life, but that doesn't have to interrupt my evening does it? People are saving lives all the time."

"You're not coming in?" Ray asked, confused.

Barratt shook his head, he was already opening the rear door of the BMW. "Not a member I'm afraid. No women, and I'm sure they would frown on queers, besides Pop wants to talk to you, and he hates it when I'm there to interrupt."

Ray frowned, not entirely sure if Barratt was joking or not "He knows I'm coming?"

"Of course, why wouldn't he? You saved his only son's life." Barratt twirled his fingers at Ray, closed the BMW's rear door and the car sped away, leaving a bemused Ray standing on the kerb. He walked up to the club entrance and pressed a bell on the side. He was expecting a sliding panel to suddenly open in the large oak entrance door, or a telescopic zoom lens to snake it's way forward, distorting his reflected image for somebody to scrutinise on a screen deep within the bowels of the building.

He was surprised therefore when the door swung open to reveal a stunning woman in her early twenties dressed in an immaculate tight, black trouser suit. A name tag on the lapel of her jacket said: Chloe. It did not say what her position was.

Chloe smiled politely. "Ray?" she said.

Ray was confused. "Yes, how would you know that?"

"Mister Green is expecting you," she replied, ignoring his inquiry. "Would you follow me please." She stepped backwards and spread out her hand allowing Ray to enter the lobby.

"Do you work for Mister Green?" Ray asked as Chloe closed the door and then took up a position in front of Ray so that he was following her.

"No," she replied. Either she was a poor conversationalist or not inclined to indulge in small talk. Ray surmised it was the latter, so decided to dispense with the chit chat.

Chloe escorted Ray through the lobby and into the main lounge of the club. A few men, most attired in expensive business suits, were drinking or chatting amiably. They paid no heed to Ray, although Chloe got more than a few casual glances. She ignored them all and kept her gaze directed straight ahead.

Cody's housed a few select private chambers where members could conduct business or relax in total privacy. A huge guy, dressed as somberley as the businessmen in the lounge stood outside one of the private rooms now. As Chloe approached he opened the door and gestured to them to step inside. Chloe, her escort duties finished, simply turned on her heel and left. Ray stepped into the room, and the huge guy shut the door silently behind him.

Sebastian Green was a slight man, with greying salt and pepper hair, cut short and a neatly trimmed goatee. Ray estimated his age to be in the early to mid-sixties. Surprisingly he was dressed down in jeans and a Jeff Banks sweatshirt. He observed Ray's look of puzzlement and laughed.

"It is one of the attributes of wealth, Mister Jessop. An attribute that defies convention, but still sidesteps scorn because of the status of the individual." Sebastian Green's voice was quite high, but there was no self-congratulatory tone about the statement, simply an astute observation.

"Please sit," Sebastian said, waving a hand towards a high-back, studded leather chair. "Would you care for a cognac?"

Ray glanced about the room. There was a second leather chair opposite the one Sebastian had indicated. Between them was a small mahogany table with exquisitely turned legs, on which sat a crystal decanter and two brandy balloons.There was a high bookcase on the far wall, lined with pristine volumes that looked as if they had never been taken down from the shelves, let alone read. The decor was exactly how Ray had imagined the interior of an exclusive club to appear.

"I'm not really one for spirits, Mister Green" Ray admitted.

"Please call me Sebastian. May I call you Ray?"

"Sure."

Sebastian poured two generous measures of brandy into the balloons and handed one to Ray.

"Trust me, Ray," he laughed. "If you baulk or splutter then I'll personally fetch you a beer from the bar. It will be frowned upon, certainly, but as you have already discovered, I am a man who purposely defies convention."

Ray took a tentative sip. He neither baulked or sputtered. It was superb, smooth without a hint of throat burn.

"Wow!" He said.

Sebastian Green laughed. "Wow indeed." He sat in the seat opposite Ray and studied him over the rim of his glass.

"You're very well informed," Ray said. He glanced at his watch. "Only thirty-five minutes have passed since I left the bar with your son, yet you appear to know about what happened and you know my name."

"I have my people follow my son, Ray. He seems to attract trouble wherever he parties, but tonight was not his fault. My people keep tabs on him but their low profile often hinders their actions. The crowds at the pub prevented them from getting to the bar before Callum had pulled the knife. Luckily you were there to intercept. I have not yet thanked you yet. How remiss of me. I really am truly grateful, Raymond, truly."

"That's okay, " Ray replied lamely. He had never handled appreciation well even when it was well intended and genuine. "I take it Callum was The Viking?"

Sebastian laughed again and took another swallow of his brandy, smacking his lips.

"A most apt description," he said. "Callum Hearst. He worked for me, felt that he was treated unfairly and decided to act recklessly by taking out his frustration on my boy."

"What was his job?" Ray asked.

A flicker of unease danced briefly on Sebastian Green's features, but it was fleeting and replaced quickly by the ready smile.

"It's not relevant, Raymond," Sebastain said and was quiet for a few seconds, swirling the cognac in his glass and staring at it. "Suffice to say that whatever Barratt told you what it was that set Callum off it was not my son's doing."

"He told me it was because his friend made a derisive comment about his beard."

Sebastian shook his head. "Hmm. Well it was not because of that. Did Barrat also tell you that he was not a member of this club because of his homosexuality?"

"Yes."

"Again, not true. This is the twenty-first century, Raymond, people don't really give a stuff about queers now. They are more prone to ostracise you for being a meat eater or member of a right wing political party."

"Or a woman?"

Sebastian Green shrugged. "Well yes, the gentlemen's club has never really been a bastion of sexual equality."

"Blustering major's with puffed up cheeks and monocles?" Ray said, taking another sip of his brandy.

Sebastian laughed. "Well quite, but even the young executive or the whizz kid financier is still bound to uphold the rules. Tradition is a fickle mistress, Raymond. You can condemn an organisation's jingoistic overtones, but once you become a member you embrace them as God's given law, believe me. Everybody criticises the gang they are not a part

289

of until the day comes when they are. Would you care for another cognac?"

Ray shook his head. "No thanks. So what happens with Callum the Viking now?"

Sebastian shook his head, momentarily perplexed. "What do you mean?"

"Are you going to punish him?"

"Personally? Dear god, my boy, I'm a respectable businessman, not an East End gangster. Callum Hearst will be handed over to the police and charged with attempted murder, I assume. It is up to them what to do with him. All I can say is that people in prison sometimes have accidents."

CHAPTER 46

Pippa got out of bed and shivered. She rummaged about in some drawers and took out see-through knickers and a bra. She dressed quickly, rubbing her hands together and performing a hopping jig with her bare feet on the cold bare floorboards.

Ray leaned across the bed and grabbed for her, but she skipped out of his reach and giggled. "Stop it," she said. "I've got to go to work."

"Work?" he replied.

"Yes, dummy. I've had a great few days, but I've got bills to pay, besides I can't go breaking engagements. You get that kind of reputation and you can kiss your steady work goodbye."

"About the money for the investigation?" Ray said.

"Stop it, Ray. I want you to find out whatever you can, and you're not going to do it for free," Pippa said, pulling on a miniscule leather mini skirt and a halter top, tied loosely at the waist.

"I don't expect to work for free, but I also have a proposal."

Pippa turned to him now. "What?"

"Work with me," Ray said. "You know the people and the area Trixie was from, you know we make a good team."

Pippa smiled wanly, not convinced by the idealistic sentimentality. "So what's in it for you?"

Ray shrugged. "I get to spend a few more days with you."

"Hmm. Tell me the rest of the story about Sebastian Green and Silk while I get ready.

Ray propped up the pillows behind him and made himself comfortable.

"Sebastian Green offered me a job. Well first he offered to buy me a new watch. He had noted my old Sekonda and said he would get me a Rolex. He would have done so too."

Pippa shrugged. "So what, he could have afforded it and you saved his son's life."

"I didn't want a Rolex, have never wanted one."

Pippa took a long, red vinyl coat down from a hook on the back of the door and buttoned it up. She gave Ray a twirl. "What do you think?" she asked.

"No wonder you're always so cold if that's all you have to wear."

Pippa laughed. "It's June, Ray. Besides, you can't expect me to turn up in a chunky sweater and thermal leggings at any time of the year. She glanced at the clock. "Shit I gotta go. I'll be about two hours. I think there's a couple of beers in the fridge." She blew him a kiss and was out the door. Ray got out of bed and walked to the window. He watched her skip down the steps. She must have known that he would be watching her, as she turned on her heel and blew him another kiss. Ray waved back.

CHAPTER 47

"I'm happy with my watch, Sebastian," Ray told him. "I know you want to reward me, but it doesn't matter. I helped your son because I was able to, and the job offer is appreciated, but I'm signed up for another two years, and then?" he shrugged. "Who knows."

"I'm a wealthy man, Raymond, " Sebastian said, setting his empty glass down on the table and standing up. "I don't wish to offend you but lavish gifts are what I can offer. Maybe it's a crude way of showing my appreciation for what you have done, but what am I to do?"

Ray smiled. "You could get me Chloe's number?"

"I could, but it would do you no good. You're not her type."

"Wrong physique?"

"Wrong sex."

"Ah."

Ray stood up and Sebastian Green laid a hand on his shoulder. He reached into his jeans pocket and took out a silver card case. He opened it and took out a card with just his name and number on it.

"This is my private number, Raymond, I give it to very few people. You ever need me, and don't think that you won't, you call me. If anybody else answers you hang up. You understand me?"

Ray nodded, but he wasn't sure that he did. As Sebastian thanked him again and led him to the exit, he pocketed the card thinking he would never call the number printed on it.

Two years later, the day after he was released from jail he rang it.

A woman's voice said, "Hello."

Ray hung up and stared at the card. He checked the number but he knew that he had punched it in right. He was debating whether or not to redial when the phone rang in his hand.

He answered it and a man's croaky voice, barely a whisper, said, "Who is this?"

"Sebastian?" Ray said hesitatingly.

There was a series of very heavy, raspy breaths on the end of the line, then the whisper once again. "Raymond, how have you been?"

Sebastian Green's idyllic country retreat was a ten bedroom detached mansion set in thirty acres of idyllic parkland in the heart of Surrey. As Ray pulled up on the front drive, with enough space to park three buses, he was amazed that one man could accumulate such individual wealth. He was greeted at the door by a nurse. She was a tall, rangy woman in her early forties. She scowled at Ray, offering him no more than a cursory glance. She told Ray that she was employed through an agency, though Ray had not volunteered any of this information. She had an air of superiority about her, that she felt obliged to share with him. She told him that Mister Green loathed doctors and hospitals, they were forever advising him to decrease his alcohol levels, and although he knew they were right, it was advice he was not about to heed.

As they walked through the hall of the house, Ray noticed that most of the rooms were shut up, furniture sheathed in sheets like spectral sculptures. The nurse stopped and looked Ray up and down as if making a calculated character observation.

"Mister Green told me that you were expected," she said needlessly. Ray didn't say anything, just nodded.

"He is in the downstairs study. It has been temporarily converted. A bed and television." Her tone implied that she disapproved of such improvisation. "He likes to look out onto the garden," she offered as a reason for this madness.

"How is he?" Ray asked as the nurse opened the door to the study.

"Dreadful," the nurse said tactlessly. "He bawls at the younger girls, they don't last much longer than a week. I myself have been here for three," she announced proudly. "He has lung cancer, terminal. He has tried all the early remedies, surgery to remove the cancerous cells, radiotherapy. He declined the chemo, because he knew, Mister Jessop. By then he knew."

"How long does he have?"

"Four, maybe six months."

They entered the study. Most of the furniture had been removed aside from the bed and a small table that was the same height. A huge plasma TV hung precariously on the wall, cables hanging like tentacles, snaking across the floor of the study and into cable boxes and printers that were arranged haphazardly on desks overflowing with paperwork and files.

The man in the bed was not Sebastian Green, Ray thought, it could not possibly be him. It had only been two years since he had first met the vibrant, sprightly man in the Park Lane club. That person bore no resemblance to the wasted, skeletal figure that lay propped up by several pillows.

Sebastian Green was asleep, his breath deep and resonant like a man sucking air through a small tube. The sound was amplified by the stillness of the room. The TV was muted to a business channel, where stock figures ran across the bottom of the screen with such alarming frequency that the eye was unable to keep up with the steady transit of information.

Sebastian appeared wrapped in a shroud. His face was creased and a deathly grey, the eye sockets sunken and red rimmed. His teeth appeared too large for his mouth and there were a few grey wisps of scraggly beard on his chin and cheeks. His once thinning hair was now completely white and lay on the pillows like soft strands of muslin.

"He sleeps a lot now," the nurse said.

"Is that a good thing?" Ray asked.

"When he is asleep he isn't in pain," the nurse said non-committedly.

"Can I wake him?"

The nurse glanced at her watch. "I suppose, if it's important." She hadn't asked Ray who he was or what business he had with her employer and Ray respected her professionalism on that. Her bedside manner needed working on though.

"Will you be sitting with him for a while?" she asked.

Ray nodded. "Yeah. Why don't you get yourself something to eat or drink, I'll shout if I need you.

The nurse nodded and cracked a smile, that appeared more of a grimace.

"Okay, thank-you. Can you see that he takes a few mouthfuls of soup when he wakes." She indicated a small thermos and bowl on the bedside table. "But not too much juice," she added. "The acidity will start one of his coughing fits."

Ray nodded and sat down on a hard-backed chair by the side of the bed.

"It's okay, you can open your eyes now, she's gone," he said.

Sebastian did so and glanced around the room to make certain that Ray was telling the truth.

"That bitch is crazy," Raymond, I'm telling you. He adjusted his position on the pillows. Ray leaned forward to help, but Sebastian waved him away.

"That damned soup. She brings it to me all hours. What am I some toothless half wit that can't chew solids anymore? Because I always leave it, she just lets it stew there in the thermos. Hand me that juice will you."

Ray picked up a small carton of orange juice off the bedside table. Sebastian took a couple of sips then started coughing. After a minute the attack abated and he slumped back onto his pillows, his eyes streaming, his grey features momentarily scarlett.

"I'm so sorry, Sebastian," Ray said.

"Don't be. You hear her say that I only have four to six months, that's optimistic, but what the hell are you going to do? All the money in the world ain't going to put up much of a defence."

Ray nodded. He had no idea what to say to somebody in this position. Condolences seemed premature, and apologies so lacking in empathy. It would be another four years before he had to tread similar, unsteady ground with Brian. But Brian was a former colleague, somebody he knew well. He had only met Sebastian Green on one occasion, although the meeting had come about under extraordinary circumstances.

"So," Sebastian said "You rang the number. I told you never to say never. I take it that this is to do with the scumbag who killed your wife and daughter?"

"It is," Ray replied. The fact that Sebastian Green knew they had been killed did not startle him. The story had been big news. It wasn't surprising that Sebastian was aware of it.

"What happened to Callum Hearst?" Ray asked.

"The Viking?" Sebastian said. "He was convicted and sent to prison."

"Did he die?"

"Yes he did."

"How?"

With a supreme effort Sebastian lifted his arms from the bed in an apathetic shrug before letting them fall once more. "How should I know?"

Ray let it go.

"I wasn't a great family man, Sebastian," Ray said. "I'm not going to pretend that I was. I wasn't abusive, not physically. I never raised a hand to my wife or daughter." He scoffed. "I say that as if it somehow had merit. My career kept me away from them for long stretches at a time, but I'm using that as an excuse. When I was on leave I was rarely at home. I abused the conditions of my marriage. I was an adequate father at best, and a lousy husband full stop. And yet it took the death of my wife and daughter to realise that. But I loved my wife and I loved my little girl, Sebastian and if their killer had shown just a shred of remorse, then maybe I could have let things lie. But he didn't. He wears my family's death like a badge of honour and I simply cannot accept that. He was a user and a dealer, part of a fucked up gang culture. These people do not care how their actions impact others. Every day I see that bastard's grinning face, the bravado, the cocksure arrogance. He fucking killed my wife and daughter and yet he treats their deaths with no more significance than if he had stolen a packet of biscuits. I cannot live with that, Sebastian."

Sebastian Green nodded very slowly. His breath came in short, hurried breaths.

"Then kill him, Raymond," he wheezed. "You don't need me to accomplish that."

"Yes I do."

"Why?"

"Because I'm afraid of getting caught. If I kill Silk when he gets out then all fingers will point at me. This is not the army anymore. I do not have the resources or the machinations to take on the deed. I would be the prime suspect from day one. I would leave trace, forensic evidence. I want the fucker dead more than anything in the world, but I'm not prepared to spend the rest of my life in prison, that isn't an option. You told me that Callum died in prison, Sebastian. He almost killed your boy. If you were able to get at him, then you could get at Silk. This is what I am asking of you, Sebastian. I can't carry on ..."

Sebastian lifted a hand and Ray stopped talking.

"Raymond you are a clever man, astute, but I think that grief may have clouded your judgement. Do you have any idea what is involved in killing a man under these circumstances? We are talking about a contract killing for a start. A hired assassin, not a couple of wide boys with a lack of morals and a piece of lead piping who will take on the job for a few grand. Twenty-five, thirty thousand minimum, my friend. Do you have that kind of money?"

"I can raise it, if needed."

Sebastain chuckled, and that led to another coughing fit. Ray reached for the juice but again Sebastian waved it away. After a few minutes the coughing abated and he slumped back onto the pillow.

"Money is not an issue here, Raymond, it's not about the money. I would gladly subsidise you any amount after what you did for me, but I just want to put things into perspective. You're talking about malice aforethought, premeditated murder, my boy and though you may not be actually delivering the killer blow, you are more than just an accomplice. You have to be aware that by taking another's life, no matter how despicable that individual is, you will have to live with the fact that you killed him.

"I know that."

"Plus you want the hit to go ahead whilst Silk is in prison, where there is no chance of the killing going unnoticed. Therefore, it would have to be somebody who has literally nothing to lose; a lifer with no chance of parole, who would firstly agree to the hit and secondly expect no remuneration personally. He may have a family that could do with a boost to their income, but for him the personal rewards are zilch. Do you see where I'm going with this Raymond?"

Ray nodded. "Of course, but what about Callum?"

"Callum Hearst was a violent psychopath with a string of other offences taken into account when he was charged with attempted murder against my son. He was convicted of armed robbery and a second count of attempted murder also. He was serving a fifteen year stretch when he had his accident. Now Silk, I believe, although callous and unremorseful does not pose a potential threat that The Viking did and I would assume he is languishing, not in high security, but a category C establishment, and you won't find many murderers or armed robbers in such an environment. And I doubt anybody doing a six month stretch for tax avoidance will be looking to take on the job at hand. Wouldn't you agree?"

"Yes," Ray agreed reluctantly.

"So," Sebastian concluded. "It would appear that a hit is totally out of the question. Therefore it would seem we have no other options?"

"Really?"

"Of course. Jeremy Silk will have a serious accident."

Two months after having this conversation with Sebastian Green he was dead. Raymond attended the funeral which was vast and lavish. Barrat had embraced him and cried on his shoulder at the graveside, and Ray was surprisingly touched. As they left the cemetery. Barrat caught up with him.

"It's done," he said, and nodded soberly. It was the first and only time that Ray noted the steely resolve in the young man's face."

"What?" he asked but Barratt simply nodded. "You know what Ray, it's done."

The next day Ray was notified that Jeremy Silk had slipped on a metal stairway on the landing of his cell block and broke his neck. He died instantly. The press called him and asked him if he had anything to say.

Ray told them he had no comment.

CHAPTER 48

Spider knew a guy from years ago; a convicted paedophile named Keith Blodwin.

It was the nature of Spider's business to mix with the most nefarious of characters. Blodwin was not a friend; as far as Spider was aware, Blodwin didn't have any. He had sacrificed that privilege following his conviction. Upon his release, Spider sought him out. Blodwin was wary and suspicious of anybody approaching him, he had served three years, mostly in solitary, and was on the sex offenders register after authorities had discoverd nearly twenty thousand indecent images of children on his laptop. Nobody wanted to associate with Blodwin, including, some might say, particularly, the villains. Paedophilia was a tainted crime, the

300

perpetrators loathed by society, and the criminals who inhabited society's netherworld were the most unforgiving.

Spider had heard that Blodwin may be privy to some information about a robbery at a bookmakers, and a reward being offered by the dodgy owners had piqued his interest. Blodwin's cousin was a regular punter at the bookies, and a suspect, so Spider went fishing for details.

It had been a wasted trip, Blodwin had baulked at the notion that he would grass on a family member, and although Spider had insisted it was not a betrayal, merely an opportunity to share the reward, Blodwin remained indignant.

"Because of what I did," he said, miserably, "I am trusted by nobody. Prison was hell on earth. I made a vow never to do anything that would incriminate anybody."

Spider had made a hasty retreat after Blodwin started to make claims, that *"none of it was my fault."* H e had tried to convince Spider that because he only downloaded the images and was not in any way involved in the physical mistreatment of the kids in the films, he could somehow be exonerated. " *I never touched any of the kids, I only looked, never touched anybody."*

Spider was a petty man himself, and not really a man of high moral standards, but Blodwin had repulsed him.

And yet.

Here he was now, in the back of the van with the missing call girl, and another girl who had become embroiled in the takedown. The third girl at the house had escaped and the boy had been killed.

Skein's goons - Oz and his two monstrous associates, Tonka and Pell, had laid into the boy with such fury that Spider had to turn away. Tonka had poleaxed him with a huge sweeping arm that caught the fleeing youngster high on the forehead. The blow had whipped his head back to such an unnatural angle that Spider was certain that his neck had snapped. Once he was on the floor, Oz stepped back, but the other two kicked him in the ribs, side and head until he stopped trying to defend himself and just lay still. Even then, the larger of the two men, Tonka, contained to stamp on the boy's face, landing devastating blow after blow until his face was a bloody pulp of torn and tattered flesh.

The Mexican girl had screamed, the hooker had stood frozen to the spot, as the thugs finally stepped back and admired their handiwork. Skein did nothing, he just looked on with stoic indifference.

In the melee the third girl had run, sidestepping the fight and bolting for the door. Spider was not certain if Skein could have made a grab for her, but he didn't even try. He simply watched her pass him and didn't even extend an arm in order to impede her escape.

So here was Spider now, unable to look Candy Girl in the eye. Was he to be considered innocent because he had simply watched and not taken part in any of the violence? He thought not. How different was he from the despicable paedophile?

They had bundled their hostages into the van, both girls were in shock and compliant. They drove for about an hour and a half, the thugs in jubilant mood. It had been a good outing for them, administering a good kicking, and picking up thousands of pounds in cash. The dead man was at their feet. They had not bothered to cover him, and the body lolled and rocked on the floor of the van like unbound cargo.

Skein sat in the passenger seat, Oz was at the wheel; occasionally the thin man would turn and offer his alarming smile to Spider, forcing the petty thief to stare back down at the floor once more. Tonka and Pell sat on either side of him, dwarfing his slight frame. The two girls sat opposite, they both had their hands bound behind their backs.

Oz pulled the van off the main road and onto a side road fringed by a dense wood on the left hand side. The van bucked and rocked as the suspension was tested vigorously on the uneven and pot-holed surface. The big men on either side of Spider exaggerated the swaying by sandwiching Spider and then laughing uproariously. The girls sitting opposite, were finding it difficult to keep their seats and almost fell onto the body that danced spasmodically like a landed fish on the deck of a trawler.

Eventually the van pulled to a stop and Oz jumped out. The side doors were opened and Spider, Tonka and Pell got out. The girls were manhandled roughly to the ground. Ricky's lifeless body was dumped unceremoniously by the side of the van.

They were outside a factory on the fringes of an industrial estate. The unit was windowless, and a large roller shutter door took up most of the front of the building. Next to it was a much smaller door. Skein stepped down from the van and stretched. He strode over to the unit and unlocked the small door, then held it open as Oz and the other two thugs pushed the captured group inside.

"Where are we?" Spider asked, bringing up the rear.

"Park Heath industrial estate, on the outskirts of Colchester," Skein said. "A safe house," he added and Spider glanced at him uncertainly. The girls were quickly secured inside, tied to seats and then left. Oz, Tonka and Pell tipped the money that they had taken from the house onto a large bench stood by a cinder block wall.

"Later," Skein said and the three men reluctantly stepped away from the table.

He pointed a long finger at Pinto. "Who are you, what were you doing at the house?"

"You killed Ricky," Pinto cried "You didn't have to do that, surely. We weren't going to take the money, honest ."

"What were you doing there?" Skein asked again patiently.

Pinto looked up and flinched at the smiling cadaverous face. Spider knew how unsettling that image was.

"We came to do her," Pinto said nodding her head at Gemma.

"Why?"

Pinto told him the story of the fight in the karaoke bar. Tonka laughed and pointed at both girls.

"Hey we should let them go at it here, naked. Wow, that would be better than snarling dogs." He nudged Pell in the ribs and was rewarded with a scowl.

Skein's phone rang and he snatched it out of his pocket.

"You've been seen," Charles Cooper said abruptly on the other end of the line. Skein walked away from the group so that he was out of earshot.

"Where?"

"In Weymouth," Charles continued. "CCTV footage of you entering the house with the whore and then leaving alone. I have contacts on the force. Weymouth P.D contacted the MET and I was notified."

Skein shrugged. "Doesn't matter, they won't have my name or my address, and I plan to leave the country tomorrow morning. Already have the flight booked, different name, new face. I'll be away for a few years. Don't sweat it."

Charles laughed and Skein felt a vein throb in his temple. The old man was pushing it here.

"You were grassed up, Skein. The pimp who you beat up. They came looking for him when they found out the girl you killed was one of his. He named you. Said you took her down to Weymouth to find the private investigator who had the photograph of Candy Girl"

Skein was incredulous. "Cole Water's snitched on me? You've got to be fucking kidding?"

"Afraid not. I think you may have to call the airline, see if you can get an overnight flight instead of a morning one."

Skein nodded absently. "Yeah, but first I need to get back to London."

"Whoa, no way. You have to finish down there first. Waters can wait."

"I can't," Skein said and disconnected. He walked back to the group and pointed at Gemma and then Spider.

"Take them into the back room, take their phones."

Spider felt ice race down his spine.

"Mister Skein, what are you talking about?" His mouth was powder dry and the question was a plaintive croak.

Skein smiled, but it was laboured. "Spider, if you ask me another dumb question, no if you actually open your stupid mouth once more I will kill you, do you understand?"

Spider nodded dumbly.

"Good." Skein turned to leave.

"What about her?" Oz asked, nodding his head towards Pinto.

Skein shrugged. "What about her? I have to get back to London, you're running the show til either I get back or Charles Cooper turns up. Got it?"

"Got it," Oz said.

Skein snatched up the keys to the van and hurried out of the factory.

"Now the fun starts," Tonka said, "Pell you take the girl, and the crip, we're going to play some games."

Pell was not comfortable taking orders from somebody he considered a subordinate

"Take her where?" he snapped

"You heard the man," Oz interjected. "One of the back rooms. How the fuck should I know, I've never been here?"

"Neither have I."

"For God's sake use your fucking initiative will you. Find an isolated room and dump them both." He headed for the front door to close it after Skein's hasty departure.

As Tonka fiddled with Gemma's bonds, he grinned, revealing twin rows of dirty, broken teeth. He was shorter than Oz but far more compact. Pell was big, but not huge like Oz or as stocky as Tonka. Pell sighed, as if he believed the whole operation was tiresome.

"When do we get paid?" he asked Oz, who turned, his face registering surprise at being barked at so rudely. Pell did not drop his gaze however, and Oz held up his hands almost apologetically.

"I have absolutely no idea," he said coolly. "That is a matter you will have to take up with Skein."

"Who doesn't happen to be here."

Oz took two steps closer to Pell, who despite his bravado, took a single step backwards.

"Who doesn't happen to be here," Oz repeated. He took out his mobile and held it at arm's length. "Maybe you would like to call him up and request that he stop whatever he deemed was urgent enough that he drop everything else and demand that he return here with your payment immediately."

Pell stared at the phone for a few long seconds then lowered his head and shook it.

"No? I thought not." He turned to Tonka. "You still fucking here?"

"I can't get the knots."

"Fuck's sake," Oz snapped.

Oz pushed him aside and worked on the knots.

"This is fucking wrong, man," Spider said, staring at Oz. "I'm part of the crew."

Oz laughed and clapped Spider on the shoulder. "Oh Spider, you never were, you fucked up spazz."

Tonka was behind Pinto now. He grabbed her breasts in his large hands and squeezed until she cried out in pain.

Spider's head dropped once again. This was not going to end well for that poor girl.

CHAPTER 49

Carly arrived home just under an hour after Gemma's abduction. She was surprised but not particularly unnerved to find the front door unlocked. She walked into the spacious hallway and called out Gemma's name.

There was no answer. The house was silent, unnervingly so in a way that large houses can be when they are unoccupied. Carly turned, closed the front door and locked it. She dumped her shopping bags on the floor and glanced around. The door to her father's study was open. Again no real issue, Gemma had the run of the house, but Carly felt that she wouldn't have really had any cause to go in there.

Unless.

Carly hurried into the study and saw the open safe and her heart sank. She emitted a low sob and sank to her knees. She cried for ten minutes. Never had she felt so utterly betrayed. Once the agony of sadness passed she felt a surge of anger and she embraced it with gusto. She walked over to the safe and slammed the door against the wall. It swung on it's hinges, the edge of the door tearing a huge chunk out of the plaster. Only then did she notice the broken window.

Had she been burgled?

No, that was a ridiculous notion. Gemma knew the combination and Gemma had taken the money and had made a half-assed attempt to make it appear as if somebody had broken in. She chided herself for wanting to believe that she had been burgled, when in her heart she realised the simple fact was that Gemma had stolen the cash and ran.

Shit, how could she have been so stupid?

She hurried out of the study and crossed the hallway into the living room. She snatched the phone up out of the cradle determined to call the police whilst her anger still held onto her emotions with a tenuous grasp.

Then she noticed the blood on the floor. There was a lot of blood.

She stared at the red pools and noticed that they were splattered over a large area of the floor. What was going on?

Carly could understand Gemma wanting to cover her own tracks by creating the burglary as an elaborate charade, but the blood seemed a step too far, and to what end? If it was Gemma's attempt to fabricate an assault, in order for Carly and the police to believe that she had been forced to give up the safes combination, then where was she? A fabricated abduction seemed wholly unnecessary. If it was Gemma's blood and for the life of her Carly couldn't think of anybody else it could belong to, then it was too much. Gemma would be dead after such a huge loss.

A seed of doubt entered her mind, and Carly embraced it, allowing it to disperse the anger like an evaporating mist.

She turned to the phone again but did not call the police, this time she punched in another number. She held the phone to her ear and waited for it to be picked up. She couldn't take her eyes off the blood. So much.

Her father answered. He sounded tired.

"Hi, babe."

"Dad we've been robbed!" She blurted out, not sure how he would react and how much of the conversation she would have to improvise.

Suddenly her father sounded wide awake. "What? Carly what are you talking about, what did they take?"

No, I'm fine dad, but thanks for asking, she thought but didn't voice the sentiment.

"The money in the safe," she said.

There was a long pause. She could hear her father breathing heavily on the end of the phone, thousands of miles away.

Eventually he said, "Carly what's going on?"

"What do you mean?"

Another long pause. ""How did they get into the safe?"

"I don't know dad, I just got in and noticed it open. Shall I call the police?"

"No, no police," her father said quickly. "Listen, I can't get away at the moment, there's just no way. I'm going to send Michael back, an overnight flight if I can arrange it."

"I don't want Michael to come back," Carly said. "I can handle it. Why don't you want me to call the police?"

"I have my reasons, Carly. Just wait until Michael gets back then you can run through with him what happened."

"What do you mean?"

She could hear the frustration rising in her father's voice and she had to bite her lip to prevent herself from crying again.

"Somebody didn't just come in and steal the money from the safe, Carly. Nobody knows that combination but family."

"What are you saying, Dad?" the tears were flowing now, but her father chose to ignore them.

"You must have told somebody Carly, who did you tell?"

"Nobody," she wailed. "It could have been you or Michael."

"We're in Cambodia."

Damn it. Cambodia, not Vietnam. Why did she know so little about her father and her brother's business? "Why don't you believe me, Dad?"

"Because I know that you're lying to me, Carly," her father said matter-of- factly.

"There's blood all over the floor," she suddenly cried out.

"What? Carly are you okay?"

"I'm fine dad, thanks for asking,"

"What do you mean about blood all over the floor, Carly? Stop this. Tell me what has happened.

Exasperated and unable to keep up the masquerade, Carly slumped onto the sofa.

"I met somebody, daddy, somebody who I thought was very special, but I think she took the money, I think she took all of it."

"You think?"

"It's the blood, daddy. I think something has gone wrong and she's probably dead or injured somewhere."

"Have you checked the rest of the house?"

"Not yet."

"Then don't. Listen, baby, I want you to get out of the house, book into a hotel for the night. Do not call the police. Wait for Michael to call you once he gets back into the country. Okay?"

"Okay."

"Go now, darling, please."

"I will. And daddy? Please make everything alright."

CHAPTER 50

Murray was confused. He looked at the photograph of Candy Girl as he sat in his car. She really was a beautiful girl. The descriptions of her (and there had been many) simply did not do her justice. He had formed a likeness in his own head of this girl who had killed his son, and despite many assurances confirming her beauty, he had conjured up a picture of Candy Girl's features twisted with bitterness and malevolence; qualities of a callous killer. His confusion was why Skein and his goons had brought the girl here, to the first unit he and Charles had ever bought, a unit that had stood empty for nearly eighteen months.

Murray trusted his brother, or at least he thought he did, but he didn't trust Skein, and Charles's insistence that they use the unstable killer to bring the girl in had set alarm bells ringing. His warning to Spider to be on his guard was only a perfunctory signal for the petty thief to remain alert. If Skein acted rashly then there would be little that Spider would be able to do to dissuade the psychopath. So when he had handed over the phone he hadn't told Spider about the tracker device secreted inside. Using the phone's smartphone technology, he called up an app, coupled with the tracker, that transmitted journey's and highlighted locations on a Google map interface.

Murray had followed the van onto the industrial estate, then parked far enough away to see what was happening but to also remain conspicuous. Half an hour after arriving, Skein hurried out, ran to the rear of the building and then sped off in the Transit.

What the fuck was going on?

Murray tossed the photograph onto the passenger seat of his car and then opened the glove compartment and took out a Glock 17 handgun. He slipped the gun in his jacket pocket then opened the driver's side and got out. The early afternoon air was balmy and fresh, the neighbouring woodland that fringed the estate, smelled of pine and damp moss. He hurried over to the unit and headed round to the rear. If Charles had insisted that Skein was to play cloak and dagger games, he would join them.

There was a rusted metal hoist to the rear of the factory, where goods were unloaded before the days of forklift trucks and conveyor belts. Below the hoist was a double wooden door that opened upwards from the ground like the entry to a pub's cellar. There was another rusted chain secured by an old padlock, looped over the handles on the door. Murray probably still had a key to this lock, he seldom threw anything away, but he didn't have it with him now. He hurried back to the car, popped the boot and took out a tyre iron. He levered the tyre iron between the links of the chain and heaved up. It was tougher than it appeared and he had to strain hard before the old links swelled and then fractured under the stress .

Murray yanked the double doors open and then headed down a small stone staircase into a musty smelling cellar.

There was sufficient light from above to allow him to negotiate between damp and mould ridden cardboard boxes. As he ventured further inside he activated the torch on his phone and located the second staircase that led up to the factory floor. As he climbed them slowly, Murray heard voices from inside the unit. He gripped the tyre iron in a tight fist and pushed open the door leading into the labyrinth of corridors that led to the many rooms housed in the old factory unit.

The building was once a storage warehouse for laminate sheets used in the manufacture of kitchen worktops. It was also a working environment and training centre, hence the several rooms that had been used as conference rooms and offices. Murray hadn't been here for ten years, but the maze of corridors had not changed that much in a decade.

They had leased the premises to several businesses in the past ten years, the last had been a mail order company exporting medical bandages and plasters. All the offices were unlocked. Murray slipped inside one of them now. It was completely empty and from this vantage point he could hear if anybody walked down the narrow corridor to any of the other rooms that ran off it. He sat down on the floor, cross-legged and waited.

CHAPTER 51

Pell led Gemma through the unit, holding her tightly by the upper arm. Spider dragged his feet at her side, his hands bound by plastic ties at the wrists.

The building was a labyrinth, Gemma thought, with corridors and many adjoining rooms, some of which were sealed with heavy steel framed doors, or in some cases, thick plastic strips that hung from the roof to the floor.

Pell pushed her inside one of the rooms, Spider followed her inside. There was a single chair inside underneath a heavy steel desk. Pell stood at the door and watched as she sat at the desk, Spider stood next to her.

"Don't you wonder what will happen to you?" he asked

"I know what will happen," Gemma replied.

Pell shook his head. "You know, I think you have no idea." He stared down at her a little longer, and then shook his head like an exasperated teacher who has finally given up on an obstinate pupil. "Good bye, Candy Girl," He ignored Spider and left the room.

Gemma knew that he was right. She really had no idea what lay in store for her. She knew that they would kill her, and she also surmised that it would not be quick. She shuddered at the thought. She glanced around. The room was little more than a cell. There were no widows and the door was reinforced steel. It looked brand new.

She still remained hopeful though, if she didn't cling to that then she would crumble. She could hear doors opening and closing within the warren that was her prison. Sometimes a loud, indecipherable voice or a harsh bark of laughter.

She felt sorry for Pinto. She didn't deserve this.

She looked up at Spider. She only knew him by reputation. He seemed to frequent most of the popular haunts, a man on the sidelines, observing. Gemma had seen him once loitering in a hotel lobby when she was meeting a client and on one occasion when she was out shopping in her own time. She had said hello to him a couple of times and he had feigned surprise, and on one bizarre occasion had offered his hand. Gemma had been so surprised that she had simply shook it, and then he had reddened and left, evidently fearing small talk or any other kind of interaction. She did not know him well enough to form an opinion of how she felt about him.

"I'm sorry," Spider said.

"Sorry for what?"

Spider paced the small room. "He paid me you know, Mister Cooper. Took me on as a team member. I think they believed that I knew more about you than most, which was partly true of course. They refer to me as the word on the street. I saw a photo of you dancing in a club and they paid me so much, so much. It was the only thing they had to go on after all these years" He paused. "They made me feel so important,"

"Will you help me now?"

Spider shook his head quickly. "How?" He sounded as if he had given up already.

"We have to get out of here. Pell left the key in the door."

Spider laughed. "So what? There is no gap under the door, so we can't get at it, and I think tunneling out is optimistic."

Gemma ignored him. She stood up and walked over to the door. She ran a hand over it's smooth surface. It was solid and although she felt Spider was probably right, she was damned if she was going to accept his negativity so early on.

"So what do you want to do, make your peace before God?"

"Maybe. Do you know the actor Richard Dreyfuss?"

Gemma stared at him.

"He was one of the main characters in Jaws, Matt Hooper. He was also in Close Encounters."

"I know who Richard Dreyfuss is."

Spider laughed nervously. "I watch a lot of movies. Anyhow Richard Dreyfuss once said that he was happiest

315

when he was a jobbing actor, before he became famous, before the nice houses and luxury cars and other extravagant shit that fame and fortune brings. It was when he sought out the roles that would pay little that he was content, because once you hit the big time, the roles were easier to come by and the sense of achievement dwindled."

He sat on the edge of the desk and laughed nervously again. "I guess he didn't say all that shit, but it was words to that effect. I should have stayed doing what I knew. I was relatively happy, but we all strive for more don't we? He paid me in cash for information about you, Mister Cooper did. Five grand. I had it on the table spread out in front of me. I just wanted to look at it, let it sink in. I was in a good place then, I felt that I had made it, was accepted. But when I saw them kill the boy without a second thought, I knew then that I couldn't be a part of this."

Gemma turned from the door. "You didn't think you were being used"?

"Not at the time."

"They are going to kill us both, Spider. We have to get out of here."

Spider shook his head. "That's impossible, even if we get through the door, there are people everywhere, so many people

"They're going to kill us!."

"We can't do anything," Spider almost groaned. "I just wish I could go back to London."

"And look at your money again?"

Spider flinched as if he'd been slapped.

"You're no angel yourself, girl. While we're in here why don't you tell me the story of how you killed Clive Cooper."

And then Murray Cooper opened the door. He was smiling, but it was the rictus grin of a man so close to the edge that the slightest breeze could send him toppling over.

"Yes, out of curiosity. I would like to hear that story, Candy."

CHAPTER 52

Cole was in a hurry.

People owed him money and he was calling it in. They weren't huge amounts but combined they were enough to get him out of the city and allow him to lay low for a while. He had to resort to threats on more than one occasion but he didn't care. The fucker's owed and he needed cash now.

He called his brother in Glasgow. Adam Waters did not sound pleased to hear from him.

"What the fuck do you want?"

Cole chewed nervously at his bottom lip. There was no love lost between Adam and himself. Cole had left his older brother in the lurch when their father had been killed over a drug bust gone bad. Neither of the siblings cared about their late junkie father, who was brash enough to bad mouth the established dealers in Govan and stupid enough to not expect there to be consequences for his actions. He had started dealing on his own and within a week his body was found drifting amongst the floating detritus in the local canal.

The atmosphere had been tense in the area for a long time following their fathers' death. Cole had hightailed it to London and left his brother to sort out any irregularities with the dealers, who having been ripped off by their erstwhile father, came looking for the next of kin in order to recuperate their losses.

"I need somewhere to crash, Adam," Cole said. "I'm coming up for a few weeks."

"Like hell," his brother snapped. "I got some major shit going down and you're not fucking invited."

"It's my fucking house as much as yours," Cole said angrily. "I don't give a fuck what you've got going down, I just need to lie low and that's it."

"I've changed the locks."

"So?"

"What's happened that you have to come back up here?" Adam asked.

"Nothing major, just give me a break will you?"

"Fuck you. You come up here and I'm going to tip off some bad people that you're back. They'll make whatever problems you've got going on down there small potatoes. I don't want you up here, Cole, now fuck off and don't call me again."

Adam disconnected, and Cole pitched his phone across the room.

"BASTARD!" he screamed.

He took several deep breaths then hurried across the room and retrieved his phone. There was a huge crack across the screen, and when he touched it, several deep coloured hues swam milkily across the surface. He managed to access the address book and breathed a sigh of relief when he punched in a number and heard it ring.

It was answered after two seconds.

"Don't fucking call me, grass" an abrupt voice snapped and the connection was ended.

Cole was stunned. This guy was a mate, or so he had thought. He stared at the handset for a few seconds, wondering if the phone was damaged and the line had disconnected because of it. But he knew this wasn't the case. Word had spread quickly that he had been to the police. His reputation, shady though it was to begin with, was in tatters. Nobody abided a grass , especially one who had snitched to The Bill. For the first time, Cole believed himself to be in serious trouble, and not just from the revenge seeking Skein.

It was so fucking unfair. Skein had thrown the rulebook out of the window when he had roughed him up and hassled him over his treatment of Trixie, though he knew now that Skein probably would have killed him anyway once he'd gotten the information he needed on the whereabouts of the detective.

When the police came calling, Cole had been characteristically cool and aloof. He had been shocked by Trixie's death. Not that he cared for her welfare but because it was a serious crimp in his cash flow. Trixie was and never would be a high earner, but she was bread and butter. She paid the rent on this battered run-down shithole of a house. With Jade missing too (she'd done a runner following the skirmish with Skein, and he had no idea where she was,) the police were quick to point the finger, so he spilled his guts, told them everything about Skein and Big Jackie, although he left out the part where he had stabbed Big Jackie and ran. He told them that Skein had stabbed the big guy for disobeying a direct order. The police were sceptical of that, but they were interested when they realised that Skein was involved. He was evidently a priority name on their hit list. They asked him about the detective too, and he'd have loved to have dropped that bastard in it up to his fucking thick neck, but he didn't want to be going off on tangents. The more information he revealed the more they would suspect him of being involved. Suffice to say they believed him once they'd seen CCTV evidence of Skein at the cottage in Weymouth. They had told him not to leave town, and Cole told them to get fucked unless they were

319

going to charge him. They said they wouldn't, but not to push his luck. Cole told them to go fuck themselves again. They really had nothing on him.

And yet?

That wasn't to say they weren't monitoring him also. Bet they put the word out themselves that he had fingered Skein, he thought.

Fuck, what a mess!

Cole didn't pack a bag. He wanted to be light on his feet. He needed cash and his gun. If the bastards were going to come at him he wanted to be able to buy or shoot his way out of trouble. He had nearly two grand in cash and he owned a Beretta M9 handgun that he had bought off a bent cop in Glasgow following an amnesty twelve years ago. He had never fired it but he loved the terror it instilled whenever he brandished it. The gun was heavy and he found it difficult to stow it in the waistband of his trousers as it slipped down and ended up in his underpants, so he had invested in a holster. The strap was over the shoulder and the gun sat snugly in it, resting against his ribcage. Cole would have worn the holster all the time because it made him feel proper gangster, but if he was picked up, they'd throw the book at him. Bad enough to be pinched with a blade on you, a gun was that much trouble ten-fold.

He tightened the holster now and hurried down the stairs through the narrow hallway and into the kitchen.

The big detective, Jessop, was sitting at the table, his hands folded in his lap.

"Jesus Christ!" Cole cried. "What the hell are you doing here?"

Ray waved an indifferent hand. "Social visit,"

"Yeah? Well excuse me for not offering you a coffee. Damn I gotta keep that front door locked."

"You in a rush?"

"What's that got to do with you?"

Ray shrugged. "Nothing, just making small talk."

"Right," Cole sneered. "I remember the last time we had a similar conversation. It ended up with me having a busted rib."

"I need some information," Ray said.

"I'm not interested."

"Where is Skein?"

Cole flinched at the mention of the name. He turned to Ray now. "Why do you think I would know where that piece of shit is?"

"I know about Trixie," Ray said standing up. Cole took an involuntary step backwards.

"Yeah? What do you know exactly ?"

"I know that Skein killed her at the cottage I was renting in Weymouth. I know that it initially looked bad for me and then you, but for now we're in the clear and Skein is being hunted by the police."

"And you want to find him first?"

Ray nodded.

"Why?"

"Not your concern."

"Why the fuck should I bother helping you?"

Ray reached inside his jacket and took out a sheath of notes. He tossed them on the table. "There's five hundred incentives there."

Cole glanced at the money and then managed a thin smile. "You know if you'd offered me cash when you first showed me the picture, I would have been much more obliging."

"Yeah, well you never gave me the chance. Maybe next time you could wait for an opportunity before flailing about with an iron bar."

Cole was silent for a few seconds, then his smile widened. "I don't like you, mister detective. Much as I'd like the money, I'm going to pass on it for the simple fact that I don't want to help you."

Ray nodded slowly. "I think the gun has bolstered your bravado, Cole but I could still break your fucking arm before you even had a chance to draw it."

Cole's smile didn't falter. "Maybe, but I still ain't going to help you. You busted me up before because I threatened you, but I ain't no fucking threat anymore and you know that, so why don't you get the fuck out and leave me alone?"

"Don't you care about what happened to Trixie?"

"No."

"What about Pippa?"

Cole shook his head, confused. "What about her?"

"What? You think I don't know?"

"Know what?"

"That she was one of your girls."

Cole said nothing.

"Seriously?" Ray said.

"I don't know what you're fucking talking about."

"I'm a a detective Cole, you think I'm stupid? You just pick a hooker's name out of the hat, apparently at random, and then after literally only knowing her for less than a day, she agrees to come away with me on some half assed wild goose chase."

322

"You don't know shit," Cole sneered. His hand hovered over the money.

"No, then why don't you enlighten me."

I don't think so. I don't have any reason to cooperate with you. You bust me up remember?"

Ray pointed at the money. "Maybe there's your incentive."

Cole smiled. "I'll tell you this, Mister smart-ass detective. Pippa was never one of my girls, never has been and never will be, I didn't even know you were in Weymouth, otherwise I'd have shopped you to Skein myself and saved myself a whole heap of trouble. That bitch double crossed me. She said she would keep me updated on your movements and then she just fucking stopped.

"Why?"

"How should I fucking know?" He then smiled knowingly. "What did you think, she fell for your magnetic charm over a plate of egg and chips. Fuck, don't you have a high opinion of yourself."

Ray nodded slowly, conceding the point. "For somebody who wasn't going to tell me shit you sure like to shoot your fucking mouth off."

"I'm not telling you what you want to hear, Jessop!" Cole said. "I know you've fallen for her, but I'm fucked if I'm going to massage your huge ego by telling you that she feels the same way She's a working girl. I paid her to tell me what you two did together, and she told me. That's it."

"Up to a point."

Cole shrugged. "Believe what you want."

"So what about Skein?"

Cole's brow creased in puzzlement, taken by surprise by the sudden change of tack in the conversation. "What about him?"

"You know where he is?"

"No."

"You know where he lives?"

"No."

"What about where he hangs out?"

Cole shrugged.

"Christ, Cole you're going to have to work a bit harder to earn that money."

"I told you I'm not interested in your fucking money."

"Bullshit."

"No it's not man. I don't like you, I'm trying to get that simple fact through to you. I'm not going to tell you anything, and the sooner you learn to grasp that simple fact the better, otherwise we're going to play this baiting game back and forth forever. So I suggest you take your fucking money and get the fuck out!"

"Or what?"

Cole laughed, a genuine, throaty, deep laugh. "Oh that's good, Jessop. What, you're going to beat me up again? Go ahead and I'll shop you without a second thought. Old Bill was well keen to hear about your exploits, believe me, especially when they realised you were staying at the cottage where they found Trixie's body. Bet you've been withholding some juicy titbits from them that I could highlight. Go ahead, tough guy, sock me a fucking good one, cos I don't give a fuck. I'm a whistleblower now, a grade A number one stool pigeon, grassing up the big boys with axes to grind and debts to settle. You think I give a flying fuck about your pathetic exploits? Be like stepping in dog shit while I wade neck deep in my own fucking shit."

There was a gentle tap at the door and both men turned quickly. Skein grinned at them both, the gun in his hand levelled between them in an arm as steady as a fixed girder.

"Oh I think that shit is up and over your head now, Cole," Skein said cheerily. "Question is, how long can you hold your breath?"

CHAPTER 53

Skein had fucked up - big time. Things had started to unravel after Big Jackie had been killed at Cole's house. They had both underestimated the skinny pimp, and that momentary lapse had cost the big man his life.

Not that that in itself concerned Skein. Big Jackie knew the risks, simple as. But Skein was angry at his own sloppiness. It was uncharacteristic; no worse, it was careless and there was no excuse for that. Carelessness got you killed in this game. Still, Skein liked to push the envelope a little. If all conquests were a pushover then life would be a real drag. When somebody's life was at risk, it was entertaining to see them fight for it, and if, on occasion, you didn't give them a sporting chance then what was the point? Might as well just shoot any fucker that pissed you off, no explanation, no need to listen to begging and pleading.

What a downer that would be.

Still, being seen at the cottage in Weymouth was a major fuck-up. He could consider himself fortunate that Charles had contacts and had been able to tip him off, giving him some time before the authorities caught up with him. He had other identities and he could change his appearance dramatically with just a few subtle changes. A new hairstyle and some facial hair could work wonders. Now was the time to think of retiring. What was it Fagin said in Oliver - *"Can a fellow be a villain all his life?"*

Obviously not. If one wasn't to kick back eventually and enjoy the spoils, what would be the point? That was Uncle Marius' philosophy, not Skein's , but he endorsed it.

What would Clint Do?

Clint Eastwood was Skein's favourite actor of all time. Uncle Marius had been friends with a guy called Mickey Stone. Mickey was a mobile projectionist, though he preferred the title: *Audio Visual Consultant* - pretentious twat.

Mickey mostly showed promotional videos, corporate and awareness films for companies that desperately needed to maintain a level footing with their employees. Again, pretentious twats, in Skein's opinion. It was not full time work and Mickey worked part-time as a projectionist in a flea-pit porno cinema in Soho. Uncle Marius loved porn and was at the cinema every time Mickey was working as the projectionist.

Skein only accompanied his uncle on one occasion and he had been horrified; not just by the graphic sex, but the overall banality; the cheapness and sordid quality, atrocious acting and appaling music. Intercourse repulsed him; a filthy pastime as intimate as picking up after your dog. He was not a virgin; his one single sexual encounter had been with a prostitute he had picked up one Saturday evening. She had led him to a strewn filled alleyway behind a Chinese restaurant. She was so drunk that he could not begin to wonder how she gleaned any satisfaction from the act. For Skein it was merely a duty bound by curiosity. He had tried smoking and could not see the point, he was not a big drinker; he disliked the taste of most beers and he found spirits totally abhorrent; fiery draughts of molten poison that did nothing to add to one's pleasure, in his opinion. The fuck was neither enjoyable or gratifying. When he had come inside the woman, she had vomited on the pavement, struggled to her feet and stood before him with her panties around her ankles and her short skirt hitched up to her waist. She wavered and laughed, clawing at her panties like a frantic climber feeling for a rope. She couldn't seem to decide whether it was best to attempt to pull them up or slip them off altogether. In her drunken state either option would have proven to be a challenge and she staggered away with her panties looped around one ankle. Skein had hit her then, a huge roundhouse swinging blow that caught her square on the jaw. She went down immediately, cracking her head on the side of a bin laden and overflowing with food waste and tendrils of grease soaked plastic wrap. She lay still, but Skein could hear her breathing. It would be so, so easy to just snuff out her life, he thought. He stood and watched her for five minutes, before she stirred and tried to right herself, then he turned and left her.

Porn aside, Skein loved movies and often frequented the glorious cinema palaces in and around Leicester Square. He enjoyed violent films like Bonnie and Clyde, A Clockwork Orange and the Wild Bunch, but it was Clint who blew him away, firstly as Harry Callahan, and then as Blondie in *The Good, the Bad and the Ugly* , Skein's favourite film of all time. It was an age before home video and the cinemas often re-ran movies and seeing the spaghetti westerns up on the big screen for the first time almost ten years after their original release dates was a dream come true for Skein. He enjoyed *A Fistful of Dollars* and *For a Few Dollars More,* but *The Good the Bad and the Ugly* was a sprawling, magnificent masterpiece that simply got better after repeated viewings.

Uncle Marius had enjoyed the movie, but at over three hours, and possessing a very limited attention span, (born out of watching far too much porn, that dictates that somebody must have his cock sucked within the first ten minutes) his mind started to wander mid way through. When the film had finished Skein had wanted to discuss it, go over the best scenes and highlight the nuances of the three main characters. Uncle Marius had declared that the film was far too long, and there wasn't any sex in it at all, most alarming for an Italian production with an X certificate.

"And besides, what do you think happened at the end?" he lamented.

Skein had not understood. The film ended with Blondie riding away, leaving a thoroughly pissed off Tuco abandoned in the military cemetery. He reiterated this to Uncle Marius who simply shook his head.

"So Tuco would take his share of the money, but then what?"

"We don't know," Skein replied. "The film ends and that is all there is to it."

"Don't you ever wonder what happens after that?"

Skein didn't, but he was intrigued where his uncle was going with the conversation so asked him to elaborate.

"I think that Blondie would have enjoyed the money, bought a ranch somewhere, maybe got married, settled down with a wife and a couple of kids, but Tuco." Uncle Marius held up a finger to emphasize his point. "Tuco would not give up the life, he would blow most of the cash on whiskey, women and gambling and within a year he would be back robbing and thieving, cos Tuco is a bad guy, and the thieving isn't about getting money, it's the act itself, the satisfaction of just taking what doesn't belong to him because he can. Crime was his life and he would not be able to give that up, some people just can't. A bad guy. Blondie wasn't exactly good, despite the title, but he was clever and he would have known when was the time to stop. A thief who spends his whole life amassing a stolen fortune, but doesn't have the good sense to invest it for the future is simply a fool. A clever thief knows when to stop and enjoy his spoils."

Skein had thought long and hard about that. He never considered Uncle Marius to be a profound or clever man, but what he had said that night after they had watched the movie together had made sense. And now as he pulled up outside Cole's house, he wondered again.

What would Clint do?

Clint would get the fuck out of Dodge, that's what Clint would do.

But first he would seek retribution.

The door was unlocked and he entered silently, taking out his makeshift gun and holding it loosely in his hand by his side. He could hear voices, one raised was Cole's. He stood outside the kitchen door for a few seconds, and smiled when he realised who Cole was talking too. He heard Cole say:

"You think I give a flying fuck about your pathetic exploits? Be like treading in dog shit whilst I wade neck deep in my own fucking shit."

Then at the most opportune time he stepped inside and pointed the gun in the direction of the two men.

CHAPTER 54

"You're lying," Murray said, his eyes never leaving Gemma.

Of all the responses Gemma had been expecting the father of the man she had killed accusing her of lying was not one of them.

"What do you mean?" she asked simply.

Murray hesitated for a few moments, he blinked rapidly a few times and chewed distractedly at his bottom lip. Gemma realised he was mulling something over.

"I've just admitted killing you son, Mister Cooper, albeit in self defence," Gemma said. "If I was going to lie about anything it would have been that."

Still Murray said nothing, then as if awaking from a deep sleep he shook his head and barked a short, humourless laugh.

"You didn't kill my son," he said matter-of-factly and made for the door.

Spider hurried over to him and grabbed his arm. Murray looked down at the fingers encircling his jacket sleeve and Spider quickly let go.

"Murray, what are you talking about?" he said.

"This girl didn't kill my son," Murray replied. "I have to go."

"Go? Go where?"

"Back to London, you can come with me." He cast a quick glance at Gemma. "Both of you if you want."

A piercing scream suddenly reverberated through the building. A girl's high pitched, terrified scream. Gemma raised her hands to her mouth.

"We can't leave her here," she whispered between her fingers.

Murray shook his head. "They are Skeins men. They may know of me, but my word counts for nothing here. They will not free the girl if they do not have to. Skein is a brutal man, and there's no reason to assume those that follow him are any different."

"We can't just leave her," Gemma said.

"Yes we can," Murray said. He turned to Spider. "Are you coming with me?"

Spider nooded, far too eagerly for Gemma's fancy. He was a cowardly man, he had made no attempt to disguise that fact earlier, but she had thought he would have helped her now, if only to assuage his treachery. Murray Cooper she could understand. Although his cryptic disclosure that he knew that she did not kill his son was baffling, there was no reason for him to aid her at all, especially as he noted that it would serve no advantage.

"So you would leave me here?" she asked.

"No," Murray replied patiently. "I have told you you can come, but we must leave now."

Gemma shook her head. "I cannot leave her."

Murray took out his gun and laid it on the desktop. "Then take this." He turned to Spider again. "Come on," he urged.

Spider stared at the gun and shook his head slowly.

"I'll help you," he said quietly and picked the gun up in his good hand. "I'll help you," he said again. Gemma smiled and nodded at him, but Murray Cooper left without another word.

CHAPTER 55

Pinto screamed when the fat man, Tonka, dropped his pants. He pawed at her jeans unable to release the button at the front and in his frustration he punched her hard in the side. That prevented Pinto from crying out again. Tonka managed to unfasten her jeans and was now pulling them down her legs. She didn't resist him. There were three of them. The unsmiling guy, Pell, stared at her with detached indifference like a man watching the conclusion to a movie in which he had already seen or worked out the end. The third man, Oz, was over the other side of the room, his phone to his ear.

Pinto felt Tonka's penis run up against her naked thigh. He pushed a large hand, with thick calloused fingers between her legs and roughly massaged her sex. She closed her eyes and blinked back the tears. He pawed her for a few seconds then slapped her naked buttocks hard a few times, grunting in frustration.

"I can't fucking get it up while you're all watching me!"

"I ain't watching you," Pell answered , "But if you've finished?"

"I haven't fucking started!"

Pell glanced down at Tonka's flaccid member. "Yeah I can see that," he sneered.

Tonka hitched up his pants and trousers. "You cheeky cunt!" He made towards Pell who held up his hands in mock surrender.

"Whoa steady big guy, I'm only fucking with you,"

Oz put his phone back in his pocket.

"I can't get any reception here. I need to get hold of Skein, or Cooper. We can't stay here forever. He glanced at Tonka and Pell who stood a few feet apart like gunslingers. Tonka's face had turned an alarming shade of red. Pell was still smirking though his hand had dropped towards the switchblade in his pocket, lest the big lug got any ideas above himself.

"I'm going outside for a bit," Oz said, taking the phone out of his pocket. "Behave yourself, the pair of you." He smirked at Tonka, who simply glared, then winked at Pell who returned the gesture.

"Pell held up his hands once ago. "Look, you want me to leave so you can have another go?" Pell said.

Tonka nodded. "I wanna fuck her hard, man."

"Sure you do, I'll go back and check on Spider and the girl. You knock yourself out. As he turned to go, Spider re-entered the room, the girl at his side. Pell threw him a puzzled glance, and then Spider drew the gun out, levelled it at Pell's chest. And pulled the trigger. The report was deafening in the large open room, the sound reverberated off the thick stone walls like repeated cymbal clashes.

The slug took Pell in the chest and he was launched off his feet and onto his back, his feet throwing up twin plumes of dust from the floor.

Tonka, who was in the process of pulling down his trousers for a second rape attempt, was in no position to offer any defence at all. He stumbled, entangling himself in his own trousers, pitched forward and fell a few feet away from the still figure of Pell.

Spider was almost hysterical with fear and anger. He fired wildly at where Tonka had been standing just before he fell and the bullet sheared off a huge chunk of breezeblock on the far wall behind. Tonka was screaming, trying to crawl away from his dead companion, his knees scraping and drawing blood on the rough floor. Spider, still shouting incoherently shot the big man in the buttock, and Tonka's screams intensified as he continued to crawl on the floor.

Gemma ran over to Pinto and lifted her up by the shoulders. Her eyes widened with shock when she saw Gemma, but she allowed herself to be guided by the other girl until they both stood. Pinto hitched up her jeans.

Spider paused and looked around. He couldn't see Oz, but he noted the open door. He swung the gun around to face Tonka, but the big man had taken advantage of Spiders momentary lapse of concentration and scurried across the floor with incredible speed and a strong hand grabbed him by the leg. Spider cried out in alarm, but was too late to raise the Glock as Tonka yanked him off his feet and Spider fell backwards. The gun skittered out of his hand and across the floor, where it lay maddeningly just out of reach, centimetres from his outstretched fingers.

Tonka fell upon him and that huge dead weight drove all the breath out of Spider's body. He heard a rib crack and the sudden pressure of Tonka's bulk was immediately suffocating. Tonka hit him hard in the ribs, and a flare of excruciating, disabling pain enveloped him. He was unable to draw a breath, and thus alleviate the agony. Tonka was climbing up him, like an enveloping evening shadow. He grabbed Spider by the shirt and pulled himself higher. Spider could not move as Tonka's bulk crushed him. He stared longingly at the gun, but knew that whilst he was pinned it may as well lay in a locked safe in another room.

Tonka grunted as his thick hands found Spider's neck and his fingers started to squeeze. Spider reached up with his good hand and attempted to pull away the death grip, but Tonka was in a frenzy and Spider knew with a clarity that was as terrifying as it was certain that the big man was going to kill him, and there was nothing he could do to prevent it.

Tonka's face was level with his own, now. He glared at Spider with thin, piggy eyes, his breath reeked of beer and pickled cabbage. Flecks of spittle hit Spider in the face and he closed his eyes as dizziness engulfed him. Brilliant flashes of light danced behind his eyes as Tonka's fingers squeezed his windpipe.

"You're supposed to be on our fucking side," Tonka spat. "Not the fucking away team!"

Then he emitted a long, surprisingly high scream and the hands fell away from Spider's throat. The relief was immediate, though he didn't suck in huge, grateful lungs of air, his windpipe was too bruised for that, and the pain from his side was so intense that he knew that a deep inhalation, even if it had been possible, would have been too excruciating to bear. Instead he breathed in blessed short blasts of oxygen, enough to alleviate the immediate pressure, and extinguish the blinding lights that danced maniacally behind his closed eyes.

He rolled over quickly when he felt Tonka slip off him like a revealing shroud; stabbing bolts of fire piercing his side like fork tines. He snatched up the gun but did not have the strength to raise it and it slipped from his fingers and clattered to the floor once more.

Gemma was standing behind Tonka. She had delivered a kick so hard between the big man's legs, aiming and hitting his exposed balls that he could do no more than simply writhe on the floor, his body stiffened to such a point that he resembled the participants of the Facebook craze, *planking*, from a few years ago. His legs shook spasmodically and his hands reached down to his crotch and cradled his swollen balls. There was a penny sized hole in his left buttock cheek where Spider had shot him earlier. Blood started to pour from Tonka's mouth and Spider realised, with horror, that he had bitten through his tongue. A fleshy piece of pink gristle lay on the floor by the side of Tonka's head. With one last incredible effort, Spider managed to raise the gun and take aim. When he pulled the trigger the slug blew off the top of the big man's head, tearing his forehead open like a page roughly ripped from a notebook. Then Spider collapsed into a world of blessed pain free unconsciousness.

CHAPTER 56

Murray was between the rear entrance of the unit and his car, slowly lowering the hatch to which he had gained entry earlier when he saw Oz step out. He was too far away for Skein's man to see him, but he wouldn't be able to get across the open ground to his car without Oz noticing him. He cursed and crouched down on the floor for a few seconds. Oz was about twenty feet away, punching in a number on his mobile. He raised the headset to his ear then snatched it away again, then held it aloft as if the extra few feet would provide him with a suitable reception. When this didn't help he stuffed the phone back in his pocket.

The first gunshot sounded in the unit, and Oz spun around as if he had been yanked by a rope. Murray cried out, and Oz briefly glanced in his direction. He didn't approach however, and instead he hurried back to the door of the unit, slowing down as he reached the door. His hand went inside his jacket pocket once more and Murray saw him take out his gun. He held it up to the side of his face and listened at the door. Murray seized the opportunity and leaped to his feet. He covered the distance quickly and almost silently on the damp grass. Oz only turned as Murray hit the gravel path leading up to the entrance door of the unit, and then it was too late; Murray was upon him.

He swung the tyre iron in a wide arc catching Oz full in the face, breaking his nose and smashing two of his front teeth. Oz dropped to his knees as Murray kicked him in the shoulder sending the big man toppling to the floor as if he was no more than a rag doll propped up in place at a child's tea party. He didn't wait to see if the man was dead. The fact that he wasn't moving was sufficient for Murray to discern that he was incapacitated.

He hurried back to his car, got in and started it up. As he sped away, he heard a second gunshot from the unit, but that wasn't his problem. He floored the accelerator and headed back to London.

Gemma knew that they would have to leave Spider for now. Between Pinto and herself they managed to drag him across the floor of the unit and sat him propped up against the wall. He was unconscious but breathing. Gemma stood up and hurried over to the door. She opened it slowly. Oz was lying down directly outside and she motioned to Pinto to tread carefully. The two girls stepped over the big man and looked around. The still, warm air was silent, the dark silhouetted panorama of the surrounding trees appeared welcoming, offering seclusion and escape. Without conferring the two girls hurried towards the treeline.

The gunshot sounded behind them, a firecracker in the stillness of a desert, and Gemma cried out as the bullet hit her in the thigh of her left leg. She buckled immediately and fell to her knees, skinning them both on the loose gravel. She turned and saw Oz waving the gun in an unsteady right hand. His other hand was cupped over his mouth, covering most of his features. The shot he had fired had been incredibly lucky. There was no attempt to aim, he barely had the muzzle pointing in the right direction, but it had hit Gemma and incapacitated her immediately. Pinto came to a skidding stop a few steps ahead. She spun around and glanced down at Gemma on the floor. She watched as Gemma tried to stand, couldn't make it and then tumbled over once again.

Oz was on his feet. He was unsteady, decidedly so, stumbling about like a boxer who had just taken a heavy hit and a count of eight, but the gun was not waving about quite so much now, and he was fixing a bead on their position.

Gemma and the killer were momentarily disposed, Pinto thought and there was a pretty damned good chance she could get away from here.

All she had to do was run for the trees.

CHAPTER 57

"Tie him to the chair," Skein said to Cole. "Hands behind his back and feet to the chair legs. Skein watched as Cole secured Ray with a roll of clothes line he found under the sink. He then shot Cole in the right knee. Cole screamed and clutched at his leg. Skein chuckled.

"Sorry, but it's difficult to keep an eye on two people at the same time." He ignored Cole and checked on Ray's bonds. Once he was satisfied they were secure he set the gun down on the drainer by the sink and sat down at the table, facing Ray. He ignored Cole who was in no state to cause him any distress.

""It's a mad, mad, mad, mad world, my friends," Skein said cheerily. "Have you ever seen that movie? All the miscreants turn up at the same place at the end, all led by greed and in order to play out the big finale." He spread his hands wide. "And here we are, all of us have had a part to play." He pointed at Ray. "The private investigator with the photograph, the catalyst that sets the chase in motion, even if the photo itself is little more than a red herring. The conniving grass," he said gesturing towards Cole. "Now I have to admit that you have come out of this the worse , because to be truthful you were nothing more than a bystander who got drawn in, which is unfortunate for you. I will have to kill you, and a lot quicker than I would have liked, but?" He shrugged. "What are you going to do?"

Cole didn't reply. He was mewling a pitiful cry over and over, his shattered knee clasped between his two hands.

"Cocky, firing a gun in a built up area," Ray said. "Regardless of what people may think, it doesn't sound like a car backfiring." He paused. "Does anybody hear a car backfiring these days?"

"No I don't believe that they do," Skein replied amiably. "Still the heart of a house will muffle the sound and it will still take time for anybody to either report it and for the authorities to act upon it. Apathy is my ally, detective."

" Former crime scene, still a risk."

Skein shrugged. "Maybe." He turned as he heard hurried footsteps on the stairs, though there was no concern about his movements. A girl in her early twenties stood at the open doorway. She had a pinched, conical face like that of a small rodent. She was dressed in a simple print pastel skirt with a tattered lace trim. Her hair was long and stringy, tied in a high ponytail that hung limply over her left shoulder.

"Well who might you be?" Skein said. The girl just stared at him, then glanced down at the writhing figure of Cole on the floor. She appeared not to notice Ray at all.

"Lettie," the girl said slowly. "What's going on, I heard a shot?"

"No, that was a car backfiring," Skein replied and laughed, making the girl blink at him a few times. He leaned back against the table and nodded towards the gun that lay on the counter. "You wanna play a game, Lettie?"

She shook her head. "No."

"Sure you do. Now do you reckon you could snatch up that gun before I reach it?"

She glanced at the gun then back at Skein. "No, you're closer than I am."

Skein shrugged and stepped away from the table until he was nearer the far end of the kitchen and slightly further from the gun than Lettie. "What about now?"

Lettie glanced at Cole who, through a veil of tears and gritted teeth, was nodding furiously at the gun.

She hesitated but didn't move. "What if I get it before you, then what?"

"Then you shoot me and save your boss."

Lettie apparently needed further clarification of the rules. "And if you reach it first?"

"Then I shoot Cole. and it's game over."

"You won't shoot me?"

"Of course not."

Lettie considered again then said: "What's to stop me just running out the front door?"

Skein held out his hands. "Absolutely nothing."

Lettie turned and ran.

Skein smiled and walked over to the counter. He picked up the gun. Then he walked over to Cole, pushed the muzzle of the gun tightly into the pimps chest and pulled the trigger twice.

"Had to do it," Skein said. He tossed the gun back on the counter.

"I guess you did," Ray agreed.

"Now what about you?" Skein said. He stepped over to Ray and stared down at him.

"Have you ever seen *The Good, The Bad And The Ugly?*"

"Of course."

"You want a showdown? You and me like in the Sad Hill cemetery."

Ray said nothing.

"You see the thing with that scene is that Clint thought himself immortal, he couldn't lose, well not at the hands of his two lowlife companions, it simply couldn't happen, even though both men are crackshots and probably feel just as confident." He tapped himself on the chest. "That is how I feel Mister Jessop. I cannot be beaten because I am the best at what I do."

"You want a gunfight?"

"Ha! What? No of course not. He performed a little jig, a nifty shoe shuffle, his expensive brogues skimming off the faded linoleum. Then he adopted an old fashioned boxers stance circling his fists theatrically in front of Ray's face.

"I say we duke it out."

Ray managed a smile. "You want a fist fight with me?"

Skein nodded eagerly. "You bet."

"Okay, untie me."

Skein laughed again. "Untie you? Whatever for?"

"I thought you wanted to be Clint."

"Clint? Fuck me, Clint wasn't a man of honour. He knew that he would win the showdown because he only had to concentrate on Angel Eyes. He had emptied Tuco's gun earlier. Both Tuco and Angel Eyes didn't know who to go for first, as they were all evenly matched. Clint however just had to shoot the bad guy, the whole thing was always going to go his way. Clint cheated. It was, and always was going to be, an unlevel playing field. Just like now. Now. Are you ready?"

CHAPTER 58

Pippa closed her eyes as her client entered her from behind. She grasped the rails of the bed frame and levered herself upwards meeting his thrusts as he gained momentum. He was reciting an indecipherable mantra; many did in an effort to stave off coming too quickly and he was alternating his speed accordingly. When you were paying for this kind of service many considered that it was a case of getting your money's worth. If it was over too quickly there would be no refunds or discounts.

The guy's name was Tom, he was not a regular, he met with Pippa maybe three or four times a year, always in a hotel room and he always fucked her from behind, over the bottom of the bed, Pippa fully clothed, him completely naked. It was one of the better scenarios for Pippa, all she had to do was wear a short skirt, take off her knickers and they were away. There was no weirdness or violence, he was quite attractive, which was always a bonus, and although now in his early fifties his body was still quite trim.

She could sense him building to a climax and she wiggled her hips as he clasped her buttiocks and quickened his thrusts, but then he slowed again which was unusual at this stage of the fuck. Pippa was experienced enough to recognise the orchestrated plays of her clients, when they were reaching the point of no return, how she could accelerate and heighten the pleasure as she sensed their approach. Now Tom came to an abrupt stop and she was dismayed to feel him soften inside her. He still held her by the buttocks, but there was no charged energy running through his fingers, he simply held her as if she was no more than stabilising his stance. His breathing relaxed and then he slipped from her unspent.

She turned slowly and he avoided her glance.

"Is everything ok, hon?" she asked. Stupid question but it had to be asked.

" *I'm* okay," Tom snapped.

That wasn't good. Tom had never complained, not once. Although he was not adventurous - he would always choose the same thing on the menu, as the girls referred to clients who never deviated from one particular fantasy, and CFNM was always a big hitter - he always enjoyed their sessions. Pippa knew that. If you thought for one second that the client wasn't getting the most out of the experience the first thing you asked yourself was - what were you doing wrong, especially, as in Tom's case, where a problem had never arisen before.

"Hey come on Tommy, I've missed you baby," Pippa purred, turning and taking his cock in her hand.

He managed a half smile but didn't tell her to remove her hand.

"It's like your mind is elsewhere," he said sullenly.

"I'm here, baby, here with you right now." She gave his cock a squeeze and was relieved to feel it stiffen slightly between her skilled fingers. "Mind and body."

"You sure? You just seem distant, Pippa."

"Not me baby, She pulled at his cock again and it began to harden. "Now what do you say we lose the rubber and I'll finish you in my mouth?"

Tom liked that idea a lot.

She was going to quit, she told herself as she left Tom, happy but not entirely placated. She knew that she wanted to be with Ray and these new, surprisingly pleasant feelings, left her unable to commit herself to her clients and Tom had noticed. She hailed a cab to King's Cross and headed over to Cole's. It was another tie she needed to sever, and she had to do that in person. Cole was not returning her calls and she knew that she had pissed him off when she told him that she didn't have anything for him.

"You fucking falling for him?" he had sneered.

"Don't be ridiculous."

343

She had wanted to tell him *yes she was* and what was the harm, but she couldn't have abided the scorn. In many eyes decisions were not hers to make, and on the rare occasions when she had offered an opinion it was often dismissed as wistful. She fucked and sucked, who gave a shit what she thought or did?

Ray does, Pippa mused as she hurried up the steps. Cole's front door was unlocked, as usual, and she stepped inside the hallway. And then into the kitchen.

She didn't recognise Ray as the bloody mass of pulped flesh tied to the chair, not at first. He was slumped against the table, his head lolling on his left shoulder, both his eyes were closed, huge swollen overripe, fruits, plum shaded and slitted. His hair was matted and greasy, swept back over his forehead, streaks of blood dripping from the fringe. It was his jacket that she recognised. If she hadn't known it was his jacket she would never have known it was her Ray. His head came up as she screamed, his unseeing eyes turned in her direction, like a blind man seeking spoken instructions. His mouth opened but no sound was emitted, only a throaty gurgle and more blood.

Skein had heard her too and he turned from where he had been standing next to Ray, his gloved hands drenched in her man's blood. He let his arms drop to his side and droplets dripped from the fingertips.

"And you are?" he asked pleasantly.

Pippa didn't reply. She took in the horror of the kitchen with widened eyes. She was aware of her throat constricting and the sound of blood in her ears akin to placing a conch shell over them. She saw Cole on the floor, evidently dead, his eyes closed tightly shut as if he had died grimacing.

"You wanna play a game?" Skein said and she turned to him. He held up his hands as if insisting that she noted that they were empty and she took a step backwards. The kitchen seemed to be closing in on her; cupboards and panels pulsating and confining. She hadn't realised that she was against the counter until she bumped against it, then she turned quickly as if she had been goosed. Her hand fell on the gun and she picked it up with one swift movement without even thinking about what she was doing. She had never held a gun in her hand, but she held it out at arms length, both hands gripping the stock.

Skein laughed and she knew that if he rushed her now, she'd drop the weapon and scream. But he just grinned at her.

"Hey, you've played before," he said. Pippa pulled the trigger then and Skein flinched at the sound but not the impact. The smile faltered, but only a little, it was the expression of one who cannot accept that the snake has bitten him, despite the fact that he recklessly continues to prod it.

For all his showboating, Skein died quietly without ceremony. There was no fanfare, no musings on the inevitably of fate or confident witticisms. At the very last moment he realised, with an incredulous and terrifying certainty, that he didn't want to die, but he was going to. He emitted a final plaintive cry and then fell at Ray's feet.

CHAPTER 59

Pinto ran Oz and shouldered into him before he had time to swing the gun round from pointing it at Gemma and levelling at her. She could see he was wrecked. His eyes were unfocused and the gun arm still tremulous. For a big guy he went down remarkably easily, though she had to concede that in his present state a gentle breeze would have been enough to send him toppling.

The gun fell to the floor and Pinto instinctively kicked it away. It disappeared in the foliage fringing the wood. Oz sat on his butt and stared at her for a few seconds. When he set an open palm on the ground beside him and attempted to push himself back up, she lashed out at him with a boot. She connected with his chin and he crashed back to the floor and was still.

Pinto turned back to Gemma who was on the floor also. Pinto could see where the bullet had hit her in the leg. There was a lot of blood. She knelt down and put her arms around Gemma's shoulder and tried to lift her, but Gemma cried out and Pinto set her down gently on the floor once more. Pinto slipped off her belt and tightened it above the bullet hole on Gemma's leg.

"Get help," Gemma wheezed. "The phones are inside. No police."

Pinto glanced at Oz, but the big man was still motionless.

"Don't worry about him, he's out, get the phone, Pinto, they're on the bench beside the chairs inside.

Pinto hurried inside. There were three phones on the bench: hers, Gemma's and Ricky's. There was nobody she could think of who could help her. She snatched up Gemma's handset and glanced at the screen. There were eight missed calls from Carly Beech and several text messages. Each one started with the words *"How could you?"* or *"I trusted you."*

She called Carly's number from the home screen but there was no signal. She hurried back outside again.

Oz was sitting astride Gemma, his hands around her throat, her feet were thrashing on the floor as he bore down on her. Pinto ran to the edge of the woods and fell to her knees. She scrambled about in the dense foliage, cursing herself for losing the gun. It was what every sappy fucking dumb bitch in

346

the movies did. Her fingers found a large fallen branch and she hefted it and turned back to Oz. Gemma was no longer kicking.

She swung the branch at Oz, amazed at how light it felt in her arms. Oz turned at the last moment and managed to raise an arm and the branch snapped like dry kindling. It must have been rotten. His ruined face broke out into a rictus grin, and Pinto noted the broken and missing teeth and jagged slash across his nose. His eyes were already starting to blacken

She looked down at the broken branch in her hand. It ended in a sharp point where it had broken across Oz's arm. Without thinking Pinto thrust forward and felt the point puncture the big man's shoulder. Oz screamed and swatted at the impaled branch. Grimacing, Pinto leaned forward and felt the wood enter a few centimetres. Oz bit down hard. His head was thrashing from side to side as he fell off Gemma. Pinto helped him on his way with another well aimed kick. She pulled Gemma away from him and sat down beside her. She was breathing but the breaths were very shallow.

I saved her, Pinto thought. *We saved each other.* For the first time since they had been snatched from Carly's house, she knew they were going to be okay. She wasn't going to die. That sudden realisation was suddenly all consuming and overwhelming. Ricky was dead, she had witnessed his horrific murder.

Pinto was tough, but she wasn't hardcore gangster; she started to cry. As she sat on the ground listening to Gemma gradually regain her composure, the phone buzzed in her hand. She jumped and almost dropped it. She glanced at the screen and saw that it was Carly calling again. She put the phone to her ear and answered it.

"Hello?"

"Why, Gemma, why?" There was a brief pause and Pinto could imagine the girl suddenly realising that it wasn't Gemma's voice.

"Who is this?" Carly asked quietly.

Pinto took a deep breath hoping to get the cries under control.

"Hey, Carly, it's me. It's Pinto."

CHAPTER 60

Charles Cooper was a man of routine. Spider would have found him an easy mark to target. It was 8.50 a.m the following day and Charles was finishing the tenth length of his pool in his home in Berkshire.

It was a large house but not necessarily so . Charles had never married and had no children so he had no need for thirty bedrooms or twenty bathrooms. What he enjoyed was opulence, he liked to flaunt his lavish lifestyle. As a man of wealth he enjoyed all the luxuries that having money provided. The house was secluded with six bedrooms, four bathrooms and the superb pool that Charles had installed five years ago. There was a snooker room and a mini cinema, but Charles was a restless man and found little time for either playing games or watching films. He did love to swim and from 8.30 every day he would complete thirty lengths of his magnificent pool before breakfast.

He alternated his strokes, starting with a crawl, that as he aged became very tiring, then ten lengths of backstroke, at a leisurely pace, before finishing with the breaststroke. He had attempted the butterfly a few years ago, but found the whole experience ridiculous and had given it up as a bad idea. As he turned onto his back now and pushed off the side he noted a figure standing at the poolside. There was nobody else in the house save for Bertrum, his personal masseuse, who was waiting to give him a rub down after his swim, but Bertrum never came into the pool room. Why would he?

Charles stopped swimming and stood up. The water only reached his chest. There was no decline as you progressed down the length of the pool; Charles had not wanted a diving area and had designed it this way specifically for length swimming. He was surprised, but not altogether concerned, when Murray waved at him from the poolside. His brother had access to the house but he had never used the pool and whenever he had wanted to meet he had always called on ahead in case Charles had gone out or had company. Murray hated to gatecrash and despite his rough exterior he always maintained a protocol that began and ended with good manners.

Charles walked to the edge of the pool and took his brother's offered hand to help him out. He marvelled at how easily Murray pulled him from the water. Even now, in his late sixties, Murray was a strong man. Charles picked up a towel and started drying himself roughly.

"Still managing thirty lengths?" Murray asked pleasantly.

Charles nodded. "Sure, but not this morning. What's up?"

"Where's Skein?"

Charles stopped drying himself off and ran his fingers through his damp hair.

"I told you, he has the girl safe."

"That's not answering my question, Charles."

"I'm not sure where Skein is at this exact moment. Something cropped up, a personal matter, and he had to leave the girl with his associates. There is nothing to worry about Murray"

"Why didn't you tell me he was taking her to the laminate factory?"

"What?" For a few seconds, Charles was so confused that he didn't actually realise that the question was a perfectly innocent one. His instructions to Skein had been exact and there is no way that Murray should be aware of this development. Everybody's phone was to be taken off them, including Spider who was the only link to Murray anyhow.

"I didn't realise that I had to divulge that to you. You left this up to me Murray, you said you wanted me to finalise everything remember, now what's this all about?"

"What was the plan, Charles? Kill the girl, dump the body and then tell me something went wrong? Spider too I guess."

Charles tossed the towel on the floor and stood with his hands on his hips. He cut an absurd figure in just his bathing trunks. His skinny frame was far from imposing, but he held his head high and when he spoke he adopted the no nonsense tone that was needed to show his younger brother just who was running the show here.

"I don't appreciate your accusations, Murray," he said loftily. "Everything that happens, happens on a need to know basis. Why should you care what we do with the girl? Suffice to say that she will be punished for what she did. If you wanted to kill her yourself then I would gladly have stepped aside, but that is not the way we do things, Murray, you know that. I take care of business, I always have and I have never let you down before. If now, at this stage in your life you wish to take up the mantle then be my guest. I'll call Skein now, have him bring the girl here and you can do what you like with her. Is that what you want Murray?"

"No Charles, I don't want that. I don't want to do anything to her because she didn't kill Clive, Skein did."

"You're crazy," Charles said, but there was a tremor in his voice, and Murray seized upon it. As Charles tried to walk past him he put a hand on his scrawny chest.

"I never had reason to doubt that the hooker killed my son, why should I? She ran and that was that. If she was innocent why run? The simple answer to that point is that she thought that she had killed him. Oh I'm not going to pretend to you that I loved him, Clive was a nasty bastard, evil and vindictive, and he probably deserved to die, but I had a right to know what happened, Charles. I was denied that and that doesn't sit well with me."

He lowered his hand and Charles sat down on the pool edge. After a few seconds Murray joined him, his feet dangling a few inches above the water. There was a hollow quality to the acoustics of the pool room and reflections danced off the rippling water onto the low ceiling.

"You made a fool of me, Charles," Murray said eventually. "That hurts me most. More than all the lies, the fact that I had to pretend that my son was missing after taking a fucking trip into the Bolivian rainforest. "

This too had been Charles' idea. Charles had never wanted to call in the police for two specific reasons. The first was the shame of dragging the family name through the mud, and possibly implicating the most important client on their books, but more importantly he had convinced Murray that there would be no real justice if the girl was apprehended by the authorities. Better they dispense their own Cooper styled payback when she was caught.

Once they had buried Clive they had forged a passport in his name, pretended he was holidaying in South America and then subsequently declared his disappearance. It was a convincing trail, with reliable informants stating that Clive had set off into the jungle but never came back. His stunt double for the trip had returned to the UK a week later on his own passport.

"Murray, please listen to me," Charles said evenly. "I can understand that you're upset, the last couple of days have been a whirlwind, but I don't know why you have suddenly convinced yourself that…"

"I've spoken to her," Murray interrupted. "I spoke to her at the factory and I know that she didn't kill Clive. Skein did."

"I see and you believe her do you?"

Murray nodded.

Charles scoffed and went to stand up but Murray grabbed his leg and yanked hard. Charles skidded on the tile floor and plunged headfirst into the pool. He broke the surface spluttering and rubbing at his eyes at the unexpected dip.

"What the fuck!" he screamed. "Have you lost your fucking mind! Who do you think you are?" He started to edge his way to the pool steps away from Murray, but his brother jumped into the water ahead of him blocking his escape. He grabbed Charles by the hair and thrust his head under. Charles beat at him feebly as he thrashed about under the water. After a minute Murray pulled him up again. Spluttering, Charles stared at his brother with imploring eyes, all the assured arrogance and bravado had disappeared in that one dunking. Charles was terrified now and he began to plead and implore as only the truly terrified can, in whimpers and plaintive cries.

"Please Murray, this is wrong. Even if you think Skein killed Clive, why kill me, please Murray."

"Skein is not an ambitious man, Charles, that is what you like about him. Did you know that he killed several high ranking mobsters in the seventies? Well, they weren't the

Krays, but they were still recognised firms, protection racketeers mainly Can you even believe that? He took them all out with football gangs, quick, decisive, ruthless strikes. He told me all this Charles, but he never elevated himself to their own positions. You want to know why?

"Please Murray."

"Because he said the higher you sit, the bigger the target you become." Murray shrugged. "Well he probably put it a little more eloquently than that, but you get the gist."

"What does that have to do with anything?" Charles asked. He wondered fleetingly if his brother had lost his mind. He had underestimated him, genuinely convinced that like every major decision that had been made in the past, Murray had left all the planning of the girl's abduction to him. And yet here was his naive, unsuspecting brother, spouting certain truths and some unfounded yet remarkably astute accusations at him. Murray had spoken to the girl also, but it was still only going to be her word against his.

"It means that Skein wouldn't have killed Clive without somebody's say so," Murray continued. "There would be nothing in it for him. A man who lacks ambition plys his trade to the highest bidder, where's the motive?"

"Look Murray, you haven't convinced me that you're right, but let's just say the whore did say that Skein killed Clive, it's going to be her word against his, we can get them both in, hold them both, what do you think?" As they talked Charles slowly inched himself around the stocky figure of his brother towards the steps. If he could just reach the steps, he could get out and Murray, fully clothed would be slowed down by the water.

But Murray lashed out again and once more forced Charles' head under the surface. This time he waited nearly two minutes before allowing his brother up for precious air. Chalrles hooted, drawing in huge shallow lungfuls of oxygen. He lay limply on the surface of the water, his head only prevented from going under once more by Murray grasping it tightly by the hair.

"You crazy fucker," Murray said and smiled. The smile was terrible and Charles knew that he was going to die that morning. "She never told me that Skein admitted to anything. It was what she didn't tell me that convinced me. It was you wasn't it, tell me the truth you fucker!"

"Yes," Charles screamed. "I told Skein, but it was for the good of the company, Murray, you must have known that. Clive was mad, think what would have happened, please, Murray."

Murray pushed Charles' head under for the final time and held it there until the thrashing stopped. Then he pulled his brother up, held him in his arms and wept.

CHAPTER 61

"I've told you the big guy, Oz and his mates killed Ricky. We were in Carly's house, me and Ricky and Gemma. These people knew about the money in the safe, they just came in and took it, Ricky put up a fight and they killed him." Pinto sat back in her chair and dropped her head.

"And this gang of heavily armed men, killed your friend, kidnapped you and Gemma Bradshaw, and held you captive, all for twenty-five grand?" Detective Inspector Billing smiled across the table at Pinto.

"Is that a question?"

"Yeah."

"I don't know. I guess so yeah."

"What do you know about Gemma ?"

"What do you mean?"

"Well did you know that she was an ex-high class call girl from London, she used the name Candy Girl?"

"No. We only met a week ago in a bar,"

This was the story that Gemma and Pinto had agreed upon. Keep it as simplistic as possible, don't fill in any gaps that the police's questions may pose.

She never mentioned Jazz. The police didn't need to know that she was at Carly's house. Pinto had shrugged when the detective had asked her about her relationship with her best friend's fiancee, citing that they were just friends who hung out.

As far as Billing was concerned Gemma was the crux of the whole debacle. It was Gemma in the photograph that Ray Jessop had shown around. Gemma who had been abducted by Skein, who had been killed in the house alongside the odious pimp. There were so many threads linking each person, who aside from a few co-stars, were all bit players in the Candy Girl show. That name had been given to him by Oz, who had told the police that they had wanted to kidnap Candy for a couple of businessmen brothers, one of whom had drowned in his own pool, the second who had disappeared.

Oz had spouted some nonsense about Candy Girl being on the run after killing Clive Cooper one of the brother's son, but records stated that Clive Cooper disappeared in Bolivia just after Christmas of last year and there was no reason to believe anything Oz said as his case was growing increasingly more serious as more evidence came to light. Pinto and Gemma both testified that he had killed Ricky at Carly's house and forensic traces on the body found at the factory unit in Colchester confirmed that the big man had more than likely been responsible for his death.

Then there was Spider, the petty thief who was also at the factory unit, who, according to Oz, was not only known to the Cooper brother's but the pimp, Cole. After he let Pinto go he called the hospital and asked if it was possible yet to speak to Ray Jessop.

"Next week," he was told.

CHAPTER 62

"Let's start with John Clyson," Billing said. "Better known as Big Jackie."

"I don't know him," Ray said. The light still hurt his eyes and although they weren't shining directly at his face the glare was enough to make him close them again and he lay back on the pillow.

He had been in hospital for just over a week since, Skein had almost beaten him to death following his idea of a Mexican Standoff. The police had visited several times, even Jackson from Weymouth had turned up twice, but they had all been sent packing by the stern, but authoritative ward sister. Ray had fallen in love with her a little.

"Come on Ray, you're supposed to be helping us here, not pulling in different directions. Billing was fifty, paunchy with long hair that suited him in that strange way that some older men have of carrying off something normally viewed as being much cooler on a younger person. Ray was beginning to tire of his whining manner.

"I don't know Big Jackie, remind me will you."

Billing referred to his notebook. "Big Jackie was found at the house in Kings Cross, the one rented by Cole Water's. He died from a single stab wound. This is the house that you yourself admit to visiting whilst conducting your enquiries into the missing girl, Helena?"

Ray nodded then winced. It hurt to nod. He had suffered a broken cheekbone, lost two teeth and his jaw had been dislocated. The worst injury however had been a globe rupture in his left eye. The beating had been so severe that the eye had deflated. Had he been treated any later then he would have lost it, the doctors assured him. He had Pippa to thank for that.

"I remember now. Cole lived there, but there wasn't anybody called Big Jackie, not that I can remember. No other girls, aside from Trixie."

Billing glanced down at his notebook again. "Yeah Trixie. Real name Sophie Watkins aged nineteen, stabbed to death at the holiday cottage you were renting."

"That almost sounds accusing, detective."

Billing smiled. "It wasn't meant to, but we're running a sweep at the station on how many of these deaths are connected to you. If we had a whiteboard, your name would be on it in capitals."

"I'm connected, but I'm in the clear, you know that. I'm helping you out aren't I?"

"Press are having a field day. If you read The Mail you'd think The Krays had been resurrected; pimps, hookers, gangsters, hitmen, seven dead in total and only one arrest."

The single arrest so far had been Oz and he was giving everything up. With nobody else about to take the blame it was all being pinned on him and he was maintaining his story that he had nothing to do with any killing.

"I've told you everything. Speak to Jackson, he'll tell you."

Billing closed his book. "I do believe you, Ray, but there are so many links to you and this girl Candy, that I wouldn't be doing my job if I didn't go over it at least eight or nine times."

Ray nodded. "I guess."

"So. This guy Skein. Pippa just shot him and he let her?"

Alone, back at the station, Billing poured himself a large scotch. Jesus, Poirot would have a fine time unraveling the clues to this case. He knew that eventually, with the exception of Oz, everybody left alive would walk. Evidence could only be corroborated if it was backed up and with the majority of the players either buddying up or denying all knowledge, the CPS were on the Met's case to tie up these loose ends and reassure the public that all these violent deaths were no more than heated turf wars amongst gangsters.

Billing felt that he could go on questioning the usual suspects for weeks but he was also aware that he would gain very little by doing so. None of them were being accused of murder and the best he could hope for was secondary midemeanours and in Spider's case an accessory to kidnapping that would be very hard to enforce since the girls who he was accused of abducting maintained that he was instrumental in helping them escape. Plus the two people that he was accused of killing were part of the kidnapping gang to begin with.

Billing drained his drink and, for the time being, he closed the file on his desk.

CHAPTER 63

Pippa came in after Billing had left Ray's hospital bedside. She bought Ray a change of clothes and a bowl of grapes which she placed on the bedside table.

She had visited him every day but they hadn't broached one particular subject. Pippa had saved Ray's life and he would be forever grateful to her for that, but there was a veil of tension between them, something that they were both aware of but had not acknowledged.

For Pippa it was time to address it.

"I'm skint," she said. "I need to go back to work."

Ray shifted himself in the bed. He was fed up with lying down and taking pain killers. He wore a patch over his left eye and his jaw had been reset. The cuts and bruises would heal and the Doctor had told him that he could probably go home in another week. He couldn't wait.

"Okay," he answered hesitatingly.

"I need to earn money, " Pippa said.

"Of course."

Pippa paused. "Do you think there is a future for us?"

Ray reached for her hand and she took his. They pondered each other for a long minute. "Pippa, you saved my life."

She stood up suddenly and his hand fell limply on the bed. "Don't you start that with me, Ray Jessop. Now you answer my question."

"Yes, I think there is,"

Pippa sat back down again though she didn't take Ray's hand. "I want to ask you one thing and then I'm done."

"Okay."

"Why were you at Cole's that night?"

"You want the truth?"

Pippa nodded.

Ray adjusted his position on the bed once so he was sitting bolt upright and facing Pippa. "I wanted to ask him why he chose you to spy on me."

Pippa was quiet for a long time and Ray let her compose herself.

"He paid me, initially," she answered eventually. "That morning we met on the steps of my apartment was prearranged. He had called me the night before, I'd never heard him so mad. I never worked for him, that much is true, but I had contact with him through the other girls, Trixie mainly. He wanted to find out where you lived. I think his idea was to get revenge on you for kicking the shit out of him. When you asked me to come to your hotel, Cole was very enthusiastic, told me that it would be a golden opportunity for me to get to know you better. If you were on to me, I guess you set that up to see where it would lead."

Ray shrugged. "Go on."

"I told him that we were getting close, this was before we went to Weymouth, He never knew about our trip. I'd stop giving him information after the night at the hotel."

"I know," Ray said.

"How did you know?"

Ray reached forward and took Pippa's hand again. "Because something changed. I was never one hundred percent certain that Cole had put you onto me, it just seemed so coincidental. When I went to see him, he didn't deny it and he assumed I knew from the off. The phone messages helped of course."

Pippa looked puzzled. "What phone messages?"

There were two answer messages on your phone at your apartment. I listened to them when you were out."

"That's sneaky."

Ray shrugged. "I'm a private investigator, I do sneaky things. Both messages were from Cole, the first demanding why you had your mobile turned off, the second one was him sounding pissed because you weren't going to relay any more information. Cole said that I was an arrogant jerk if he thought that you had fallen for me over such a short period of time."

"You are an arrogant jerk. Why did you take me away with you if you knew that I was reporting back to Cole."

Ray held up a finger. "I told you, I wasn't a hundred per-cent sure, and besides I never told you anything of importance, nothing that would lead Cole back to me."

"You told me about your wife and daughter and what happened to Matthew Silk"

Ray nodded. "That was different. I realised by then."

"That you had fallen for me?" Pippa asked.

"No that was when I realised that you had fallen for me."

She swung at him playfully and he caught her wrist and pulled her into an embrace. They kissed very gently then Pippa leaned back and studied him seriously.

"So what now?"

"You want to play detective, we'd make a good team."

"Don't make jokes, Ray."

"Who's joking? It's not easy, but with my contacts and army training and your street wises , not to mention your acting skills we could be formidable."

"No more lying on my back?"

"Definitely not."

Pippa stood up. "Okay let's do it." She held out a hand. Ray took it and they shook. Pippa glanced out of the hospital window.

"So all we have to do now is decide who's name goes first on the door.

CHAPTER 64

"Thank-you for meeting with me," Carol Harrier said. She stood up but didn't offer her hand. Ray nodded and sat at the small table. There was a dish filled with small pebbles on the centre and the condiments were shaped as bowler hats. They were outside; a small cafe overlooking the harbour. From where he sat Ray could look across the narrow channel and see the cafe where he had had breakfast with Brian back in April.

Carol stared at him for a moment then sipped her coffee. Her hands shook and she spilled some of it into her saucer. She sat down as a waitress came over and Ray ordered a coffee for himself.

"What happened to your face?" Carol asked.

"It doesn't matter," Ray said. They had released him from the hospital last friday, and Carol had called him the next day. On a whim he had asked Pippa if she wanted to come to Weymouth for a break for a few days. They could catch a movie, have a few meals, go for a drink. Pippa thought that was a great idea providing there were no strings. They both laughed at that. She was at the hotel whilst Ray met with Carol.

"To be honest, I was thinking that you may have contacted me, Carol said."

Ray leaned back in the chair. Gulls swooped low over the still water and fishing boats bobbed gently on the surface. An alarm sounded, signalling the raising of the bridge and everybody stopped what they were doing to turn and watch.

"Why would you think that?" he asked.

"Well I was thinking that you may have told Brian's brother, Michael what happened," She was struggling to stop the tears, a combination of fear, bitterness and anguish, Ray guessed.

"That would achieve nothing," Ray said. He thanked the waitress when she set his coffee down. "Any retribution I wanted to lay down would only further tarnish Brian's memory. If I wanted to reveal to his family that he was being blackmailed by his own daughter, a fact that his wife was aware of, then all the sordid details about what he was being blackmailed for would come out. How would that achieve anything?"

Carol considered this for a moment. "Thank-you," she said.

"Don't. Like I said I'm not doing it for you, or you fucking daughter."

She winced at that, but Ray didn't care.

"When did you find out?" Ray asked.

"About a couple of days after I'd employed you. Lucy came back from the Island and went crazy when I told her what I had done. I didn't understand why at the time. A few days later we were talking about the girl, Helena, in the video and she called her Zoe. I said *who the hell is Zoe?* and she just froze, Mister Jessop and then I knew. She told me later, Told me that she hated her father. She said that he had abused her."

"Did you believe her?"

Carol took a sip of coffee, her hand was steadier now and Ray realised that she was envisioning their meeting drawing to a close and this single notion empowered her a little, especially now that she was aware that there would be no personal recriminations.

"No I did not."

"Did you tell Lucy that?"

Carol glared at him for a second, but then lowered her gaze. "She is all I have left now, MIster Jessop, our relationship is damaged, possibly irreparably, but if I went to the police she would be arrested and jailed. I can't do that, I'm her mother."

"That's your decision," Ray said standing up.

"And my burden," Carol countered.

Ray nodded slowly. He turned and left.

CHAPTER 65

Spider didn't like the sun. It was mid August and though dressed in shorts and t-shirt, and looking faintly ridiculous, in his opinion, he was still perspiring. He had been wandering the sea front at Cromer for nearly an hour, seemingly walking against the crowds, who, oblivious to his presence, ambled, sauntered, and generally took a lot of time to get from A to B.

Holidaymakers.

Although he walked all the time in London, this was a unique experience for Spider. There was always a purpose when he was on the grimy streets of the capital, whether it was seeking out a perspective mark or weighing up potential, congregating crowds, his hurried, scurrying, weaving in and out of the crowds was rarely noticed. Dips loved the seaside towns, of course, but Spider wasn't one of them. Seafronts and esplanades, although bustling were still open expanses, with few escape routes. Spider liked narrow alleyways shrouded shop fronts and the nether world of The Underground network.

Still he wasn't here to work.

He spotted the small cafe/bar and stopped. It was in a prestigious spot, sandwiched between an ice cream vendor and a small stall selling beach toys, all three in a row opposite the pier.

It was called Candy's.

Spider walked to the entrance. It was a little after three o' clock in the afternoon and most of the dinner time trade had left, though there were a few people drinking coffee and snacking on cakes as they gazed out onto the beach. Spider didn't take a seat, just stood and waited until a waitress caught his eye. She walked over to him and smiled.

"If you'd like to take a seat, sir, I can take your order."

Spider shook his head. "No, thanks. Is Gemma here?"

"Gemma is the owner, sir," the waitress said, a little confusingly. She tilted her head as if she couldn't imagine what Spider would have to discuss with Gemma.

"Can you tell her that Spider is here, please."

"Spider?"

He nodded and the girl left shaking her head. He heard a muted conversation in the back and then Gemma appeared at the doorway behind a small bar, the waitress at her side. Then she broke into a quick trot and flung herself at him. Spider managed to keep his feet and they embraced. Gemma was crying, but she wouldn't release him and he felt himself well up. He caught sight of the stunned waitress and that image alone made him smile.

"Where have you been?" Gemma said as they sat together in a window seat, both sipping coffee. "After the investigation, you just disappeared, I was worried you'd never call."

Spider nodded. "I'm not used to such scrutiny," he admitted. "The police were desperate to pin something on me, but I think they realised that I was little more than a pawn. I was lucky, but there you go."

"I could do with a barman," Gemma said nodding towards the bar.

"Are you offering me a job?" Spider asked, surprised and yet flattered by the offer.

"If you want it."

Spider smiled. "After what happened the last time I was offered to work for somebody, I think I will decline, but thanks. How's the leg?"

"I've got a limp, perhaps I always will. It doesn't hurt now. Hey you want to see something cool"

Spider nodded. "Sure."

Gemma got up and walked over to the bar. If she did have a limp, Spider didn't notice it. She reached up to a high shelf above the bar and took down a thick resin cube that sat next to an alarmingly hideous monkey with a pair of dull cymbals in each hand. She handed it over to Spider who turned it in his good hand. Deep inside the resin was a flattened bullet.

Gemma laughed. "I asked the surgeon for it. I think he was pissed because he wanted to keep it for himself."

"Quite a memento," Spider admitted. He set the cube down on the table. "Have you seen Pinto?"

Gemma smiled. "Yes, Spider, we're partners."

Spider looked around. " What, this place? Congratulations."

"Not business partners."

"Oh. Oh right, I see."

Gemma took a sip of coffee and Spider was wondering how much she was prepared to tell him.

"After the abduction and what happened at the factory, we kind of bonded. When you go through something as traumatic as that you have a kinship. Some nights one or both of us will wake up screaming. It's nice that the other person is able to empathise rather than just reassure. And we have a great conversation opener whenever people ask us how we met. "

"So what happened with Carly?" Spider asked. He caught Gemma's frown and reddened. "I'm sorry that was tactless and bloody nosey too."

Gemma waved a hand, "No, no it's okay. She moved to the U.S to be with her mum. We were together for a bit, but it was a very strange triangle. Jazz hung about for a while, but she was a spent force. Pinto said that she took Ricky's death surprisingly well, but the fight had gone out of her and the last she heard is that she had moved in with a bunch of travelers. She could be anywhere now. Pinto though is a changed woman. Unfortunately, she is still the girl who bullied Carly at school, and Carly couldn't see past that. I don't think she could accept that I had feelings for Pinto also. I guess she saw it as a kind of betrayal." She sighed and took another sip of coffee. "Uh, that's cold. Do you want another?"

Spider shook his head. "No, I'll be going soon. The reason that I took so long to come and see you is because." He paused and lowered his voice a little. "I've been helping Murray Cooper out."

Gemma's eyes widened in surprise. "What?"

"I know, it's crazy. But he has set me up financially. He's living abroad, and don't ask me where because I won't tell you. Jesus, you wouldn't believe the contacts that man has. Suffice to say that he won't be coming home again. I was his gopher and I enjoyed it, Gemma, but he's settled now and our arrangement is over. He offered me full time work but you know me, I'm my own man and I miss London too much. Anyway, he left this for you."

He reached into his pocket and took out a creased envelope. Gemma took it from him.

What is it?" she asked.

Spider shrugged. "I don't know. He stood up and they embraced again. He nodded at the envelope in her hand and shrugged. "An explanation maybe?"

CHAPTER 66

Gemma watched the sun go down and the lights come on. The theatre on the pier was holding a *"Vaudeville*

Extravaganza," and ticket sales had been high. She didn't open the cafe at night and she sat alone enjoying the solitude.

Spider had left a few hours ago and as she sat at the same table, the envelope was still unopened in her hands. She pondered what an extraordinary year it had been. Pinto came in from the back room and walked behind the bar. She held up a bottle of wine and Gemma nodded.

"Aren't you going to open it?" she asked.

Gemma nodded. "I guess." She opened the envelope and took out a single typed sheet of paper.

Dear Miss Bradshaw,

First off, this is not an apology. I don't feel that I owe you one and I don't believe that you would be expecting one. What I do feel you deserve is an explanation. I'm not going to admit to anything myself, especially in writing, suffice to say that you have read the newspapers and you can make your own assumptions as to what happened to the people mixed up in our saga. Skein killed my son a few hours after you fled your flat. He was working under the instruction of my brother, Charles. The only reason I can offer as to why he would do such a thing is to prevent Clive, as the only heir, of inheriting the company upon our deaths. Charles was tremendously proud and protective of the family business, and he hated the notion of a waster such as Clive taking up that mantle. My son was an evil person, as I'm sure you yourself was aware, but he was still my son, and Charles took him away from me. I don't believe that it was premeditated. Charles had sent Skein to your flat that morning simply to check on his whereabouts. What I know for certain happened next is sketchy, but it absolves you. Clive's body was found in the kitchen, and not in the living room as you told me.

Also the Jack Daniels bottle was smashed after you had already stated that you placed it down on the coffee table. There is no reason why you would have lied about these particular details. Therefore the only logical explanation left is that Clive was alive when you ran. Skein, after consulting with Charles seized the initiative and killed my son using the bottle to deliver the fatal blow and laying the blame at your feet. My brother had always been so keen to find you, more so than me. I became suspicious when I found out you were being held in the factory without my knowledge. He would have killed you, I'm certain of that and would have stated that it was an accident, or an over zealous thug. That is it, Miss Bradshaw. I will not communicate with you again and please be aware that I will no longer be pursuing you.
M.C.

Pinto came over and placed two glasses of wine on the table. She stood behind Gemma and placed her hands on her shoulders. Gemma reached around and handed her the letter. Pinto read it aloud.

"That's that," she said.

Gemma nodded and gazed out of the window once more as the crowds gathered on the pier for the evening show.

"You want to go out?" Pinto asked.

Gemma smiled and picked up her wine glass.

"No, not tonight I fancy a quiet night in."

EPILOGUE

The girl was cold. The heater, the man with the dark beard had left her, had stopped working. She heard a pop and there was a puff of dark smoke that rose out of the back of the heater and then the room started to get cold very quickly.

She was naked. She was always naked now. She had no idea what he had done with her clothes or if he was ever going to provide her with more. The men who came and took turns with her didn't comment. She only pleaded with one of them to help her. He had appeared nicer than the usual filthy, unwashed rabble and she felt that maybe he could be trusted to get a message to somebody outside. But he had evidently told the man with the dark beard, because within minutes after confiding in him, the man with the dark beard stormed in and beat her until she cried and huddled in the corner, terrified and shaking.

There had been no men today, not yet, but it was still early. The man with the dark beard had left before it was light outside, she had heard his heavy step on the bare boards on the stairs and then the door had opened and slammed. She had no idea how long she had been here, but it was probably no more than a couple of weeks. He lured her off the streets with food and the promise of a warm bed. She was at her lowest then, regretting her decision to run from home, not even able to remember what the arguments had been about.

She could hear footfalls on the stairs now, but a pacy, lighter step, quick. A woman perhaps.

Whoever it was paused outside the door, then she saw the wood begin to splinter around the keyhole as a long tool, possibly a crow bar, was pushed into the jam. It took only a few seconds for the door to be levered open and a pretty woman stepped inside, glancing around quickly. The girl sat on the bed, crossed her arms over her small breasts and stared at her wide-eyed.

Pippa recognised the girl immediately from the photograph. Her name was Hannah Glass and she was fifteen. She had left her foster parents home nearly four weeks ago after a bitter argument with her foster mother over some inappropriate online photographs the girl had posted of herself. The usual accusations were tossed about.

"You have no idea who is out there watching this!" *You're only fifteen, for God's sake!"*

The girl countered with: *"It's my body!"* and that perennial favourite - *"You're not my mother!"*

Pippa took off her coat and held it out to Hannah, who stood up quickly and slipped it on.

"Who are you?" she asked, on the verge of tears.

"I'm Pippa, Hannah, your mother hired me to find you."

"What are you a secret agent?"

Pippa chuckled. "Something like that."

The front door opened and Hannah cried out as she recognised the man with the dark beard's heavy steps. She turned from Pippa and retreated to the sanctuary of her corner, drawing the coat tightly around her thin frame.

The man with the dark beard was thin and wiry, dressed in tracksuit bottoms and a thick blue fleece. Pippa guessed him to be in his mid-thirties. He stared firstly at her and then at the splintered door.

"The fuck…" he said.

"It was all he managed to utter before Ray swept a huge arm around his throat and lifted him off the ground. The man with the dark beard spluttered and clawed at the arm but Ray simply tightened his grip and the man went limp. He dropped him to the ground and secured his wrists and ankles with plastic ties. He glanced quickly at the girl, but she had her head buried in her lap.

"Is it her?" he asked.

PIppa nodded. "Yes. Police on the way?"

"Just called them, be about ten minutes. He glanced at the cowering girl again, then dragged the unconscious form of the man out of the room leaving the two girls alone.

Slowly, Hannah Glass got up and walked over to where Pippa sat on the bed. She sat down beside her and managed a small smile.

"I want to go home," she said quietly.

Pippa reached out and brushed a strand of hair out of the girl's eye.

"I know, honey. Soon, okay? Very soon."

Printed in Great Britain
by Amazon